THE REIMAGINING OF THORNWOOD HOUSE

THE REIMAGINING OF THORNWOOD HOUSE

JALEIGH JOHNSON

ACE · NEW YORK

ACE
Published by Berkley
An imprint of Penguin Random House LLC
1745 Broadway, New York, NY 10019
penguinrandomhouse.com

Book design by Daniel Brount

Export edition ISBN: 9798217193721

Library of Congress Cataloging-in-Publication Data

Names: Johnson, Jaleigh author
Title: The reimagining of Thornwood House / Jaleigh Johnson.
Description: New York: Ace, 2026.
Identifiers: LCCN 2025039778 (print) | LCCN 2025039779 (ebook) |
ISBN 9798217188819 hardcover | ISBN 9798217188826 ebook
Subjects: LCGFT: Fiction | Witch fiction | Fantasy fiction | Novels
Classification: LCC PS3610.O35438 R45 2026 (print) | LCC PS3610.O35438 (ebook)
LC record available at https://lccn.loc.gov/2025039778
LC ebook record available at https://lccn.loc.gov/2025039779

Printed in the United States of America
1st Printing

The authorized representative in the EU for product safety and compliance is Penguin Random House Ireland, Morrison Chambers, 32 Nassau Street, Dublin D02 YH68, Ireland, https://eu-contact.penguin.ie.

For Tim

This book means many things to me, but it's also the love letter I've always wanted to write you. It only took twenty years or so. Thank you for being patient.

THE REIMAGINING OF THORNWOOD HOUSE

Prologue

To: Ms. Evelyn Sharpe
ECRA Headquarters
1025 Banner Square
Dorna City

Dear Ms. Sharpe,

I was delighted to receive your application for the position of caretaker of Thornwood house. I must say, I never expected a land witch of your caliber to take an interest in our little village and its sentient abode. Our previous caretaker sadly passed away six months ago, and I'm anxious to fill the vacancy; therefore, allow me to formally offer you the position.

While I am eager to bring you to Iskendra as soon as possible, I feel it is my responsibility to caution you that we've had some difficulties with the house. Since the previous caretaker's passing, it has rejected all candidates for a replacement and, as a result, has fallen into a state of significant disrepair. It will require a great deal of time, patience, and magical resources in order to properly restore the structure.

Having said that, I believe you are more than equal to this task. If you give the house a chance, it and our village could turn out to be exactly what you're looking for in a new home. Please know that I and the rest of the village would be happy to welcome you to Iskendra and to Thornwood house.

Sincerely,
Cinda Cartwright
Village Mayor
Iskendra

One

I must say, I find your conduct disappointing, Ms. Sharpe," said Mr. Cinton, who peered across the table at Evie with a beady-eyed stare. The chairman of the Environmental Crisis Response Agency's adoption committee had feathery white hair that reminded Evie of a messy cloud bank. Tiny wire-frame glasses perched on the tip of his thin nose. "For you to go behind our backs in this manner is disrespectful and highly irregular."

The rest of the committee, which included Mr. Tansling, the child advocate, and Mrs. Shields, the head of departmental resources, sat on either side of Cinton, their hands folded on the heavy oak table that divided them from Evie.

They were waiting for her to speak. Evie drew herself up and took a steadying breath. You can do this, she reminded herself. The wheels were already in motion. Now she just had to follow through, for herself and for Ruby.

"I apologize for any misunderstanding," Evie began, "but I fail to see how I've offered the ECRA any disrespect in this matter." She looked at each of the committee members in turn. "I've acted completely within the agency's rules in applying for a new position as caretaker of Thornwood house."

"Your *position* is that of an earthwalker," Mr. Cinton insisted, as if Evie could have possibly forgotten the job title she'd held for the past seven years. "The ECRA has trained you to be among the first teams on the ground in the event of a natural disaster. Your magic and expertise are put to their best use in that capacity." He waved the letter that Cinda Cartwright had sent to Evie. "Now, after the considerable amount of time and care this organization has invested in you, you've taken it upon yourself to cast it all aside in order to travel to a remote village, for no better reason than to act as a country healer and renovate a *house*."

"A *sentient* house," Evie pointed out, emphasizing the distinction. She'd spent countless late nights studying the ECRA's policies and employee regulations, at the same time poring over her own contract to look for a way to quit the agency.

There hadn't been one.

According to the terms of an agreement she'd signed when she was eighteen years old and believed in the ECRA's mission with all her naïve little heart, she was yoked to the agency for a period of not less than twenty years.

Unless.

Evie had grabbed that one little word and held on to it for dear life.

Unless she transferred to a position that directly supported the ECRA's ancillary mission of preserving and protecting magical resources throughout the world.

"According to agency records," Evie went on, "there are fewer than twenty sentient houses remaining in the world. The ECRA have made multiple public statements showing their commitment to preserving these magical phenomena."

She looked to the rest of the committee for support. Even if Cinton missed the implication of what she'd said, she hoped the others wouldn't be so obtuse. "Surely, there can be no objection to me embracing the importance of that commitment, even if it means relinquishing my current role within the agency."

"Is that what this is really about?" Mrs. Shields asked, speaking for the first time since the proceedings had begun. The older woman's silky gray hair was coiled in tight braids atop her head, woven with ribbons that set off her tawny skin. A crystal-topped cane that doubled as a wand rested near her chair.

People often said that Evie possessed a penetrating stare, that her blue eyes darkened to storm gray when she was angry. Evie thought this was an exaggeration and that the people who had made those observations had never come under the power of Mrs. Shields's sharp, assessing gaze.

"Did you apply for the position as caretaker because you truly believe in that cause," Mrs. Shields continued her questioning, "or did you do it because the committee expressed misgivings about approving the adoption of your apprentice and ward, Ruby Keeler?"

Evie's palms were sweating as she inclined her head in Mrs. Shields's direction, trying not to betray her nervousness. She couldn't afford a misstep here. "It's true, when the committee expressed their concerns regarding the dangers of my position as an earthwalker, and how that might make me an . . . *undesirable* candidate to adopt

Ruby, I took those words to heart." Evie tried to ignore the bitter taste in her mouth.

Undesirable. They'd actually used that word.

"However," she went on, "though the committee's concerns played a part in my decision, I did not make the choice to leave lightly, and I do believe the preservation of magical phenomena like Thornwood house is of vital importance." She lifted her chin, ready to deliver the final blow. "Consider my background and family history, if you need further proof."

Her words had the desired effect. Tansling and Cinton exchanged glances, and Evie thought she detected a spark of approval in Mrs. Shields's gaze as she tapped an aqua-colored fingernail against the head of her cane. Evie didn't like invoking her family's position in the magical community. It was a part of her life she'd left behind. But for Ruby, she would use every advantage she had.

"The committee notes your words," Mrs. Shields said. She looked down the table at Mr. Tansling. "In light of these developments, would the advocate care to speak on the status of the adoption?"

The final hurdle, Evie thought, forcing herself to breathe normally. Everything she and Ruby had worked for, planned for, since Ruby had been assigned to her four years ago—all their hopes rested on Mr. Tansling's judgment.

Mr. Tansling looked to be in his late thirties, with straight, sandy hair and dark-brown eyes, impeccably dressed in a crisp gray suit and matching tie. He smiled a great deal and had an amiable air in general. Evie hadn't had as many interactions with him as Ruby had over the past several months. What stood out to her was something Ruby had observed after she'd first met the man.

"It feels like he already has the next thing he's going to say planned out, no matter what I tell him," she'd said.

Mr. Tansling shuffled some papers and glanced over at Evie with a smile that was probably intended to be kind, except it looked like he'd practiced the expression by studying a wax doll.

"I'm sure you and Miss Keeler are anxious to have this matter resolved," he said. "While it's true that you've assuaged some of my concerns regarding your fitness to adopt Miss Keeler, I'm afraid there are certain doubts that remain."

"Oh?" Evie felt a flush creep up her neck, but she forced herself to ignore his patronizing tone and spoke with all the politeness she could summon. "I wonder that there can be any doubts about my capabilities. Ruby came into my care when she was seven years old. She's eleven now, and has become a capable farseer witch under my tutelage—"

Mr. Tansling raised his hand to stop her, that facsimile of a smile still fixed in place. "Rest assured, all that has been taken into consideration." He cleared his throat. "Forgive me for stating the matter bluntly, but being her teacher is not the same as being her parent. Your inexperience in that area is one of my concerns, and, as Mr. Cinton pointed out, going behind the committee's back and applying for a position outside the ECRA's jurisdiction hardly does you credit. It points to a lack of maturity, which isn't surprising, given that you're only twenty-five years old."

"I didn't go behind anyone's back—" Evie cut herself off. Her voice had risen in frustration, causing Mr. Tansling's brow to arch.

And just like that, she was losing control of the conversation. Were they really going to deny her this, after everything she'd given the ECRA? She hadn't been considered too young to risk her life for the agency, and she'd done so countless times over the last seven years. She'd earned pebble-like scars along her collarbone from hurricane debris, walked through forest fire smoke as black as her hair, and broken more bones than she cared to count. Even if they never acknowledged it, she knew she was one of the best earthwalkers they had.

She'd never asked for a single thing from them in return, until now.

"In addition"—Mr. Cinton again waved the letter from the mayor of Iskendra—"it sounds as if this position as caretaker is a tenuous offer at best. Ms. Cartwright admits in her correspondence that the house has rejected all previous applicants." He sniffed. "What makes you believe you will succeed where others have failed?"

Evie met his gaze. In this, at least, she could summon confidence. "I may be inexperienced as a parent"—*four years, I've cared for Ruby, raising her as my own*—"but my record as a land witch and an earthwalker in the ECRA is exemplary, and I possess all the traits Ms. Cartwright spoke of as necessary to restore Thornwood house." She raised an eyebrow. "Am I wrong in that assessment?"

"You are not," Mrs. Shields acknowledged. "The committee has taken that into consideration as well, and we have decided to put forth this compromise." She glanced at the other members, who nodded for her to continue, though Cinton seemed as if he would have liked to keep on lecturing Evie. "We will grant you leave to pursue the position in Iskendra on a trial basis for the next four months. If you are accepted as caretaker, the leave will become permanent, and we will release you from your contract."

Evie held her breath. It sounded too good to be true. "And the adoption?" she pressed.

Mr. Cinton and Mr. Tansling shared a glance, but it was Cinton who spoke. "As advocate, Mr. Tansling will conduct a final interview with Miss Keeler before you leave. Provided the adoption is still what she wants, we will approve it, on the condition that you are accepted as caretaker of Thornwood house. However . . ."

Here it comes, Evie thought.

"If, for any reason, you are unable to secure the position of caretaker, you and Miss Keeler will return to the ECRA, where you will stay with the agency as an earthwalker, for the duration of your contract, without seeking employment elsewhere."

Evie remained silent, turning the offer over in her mind. This was a gray area, and everyone here knew it. Not that it came as a shock to her. Gray areas were where the ECRA lived and breathed.

Technically, they were within their rights to summon Evie back if she wasn't accepted as caretaker, but they didn't have the authority to prevent her from seeking employment with a different organization that worked toward the preservation of magical resources.

No, this was all about control. Now that she'd found a loophole in her contract, the ECRA wanted to close it. They didn't like surrendering power, and they didn't want to lose one of their best earthwalkers, not to mention a farseer like Ruby.

That wasn't the worst of it. If she and Ruby were forced to return, if Evie had to continue as an earthwalker, with all the dangers that job entailed, the committee would have the justification they needed to deny the adoption and separate them for good.

It was unimaginable. Evie knew if she let herself think about that outcome, it would destroy the facade of calm she'd built to face the committee.

Gray areas and a devil's bargain—she should have expected nothing less from the ECRA.

But if she agreed to their terms and successfully became the caretaker . . .

Evie didn't even have to consider it. If it meant that Ruby would be her daughter, forever and always, she'd promise the ECRA the moon, and then she'd find a way to get it for them.

In the end, what she was actually promising was going to be much easier—not to mention more pleasurable—to accomplish. She just had to become the caretaker to an aging sentient house, in a quiet little village, far from the ECRA's influence. Cinda Cartwright had declared that all it would take was time, patience, and magical resources.

Evie had those in abundance. Compared to what she had faced being an earthwalker, this job would be a dream.

"I'll do it," she vowed.

Two

Evie held her battered brown suitcase in one hand and a fistful of earth in the other. A warm pulse snaked up her arm from the loamy soil. It spoke to her of spreading roots, of primrose and milkweed flourishing in patches by the roadside. It was a greeting, and though it wasn't expressed in words, Evie felt the welcome in it, and her magic responded. The land here was very *present*. Curious and watchful.

In a similar vein, Ruby observed her from beneath her strawberry-blond bangs. The rest of her hair spilled halfway down her back, tied with a small, shimmery green scarf. She had a round face and watchful blue eyes and carried a patched cloth travel bag that she shifted from one shoulder to the other. "What do you think?" she asked hopefully. "Is it a good place?"

"Yes, I think so." Evie let the expressive soil sift through her fingers. Earthworms and summer rains—the feelings drifted away on the wind. "We should get going," she said, indicating the narrow gravel track that curved south along the outskirts of the Thornwood. "It's about two miles from here to the house. Do you want me to carry your bag for you?"

"I've got it," Ruby said. The child's eyes sparkled. She was already bouncing on the balls of her feet, like a deer eager to play. It had been a long train ride for an eleven-year-old, though Evie felt much the same. She was more than ready to stretch her legs.

In the distance, the train gave one final, piercing whistle as it lumbered away from the station, severing their last link to Dorna City. Evie closed her eyes and let out a long, slow breath. Her shoulders loosened; the tension in her neck and jaw eased. And for a moment, the land sighed with her, as if it too had felt her lingering anxiety.

If this was how she reacted just getting off the train, she was going to be a mess when she actually set eyes on the house and village.

But wasn't that how it always went? You don't realize how much you need to get away—from a city, a job, something that's been slowly draining you—until you actually take the first steps.

Evie should have tried to leave years ago, and she knew it.

None of that mattered now. They'd taken those steps. Maybe they'd been shaky, and there'd been plenty of scrapes and stumbles along the way, but that didn't matter either. What mattered was that they were *here*, and the land had welcomed them.

Maybe this time, maybe this place, would be what she'd been searching for.

Ruby trotted ahead down the path. The gravel crunched beneath their walking boots, and Evie was grateful she'd chosen a thinner, lighter skirt. The summer heat was already settling in, the sun like a warm hand pressed against her back.

The main road from the train station led straight to Iskendra. Cinda Cartwright had offered to meet them and take them to lunch in the village, but Evie had opted to take the lesser-used path to the house first. She'd also wanted the chance to reach out to the Thornwood along the way. It was important to make a good first impression, especially with a wood as old as this one.

She let her magic brush searchingly against the dense clusters of oaks bordering the path, though she kept her hands to herself. The Thornwood had been named not for any actual thorns but for the unique bark of the oaks that stood alongside the beech and ash trees in the wood. As the oaks aged, their bark thickened and cracked, creating jagged-edged plates, a natural armor that could easily cut skin. By all accounts Evie had read, the process took centuries. So, whatever it had once been called, the wood was now known only as the Thornwood.

But far from making the place unwelcoming, the change simply taught the villagers of Iskendra and all subsequent generations to take precautions when they hunted there, and to teach their children which trees were safe for climbing and which were to be avoided. Village and wood had existed in harmony in this way for many more centuries, and Evie could feel how that peace had helped the land thrive.

The mayor had sent her several books on the history of the area—some of which were tedious and dry—but Evie had dutifully read them all. She wanted to make a good impression not only with the house and the Thornwood but also with the villagers she'd be taking into her care.

She would do whatever was necessary to make this work, for Ruby's sake and for her own.

"Will there be a mailbox at the house?" Ruby asked, swinging her bag around, letting its weight spin her in wobbly circles.

Evie watched her in amusement. "The village is smaller than Dorna City, but it's not *that* small," she said. "Yes, there will be a mailbox, and all our letters are being forwarded." She couldn't help adding, "But I don't expect to hear from the agency, if that's what you're worried about. They gave us four months for the trial period, after all." The ECRA had no reason to contact them before that time was up.

Ruby skidded on the loose gravel but managed to stay on her feet. "Good," she said, wrinkling her freckled nose. "It's about time they left us alone."

Evie couldn't have agreed more.

"Do you think the house will like us?" Ruby continued, switching subjects with the speed of the honeybees working a patch of white clover by the path.

"That's a more complicated question," Evie said.

And as little as a year ago, Ruby might not have asked it. She'd have used her magic to look for herself. It was a good sign. She was learning restraint.

"Going by the mayor's letter, I think we'll have our work cut out for us in the beginning," Evie continued. She shifted her suitcase to her other hand. "I wouldn't take it personally. The house is grieving its caretaker. They were bonded for nearly seventy years."

According to the archives in the Dorna City Library, Thornwood house was one of the oldest sentient houses still in existence, though scholars couldn't agree on its exact age. All anyone knew for certain was that it had bonded with over a dozen caretakers through the centuries. Each of these witches had in turn kept up the house and also acted as village healer for the people of Iskendra.

Normally, the transition from one caretaker to the next was made easier by the witch naming their successor years in advance, bringing them to live and train in the house. When the time came, everyone would be prepared for the change, so there was as little suffering as possible.

But Amelia Howell, the witch who had lived in and cared for Thornwood house her whole life, had not chosen a successor before her death, leaving the house without a caretaker and the village of Iskendra without a witch. It was a mystery that Mayor Cartwright had tried to downplay in her subsequent letters, but Evie had sensed the woman's frustration, and she could only imagine the upheaval it had caused in the village. It was going to be hard for everyone to get used to an outsider taking on the caretaker position, especially one from so far away, with no family connections to Iskendra. But Evie was convinced she could manage it.

"A house shows its grief by letting itself get run-down and shabby," Ruby said, frowning. "At least that's what it said in those ratty old books. That's not very nice, is it?" She kicked at a jutting rock, sending it skittering down the path ahead of them. "Of course you're not going to be at your best when you're hurting. No one expects it of a person. Why would they expect it of a house?"

"You're exactly right," Evie said, "but it isn't just grief that damages the house. Without a witch acting as caretaker, its magic falters and fades over time. They're connected, you see. The house is the witch's haven, her place of power. In return, she shares her magic and vitality with it to keep it strong." That cycle had been interrupted at Thornwood house, and it was Evie's job to put it right again. "We'll take things slow," Evie promised. "We won't expect more from the house than it's willing to give us."

The wood continued to loom large and attentive on the right side of the path, as if the trees were listening to their conversation. Warm wind rustled through the branches, like excited chatter in a language Evie couldn't quite make out, but she loved listening to it anyway.

To their left, open fields and swaying grasses slowly gave way to rows of mature apple trees, lined up tall and proud. Evie recalled from Mayor Cartwright's description of the area that Thornwood house had only one close neighbor—a Mr. Weaver—who owned an orchard that had been in his family for generations.

If they'd reached the orchard, that meant they must be close to Thornwood house.

Ruby felt it too. The girl's steps quickened, and so did Evie's, her excitement getting the better of her as they rounded a sharp bend in the path.

The first thing Evie saw was an open clearing, with two plots of land that rose and fell into a comfortable hollow of green grass and thick clover, nestling in the shadow of the Thornwood. The first plot held a small stone cottage, with a peaked, moss-covered roof that made it look as if the cottage was swaddled in a fluffy green blanket. A weather vane perched on the roof, topped by a shiny copper apple, but the central pole had been bent almost in half, the fruit now sad and drooping. A carpet of delicate ferns sat in the shadow of the eaves, and a wind chime tinkled softly from the front porch.

"Our neighbor," Evie said distractedly, for her attention was caught by the bigger plot of land next door to the cottage, the place where Thornwood house, their new home, *should* have been waiting for them.

Except the house was gone.

Three

It was fair to say that Evie and Ruby had encountered more than their share of obstacles in the pursuit of this new life they'd chosen. But after everything they'd gone through, the one thing Evie had *never* expected was to arrive at her new home only to find it missing.

The foundation was still there, and a handful of loose boards and shingles had been left scattered around the yard, but the rest of the structure was gone.

Fortunately, their neighbor's cottage was still standing tall and undamaged, and there weren't any limbs down from the surrounding trees, so Evie had no reason to suspect a storm or other natural disaster had struck the area recently. That was promising. In the unlikely event Thornwood house had been the victim of some other catastrophe, surely there would have been more evidence of its remains. Since that wasn't the case, there was nothing left for her to conclude, except—

"The house appears to have run away," Evie observed, and had the sudden, inexplicable urge to laugh.

And cry.

She swallowed both of those urges as they approached the rickety gate. A waist-high stone wall rambled around the property, enlivened by tangles of ivy and ruby-red honeysuckle. To their left stood a voluminous weeping willow tree. Ground-sweeping branches enclosed a small pond, its slender leaves kissing the surface and sending ripples out to the shore. Spanning the pond's length was a little wooden footbridge. A charming detail, except it was badly in need of new planks and a good coat of paint.

On the opposite side of the yard there was an expansive, untended garden. Thick patches of basil had gone coarse with flowers, the rosemary was tall and spiky, the lavender flourishing. Surrounding the herbs were clusters of bee balm, catmint, and other colorful flowers slowly being consumed by weeds. A stone path bisected the yard, leading to a set of dilapidated steps that ended in jagged-edged boards.

A long curtain of ivy that had probably once clung to the side of the house now lay draped across the yard like a cloak put out to dry. Sparrows and squirrels picked excitedly through the remnants, searching for treasures. At the back of the property, beyond the stone wall, jagged furrows marred the ground, jutting off in sets of three like tracks left by a giant chicken. The rough trail led right up to the edge of the Thornwood.

Ruby's brow creased in consternation. "I didn't know houses could do that—run away, I mean." She went over to examine the mailbox, which was still in place beside the gate, huddled in ivy and doing its best to keep its head above the copious weeds. But the rusted metal door opened obligingly when Ruby tried it, and a spider crawled out and scuttled into the bushes.

"As a rule, they don't," Evie said, setting her suitcase on the flattest part of the wall.

"This isn't good." Ruby followed Evie anxiously through the gate and up the stone path. "If the house isn't here, that means you can't bond with it, and if you can't bond with it, you can't be its caretaker, and we'll have to leave and the adoption won't— "

"Let's not get ahead of ourselves," Evie soothed, with a calm she could fake if not feel. "We just got here. I'm sure there's a reasonable explanation for this."

For a runaway house. Of course there was.

Ruby glanced around the yard. "Where do you think it went?"

Evie nodded to the torn ground. "It looks like it went into the wood." The marks were fairly fresh, though it was impossible to tell exactly how long the house had been gone. It might have been hours or days.

Ruby appeared doubtful. "But how could it fit? Even if there was a path, it'd be too small for the house, unless it knocked over some of the trees."

That was a fair point. And there was no sign that the wood had been in any way disturbed. Beyond the tree line, the chicken-foot trail just stopped, and everything appeared normal. Blue jays jeered and insects buzzed in the steamy afternoon. A welcome breeze blew through Evie's long, wavy black hair and set their neighbor's wind chime tinkling again.

Ruby turned to stare at the chime, getting that faraway look in her eyes that meant she was seeing something familiar, even though she'd never been here before.

"Are you all right?" Evie asked, laying a hand on her shoulder.

"Y-yes," Ruby said after a moment. She looked up at Evie, her expression unreadable. "I was just . . . Yes, I'm all right."

Evie nodded and didn't press her. It was bad manners to ask a farseer witch to talk about their visions before they were ready. Still, she was surprised. Ruby was usually eager to share her glimpses of the future with Evie, so that she could better understand their meaning. This was the first time Evie could remember her hesitating.

Things were changing so much, so fast—for the both of them. It wasn't just that they were moving to a new home. Ruby was growing up and coming into her own power. Evie had known these days were near. She just wished she felt more prepared for them.

Because she obviously hadn't been prepared for this situation with Thornwood house.

"To answer your question, I don't know how the house passed through the wood without leaving a trace," Evie said. "Maybe the Thornwood made space for it and then covered its tracks." It wasn't unheard-of—the wood was as alive and aware as the land around them—but trees didn't usually move to accommodate a building, even if it was sentient.

Her gaze rested on the wind chime again. "Maybe we should introduce ourselves to our neighbor, see if he can tell us what happened here."

Ruby followed her gaze and nodded slowly. "That's a good idea," she said, but her cautious tone again made Evie wonder just what she'd seen in her vision.

Together, they retraced their steps down the path and walked next door. Evie glanced up at the bent weather vane, shading her eyes against the afternoon sun. Had the house done that when it pulled itself up and ran away? She hoped not, but at least nothing else on the property appeared to be damaged. Silently, Evie added "weather vane" to the list of possible repairs she was going to have to make—assuming she could get Thornwood house back to its proper place.

One step at a time.

The neighbor's door was set with a small stained-glass panel featuring a basket of apples. Rarely shy, Ruby skipped ahead of Evie and knocked. They waited, watching a blue-winged dragonfly flit among the ferns, the wind chime filling the air with its soft music.

Evie thought she heard movement from somewhere within the house, but the door remained shut. Ruby glanced up at her for permission, then knocked again. The seconds became a minute. Then two.

"Looks like there's no one home," Evie said briskly, trying to ignore a pull of uneasiness.

As they turned to go, Evie caught movement out of the corner of her eye. At first she thought it was just the sun reflecting off the copper apple on the weather vane, but then she realized it had come from one of the upstairs windows.

She looked up. A face watched her from the other side of the glass. It was a handsome face, what little Evie saw of it before it disappeared behind a curtain. She was left with the impression of unruly chestnut hair, a thick matching beard—and a glare that made her insides clench.

The message in it was clear enough: *Go away. You're not welcome here.*

Maybe the runaway Thornwood house *had* been responsible for damaging the weather vane. And their new neighbor was not happy about it.

Evie's shoulders slumped as they walked away, and a dull ache settled behind her eyes. The exhaustion of the long, hot travel day was catching up to her, and this was the opposite of the good first impression she'd been hoping to make in her new community.

She'd been so sure that once they got here, everything would be all right. But it obviously wasn't, and things were turning out to be more complicated than she'd imagined.

Fortunately, Ruby didn't seem to have noticed the glaring face in the window. She ran ahead, kicking rocks and picking wildflowers, her energy boundless. "Where are we going to sleep tonight?" she asked as they returned to the spot on the wall where they'd left their luggage. "Can we go into the village?"

Evie considered that. Maybe they should venture into Iskendra. Someone there might have seen the house or know where it had gone.

Or maybe the house had gone straight through the wood and into the village, and was even now rampaging through the streets and menacing the townsfolk.

Evie felt her headache worsening. No, there was no reason to think that. Going by the trail, the house had gone into the wood, so it was probably still out there somewhere. She could salvage this. "We're going to sleep in our new home tonight," she told Ruby firmly, squaring her shoulders. "Just as soon as I bring it back."

"I could look," Ruby offered hesitantly. Her gaze swung in the direction of the Thornwood. "I might be able to see where it went, without seeing too much."

Evie didn't immediately answer. She went to sit on the ivy-covered wall, helping Ruby up to straddle the wall next to her. "Is that what you really want to do?" she asked. "It's our first day here, after all. You might want to give it some time."

Ruby made a face. "That's your way of saying I shouldn't."

Evie shook her head. "I'm saying it's your choice, but what's the first lesson of farseeing, the one we return to time and again?"

"Don't try to force the power to show the future," Ruby recited impatiently. "Listen to what it's trying to tell *you* instead. I *know* that." She fidgeted, picking at a patch of dried mud on the stones. "But if it helps us stay here—"

"We're *not* leaving." Evie put her hand out, and after a pause, Ruby grasped it. Their magic stirred and entwined. Green and gold light blended with Ruby's pale-pink aura. "I promised you, remember?"

Ruby nodded, but as she pulled away, she wouldn't meet Evie's eyes. "It's just that I already like this place," she said, "and there's not even a house yet." She sighed. "I guess I don't really want to look, not right now. I think the magic's telling me to wait."

"Then let's listen to it," Evie advised. "We'll figure out another way."

"If you say so." Suddenly, Ruby wrinkled her nose. "I think the Thornwood is listening," she muttered. "It's really nosy."

"We're new here," Evie said. "We're going to be a novelty for a while." She let her awareness expand past Ruby and into the wood, feeling for some sign of the house.

There was another trail. Invisible to the eye, but if she focused, she could just pick it out. Flecks of silver, delicate as rose petals, scattered in the shape of chicken feet. It sank into the earth, careful but urgent, imploring—*Will you please let me pass?*

And the land had responded, the living curtain reshaping itself for just an instant. The wood had indeed created space for the house, allowing it to make its way deep into the trees before something stopped it. But what could that have been?

In her mind's eye, Evie saw a flash of rushing water, a pewter ribbon weaving through the wood, vibrant with bullfrogs and dragonflies gliding along the water.

Ah. The river.

"Come on," Evie said, smiling. She hopped off the wall and waited for Ruby to do the same. "I think I know where to find our wayward house."

Four

It took some searching, but eventually they found an uneven dirt track that roughly paralleled the house's trail into the wood. Threads of unfamiliar magic, so faint they'd become colorless, were worn into the land here like footprints. But they still made the dandelions shimmer and the wild violets gleam. It made Evie think this was a path the old witch must have trod whenever she went into the Thornwood. Was there a grove in the wood that Amelia Howell had claimed as her own? A secret place to commune with the trees? Was that where the house had gone out of grief?

"Stay close," Evie said as Ruby drifted to the edge of the path. She wasn't worried about potential dangers in the wood, but she didn't want Ruby wandering off and getting lost, not before Evie had had the chance to map the wood thoroughly with her own magic.

When a witch became a true caretaker of a house and village, they would know where everyone in the community was at all times, bound to them like the blossoms in a chain of forget-me-nots. Evie understood that it would take time for her to get to that point, but there was no better time to start learning this new place, to weave her magic among the trees so that they might know her and know that her intentions were good.

She let her awareness expand again, greeting the wood and following the sparkling silver trail left behind by the house's magic. In response, the trees swayed and bent, subtly pulling back from the path to make room for them. Wind hissed through the leaves as if to say, *This way.*

Evie had never had the land act as a guide for her like this. The feeling was new and thrilling. In Dorna City, the land's presence was muted by all the things that made a city thrive. Here, it was unfettered and so very strong. She would have to get used to that too.

They'd gone roughly two miles in before the house's trail diverged from the dirt path and began to roam in aimless circles, as if the house had lost its way. Evie felt the leftover frustration rising from the soil. It sat there, leaving a large echo of magic, as if the house had stayed in one place for several hours. When it finally continued, it was moving in a straight line again, but the trail faltered, the silver light diminishing like a candle flame sinking in a pool of wax.

A sudden chill crept over Evie's skin. "Something's not right," she whispered, which made Ruby turn to look at her in alarm. "It's not a danger to us," Evie hurried to reassure her. "It's the house's magic. It's . . . severely weakened." More than it should have been, even accounting for the time it had spent roaming the wood without a caretaker.

Ruby's eyes widened. "How did that happen?" she asked.

"I don't know."

The more she examined those faint motes of power, the more Evie's uneasiness grew. It was shocking, how little magic the house had left. She suddenly understood why the mayor had been so anxious to find a replacement caretaker, why she'd accepted Evie's application at once, without so much as a face-to-face meeting.

The house wasn't just grieving. It was sick. It needed help.

"Hold on," Evie murmured, forgetting her headache and her fatigue as she hiked up her skirt to plow through the trees. "We're coming."

They approached the river Aglin. Evie heard the burbling sounds before she glimpsed the sun-dappled water through the leaves. Ahead of her, the trees thinned, gradually revealing a wide, rocky clearing that spilled down a sloping embankment to the water's edge.

Thornwood house huddled at the top of the embankment on a pair of wooden chicken feet that it had constructed out of itself. Its eaves and joists scrunched into a grating, unhappy tangle as it surveyed the river blocking its path.

Evie had no trouble seeing the echo of what a fine house it had once been. Two stories, with a cedar-shingled roof and windowed turret that leaned precariously to one side, as if it was about to snap off. What was left of the grand wraparound porch was full of gaps and splintered wood, like a mouthful of broken teeth. Pale yellow paint peeled off walls stained green from the moss and ivy that the house had ripped away when it made its escape.

Connected to the U-shaped rear of the structure was a small glasshouse framed in wrought iron. Most of its panes were cracked or shattered, leaving a trail of glittering fragments from the house to where Evie and Ruby stood. Near the peak of the glasshouse, there were the remains of a panel of stained glass, though it was impossible to tell from the jagged shards what had been depicted in it.

"What should we do?" Ruby asked in a strained whisper. "It doesn't look like it wants us here."

She wasn't wrong. Caught between the rushing river and the two witches, the house hunched into a protective mass, popping nails and snapping boards as if it didn't care how much damage it did to itself.

This was worse than Evie had thought. The house was obviously suffering, and if it wouldn't let her get close enough to help, if it tried to run again, the damage might be irreparable.

She took a cautious step forward, into the clearing. The sun was hot and bright on the top of her head. Clouds of gnats hummed in the air, and the smells of algae and mud drifted up from the riverbank. The branches of the nearby trees creaked in the wind. It felt as if they were leaning in to watch the drama unfold.

"Hello." Evie kept her movements slow, her voice gentle. "I'm Evie, and this is Ruby. We're the new caretakers."

As soon as the words were out, Evie realized she'd said the wrong thing. The turret swung sharply in their direction, shattering the remaining windows and spraying more glass all over the embankment. Empty black pits stared down at them like baleful eyes. The scent of rotten fruit suddenly filled the air.

Ruby gulped. "I don't think it likes us." She nudged Evie's arm. "Say something better."

"I'm trying," Evie muttered. Her magical education hadn't

included lessons on how to approach a hostile runaway house. There wasn't a handbook for this sort of situation.

Except, maybe she *did* know what to do, Evie realized with a jolt. Hadn't she just said it to Ruby earlier?

She stared up at the turret steadily. "We're so very sorry for your loss," she said. "We didn't know Amelia Howell, but Mayor Cartwright said in her letters that she was a wonderful woman. I wish I could have gotten to meet her."

The house went still.

Evie waited, and slowly, the turret shied away from them. The rotten scent faded, and the sense of hostility lifted. In its place, she felt grief ripple the house's shingles, pain and something else—*fear*—contracting the walls.

The fear gave Evie pause. Living houses didn't communicate in words. It was part of the reason they were so tricky to bond with, even for a seasoned witch. But they had moods, emotions that could be smelled or felt like a breeze on your face if you knew how to open yourself up to them.

She didn't try to move closer to the house. Its grief she understood, but the last thing she wanted was for the house to be afraid of her.

What had gone on here in the six months since the old witch's passing? Was there something the mayor hadn't told her? Evie didn't like being in the dark, but for the moment, her questions would have to wait. The house needed her, whether it wanted to admit it or not.

She took a moment to listen to the wind rustling through the trees, rattling the loose boards on the broken porch. Ruby stood close beside her, her magic a bright, familiar pink glow in the clearing. Evie took strength from it and addressed the house again.

"We're not here to make you do anything you don't want to do," she said. "We just want to help you, give you magic so you can recover."

And to keep the house from falling apart, which looked like a distinct possibility at the moment. Thank goodness it hadn't tried to cross the river. The current and flooding would have torn the structure to pieces.

Where had the house been trying to go? That was another question that nagged at Evie.

Beside her, Ruby stirred. Evie looked down at her. "Something you want to add? Go ahead."

Cautiously, Ruby stepped forward and drew herself up to address the house. "I think you should come back with us," she said. "It's going to be dark soon, and we don't want you to get lost." She hesitated and added, "I can't wait to get to know you. When you're ready, I mean. We'll be here."

Pride swelled in Evie's chest. "Well said," she whispered. She didn't know if the house was going to accept the invitation, but Ruby's words had given her an idea.

She took a few steps back, drawing Ruby with her to give the house some space. Going down on her knees, she buried her hands in a patch of wildflowers in the clearing, entwining her fingers with the feathery white yarrow and butter-yellow dandelions nodding in the breeze. The connection from the land to her own power was immediate and strong. It flowed through pistils and stamens and made petals shiver. Once again, Evie felt the close scrutiny of the

Thornwood from over her shoulder, as if it observed their every move.

Was she doing what was right? Or should she be leaving the house alone?

But the trees kept their feelings to themselves and offered no judgment either way.

Well, all she could do was try.

Gently, Evie tipped some of her magic into the soil, letting it gather and pool into an invisible pot. The grass under her fingers shivered and deepened to a rich, dark green, the yarrow multiplied, and the dandelions grew a foot taller, their heads expanding to the size of dinner plates. The thickened stems swayed drunkenly with the sudden surplus of magic.

There, that should be enough.

Evie stood up carefully, feeling a soft wave of lightheadedness. She'd given a bit more power than she should have after the long day of travel, but the house needed it, and more.

"We'll leave this here for you," Evie offered, backing away. Ruby followed, her fingers grazing the giant dandelions in delight. "When you're ready, please take it. It will help."

The house didn't stir. Evie wanted to say something else, to reassure it somehow, but in the end, she decided not to press. She didn't want to overwhelm the house or make it mistrust them any more than it already did.

They left the clearing and retraced their steps through the wood in silence. By the time they reached the stone wall that marked the edge of their property, the sky was turning a fiery orange with sunset, the heat of the day slowly giving way to evening coolness.

"It's getting dark," Ruby said. "Do you think the house will come back before bedtime?"

"I hope so." But Evie wasn't counting on it. And even if the house did come back tonight, she wasn't sure the structure was safe to sleep in. Not without more magical reinforcement.

That left them with limited options. The practical thing to do would be to walk into the village and stay at an inn or bed-and-breakfast for the night, but somehow that didn't sit right with Evie, not while Thornwood house was out in the wood by itself. She wanted to be here if it came back, to make sure it wasn't alone.

Yet, she'd told Ruby they'd be sleeping in their new home tonight. How could Evie expect to take care of her, to keep the bigger promises she'd made, if she couldn't even deliver on the simple ones?

"Being her teacher is not the same as being her parent."

The words echoed mockingly in her mind, and Evie was suddenly swept back into that stuffy chamber, facing down the ECRA adoption committee like a magical firing squad.

We're past that now, Evie reminded herself. The ECRA was far away. They couldn't hurl those words at her anymore.

And she was still a powerful land witch. No one had ever doubted that.

Which meant she *could* give Ruby a comfortable place to sleep, Evie realized, even if it wasn't in a traditional bed. It wasn't as if they'd never been camping before, and Evie was used to sleeping rough at her old job.

"Come on." She led Ruby to the rear of the property. She hadn't had a chance to explore back here earlier, but now she saw the empty impression where the glasshouse had once stood. Nearby, a short, winding path led down rows of a vegetable gárden that had been planted but not tended. The lettuces and onions had grown thick and been sampled by many forest critters. Wild mint ran riot along the back wall.

To Evie's surprise and delight, there was even a crescent-shaped mood garden that flowed across the yard to their left. She'd never seen one in Dorna City, even in the ECRA gardens. The magical plants reacted to the emotions of anyone passing through, feeding on the feelings the way other plants reached for the sunlight.

As she and Ruby approached, delicate lavender mirth blossoms swiveled in their direction, the trumpet-shaped flowers soaking up the enjoyment Evie felt at this new discovery, while the yellow rosettes of the vex plant swayed and shivered, absorbing their lingering worries.

It was a garden that fed on *all* emotions and counted even the negative ones as something precious and vital. Evie had always liked that way of looking at the bad feelings that sometimes swirled inside her. Mood gardens were a reminder that even the emotions people thought were ugly, the parts of themselves that they saw as weak or unkind, were necessary to the cycle of living things. Love and anger, fear and serenity, were all a part of this space.

An unexpected ache took root inside Evie as she absorbed the scene. In her mind, she placed a white wooden bench in the clasp of the mood garden and saw herself sitting there with a cup of cocoa on an autumn night. There would be star-shaped coral yearns growing beneath the bench, blossoming under the tender weight of hopes newly realized. The image was so clear, she could almost smell the steaming chocolate and feel the brisk October chill on her bare, pale shoulders.

Could this really be her place, a place where she and Ruby belonged?

Only if she became the caretaker, if she could bond with the house. Right now that goal seemed far out of reach.

Evie blinked, and the image vanished. Dreams like that were best saved for the future. Right now, she had work to do.

The sun was setting, but she had just enough light to see. Evie made a sweeping gesture with her right hand, fingertips grazing a thick strawberry patch, coaxing the plants to bend and twist, curving upward into a half arch. With her left hand, she beckoned the pale-white ease lilies in the mood garden to awaken and rise, petals slotting into place to form the other half of the arch. Together they created a dense canopy of red and white, of fragrant fruit and flowers.

That done, Evie knelt and thickened the grass beneath the canopy, drawing the slender green strands up between her fingers. Then she laid her palms flush against the earth, pressing magic into the ground to make it spongy and soft like the plushest mattress.

She fought off another swell of dizziness. All right, that was officially enough power spent for one evening.

Watching her, Ruby giggled and plucked one of the strawberries, holding the bright-red fruit in her freckled hand. "At least we have something for dinner," she said.

"True, and I still have part of that loaf of rye bread from the train's meal cart," Evie recalled, "but we'll get a big breakfast in the morning."

They hauled their luggage to the backyard and pulled out some blankets and light sweaters to keep warm in their impromptu camp. The rest of their clothes and furniture wouldn't be arriving until the next day, but Evie was glad she'd thought to pack these necessities. Soon they were settled beneath the canopy, the scent of strawberries filling the air as they laid out their picnic and ate.

When darkness closed in and the moon was high and milky in the sky, their contentment made the ease lilies open fully, their gossamer blossoms like a curtain of sparkling lace cast over the arch. Lying on her back, Evie reached out and cupped the closest bloom, feeling its softness tickling her palm like a butterfly's wing. Across the yard, patches of the mood garden glowed with bioluminescence, pink flummox and blue hush shining against the dark grass. The latter could be harvested for calming potions to help the anxious sleeper. Evie felt their power peaking. In a few days, their magic would diminish and fade.

The old witch was gone, but someone had been in her gardens, planting new vegetables and herbs, making sure the flowers were healthy, even if they were losing the battle against the weeds and the rabbits. Evie wondered if it was the mysterious Mr. Weaver next door, or perhaps someone from the village.

Next to her, Ruby wrapped herself in a plaid blanket and turned to face Evie. "Will you read to me?" she whispered.

Evie went as still as the house had been at the edge of the river. Her emotions rippled through the mood garden, so fast she couldn't identify all the flowers that bloomed to the sudden drum of her heartbeat in the quiet night.

It wasn't the first time they'd shared a book. Evie's library in Dorna City had been extensive, and perusing the shelves was one of Ruby's favorite activities. But most of the time, Ruby had been reading on her own as part of her magical studies. She would ask Evie questions about the texts, and they would discuss them as teacher and student. It was comfortable, familiar.

Only recently had Ruby started asking Evie to read her bedtime stories—fantastic tales of other worlds, impossible quests, and reluctant heroes. Evie recalled vividly the night she'd opened their first book together and started reading. Though nothing had changed outwardly, she'd felt a seismic shift inside her chest. Because when Evie read to Ruby that night, for the first time, she hadn't felt like a teacher reading to a student, but a parent reading to a daughter.

Now, each time Ruby asked for a story, it smote Evie right through the heart. She tucked the feeling away inside her, as delicate and precious as the blossom she'd just held in her hand. She would make a bouquet of them, let them grow inside her forever.

"Of course," she whispered back.

Her brown suitcase lay open on the grass nearby. Evie sat up and rummaged through it, taking a moment to collect herself while she located the book they'd started reading together. They resettled themselves, and Evie propped the book on her stomach. She opened it to where they'd left off.

"The blue-eyed rabbit and the singing goose met at midnight beneath the boughs of the yew tree," she began. "There, they were assured no one would overhear their plans for the great heist."

As Evie read, the sound of their neighbor's wind chime drifted across the gap between properties. Evie paused in the story long enough to glance over at the Weaver house. There was a light in the downstairs window near the back door, but no face, glowering or otherwise, gazed out at her. Still, she had the strange impression that just for a moment, someone had been there, perhaps listening to the rabbit and the goose conspiring.

Despite the promise of a heist, it took only a handful of pages before Ruby's breathing deepened and she sprawled on her back with her blanket wrapped around her and her mouth slightly open. Evie was about to close the book and put it away when she heard the sounds.

A rumbling, a thump, and a sustained scraping coming from the front yard, like a lumbering giant trying and failing to sneak up on them. It startled a flock of starlings that had just gotten settled in the trees, sending them into panicked flight. At the same time, Evie felt the familiar presence of the house's magic, stronger now than when she'd sensed it earlier.

On instinct, Evie cleared her throat and kept reading, not turning to look. She was afraid if she stopped, if she paid the house any attention at all, it would get scared and run off again. She didn't want that to happen.

So Evie continued to read, while ever so slowly, Thornwood house made its way over the stone wall and back to the place where it had been built. Evie kept on reading even when the house settled back onto its foundation with a disconcertingly loud *boom*, the crunch of breaking glass and bending iron heralding the little glasshouse's arrival as well.

Ruby slept through it all, of course. She could sleep through a tornado and not feel a thing.

Then all was quiet. A cloud of dust hung in the air in the wake of the house's return.

While she read, Evie stretched out a tendril of magic to assess the house's well-being. There was still grief in abundance, but that sharp pain and fear had ebbed a bit, and Evie was relieved to discover that the house had accepted all of her gift. Her own magic swirled in its walls and settled into the shingles and shutters, beginning the painstaking process of repairing what had been damaged.

One step at a time.

Evie kept on reading the story aloud while her daughter slept beside her, and she would have sworn that the house, battered and exhausted as it was, leaned in just slightly in order to hear how the chapter ended.

Five

When Evie woke the next morning, rubbing the sleep from her bleary eyes, her first sight was a perfect, curling strawberry vine resting near her face, its bright-red berry glistening with morning dew. Ruby was still asleep, snoring quietly beside her.

As the memories of the previous day returned, Evie sat up and cautiously parted the strawberry vines, looking to see if Thornwood house had remained in its place overnight.

To her relief, the house was still there, sitting stiffly despite the damage to its walls, as if trying to pretend nothing had happened, while at the same time giving off a faint air of sheepishness.

Determined to act calm and casual, Evie stood and indulged in a long, back-bowing stretch before going over the garden wall and into a cluster of trees for a moment of privacy. When she returned, Ruby was awake and prancing through the gardens like a fairy, her blanket flapping around her shoulders like wings in the chill of the morning.

"The house came back!" she squealed, bouncing up and down in front of Evie excitedly. Her hair stuck out from her head in wild blond spikes peppered with clover and blades of grass. Evie didn't want to know how her own must look.

"I'm so glad." Evie pitched her words just loud enough to carry across the yard to the house. She put out a hand and gently lifted her magic from the strawberry patch and the ease lilies, allowing them to sink back to their normal size and shape in their respective gardens. Power flowed into her, tingling at her fingertips and clearing the last of the sleepy fog from her mind.

Now that the house was back, they had a long day ahead of them, and this first part would be the hardest, Evie thought as she followed Ruby through the yard to the front of the house. They needed to get inside and assess the extent of the damage and any repairs the house had managed to make using Evie's magic. She'd given as much as she could for now. Magic was not an infinite resource, either in her own body or in the land around them. It needed time to replenish itself before she could share any more with the house.

"Can we go inside?" Ruby paced at the foot of the steps leading up to the wraparound porch. Evie noticed immediately that the house had not repaired those steps, and the porch was little more than gaping holes and jutting boards with rusty nails sticking out of them. A no trespassing sign wouldn't have been any clearer.

"We need to come to an understanding first," Evie said, glancing up at the house's turret. The vacant windows were angled away from them, pointing across the lawn as if the house was averting its gaze. Evie addressed it anyway. "I want to help you recover and replenish your magic," she declared. She braced herself, scraping together her courage, but no matter how hard she tried, she couldn't get the next words out, the ones she truly needed to say.

I don't have to do this. I could force the bond.

Shame flooded Evie at the thought, but that didn't make it untrue. She had enough power. She'd been an earthwalker of the ECRA. She could *make* this work, whether the house wanted her there or not. It would secure her and Ruby's future and ensure that they were never separated. Surely, that was her most important responsibility now as a parent, and it was worth any guilt or regret she might have to live with.

But it made her no better than the ECRA.

Evie took a ragged breath and plunged ahead before she could change her mind. "Once you've recovered, what happens after that . . . is entirely up to you. If you want us to leave, we will, and the search for a new caretaker for you and the villagers will go on."

Ruby stopped prancing around the yard. Evie felt a sudden, palpable tension radiating off the girl. But as much as she wanted to, she couldn't take back the words.

Whatever happened next, it had to be the house's choice. She'd made a promise to Ruby that they would stay, but she also knew that no witch should ever try to be a caretaker for an unwilling house. The relationship would be doomed to disaster from the start, and there could be no true happiness in a home like that.

"What'll we do if— " Ruby started, but seeing the determined set to Evie's face, the girl fell quiet. She wrapped her arms around herself and stood staring down at the stone path, trying and failing to keep a look of misery off her face. Evie fought the urge to go to her, to tell her that everything would be all right. But she couldn't lie about this. It wouldn't be fair to either of them.

A strange thing happened then. Evie watched as the house's turret dipped ponderously in Ruby's direction, its attention caught by the girl's posture and somberness. Her eyes downcast, Ruby didn't notice the house's interest. The turret creaked and groaned as it considered the young witch. Finally, its walls expanded and contracted, as if the house was letting out a gusty sigh.

The turret pulled back, and the porch and stairs began to repair themselves.

Evie put her hand on Ruby's shoulder, drawing the girl back a safe distance while the floorboards re-formed and snapped into place, nails squealing as they flaked off their rusty coats and burrowed back into the wood. A railing sprang up around the porch, spindles locking into place straight as piano keys. The rail extended all the way down the front steps, whose treads were taking shape one by one. A fresh coat of white paint flowed over the bare boards like cream, sealing and drying in less than a minute.

When it was all done, the house drew itself up, displaying the restored porch like a child preening in a new skirt.

Ruby gasped at the transformation. A small, hopeful smile quivered across her lips. Evie thought that would be the end of the show, but the house seemed unsatisfied with the girl's reaction. It gave a tiny allover shake, from shingles to foundation. The movement caused two sets of chains to fall from the roof of the porch, and a pile of discarded wood rose to meet them in a mini tornado that eventually resolved itself into a wooden swing big enough to seat three. Then the house paused, as if waiting for something.

Evie figured out what it was at the same moment Ruby did.

"Green?" the girl suggested.

A green dot sprouted on the seat like clover, and with a soft *splooshing* sound, a wave of green paint overtook the porch swing. At the same time, a pair of green flower boxes assembled and attached themselves to the railing on either side of the front steps. A rumpled brown rug unrolled itself in front of the door.

Then it was over. The porch had been thoroughly redone.

"Oh, it's perfect!" Ruby burst out. Without hesitating, she dashed up the steps and dove onto the swing, using her feet to push herself back and forth. She flashed Evie a brilliant smile. "Come and see, Evie! I've always wanted a house with a porch swing!"

"I know," Evie managed, swallowing thickly. "Be gentle with it. I'll be there in a minute."

She looked up at the turret, which had carefully averted its gaze again, though Evie wasn't fooled. The house was still preening and pleased. The same grieving house that had run off into the wood, glowered at them, and then cowered in fear had used some of Evie's magical gift to fix its porch.

All because it hadn't been able to stand seeing Ruby sad.

Evie crossed the yard and slowly began to ascend the new steps. The wood creaked softly beneath her feet. She took her time, wanting to give the house the opportunity to rescind its welcome if it started having second thoughts. She was almost to the top and starting to feel confident—

The risers shivered beneath her boots, making her teeter in place. Evie froze on the steps, gripping the newly restored railing to keep her balance. She glanced up at Ruby, but the girl was occupied playing on the swing and hadn't noticed the disturbance.

Evie's thoughts raced. Was that a threat on the house's part? Or a test?

Or was the house still afraid?

Suspended between one moment and the next, Evie waited, willing the house to give her some sign of what it wanted. Wind blew across the porch, making a hollow echo, but everything else stayed as it was. Cautiously, Evie lifted her foot, braced for the steps to start trembling again, but they didn't. She went up the stairs one at a time, feeling like a young child just learning to walk, but soon enough, Evie was standing before the front door. Ruby perched on the swing, watching her curiously.

Well, here goes nothing. Evie reached out, grasped the brass knob, and turned it.

The door swung open.

Evie let out a breath. She supposed that was progress.

Of course, Evie hadn't expected the rest of the house to be repaired as quickly as the porch had been. The magic she'd given it would only go so far before she would have to replenish it. Still, nothing quite prepared her for the extent of the mess inside the house.

Most of Amelia Howell's furniture and common household items remained. While they'd been living in the ECRA's housing, almost all of Evie and Ruby's furniture had been provided for them, so they hadn't had much to bring with them when they left. Having the house come fully furnished had suited them well. The old witch's personal effects had already been boxed up and taken away.

But the furnishings and decorations that remained in the house had suffered as much from its running away as if an earthquake had struck, and the structure itself still didn't look entirely stable. A multitude of cracks skittered up the walls and made jagged cuts across the white ceiling. To the right of the foyer, a pair of glass-paneled doors hung off their hinges, the panels broken, leaving a carpet of glittering shards strewn over the floor. Through the ruined doors, Evie could see the kitchen was even more of a disaster. Most of the cupboards had come off the walls or dangled open, dishes spilled out and shattered on the floor. The iron chandelier that had hung in the center of the room had fallen and broken the kitchen table in half before coming to rest in front of the large stove in the corner.

Evie decided to leave it for now. They could eat their meals in Iskendra for a few days.

A staircase hugged the wall opposite the glass doors, but a large chunk was missing from the middle, making the second floor inaccessible. To her immediate left, a pocket door opened into the living room, which had a fireplace, a couch, and several plush chairs. The couch had been overturned and lay in a pile with the chairs, along with the remains of several plants. The fireplace had emptied ash and soot all over the room, much of it now ground into the rugs. There was what looked like a small bathroom off the back of the living room, but Evie was too far away to assess its condition, and really, she'd seen enough already.

"We have our work cut out for us," she warned as Ruby came up behind her and peered around her shoulder into the gloomy interior.

The house made no objection when Evie stepped inside, though she made a conscious decision to leave the door ajar for now, just in case the house turned unfriendly. "Watch your step," she cautioned, and again she was grateful for their thick boots as they moved into the living room, crunching on broken glass, splintered wood, and other unidentifiable debris.

Evie understood that the house was grieving and reluctant to take on a new caretaker after the old witch's death. But she had never heard of a house reacting like *this* to a change in circumstances. It didn't make sense.

There was more going on here than grief. Evie could feel it in every crack and cornice.

But the house was letting them stay, at least for the time being. And now that she was across the threshold, Evie was determined not to be intimidated by whatever was waiting for her here. She would not only help restore the house but also find out what had happened to it after Amelia Howell died.

Six

Now that they'd been allowed inside the house, Evie and Ruby began attending to some of the practical considerations of moving in. They hauled their luggage into the living room, and upon investigating the small bathroom, Evie was pleased to discover that the plumbing was functional, so she and Ruby could each have a bath and change clothes. The room had also been cleaned, the cracks in the walls sealed over. Evie sensed her own magic flowing through the bathroom walls. The house had obviously allocated a bit of power to see that they were as comfortable as they could be, under the circumstances.

Again, Evie was grateful, and it made her suspect that the house's earlier anger and fear weren't directed at her and Ruby specifically. They had just been caught up in it.

As Evie soaked her sore muscles in the small claw-foot tub, she debated asking the house why it had run away. It wouldn't be able to tell her directly. At best, its emotions might give her some insight into what had made it afraid. At worst, the question might cause the house to retreat into silence and cut itself off from her and her magic. In the end, Evie decided not to risk the progress she'd already made toward earning its trust.

Reluctantly, Evie stood, leaving the warm bathwater behind and reaching for a fluffy towel she'd found in a cupboard by the sink. As she dried herself, she noticed a small pile of what looked like wood shavings scattered on the floor beside the tub. In the otherwise clean bathroom, they were strangely out of place, and Evie was positive they hadn't been there when she'd gotten into the bath.

Wrapping the towel around herself, Evie bent to pick up a handful of the shavings. They were a dark, bluish gray, warm to the touch, with the tiniest threads of silver running through them. She felt the house's magic in them, faint but unmistakable.

A prickle tugged at Evie's scalp, and she sensed the house's attention suddenly fixed on her. Spikes of anxiousness filled the air, sweeping away the lavender-scented steam from the bath and leaving the reek of sour milk in its place.

I wasn't meant to see this, Evie realized. This *shedding*, or whatever it was, was something the house had been trying to hide from her.

"What is this?" she asked quietly, putting aside her caution for the moment. "Is something hurting you that I can't sense?"

As she'd feared, the house recoiled. A sourceless wind swept through the room, fluttering her towel and blowing the shavings out of her hand. Evie closed her eyes against the sudden, swirling gale. When she opened them, the shavings were gone, the bathtub had been drained, and her clothes lay in a rumpled heap on the floor.

"That was rude," Evie said mildly. "I'm only trying to help."

But the house was ignoring her now, and she got no answer.

By the time she'd dressed, brushed the tangles from her inky black hair, and found Ruby playing outside beneath the willow tree, Evie was ravenous. "How about a walk into the village for breakfast?" she suggested.

Before Ruby could reply, there came the sound of wheels crunching gravel on the road toward the house. A bright ladybug-red bicycle drew to a stop just outside their gate, carrying an older woman with braids of steel gray hair and dark-brown skin. Seeing Evie and Ruby, she waved and smiled.

"Good morning and welcome to you!" she called, getting off the bike and leaning it against the stone wall. She wore a plain, scoop-necked brown shirt, but her loose trousers were a multicolored patchwork of fabrics, the cuffs rolled to the ankles. "I'm Cinda Cartwright. I'm so sorry I wasn't able to visit you yesterday." She came right up to Evie and seized her hand, shaking it in a firm grip. "I can't tell you how glad I am that you're here. How was the train ride? Did you have any trouble finding the house?"

"Only a bit," Evie said dryly. "It's nice to finally meet you in person, Mayor Cartwright."

"Oh, none of that!" The mayor beamed. "We're done with all that formal stuff now. Call me Cinda, please. And this must be Ruby!" she added as Ruby came bursting out from behind a curtain of willow branches.

"We were going into the village for breakfast," Ruby informed her. "We're starving!"

"Well, of course you are, after that long trip yesterday." Cinda hooked a thumb toward the road. "Come on with me, and I'll take you to Ben and Shara Green's place. Their café serves biscuits and gravy that are to die for."

Evie's stomach growled loudly at that promise. "It sounds wonderful," she said, and added, with a pointed look at the mayor, "Maybe on the way, you can tell us a little bit more about the situation with the house. We had some . . . challenges when we arrived yesterday."

Cinda's gaze lifted over Evie's shoulder, and she took her first real look at the house since she'd pulled up. Her mouth twisted in dismay. "Oh, dear," she said quietly. She looked back at Evie. "I can see you've already been at work fixing things, but there's new damage too. The house ran off again, didn't it?"

Again. Evie was taken aback. "This has happened before?"

Cinda's cheeks flushed with guilt. "Yes, and I should have told you about it, I know, but please, I . . . I wanted a chance to explain in person. I was afraid if I put it all in a letter, you'd never come and give us a chance." She wiped sweat from her forehead with the back of her hand. The early morning coolness was already giving way to another hot, humid day.

"It happened the first time about a month after Amelia died," Cinda said. "The second time was just last week." She collected her bike and began walking alongside it. "Come on. Better if I show you."

FOR THE FIRST PART OF THE WALK INTO THE VILLAGE, EVIE found it difficult to concentrate. She kept turning and looking back at the house, growing smaller and smaller in the distance.

Would it stay put while they were gone? Or would it drag itself back into the Thornwood at the first opportunity? Evie knew she couldn't keep an eye on the house all the time, and she couldn't do anything to stop it if it did decide to run off again, but the mayor's revelation that this was not the first but the *third* time it had happened had made her even more concerned, and not just about the house's welfare.

She couldn't believe Cinda had kept this from her. Evie tried to stifle her frustration and anger. If she'd known that the house was this unsettled, she might not have gotten her hopes up, and Ruby's too, about coming here.

She might have considered more carefully her devil's bargain with the ECRA.

Evie had been so sure that she could handle the house with her magic. That had been a mistake. She'd gambled their future on a situation that she was now realizing she knew nothing about.

Cinda noticed her restlessness. "I truly am sorry for not telling you everything that's been happening," she said. "I just wasn't prepared for the house to take Amelia's death so hard." She tightened her grip on the bike's handlebars. "It's never acted this way before. It used to be such a welcoming place. The village children would come and go as they pleased, playing in the gardens or swimming in the pond, and the house would watch over them. It was very protective." She shook her head sadly. "Now it won't let anyone near it."

"Who's been working in the gardens, then?" Evie asked, puzzled. "I noticed someone planted new vegetables and herbs."

"That was me," Cinda admitted. "The house tolerates me coming into the yard sometimes, mostly because it knows I'm stubborn as the oaks in the wood and won't be driven off by its tantrums. But I've only got time to do so much, and Amelia was always better at such things. I just couldn't stand to see all the work she'd done go to waste." Cinda's wrinkled face folded in sorrow.

"You were close," Evie realized. She felt some of her frustration ebb. "I'm sorry for your loss. I should have said so before."

"Thank you." Cinda dug a handkerchief out of her pocket and swiped at her eyes impatiently. "Much as I miss the old girl, she's put us all in a mess. Wasn't like her to leave things unfinished like she did."

"You mean because she didn't choose a successor?" Evie's brow furrowed. "Do you have any idea why? She must have said something."

"She was too sick at the end to say much." Cinda sighed. "Tell you the truth, most of us thought things were settled long ago, that she was going to choose Ig to take over after her."

"Who's Ig?" Ruby spoke up from behind them. It was clear she'd been listening, at the same time wandering from one side of the road to the other, so she wouldn't miss any of the sights as they made their way toward the village.

"Ignatius Smythe. His family founded Iskendra—as if he'd let any of us forget it—but his parents died years ago, and Ig's the only Smythe witch still living here, so he carries on the family's responsibilities in the village." She looked at Evie. "He was also set to be Amelia's successor as caretaker, or so we all thought. She spent a lot of time training him too, even sharing some of her duties with him when she wasn't moving around so well."

"Then why didn't she choose him as the next caretaker?" Evie asked. "Did something happen between the two of them? Or did the house reject him?"

"As far as I know, he got along with the house just fine—Ig was one of the ones who used to play there as a child," Cinda explained. "He was sweet when he was a boy, though he soured as he got older." She scowled and shook her head. "No, Amelia wouldn't say what happened, not even to me." Evie could tell by the crease in Cinda's brow that this was a source of hurt for the woman. "She came to me one day, not long before she died, and said, 'It's not going to be the boy, Cinda, or anyone else in the village. You need to advertise after I'm gone.' She looked like she was sad about it, and I can tell you Ignatius wasn't happy either, but that was the end of it. I couldn't talk her into changing her mind." Cinda brightened. "Ah, but here's the village coming up. We'll talk more later, but I want to give you the grand tour."

Evie looked up and got her first glimpse of Iskendra. Small farms and cottages dotted the outskirts, but in the village proper, the buildings were mostly brick and arranged closer together, forming a rough horseshoe around a sizable park. A tall spire poked out above the trees, attached to an impressive building of gray stone. Cinda explained that it was a former church and now the village library. The community building with the mayor's and councilors' offices sat on the opposite side of the park. The main street had been closed off, and the market was in full swing, with local businesses running stalls while children ran around playing.

One particular stall with a big red apple painted on the signboard caught Evie's attention as they walked past. Beneath the apple were the words WEAVER ORCHARD painted in green. The stall was empty, though, no apples or Weavers to be seen.

Evie nodded toward the stall. "I believe that's our neighbor," she said, "though we haven't had the pleasure of meeting him yet. Will he be at the market today?"

Cinda glanced over and harrumphed. "That's odd. The boy doesn't usually skip market day. He likes being around the people too much. Probably he's just running late and Ben set up the stall for him."

They continued on, but Evie kept glancing back at the stall, just as she'd done with the house. Maybe she was making too much of this. Maybe Mr. Weaver was sick at home, and that's why he hadn't gone out and wasn't answering his door. Still, Evie couldn't ignore the feeling that something wasn't right there either.

Past the park, at the edge of the village, there were a few more businesses, including a large warehouse whose roof had been partially caved in.

"That's Caleb Bearn's place," Cinda said, nodding to the damaged building. "He runs a glassblowing school and shop in there. As I said, about a month after Amelia's death, the house picked itself up and walked around the outskirts of the village. That time it didn't do any damage, just scared some people out of their wits. But last week, it went roving again and took out part of Caleb's roof."

"Why would it do that?" Ruby asked, walking up beside Evie to get a better look at the damage.

"I didn't see it myself, but some folks who did said it looked like an accident. Said that right afterward, the house turned and went back the way it'd come." Cinda slowed to let another bicyclist pass in front of their group.

The rider stopped and swiveled in his seat, giving them a nod. "Morning, Mayor Cartwright," he greeted Cinda. His gaze slid to Evie. "That the new witch you've got with you?"

"It is, Caleb," Cinda said. "I've just been telling her about your roof." She nodded to the man. "Caleb Bearn, meet Evie Sharpe and her daughter, Ruby."

Evie warmed at hearing Cinda introduce them this way, and she noticed that Ruby perked up, a hesitant smile spreading across her face. But when she turned her attention to Caleb, she caught the man staring at her with a decidedly unfriendly expression. He looked to be in his late fifties, his grayish brown hair combed neatly across his forehead, with a speckling of shiny burn scars on the backs of his pale hands. "I'm so sorry about the damage to your property, Mr. Bearn," she said. "If you don't mind, I'd like to have a closer look, see if I can do anything to help with repairs."

The man sniffed. "Mr. Smythe already offered to send part of his crew over later today to fix the roof," he informed her. "It'll slow down the renovations on the library, but he wouldn't take no for an answer. Watches out for the community, that one does." He looked Evie up and down. "Unless you can put a dozen vases and sculptures back together so I can sell them, I've got no use for you." He turned his bike and rode away without waiting for Evie to reply.

"Caleb Bearn, next time you're in my presence, you'd better remember your manners!" Cinda shouted after the man. She clucked her tongue disapprovingly. "Don't pay any attention to him," she said. "He lost a fair bit of money between the damage to his stock and roof, and he can't yell at a house. Well, he could, but he hasn't got the spine for it. He's been looking for someone to blame for a week."

"It's all right. Maybe I'll go and visit him later," Evie said, trying to quell her dismay as Cinda turned them down a shady side street. Flower boxes hung off the windowsills of the various shops and cafés. "There might still be something I can do for him."

"I'm sure he'd appreciate that," Cinda said, "though you're under no obligation to do so, especially after that display. You're not responsible for things that happened in Iskendra before you arrived."

Evie was happy to have the mayor's support. It took some of the sting out of the glassblower's dismissal, though she wished that Ruby hadn't been there to see it. The girl stayed close to Evie, looking around the quiet street as if waiting for someone else to step out and confront them.

Luckily, a distraction came when Cinda parked her bike next to a two-story brick building covered in what had to be a foot-deep curtain of green ivy. As the three of them gathered by the weathered front door, Evie noticed the sign on it: GREEN BOOT CAFÉ.

"Plenty of time to finish the tour after we've had breakfast," Cinda declared.

She opened the door, and the heavenly aromas of coffee and fresh-baked cinnamon rolls wafted over them. Evie closed her eyes and suppressed a moan as her stomach growled again.

They entered a cheerful room with yellow walls, lace curtains tucked up against the windows, and potted plants of all shapes and sizes sitting on the wide sills. A well-stocked coffee bar took up most of the back of the room. Green booths lined two walls, and walnut tables were arranged in the middle of the room around an open stone fireplace. Cinda led them to a booth and, in no time at all, two orders of biscuits and gravy were delivered to their table, along with a stack of fluffy pancakes for Ruby. The coffee was hot and delicious, served in large, bright-red mugs.

"I can't remember the last time I had a breakfast like this," Evie said. The ECRA's commissary was serviceable but nothing special, and she'd never been a very good cook. At eleven, Ruby was already better and more patient in the kitchen.

Cinda beamed her approval. "It's all down to Ben and Shara. Ben's running the market stall today, but Shara's cooking and looking after her nephew. He's staying with them for the summer and came down with a fever two nights ago. Poor thing hasn't been able to shake it." She gave Evie a hopeful look. "I know you've only just arrived, and you already have your hands full with the house, but I was wondering . . ."

"I'd be glad to take a look at the boy, but only if it's all right with his aunt and uncle," Evie clarified. After seeing Caleb Bearn's reaction to the new witch in town, her guard was up, and she didn't want to intrude where she wasn't welcome.

Cinda looked relieved. "Finish your breakfast first. Afterward, I'll go and have a quick word with Shara." Seeming to sense Evie's hesitation, she waved a hand. "You'll like the Greens. They're as good-natured as any folks you'll meet. They've been asking about you both for days, pestering me about when you'd be arriving." She smiled at Ruby. "And they have a daughter about your age."

"I know," Ruby said, her eyes alight. "Her name's Trin." She bit her lip and shot Evie a guilty look. "I peeked," she admitted. "I'm sorry! I couldn't help it."

"It's all right." Evie hid her smile behind her coffee cup. She'd been expecting this. "I'd be shocked if you didn't peek at the future before moving to a new place. I know I'd be tempted." She looked at Ruby askance. "Are you and Trin going to be friends, then?"

If a person could grin with their entire body, that's what Ruby was doing now as she shifted forward in the booth, kicking the table leg in her excitement. "*Yes,*" she said, "good friends."

That grin, and the obvious happiness radiating from her, made Evie put aside her uncertainties, at least for now. She might have come here underprepared, but she was serious about being a caretaker. She would just have to convince the house, and the villagers, to give her a chance.

Cinda blinked at Ruby. "Are you a farseer witch, then?" she asked. "I didn't realize." Her gaze turned thoughtful. "Well, it must have been hard for the ECRA to let you go. They don't get many farseers in their ranks, do they?"

"Currently, they don't have any," Evie informed her.

Farsight was a gift that was much sought-after. Glimpses of the future, when correctly interpreted, were more valuable than gold. It also meant that farseers were the most heavily exploited of all witches. Especially by the ECRA.

Evie met the older woman's eyes as Ruby slumped in her seat, trying to communicate that this wasn't a subject either of them wanted to pursue.

To her credit, Cinda was quick. She caught the look and gave a tiny nod of acknowledgment. She glanced at Ruby. "You're in good company here, you know. Both of you. Everyone knew Amelia was a land witch to the bone, but for years, I suspected that she had a bit of the farsight in her too. Stubborn old girl never would confirm it, though." She thumped the table with her fist and smiled fondly.

"Is that so?" Evie was surprised. It was rare for witch magic to overlap. And even witches with only a hint of farsight usually ended up working for city governments or as consultants for wealthy families who lived in the Quiet Lands, where glimpses of the future were especially prized.

Cinda shrugged. "It could just be a fancy on my part," she said. "Still, I did wonder . . ." She gave Evie a significant look. "But what folks choose to do with their own magic should be their business, as far as I'm concerned."

"Agreed," Evie said, relaxing in her seat. She found the more she talked to the mayor, the more she liked her. It was clear Cinda Cartwright wanted them here. Though Evie wished the mayor had warned her about the full extent of the problems with Thornwood house, she understood why she had kept those details a secret. Dealing with a runaway house was not a problem the villagers or the mayor had ever had to face, and Cinda had admitted in her letters that other applicants had been turned off by the challenges.

While they ate, Evie thought about the house and Caleb Bearn's roof. "Cinda," she said, stabbing a piece of sausage with her fork, "do you have any idea why the house came into the village those times, or where it was intending to go?"

Cinda wiped her mouth with her napkin. "Tell you the truth, there was so much upheaval among folks when it showed up, I spent most of my time calming everyone down and didn't get the chance to see what it might be after. The first time, it came through Jinny Teel's farm, pulling itself along on those wooden chicken legs. Left these long tracks all over her bean field." She demonstrated by slicing her butter knife through her biscuit.

"What direction did it go from there?" Evie pressed.

Cinda put her knife down. "Southwest, I think." She nodded vigorously. "Yes, it was southwest. It came in through a different field the second time, when it hit the warehouse, but it was going in the same direction. Can't imagine why."

"Surely, there must have been some reason," Evie said, handing Ruby an extra napkin to wipe the syrup off her hands. "What's in that area?"

"Nothing a magical house would be interested in," Cinda assured her. "There's a thrift shop, some storage sheds, and a back road that goes into the park. Some houses here and there, but that's pretty much it."

Ruby nudged Evie's arm. Evie followed the child's gaze to the café door, which had just swung open to admit a rangy man with light, wavy blond hair and round spectacles sliding down his nose. An older, taller man in stained work clothes with dark stubble on his pale cheeks stepped into the doorway behind him. His muscled frame filled up the space.

Cinda turned to look and winced. "Well, it was bound to happen sooner or later," she muttered.

"Who is that?" Evie asked. The blond man was already looking in their direction. His gaze wasn't unfriendly, but it wasn't welcoming either, and the large man standing behind him had his face set in a grim frown.

"Ig, er, Ignatius Smythe, head of the Smythe family." Cinda sounded resigned. "I thought it would take a little longer for him to hear you were in the village, but he has gossips everywhere."

Evie's breakfast was suddenly heavy in her stomach as a flutter of nerves went through her. She had no idea what sort of reception she could expect from the man, but she had a feeling it wouldn't be any warmer than Caleb Bearn's had been.

"What about the man with him?" Evie asked.

Cinda snorted. "That's Veld Tapper, head of the crew Ignatius hired for the library renovations. He used to work for Ignatius's father, and he's just as pleasant as he looks."

Some of the other diners looked up briefly from their breakfasts as Ignatius moved through the room, giving him a respectful nod. Evie smiled politely and tried to relax as the men approached their booth.

"Cinda, you should have told me you were bringing the new land witch into the village today," Ignatius admonished. "I wanted the chance to welcome her properly, see if she needed any help getting settled."

"Well, here she is, Ig." The young man scowled at the nickname, but Cinda just smiled sweetly. "Somehow, I knew you'd arrange an introduction, with or without my help."

Now that she viewed him up close, Evie realized Ignatius was younger than she'd first thought. He had to be in his late twenties or early thirties, not much older than her. He held himself stiffly, and there was a defiant tilt to his pointed chin. He stared at her curiously as his companion wandered over to the bar to order a coffee.

She also caught the hint of reddish magic swirling around him. It was hearth magic—a gentler way of saying he was a fire witch—a power that had a pleasant woodsmoke scent. The magic wasn't strong, but it was old. A presence long established, something that had been in the village for generations.

Long enough to feel as if it owned the place and was protecting its territory.

"Evie Sharpe," Evie said, standing and holding out her hand to the man. He took it, and she could feel him immediately pressing through the connection, trying to gauge how much power she had.

Well, now, that was just rude.

With a charming grin, she allowed a bit of her magic to sink into the handshake. It jolted up Ignatius's arm, not painfully, but strong enough to make his eyes widen behind his glasses. "Nice to meet you," she said.

Seven

The man dropped her hand like it was a damp sponge. He cleared his throat. "Ignatius Smythe," he said. "Welcome to Iskendra." He hesitated, his pale features twisting in sympathy. "Though I suppose I should be apologizing instead."

"Really? What for?" Evie asked.

"For the house, of course," Ignatius said, as if it should have been obvious. "You've had to endure more than a bit of disappointment where your new home is concerned, what with it running amok these past few months. I'm sure the place is a wreck inside." He tilted his head. "Or did it even let you inside? I understand none of the other applicants made it past the front door."

Out of the corner of her eye, Evie noticed Cinda stiffen. Evie waved her hand dismissively. "It did let us in, and I wasn't disappointed at all," she assured him, resuming her seat and picking up her coffee mug. "It's true the house has been damaged, but we're going to fix that, aren't we?" She bumped Ruby's shoulder, and the girl giggled. "Besides, there are always challenges moving to a new place."

"If you say so." Ignatius glanced away, pushing his glasses up the bridge of his nose. When he looked back, he wore an expression Evie couldn't quite interpret. "But then, you found everything you needed? In the house, I mean. Amelia's instructions—"

"Yes, I was getting to that part, Ig," Cinda said, an edge of impatience in her voice. "Really, they've only just arrived, and the house ran off again, so it's been a bit hectic—"

"It ran off *again*?" Ignatius interrupted, his gaze darkening. "When?"

Evie could practically feel the other diners leaning in to listen to their conversation. Well, there was nothing she could do about that. "It was in the Thornwood when we arrived late yesterday afternoon," she informed Ignatius. "I'm not sure how long it had been gone—probably no more than a day. It came back at nightfall." She glanced at Cinda, hoping to shift the direction of the conversation. "What's this about instructions?"

"Amelia left a diary for her successor," Cinda explained, holding out her coffee cup for a refill when the server came back by their table. "It's a tradition among caretakers here, to pass on things you'll need to know about the house and the village."

"I put it in her study after she was gone," Ignatius said. "Did you find it?"

Though he tried to hide it, Evie thought she detected an odd note of urgency in his voice. Was he worried she wouldn't be able to handle the house on her own? It irked her—especially since he might be right—but she kept her expression neutral.

"I'm afraid we've only explored a couple of the front rooms so far," Evie said. "But now that I know to look out for it, I'm sure I'll find the diary soon." She glanced at Cinda, her gaze softening. "That was thoughtful of Amelia to carry on the tradition for a witch she didn't even know."

Cinda smiled, though there was an edge of sadness to it. "I wish you could have gotten a chance to meet her. She was a tough old girl, but she was sweet. Most people didn't get to see that side of her."

"Full of surprises too," Ignatius put in with a thin smile. "The fact that she'd choose a stranger to replace her shocked us all." He looked at Evie, his gaze turning speculative. "I confess, I've been curious about you. Cinda told me that you come from Dorna City, but she was sparse on the rest of the details."

Evie found herself liking the mayor even more.

"That's quite the change, moving from a metropolis of thousands to our quiet little village," Ignatius droned on. "What did you do when you lived there?"

Evie hesitated. What she used to do for a living wasn't a secret, but it also wasn't something she wanted to advertise, especially now that she'd decided to leave that life behind her. But a family as old and influential as the Smythes probably had ways of finding out her history on their own, so she might as well not dissemble. It would only make it appear as if she had something to hide. "I worked for a branch of the ECRA," she hedged. It was the truth, if not the whole story.

"Ah, an agency witch," Ignatius said, nodding as if he'd solved some mystery. "Probably in administration, yes? A land witch who wanted to get out of the office and back to nature?"

"Something like that," Evie murmured into her coffee mug. Across from her, Cinda's lips twitched, but she didn't say anything.

"We've already started fixing the house," Ruby spoke up. "It has a brand-new porch *and* a swing."

Ignatius gave her an indulgent smile. "Well, that's a good little piece of magic for your first day here," he said, as Evie gritted her teeth. "At that rate, you should have the house back to its original condition within the year. Assuming it doesn't keep running off and undoing all your hard work, of course."

"It's upset," Ruby said, leaning her elbows on the table as she frowned at Ignatius. "It's not its fault that it lost its caretaker."

The man had grace enough to flush under Ruby's censure. "You're right," he said. "If there's any blame to be laid for the current situation, we should put it where it belongs."

"That's enough, Ig." Cinda put her coffee cup down in its saucer with a *thunk*. "There's no need to speak ill of the dead."

Ignatius's cool demeanor cracked. "I've told you before not to call me that," he snapped. "I'm not a child—"

"Oh, I beg to differ, lamb," Cinda said, stabbing a finger at his chest. "I've known you since you were skinning your knees and riding around the park on your brother's shoulders, and you were acting the same way then as you are now." She sat back. "What's done is done, it's a fine day outside, and I'd like you to leave these ladies to finish their breakfast in peace. If you really want to help, you can see them later."

Ignatius opened his mouth, a look of outrage flashing across his face, but Cinda's intimidating countenance stopped him from saying whatever he'd been about to say. Instead, he gestured imperiously to his companion at the bar. "Veld, let's go. We still need to meet with the carpenter about Mr. Bearn's roof." He nodded stiffly to Evie. "Enjoy your breakfast. If you need any help in your new role, I'd be happy to provide it."

"I appreciate that," Evie said, trying to salvage some of the conversation. No matter how unpleasant Ignatius might be, the last thing she wanted was to make an enemy her first day in the village. "Before you go, I was just asking Cinda if she had any idea why Thornwood house would want to run off. What's your opinion?"

For a second, Ignatius's anger faltered, and he looked torn. He opened his mouth to say something, then, glancing around and seeing the other diners not-so-casually listening in, he sighed and shook his head. "My opinion is it's nothing more than grief run rampant," he replied. "But grief can make us reckless. Porch swings are fine for a little fun, but sooner or later, the house is going to need a strong, competent hand to control it. In the meantime, my advice is, don't turn your back on it."

With those ominous words ringing in the air, he left them. Veld slid off his stool and lumbered after, coffee in hand. When the door swung shut behind them, Evie exchanged a resigned glance with Ruby. "That went about as well as could be expected, I suppose."

"I'm sorry," Cinda said, glowering after Ignatius. "That man needs the chip knocked off his shoulder and has for a long time."

"I'm sure these past few months have been hard for him," Evie allowed. "He expected to follow in his mentor's footsteps, only to find out that a stranger was going to take the caretaker's position instead. It must have been hard for a lot of the villagers."

Evie was beginning to wonder how many of them would be set against her, if the oldest family in Iskendra already had a grudge.

"They'll get used to it," Cinda insisted. "A lot of us are truly glad you've come, and if you ask me, we could use a shake-up around here. We've gotten too comfortable."

"In any case, if I want to prove myself, I'd better get started as soon as possible," Evie decided. She looked down at Ruby, who was still scowling at the door, as if she expected Ignatius to walk back through. "What do you think? Is it time to meet this famous Trin and the rest of her family?"

"Yes!" Ruby's scowl vanished, and she practically climbed over Evie to get out of the booth.

CINDA STUCK HER HEAD IN THE CAFÉ'S KITCHEN, AND AFTER A brief, muffled conversation, a short woman with wide, muscled shoulders and frizzy blond hair sticking out of a kerchief came out to greet them. She wore a stained apron with a bright-green boot stitched on it and the name of the café in swirly letters up above. She was wiping her hands on a towel as she smiled warmly at Evie.

"Shara Green," she said, shaking Evie's hand. "I can't tell you how good it is to finally meet you. We've never gone so long without a witch to look after the community, and we've all felt the loss." She exchanged a quick look with Cinda.

"I already told her about Jamie," Cinda confirmed with a nod.

"I'd be happy to take a look at him," Evie assured her, noticing the tension around the woman's eyes and bow-shaped mouth. "Has there been any improvement with his fever?"

"It spiked in the middle of the night and then broke first thing this morning," Shara said, leading them down a short hall off the kitchen that ended in a set of narrow stairs. She paused at the bottom, worrying her apron in her fists. "We live in the rooms upstairs. I've had Trin sitting with Jamie while I prep the lunch menu, but she came down a few minutes ago and said it looked like the fever was back again. It's got me worried because Jamie usually shrugs off any illness right away, especially a summer fever. I'm not sure whether I should send for his parents."

"Let me have a look first," Evie urged as they climbed the steps. On the landing, Shara turned to the first door on the right, gave a warning knock, then led them all inside.

The bedroom was warm, sunlight streaming through the windows, which had been cracked to let in a soft breeze. A freckled boy who looked to be about thirteen or fourteen was lying on the bed, the blankets balled up next to him, as if he'd been tossing and turning and twisting them all night. He was asleep but restless, shivering and mumbling in his sleep.

Sitting next to the bed was a slightly younger girl with dark-brown eyes and a thick fall of blond hair gathered over one shoulder. This must be Trin, Evie thought, as the girl looked just like her mother, especially through the eyes and the heart-shaped face. She wore a peach button-down shirt and pale-green trousers.

In a rare display of shyness, Ruby hung back, hiding behind Evie. That was interesting. If Ruby was nervous, it meant she'd been anticipating this encounter for some time. It made Evie even more curious to meet the girl.

Trin stirred when they entered the room, her eyes widening at seeing the strangers, but then she looked up at her mother with a worried expression.

"He's no worse, but not any better," she said. "I was just about to come and get you. I wasn't sure—"

"It's all right," Shara said, putting her hands on her daughter's shoulders. "The witch is here now." She glanced over at Evie. "This is my daughter, Trin."

"A pleasure to meet you," Evie said, nodding to the girl. It hadn't occurred to her until just then, but for the first time, she was in the position of presenting herself and Ruby to another mother and daughter. She kept her expression composed, but she felt the weight of the moment, even if no one else in the room did.

They'd talked a bit about what Ruby would call her after the adoption. For so long, she'd simply been "Evie" to her. It felt easy and right, and above all, Evie had wanted Ruby to feel comfortable. But there was more to it than that. The adoption was so new, a shared dream that had come perilously close to not happening at all, and one that was still contingent on Evie bonding with Thornwood house. They were both navigating their feelings about that, and the changes that had taken place in their lives. There was no need to rush things.

But standing here now, before this gathering of women, Evie had the sudden urge to shout it from the rooftops. "*This is my daughter. I'm her mother. Her mother! Isn't that wonderful?*"

No one had prepared her for these moments, the feelings that swept her along like an unruly sea. But she would learn to swim and not sink.

Gently, she prodded Ruby forward. "I'm Evie," she said. "This is my daughter, Ruby. She's your age, Trin."

"It's nice to meet you," Trin said. She stayed close beside her mother, but she was watching Ruby curiously.

"Why don't you two girls go downstairs?" Cinda suggested. "Trin, I'm sure Ruby would love to know more about the village. She'll start school here in the fall and will probably be in your class."

"Sure." Trin smiled hesitantly, and that seemed to be all it took for Ruby to relax. The two of them went downstairs, leaving Evie, Shara, and Cinda to surround Jamie's sickbed. All business now, Evie sat in the chair Trin had vacated and laid her hand on the boy's forehead.

Immediately, she felt the inflammation, sensed his body struggling to purge an infection. It didn't take her long to find the source. A cloth bandage covered the tender skin between his thumb and index finger. When she gingerly unwrapped it, she saw the angry red mark.

"Where did he get that cut?" Evie asked.

"In the Thornwood," Shara said. "He went fishing by himself down at the river a couple of days ago." She pulled up a chair for Cinda and then perched on the opposite side of the bed. "There's a footbridge that goes across the river just outside the village," she added for Evie's benefit. "The local kids go underneath it to fish, and sometimes they wander into the wood to play, but we always make them stay within sight of the bridge so they don't get lost. They've gotten cuts from the oak bark before, and they never got sick."

"Some of the oldest trees have poisonous sap that can cause fevers like this," Evie explained, "but those would most likely lie deep within the wood."

Shara frowned. "He swore he never left the bridge, though he seemed a little confused when he got home that evening. I blamed it on the fever."

"He probably got curious and wandered farther than he should have," Cinda said. "They all do it sooner or later, but they make their way home."

Evie laid a hand on the boy's chest. Jamie's heartbeat thumped beneath her fingers as she sank into her connection with the land around her, from the flowers lined up neatly in boxes all along the street, to the ivy snaking up the building's walls. Her thoughts spiraled outward, all the way to the distant Thornwood and the ever-present, listening trees. Taking a breath, she let her awareness deepen, feeling the same pulse of life from every person in the village.

It was the first time she'd let her magic encompass a large group of people since she'd left Dorna City. She sensed a vibrant community, happy in a general way, but like all human hearts, there were fissures and cracks, pockets of uncertainty and maliciousness, aching sadness and overwhelming joy. She took it all inside her for a brief moment, just to feel the shape of it, knowing she couldn't hold it for long.

Gradually, she withdrew her power, letting all the other lives slip away, until there was only the boy in front of her. Her magic touched each raw, burning place inside him, soothing them like a cool compress. Offering a bit of her own vitality, bolstered by her connection to the land, she drew out the infection.

When she was done, she sat back in her chair, aware of the wood creaking beneath her, blinking as the room slowly came back into focus. Jamie had turned onto his side and appeared to be sleeping deeply now, one arm tucked under his pillow, with none of the restless twitching she'd seen when she'd first come into the bedroom.

Evie turned to the basin by the bed and poured fresh water into it from the cream-colored pitcher. She soaked a rag and used it to wipe Jamie's face.

"It'll take a few days for him to fully recover his strength," Evie cautioned the women, "but the fever won't come back. He'll be fine."

"Really?" Relief made Shara's voice wobble. "Oh, thank you. That's such a weight off my mind." She straightened out the blankets on the bed and pulled the sheet over Jamie. "You are staying, aren't you?" she entreated Evie. "In Iskendra, I mean. I know the house hasn't taken to any of the other applicants, but surely . . ." Her voice trailed off as she glanced at Cinda.

"I want her to stay as much as you do," the mayor said with a rueful chuckle, "but in the end, you know it's the house's decision, and Evie's."

"The house and I have come to an understanding," Evie said carefully. "We're taking things day by day, to see if it will eventually accept me as the new caretaker." She hesitated but decided to be honest. "I hope it does, because Ruby and I would very much like to stay."

Shara might have heard the note of longing in Evie's voice, for she smiled. "My family and I would love to have you over for dinner next week, if you and Ruby are able to come? It'll give you some time to settle in first."

"We'd be delighted," Evie said, touched by the invitation. This was the welcome she had dreamed about when she'd first contacted Cinda about the position. It gave her hope that she might yet win over the rest of the villagers.

And the house.

Evie hung the washrag on the side of the basin and was just about to stand, when Jamie shifted in his sleep. The sleeve of his nightshirt pushed up, revealing part of his forearm and wrist. A dark rash covered the skin there, on the same arm where he'd been cut by the tree bark. But instead of being red with inflammation, there was a distinct bluish cast to that patch of skin, threaded with veins of silver.

A chill ran up Evie's spine as she leaned over the bed to get a closer look. The rash was fading now, probably as a result of her healing magic, but it bore a striking resemblance to the shavings she'd found on the bathroom floor of Thornwood house that morning.

How was that possible?

She reached out, questing with her magic again, this time focusing on that single spot of rash instead of the boy's entire body. It took her a moment, but . . .

There – something lurking just beneath the surface of the skin. It wasn't a poison from the ancient oaks' sap, as she'd first thought. This was something older, a more potent form of magic. Evie had never felt anything like it before.

"What is that?" Cinda asked sharply, noticing the rash. "Shara, did he have that when the fever started?"

"No," Shara said, shaking her head in bewilderment. "It must have come on later. Is that what made him sick?"

"I don't think so," Evie said. "He might have gotten into some merkyl plants while he was fishing. They grow along the shoreline and can cause a rash like this." It wasn't entirely a lie. The waxy leaves of the merkyl plants *could* cause a rash, but not one that bore threads of silver. "My magic will heal this too, given enough time to work," she hastened to reassure them. "Don't worry."

Both women visibly relaxed. Evie rolled up both Jamie's sleeves and checked the rest of his exposed skin to make sure the rash hadn't spread any farther than his arm, but there was no sign that it had. She pulled the sheet back over him and stood.

"Cinda, would it be all right if we continued the village tour another time?" she asked. "I think I'd better collect Ruby and go check on the house, just to make sure it's . . . staying put." Now, that was a sentence she never thought she'd say about a house.

"Of course," Cinda said. "I'll get my bike and see you home."

"Oh, thank you, but that's not necessary," Evie said, waving her off. "I'm sure you have other things to do, and I know the way now."

"It's a nice walk between the village and your house," Shara agreed.

Evie smiled and bid the women a distracted goodbye. Her thoughts were racing. She wished she'd gotten a chance to use her magic to examine the shavings in the bathroom before the house had destroyed them. Would they have contained the same traces of old magic she'd felt in Jamie? Or was it just a coincidence?

". . . my advice is, don't turn your back on it."

Ignatius's words rang a warning in her head. Just what was going on at Thornwood house?

EIGHT

They left the café, Evie leading Ruby back through the village the way they'd come. Her daughter chattered happily the whole way, bouncing along the sidewalk and regaling Evie with tales of Trin and how she and Ruby were already best friends.

"Trin's an artist," Ruby was saying as they turned down the street where the glassblower's shop was. "She has drawings all over her bedroom walls. I saw some of them in my vision, but there are lots more, and they're even better up close! She did some of Thornwood house too."

Evie was impressed. "I'd like to see those. It would be nice to have a comparison of how the house looked before it was damaged. It might help us with the repairs."

She slowed as they approached the glassblower's so she could get a better view of the damaged warehouse.

"What are you looking at?" Ruby asked, seeing her intent expression.

"I'm looking for old magic, but I'm not feeling anything," Evie admitted. It had been a long shot, but she'd wondered if that strange magic she'd sensed earlier might have been what drew the house into the village. As they approached the shop door, Evie filled Ruby in on what she'd discovered in the bathroom that morning and its similarity to the rash she'd seen on Jamie.

"Do you think there's something bad happening?" Ruby asked, her excitement fading. "Magic that's hurting the house and the people here?"

"I don't know yet," Evie said. "It might not be good *or* bad." Magic was rarely one or the other. It came down to how people used it. "Right now I'm just trying to get more information."

She tried the shop door, only to find it locked. There was a small handwritten sign on the door that said Mr. Bearn had a class in progress and the shop was temporarily closed. "Doesn't look like we'll get to speak to the glassblower right now," she said ruefully. She'd wanted to see what she could do to help him, but that would have to wait for another day. "We really do need to get back to check on the house."

"Don't worry, it's still there," called a voice from behind them.

Evie turned to see a woman about her age riding toward them on a beautiful lemon yellow bicycle. A brown wicker basket attached to the handlebars was overflowing with books. As the woman rolled to a stop in front of them, one of the books slid out and landed with a smack on the pavement.

"Oops, sorry about that," the woman said, as Ruby bent to pick up the book. "I always try to take too many."

"No such thing," Evie said, smiling. "I love your bicycle."

"Thank you." The woman beamed. She wore sandals and ankle-length red pants with a white blouse. Her short brown hair was tucked beneath a wide-brimmed straw hat, secured at her chin with a tie. Evie noticed the books in her basket were all marked with the same sticker on the spines: *Iskendra Public Library*.

"I'm Gemma Gray," the woman said, holding out her hand. Evie shook it. "Village librarian—well, one of them anyway, along with my sister. But I handle all the book deliveries for people outside the village. That's how I know your house is still there." She wrinkled her nose. "That probably sounded odd, didn't it? Like I was spying on your house. I really wasn't! I just had a book delivery for Gil Weaver, but he wasn't home, and when I came back by, the house was sitting right where it should be." She took a breath. "Sorry, I'll stop talking. I'm always a little nervous meeting new people."

"No, that's . . . thank you for setting my mind at ease," Evie said. "I'm Evie Sharpe, and this is my daughter, Ruby." She let go of the woman's hand, but an echo of power lingered in the air, a unique twist of purplish magic that smelled of old books and sounded like the ticking of a clock in a quiet room. It was familiar and unmistakably—

"Time magic," Ruby piped up excitedly, sensing it too. "You're a time witch!"

"Ruby," Evie admonished gently, "that's not polite, remember?"

Not all witches wanted to discuss their powers openly, and some of them actively concealed the colors of their magical essences, which were normally visible to other witches and those sensitive to magic, in order to avoid being exploited for their abilities.

"Sorry," Ruby said, color flooding her cheeks as she handed the book back to the woman. "It was just so strong, and it felt exactly like it said in my study books."

"It's all right," Gemma said, smiling. She tucked the book securely into her basket. "It's not a secret. My sister has the same gift." She glanced back at Ruby. "Have you never met a time witch before?" she asked. "That's strange. We're not so rare."

That was true, but the ECRA had almost as much difficulty recruiting time witches as they did farseers. Having spent so much of her life on the ECRA campus, Ruby had never encountered one. Evie had met one only once before, many years ago.

"We're pleased to meet you now," Evie said.

Ruby nodded eagerly. "Can I see some of your magic?" she asked, glancing at Evie to make sure she hadn't overstepped again.

"Of course," Gemma said before Evie could reply. She fished a large hardcover book out of her basket, balanced it on her open palm, and began thumbing quickly through the pages. Her eyes took on a faraway cast. Suddenly, the turning pages gleamed with a purple radiance and began to slow, passing from one half of the book to the other like they were moving through water. Eventually, they stopped altogether, each one frozen straight up in the air, caught between one moment and the next. It was a simple yet elegant display, the work of someone confident in their power.

Ruby was entranced. "Did you just make time stop?" she demanded. "How am I still moving, then? How are we all still moving?"

Gemma chuckled. "No one can truly stop time, not on that kind of scale," she said. "Time witches manipulate the forces around people and objects and their *relationship* to time. It's how we're able to look into the past. We shift our minds back to moments that have already happened and inhabit the empty spaces within them for brief periods, while no time at all passes for our bodies in the present."

She let the magic go, and the pages fell to either side of the book. She closed it with a snap, tossed the book into the air, and waited as it slowly drifted back down and came to rest in her hands. The purple light faded. "It takes a great deal of magic," she said, "but fortunately, objects are a lot less draining to affect than ourselves."

Ruby continued to stare at the book in fascination as Gemma put it away. "I wish I could do that," she murmured. "It's amazing."

"It is," Evie agreed. She put her hand on Ruby's shoulder. "Please tell Gemma thank you for sharing her magic with you. She didn't have to."

"Thank you," Ruby said breathlessly. "That was great!"

"You're welcome," Gemma said. "Anytime you want to learn more, I'm at the library most days, unless I'm making deliveries. My sister and I live on the top floor, in the old belfry."

"That's very kind of you," Evie said. "We haven't had a chance to visit the library yet, but we saw the building from a distance. It's stunning."

"Oldest and tallest structure in Iskendra," Gemma said proudly, leaning over her handlebars. "Just wait, it'll really be something once the renovations are complete. That won't be until the end of summer, unfortunately, but you should still come by sometime and let me give you a tour." She raised her hands. "No rush, though. I understand you've probably got your hands full moving in, and the house isn't exactly . . ." She let the thought trail off, looking suddenly uncomfortable.

"It's a challenge," Evie agreed. "We weren't expecting the house to be quite so *mobile*, were we?" She looked down at Ruby.

"Yes, it's just been the strangest thing." Gemma rocked her bike forward and back in agitation. "Thornwood house never used to behave like this. I mean, of course it's going through a difficult time, but to push people away like it has—it's so sad."

"The house let *us* in," Ruby said staunchly. "Maybe something's changing."

"Well, that's a credit to you two," Gemma said, "because no one else has gotten so far. But is it safe inside? You haven't noticed anything strange, anything that might be causing the house to act like it has?"

Much like Ignatius, Gemma seemed awfully interested in the fact that Evie and Ruby had managed to get inside Thornwood house. Was it just curiosity, or did they know something Evie didn't? Once again, Evie was reminded that she and Ruby were outsiders here. She knew it was only natural to feel that way, but it wasn't something she enjoyed.

"We haven't noticed anything strange, but we've only just begun to explore the place," Evie said. "I've been asking some of the other villagers if they have any theories about why the house is running off. What do you think?"

"I'm afraid I'm not as familiar with the house or its history as most of the rest of the village," Gemma explained, "so I couldn't speculate. My sister and I only moved here a couple of years ago, and we've spent most of our time and attention on the library. I'd be happy to hunt down some books on sentient houses, though, if you think that might be a help to you."

"That would be wonderful," Evie said, "thank you." She looked off toward the road home. "We really should get going, but I wonder if we might ask another favor."

"Anything," Gemma said brightly. "How can I help?"

"Where did you get your lovely bicycle?"

Gemma grinned. She hopped off her bike, turned it around, and began walking alongside it. "Follow me," she said. "I've got just the place for you."

Nine

It was after lunch by the time Evie and Ruby arrived back at the house, but they did so riding a pair of shiny secondhand bicycles from Vera's Wheels and Heels—purveyors of fine bicycles *and* shoes, as it turned out. Ruby had selected a sky-blue bicycle with a white wicker basket, while Evie had opted for lavender and cream.

With the fine weather and the breeze, the bike was perfect. It made her feel like a child again, riding on those long summer days that seem to last forever. She sailed down the road next to her daughter, the gravel crunching under their tires, sun on their faces, and Ruby pedaling like mad after challenging Evie to a race.

Out of breath and laughing, they rolled up to their gate, only to discover that the rest of their belongings had been delivered in their absence. The various boxes and sheet-wrapped pieces of furniture had been unceremoniously dumped just inside the wall, as far away from the house as possible. At a glance, nothing appeared to be broken or damaged, but the movers obviously hadn't found a warm welcome from Thornwood house.

Shingles lay scattered throughout the yard. A couple of the shutters had been torn off the front windows and were now floating in the willow pond. The house itself crouched, sullen and silent, exactly where they'd left it, but it did swivel its turret minutely toward them as they got off their bikes.

Ruby, still glowing from the trip into the village, making a new friend, and getting her own bike, was undeterred by the mess. She immediately set to work sorting everything. Evie decided to follow her example, ignoring the debris and the house for now as she carried an armful of bags inside.

They'd stopped at the general store for supplies. Luckily, the refrigerator in the corner of the kitchen was still working, and the house's electricity was up and running, so they could keep the food Evie had bought chilled and fresh. She had also attempted to call on Caleb Bearn again before they left the village, but the glassblower had still been in his private lesson and wouldn't come out to speak to her. It had been discouraging, but Evie vowed to keep trying. For now, she wanted to focus her energies on the house.

It would take time to gain the place's trust, but Evie couldn't help feeling a sense of urgency. The more she thought about it, the more convinced she was that something had happened in the months after the old witch's death, something that had caused the house to lash out and distressed it enough to make it run to the village and the Thornwood. But what was it? And was it related to the strange magic she'd discovered in the house and on Jamie?

Evie needed to know what she was facing. The sooner she could get the house to open up to her, bond with her, the sooner she and Ruby would be secure, and Evie could help put right whatever had gone wrong.

Since Evie had already given the house all the magic she could for now, she decided the first step today was to address the problems they could fix without the help of magic. To that end, they set to work sweeping up debris on the first floor, salvaging what could be salvaged, and hauling the rest outside to be taken away.

While they cleaned, Evie kept an eye out for the diary that Ignatius and Cinda had told her about. She was curious what words of wisdom Amelia Howell might have left for her, and she would take all the help she could get dealing with the house and its situation.

But the afternoon wore on, and there was no sign of a diary or instructions of any kind. Ignatius had said it was in Amelia's study. Since there was no room that fit that description on the first floor, it must be upstairs, which was still inaccessible because of the broken staircase. That was a frustrating setback, but Evie reminded herself to be patient. They would get up there eventually.

In the meantime, they rehung the chandelier in the kitchen and hauled away the broken cabinets and the two ruined halves of the kitchen table. By midafternoon, the downstairs was clean enough to bring in some of their own things, so together, Evie and Ruby muscled in the heavy round dining table they'd brought from the city, one of the few pieces of furniture that they'd owned themselves. Evie had painted it periwinkle blue, except in the center, where Ruby had left yellow handprints on it when she was eight. It looked right at home in the corner of the kitchen, where two sets of diamond-gridded windows met and an L-shaped bench and a handful of chairs provided plenty of seating.

After that, they were well and truly exhausted. So, while the evening sun cast its ruddy light through the newly cleaned windows, Evie and Ruby sat at their table and ate chicken sandwiches dressed with pickles and onion and drank cold lemonade.

They were sweaty, dirty, and sore. But it wasn't the soul-bled feeling that Evie had had working for the ECRA, giving every ounce of her magic, knowing that they would continue to demand more. This was the best sort of tired, an *earned* feeling that happened on their own terms. A long day of hard work and progress toward building their new life.

There were still some structural issues in the living room that needed to be addressed with magic, but overall, Evie couldn't have been more pleased. It had been a good day and, unlike with the movers, the house had shown no signs of distress or displeasure at any of their activities.

In fact, the longer they'd worked, the more Evie felt a stirring of interest from the house. She'd noticed it while she stood at the kitchen counter, preparing mint tea for the first time since they'd arrived. She measured out the fragrant leaves and poured hot water into the pot, marveling at how the familiar ritual, when performed in a new space, changed the experience.

In their old place, she always made tea first thing in the morning. There'd been no windows in their tiny galley kitchen, and the walls were thin enough that Evie could hear the other residents moving around their apartments, turning on showers and getting ready for work. She'd used those small sounds in a meditative way, letting them ground and soothe her as she gathered her power for whatever would be required of her that day.

Here, as she put two of their favorite, daisy-yellow tea mugs they'd brought from the city on the counter, she became aware of finch song drifting through the open windows. Of how the sun pooled in various spots on the flagstone floor, changing the temperature beneath her feet as she moved from the refrigerator to the stove.

The steps of the preparation hadn't changed. Yet in that moment, Evie felt like it was the first pot of tea she'd ever made.

And as the air filled with fragrant steam and Evie savored that first sip, she could have sworn she heard a contented sigh pass through the kitchen, making the curtains flutter and the repaired chandelier dance.

They'd felt the house's presence again when she and Ruby had struggled to arrange a mossy green area rug in the center of the living room floor. The thing was heavy and unwieldy, and Evie felt the frustration bubbling up between her and Ruby as they tried to agree on how to position it properly. Then, just when tempers were starting to fray, the house had unexpectedly flexed its creaky floorboards to help unroll the rug in the perfect spot.

They were small things, but Evie counted each one a victory.

After dinner, Evie wiped down the table and helped Ruby stack the dishes in the deep sink. Then she went into the living room and was just about to use her magic on the cracks in the walls when she caught something out of the corner of her eye. She turned toward the back of the living room and noticed a narrow door at the rear of the house, just off the hallway where the bathroom was.

There was nothing ornate or otherwise out of the ordinary about the door. It was a simple wooden rectangle with a rusted iron latch, but Evie's scalp prickled the moment she laid eyes on it.

Because she was certain the door hadn't been there before.

Ruby came down the hall while Evie was standing in front of the door, wiping her damp hands on her pants. She stopped and stared. "Where did that come from?"

Well, at least she wasn't imagining things. "I have a feeling it's always been here," Evie said. "The more time we spend in the house, the more our power acclimates to it, which means we can start to see its magic . . . including any illusions it might create."

She'd read about the process when she'd applied for the caretaker position, but seeing it in action was something else. She hadn't known the house could use its powers to conceal an entire room.

"But why?" Ruby asked, addressing her question to the house by looking up at the ceiling. "Why would you make the door disappear?"

They waited, but there was no response. Evie reached out and tried the latch. She pressed her weight into it, but the door was stuck tight.

"It's going to take magic to open this, I'm afraid," Evie said.

She'd only been making an observation. She hadn't actually intended to try using her power on the door, but the house must have thought otherwise. Suddenly, the lights on the crystal-and-brass fixture hanging above their heads strobed painfully. A hot wind gusted through the hall, accompanied by a wave of anger that filled the air with the reek of rotten fruit.

Evie released the latch at once and stepped back from the door. "It doesn't want us in there." That was an understatement. She could practically feel the walls quivering with emotion. "We'll respect your wishes," she said, addressing the house. "We didn't mean any harm."

But the anger was slow to fade, and with it went the house's presence. She'd driven it away again. Frustration warred with sympathy in Evie. She knew she needed to be patient, but she'd also never expected the house to hide something like this from them.

How could she create a bond between them if Evie couldn't trust the house?

"What do you think is in there?" Ruby whispered, as if afraid the house was still listening.

"I don't know," Evie said. She hoped it wasn't Amelia Howell's study, the place where she'd left her diary and instructions for her successor. But surely that couldn't be the case. Why would the house try to hide a room that the old witch had obviously *meant* for someone to enter?

A shiver of unease went through Evie as she looked over at the door again. "Come on," she told Ruby, "let's go outside and talk."

She gathered up a load of trash and headed out to the yard, Ruby following at her heels. She managed to cram the last of the debris in the trash cans, but when she stood up straight, she noticed Ruby frowning.

"I think I should look into the house's future," Ruby said, sounding more certain now than she had the day before. She perched on the mossy wall next to the road and squinted up at the house. "We need to find out what's going on here."

"Is that what the magic is telling you?" Evie asked.

"I'm not sure," Ruby admitted. "But I have this . . . fizziness . . . in my head, and I just *want* to look. I won't dig too deep," she promised.

Evie leaned against the cool stone wall next to her daughter. Misgivings churned in her stomach. Being a farseer witch was a double-edged sword at the best of times, but being the teacher of a farseer also came with its own unique challenges. It would be so easy to let Ruby look, in the hopes of getting a shortcut to the mystery. But knowledge of the future came with a price, and Evie's first instinct was to protect and shield Ruby, to carry all the burden herself.

Ruby cocked her head, as if sensing Evie's indecision. "You're always worried about using me for my magic," she said, "but you never have."

"Then I've done the bare minimum as your teacher," Evie said. She ran her fingers over the cool moss, letting the connection to nature soothe and ground her. "Farseer magic is one of the most valuable magics that exist. The world will find so many ways to try to use you for your power, Ruby. I want *you* to always have the power to say no."

"But you're my—" Ruby stopped, her small fists clenching nervously as she tried to find the words she wanted. "We decided to be a family," she said at last. "Right?"

Evie felt that shift in her chest again, the weight of another moment, of change sinking in as they sat outside the house they were trying to shape into a home. "That's right," she said. "But it's okay for you to take the time to figure out what that means."

Ruby lifted her chin. "It means I *want* to help you."

"I know, and you're brave and wonderful for it, but that makes this situation even more of a slippery slope," Evie said. "Sometimes we'll do the most foolish things for the ones we care about."

"You've been used for your magic too," Ruby said quietly, "by the ECRA."

Evie didn't deny it. "That's behind us now."

Ruby shook her head, looking faintly exasperated. "I just mean, you know what it's like to be used for your power, so I think you'll do your best not to do that to me." She met Evie's eyes. "Don't you think?"

Evie smiled, though she still felt a lingering ache in her chest. "You're becoming quite the wise witch, you know that? I'm not sure I'm ready for how grown-up you sound."

Ruby's cheeks reddened, but Evie could tell she was pleased. "So, come on! Let me look!"

"If that's truly what you want, I won't stop you," Evie said. "Just remember that there's a limit to the number of times you can look, and you won't know—"

"Where that limit is," Ruby finished for her. "I know." She winced. "I learned my lesson the last time."

Evie nodded and let it go. She'd said what she needed to say. Whether as a parent or a teacher, or both, all she could do now was wait as Ruby closed her eyes, laying her palms flat on the stone wall to connect herself to the property. It wasn't the same as the connection Evie made with the land for her own magic, but it was just as important to following the threads of possible futures.

The sun had already set, but there was still enough light in the sky that Evie could see the intense concentration on Ruby's face and the burgeoning pink aura that haloed her. She not only sounded grown-up; she looked it too. In her mind's eye, Evie glimpsed the shadow of the witch her daughter was yet to become, a notion brief but strong.

Time was going so fast now, Evie thought in wonder. It had gone even faster in the city, when every day had been a blur of work, moving from one crisis to the next, with no time to slow down and enjoy a summer night like this.

Once again, a sense of longing washed over her. Could they really keep this slower-paced life?

Ruby opened her eyes and exhaled. Her lips were sealed in displeasure.

"Are you all right?" Evie asked, laying her hand on the girl's arm.

"I'm fine," Ruby said, but she didn't sound like it. "All I saw was a tree. It was a strange tree, like something out of a fairy tale. There was nothing to do with the house."

A fairy-tale tree.

The hairs on Evie's arms rose, and a memory surfaced from the back of her mind. It had been weeks ago, when she'd first started reading about Iskendra and its history, a tiny footnote in an obscure text discussing the extinct flora and fauna of the area. "What did the tree look like?" she asked.

"It was silver," Ruby said, "like there was starlight shining from inside it. Its leaves were shaped like oak leaves, but the color was different. They were dark. So dark. Almost . . ."

"Blue?"

Ruby looked at her in surprise. "How did you know?"

Blue and silver—like the shavings in the bathroom. Like Jamie's rash.

"I think you found exactly what I'm looking for," Evie said with a burgeoning excitement. "The missing clue in all this." She turned her gaze to the tree line. "I need to go into the Thornwood tonight." She looked back at her daughter. "Would you be all right staying at the house by yourself?"

"Why can't I go with you?" Ruby demanded, hopping off the wall. "Is it dangerous? If it is, you'll need someone to watch your back."

"It's not going to be dangerous," Evie assured her. "I'm asking you to stay here because I believe if you're at the house, it won't go roaming again. I don't know about you, but I have no desire to clean up another mess, or to lose the bits of furniture we have left."

Ruby grimaced. "That's true," she said, but she still looked anxious. "What are you looking for in the Thornwood?"

"I'm looking for the tree in your vision," Evie explained. "It's an oak, like you said, but an old one and very rare."

"Is it magical?" Ruby asked. "I thought there were only regular oaks in the Thornwood."

"So did I," Evie said, "and, yes, it's definitely magical. If I'm right about what you saw, it's called a Star Oak. Its magic shines silver and blue, like its appearance."

The trees were such a rarity in the world now that they were more the stuff of legends and myth than reality. There were a few tiny specimens left in museums and magical botanical gardens, but those were pale shadows of the glory of those ancient oaks.

They'd become endangered long ago because every part of them could be used for amazing magical effects. Their leaves could be stripped for healing poultices that were said to staunch heavy bleeding and cure mortal wounds. Elixirs brewed from their crushed acorns or strips of bark could make a person live many years longer than they might otherwise have, and with a better quality of life. It was said that one of the last full-grown Star Oaks had helped to keep a mind witch alive until their one hundred and forty-fifth birthday.

Even with all that, by far, the Star Oaks' most sought-after resource was their silver branches, because they could be cut and shaped into powerful wands, instruments that could amplify a person's magic tenfold, easily making them the most powerful witch of their kind. Competition to create such items had driven the trees to the brink of extinction.

To find a Star Oak untouched and thriving in the wild today would be like seeing a unicorn, or a dragon, or some other creature straight out of a storybook. The magical community would go into a froth over such a discovery.

The implications of Ruby's vision crashed over Evie in a dizzying wave. If what she had seen was true, then they had more here to protect than just Thornwood house. If there was a Star Oak in the wood, and they didn't act to guard it, it was only a matter of time before a witch would come hunting for its magic. Wars had been fought over that kind of power.

The world had enough problems, Evie thought. It didn't need that temptation.

One step at a time, she reminded herself.

"I believe the Star Oak is what the house was looking for when it ran away into the Thornwood," Evie said, pulling herself back to the present. "I have to see if I'm right."

"But why would the house be looking for a magic tree?" Ruby asked. "It doesn't make sense."

Oh, but it did. Evie just hadn't considered the possibility before. "I suspect it's related to why the house has fallen into so much disrepair," she said. "Do you remember what we read about sentient houses, that day we went to the library in Dorna City to research Iskendra?"

Ruby nodded. "They're made from ancient stone or wood, things that have old magic." She gasped. "Was Thornwood house made from a Star Oak?"

"That's what I'm beginning to think." If so, the house had likely gone into the wood seeking another tree of its kind to heal itself and replenish its power. But if that was the case, why had it gone into the village those first two times it ran off? Why hadn't it gone straight into the Thornwood?

If she was able to locate the Star Oak, it might give her some answers. But no matter what, she had to make sure it was safe. Evie glanced up at the sky. "I'll need to wait until near midnight to go."

"But why so late?" Ruby pressed. "Why can't you go now while there's still some light?"

"The rule of three," Evie told her. The old lessons were sunk deep into her bones. She recited them from memory. "The night is made of threes, like the fairy tales. The three minutes after midnight are when hidden things show themselves. Three o'clock in the morning is when your fears nudge you awake, and you have to decide whether to sit up with them, quell them with a cup of tea, or let them chip away at you. Three minutes before dawn is when your magic is at its most powerful. Untouched and deep, like a clear pool in the heart of a forest."

Ruby considered her words. "So, you need to go after midnight because you think the Star Oak is hidden?"

"I'm certain it is."

It would have to be, for it to have survived so long.

But the house had been looking for it. And young Jamie had probably found it by accident. The fever and rash were side effects of the tree's ancient magic, a power used to make the boy forget what he'd seen and where he'd been, to protect the tree's location from those who might try to strip it and take its power for themselves.

Evie gazed up at the house and its turret. If she was right, there were more secrets in the Thornwood—and in the house—than she'd ever dreamed.

TEN

Later that night, Evie left Ruby fast asleep on the living room couch, buried underneath her favorite patchwork quilt. All the work they'd done that day had been worth it. The downstairs rooms had been completely transformed. In addition to all the cleaning they'd done in the foyer and kitchen, they'd rearranged the living room furniture, bringing in their own few pieces to add to what was already there, and rescued all the plants that had been dumped from their pots. Evie had given a bit more of her magic to fix the structural damage, sealing cracks and mending broken beams and buckled floors. A fresh coat of rich autumn-yellow paint gleamed from the walls, contrasting perfectly with the exposed ceiling beams arching above their heads.

Next, she would begin work on mending the staircase so they could reach the upper floors and assess the damage there. Hopefully, they would also find Amelia Howell's diary.

Evie paused at the gate, shifting her medicine bag on her shoulder. She wasn't sure what instinct had made her grab it on her way out the door, but she rarely regretted listening to her intuition.

She turned back to look at the house's turret. Moonlight gleamed off the jagged edges of its broken windows. It was a watchful presence hovering over her, but not in a menacing way. It seemed almost . . . hopeful.

That would certainly be a change.

"I know you have secrets," Evie told the house. "I know you don't trust me." Her voice gentled. "And I know you're hurting. I think I'm starting to understand a bit more, and I'm going to help you, if you'll let me." She hesitated, her gaze flicking to the living room windows. "But that's my daughter in there, and I won't let any harm come to her. I need you to stay put. Do you understand?"

Slowly, the turret swiveled in Evie's direction, regarding her gravely for a moment before it gave a tiny bob of acknowledgment. A wave of emotion enveloped Evie with the night breeze, feeling like a cozy blanket or a warm fire on a cold winter's night. It was easy enough for Evie to translate the house's intent.

Safe.

She is safe with me.

Evie swallowed hard. She cleared her throat and nodded. "Thank you."

She slipped into the wood, following the well-worn track back to the clearing where they'd first encountered the house. This time, Evie went all the way down the uneven embankment to the river, pausing to watch the moonlight cast silvery streaks across the dark water. Bullfrogs croaked their *jug-o'-rum* song into the night, and a raccoon peeked out of the underbrush at her, rubbing its paws together, eyes gleaming with curiosity. It was a warm night, and the gentle rush of the river tempted Evie to kick off her boots and sit on the sandy bank, to let the cool water run over her toes. She wasn't a water witch, but she still enjoyed those simple pleasures.

Another night, she promised herself, and instead turned left and followed the river in the direction of the village. Shara Green had said there was a footbridge, and sure enough, a few minutes later she saw it, rising out of the darkness in a broad arch over the river. She felt its peeling paint beneath her fingers as she gripped the railing. The bridge had obviously seen better days, but it was sturdy beneath Evie's feet as she crossed to the other side and ducked back into the trees.

The sound of the river dropped away as she walked, and a sense of calm and stillness settled over her. The farther she went, the taller and wider the trees became, dense clusters of them pressing in from all sides, but not in a way that made her feel afraid or claustrophobic. Evie was careful not to touch the sharp bark, but she didn't hesitate to reach out with her magic, to let it stir the leaves in a quiet greeting.

It's me. I'm here. I just wanted to say hello.

The branches above her head creaked, their leaves rustling, and Evie again felt the trees parting ever so slightly to make a path for her to pass deeper into the Thornwood. It was nearly midnight, but the trees surrounding her all looked the same—normal oaks, to a one. They were stately, beautiful trees, and under other circumstances, Evie would have lingered to appreciate them.

But tonight she had a mission.

"I've come seeking a Star Oak hidden in the wood," she said aloud. The darkness swallowed her words. Even the moonlight had difficulty penetrating the thick canopy. Evie was undeterred. "I've been an earthwalker of the Environmental Crisis Response Agency, and I'm now preparing to be the caretaker of Thornwood house. I swear to guard your secrets with my life. Will you show me the way?"

Silence met her request, but Evie thought it was a listening kind of silence. The wood had heard her. She could only hope it was considering what she'd said.

She sank to the ground to wait, burying her hands in the leaf fall and soil, breathing in the warm night air. Her thoughts wandered back to Thornwood house and her theory that it had been built from a Star Oak.

Had the old witch or her predecessors known about the house's origin? Evie found it hard to believe they wouldn't have, considering how rare and precious the trees were. Now that she thought about it, a Star Oak would probably be exactly the sort of tree that would choose to become a sentient house.

Because it *was* a choice. Evie had also learned that in her research before coming here. When the ancient trees or the oldest stones had grown weary of their forms, they succumbed either to death or to the ravages of time that wore even mountains down to dust.

But sometimes, rarely, they chose a different path. They cast off their old skins and let themselves be made anew, to live in a way they never had before.

What made a tree want to become that kind of home? Evie wondered. For a tree already could be host to the sparrows and the hawks, a burrow for squirrels or any number of other creatures. What inspired them to be a sentient home for human beings?

Evie lay back on the mossy ground, running her fingers over a patch of white mushrooms growing beneath a bush. Was it because of the pact sworn between them and the witches whose magic helped make the transformation possible? Or was it simply that they had watched humans for so long, living their brief, vibrant lives, so fragile and flawed, that they wanted to see for themselves what all the fuss was about?

Did Thornwood house remember what it had been like to be a Star Oak, once upon a time? Had it run into the wood because it needed to return to the place where it had been born?

Suddenly, a distant, mournful howl broke the stillness, sending an icy shiver down Evie's spine. An animal in distress—a dog or a coyote, maybe even a fox. She instinctively jumped to her feet and turned toward the sound, but the movement broke her contact with the presence in the trees.

She had no time for regrets. Evie took two uncertain steps forward and stopped, listening. The howl came again, punctuated by a high-pitched yelp that made her break into a run.

Leaves crackled and twigs snapped underfoot as she followed the sound deeper into the wood. Animals scurried away at her approach, little more than shadows darting into their hidey-holes. The trees drew closer together, trunks wider now than the span of her arms. Their arching branches blotted out the moonlit sky, and the darkness closed in around her, until she could barely see the path ahead.

She slowed her pace, picking her footing with care, and finally the trees parted. A sliver of moonlight revealed a small clearing. A dilapidated shed stood in its center, leaning precariously to one side, as if it were one stiff breeze away from collapsing in on itself. It was the last thing Evie had expected, seeing the little building in the middle of the wood. Had there once been a cottage nearby? Another witch's sanctuary within the wood? If so, it looked like this was all that remained.

Evie approached cautiously, just as the howl rang out again, muffled but clearly coming from within the shed. This close, the mournful sound tore at her heart.

Evie went up to the structure and yanked on the rusted latch. The shed wasn't locked, but the door was stuck tight in its frame. She didn't waste time or strength trying to force it. Instead, Evie laid both her hands flat against the door and closed her eyes. Power swirled inside her, rising and gathering in her hands, making the tips of her fingers tingle as magic passed into the door and settled. It didn't take much. The wood was soft, already rotting.

Quietly, she spoke, coaxing the old wood to hear the call of the soil beneath it. It was time to return to that place, to rest and feed a new cycle.

With a faint groan, a sound that was almost like relief, the door gave in, disintegrating beneath her hands. The latch, a pile of nails, and three rusted hinges fell to the ground in its wake.

Evie wiped her fingers on her shirttail and peered into the dark interior. Moonlight coming in through large gaps in the roof revealed racks of empty shelves lining the back wall, chipped and stained by the remnants of whatever had once been stored there. A lumpy pile of whitish rags had been thrown in the far corner.

Except they weren't rags. As Evie watched, the pile shifted and shrank against the wall. A furry face and body turned in her direction, revealing a male dog with a long, wolflike snout and the most beautiful golden eyes Evie had ever seen. His coat was white—or it would have been, were it not filthy and matted with dirt and leaves. Dried blood coated his right hind leg, and when he tried to move it, pain flashed in those stunning eyes.

"It's all right," Evie whispered, slowly going down on her knees.

The last thing she wanted to do was frighten him. "I'm not going to hurt you."

The dog bared his teeth in an attempt at a growl, but the sound dissolved into another yelp of pain.

Evie fumbled in her medicine bag, removing a small glass jar. She unscrewed the metal cap, and the smell of citrus and cinnamon filled the air. In its wake came a subtle curl of magic from the yellow serenity petals swirling in the ointment. When harvested at the peak of their bloom, under a midday sun, they could be used in concoctions like this one, calming and soothing the nerves. And though it couldn't cure it, the smell of the ointment could often take the bite out of raw fear.

The dog sniffed the air once, then again. His eyelids drooped, and some of the rigidness went out of his body.

"That's right. That's good," Evie soothed, crawling into the shed to reach him. She held out her hand to let him sniff her. "I'm here to help."

The dog's nose pressed against her palm. A warm tongue slicked across her fingers, and the animal stared up at her with the kind of pure trust and adoration that only dogs seemed able to manage. He looked at her as if to say, *Finally, you're here to fix things.*

Taking the invitation, Evie ran her hands gently over the dog's body, making sure there were no other injuries before moving to examine the leg. Power waited, aching in her fingertips, ready to be put to use. She let it sink into the wound, drawing on her vitality to heal it. She'd already used some to help Jamie earlier, and she felt the pull of fatigue in her limbs. It helped that the dog's leg wasn't broken, only bruised. There were several shallow cuts along the leg that explained the blood.

As a bit of her own essence passed into the dog, Evie rode the connection, gently reaching out to touch the animal's thoughts. She could only do this with animals and plants. Humans were too complex; she couldn't follow their overlapping thoughts and memories to see anything clearly. Only mind witches were that skilled.

The dog's memory was straightforward. Evie rode past a flash of fear, and beyond it she saw a large man, his blurry shadow looming over the animal. The details of his face sharpened briefly, and Evie recognized him.

It was Veld Tapper, the man who'd come into the café with Ignatius Smythe. What had he been doing so far out in the wood?

"Go on, get out of here!" The garbled words were accompanied by a swift kick. There was a pained yelp, and the dog limped away, stumbling and lost in the wood until he found the old shed and squirmed his way inside the half-open door. He'd fallen asleep, and when he woke, the door had blown shut, trapping him inside.

"You poor thing." Evie withdrew her magic. The dog's tail twitched as he readjusted and tucked his newly healed leg underneath him. Evie put the ointment away and reached into her bag, pulling out an apple and a paring knife. The dog's eyes sharpened, his tongue lolling out as she carved up the bright-red fruit. She fed it to him in slivers, and a good thing too. The dog gulped the fruit down as fast as she could get it to him.

Stroking his feather-soft ears, she noticed a blue collar buried in the fur around his neck. Evie wiped away the dirt clinging to the tags so she could read the dog's name: Snow. The address underneath was one she recognized.

"The Weaver house," she murmured. Suddenly, the glaring face in the upstairs window, the empty market stall in the village, and the undelivered books all began to make sense. "If I'm not mistaken, I believe your Mr. Weaver is very worried about you, Snow," she told him. "He's been out looking for you for some time. How about I take you home to him?"

Hearing his name, the dog pushed up to his feet and nudged his head against her chest, at the same time snuffling around her bag for more food.

"Sorry," Evie said, scratching behind his ears one more time as she got to her feet. "I've got no more food with me. Come on, let's put your person out of his misery."

Snow followed her eagerly out of the shed. Evie glanced up at the moon and the trees surrounding her. It was well after midnight now. The connection she'd been trying to establish was gone, and the Thornwood was withdrawn and silent. She would learn no secrets tonight, and the Star Oak, if it was somewhere out there in the wood, remained hidden from her.

But that didn't mean the night had been a failure. She *had* found something hidden, something that was lost. She leaned down and patted Snow as they made their way through the wood toward home.

Eleven

It was nearly two in the morning by the time Evie and Snow broke the tree line and approached the Weaver house. They'd gone slowly, stopping at a small stream so the dog could get some much-needed water. Evie would have carried him, but he was far too big, and the closer they got to home, the more energy returned to him.

Evie felt a twinge of guilt as she rapped loudly on her neighbor's door. She hated to wake the man in the middle of the night, but if it had been her dog lost in the Thornwood, she wouldn't have been able to sleep at all.

The wind chime tinkled softly at her shoulder, but there was no response or stirring of movement from within the house. Evie waited a moment, then raised her hand to knock again.

Snow, unable to contain himself now that he was home, began to bark, turning in tight circles and lashing Evie's legs with his fluffy tail.

The effect this time was instant. Lights blazed on inside the house, spilling buttery glows onto the front stoop. Evie put a hand on Snow's back to calm him just as the door burst open, and a man peered out at them.

It was the same face she'd seen glaring from the upstairs window, a face Evie now noticed was about her own age, with strong angles and pale skin tanned pinkish by the summer sun. But her neighbor wasn't glaring now. His bearded jaw had gone slack with astonishment. He stared down at the dog in frozen silence, as if he thought his eyes might be playing tricks on him.

"Mr. Weaver?" she asked, offering him a cautious smile. "I'm sorry to disturb you so late, but—"

Snow's delighted bark cut her off, and the dog launched himself at the man. Mr. Weaver absorbed the impact of the animal against his chest, taking several enthusiastic licks to his cheeks and chin before he sank to his knees on the threshold, burying his face in the dog's fur. Evie couldn't make out much of what he murmured to Snow as he ran his hands through the thick white fur, but the dog's entire body vibrated with happiness.

Evie's throat tightened as she watched the two of them. She took a step back and turned away, intending to leave them to their reunion, when the man's voice called after her. "Wait, please."

She paused and turned back to where the man was now rubbing Snow's belly while the dog lay in a puddle of ecstasy on the ground. She laughed at the sight. "Even if he didn't have a collar, there'd be no doubt he belongs at the Weaver house. I'm Evie Sharpe," she added, "your new neighbor."

"I know who you are." The man stood. He was a few inches

taller than she was, and broader than she'd realized when he first answered the door. His thick chestnut hair was curly and sleep-matted on one side. He stood on the threshold in his bare feet, wearing a pair of loose-fitting pants and a rumpled blue shirt with the neck laces open, as if he'd just tossed the clothes on before coming to the door. "You found Snow," he said. "He's been missing for two days. I've been looking everywhere. I was afraid . . ." The man swallowed, his throat bobbing. He was more unsettled than Evie had realized.

"He's all right," she assured him. "He was trapped in an old shed in the Thornwood, a few miles west of the village. His leg was hurt, but I healed it. He just needs more food and water—definitely a bath—and some rest in his own bed." She was glad she'd cleaned the dried blood off Snow's leg in the stream on their way back. She didn't want to alarm him.

"I can't begin to thank you." Color suffused the man's cheeks, but he held her gaze. "You came to my door before, and I didn't answer."

"I know," she said. "I thought maybe you were angry about the house running off and damaging your weather vane."

"What? Oh, no, the weather vane's been like that for a while." He waved it away. "But the house . . . when it uprooted itself the last time, it scared Snow. He chased it into the wood. I tried to follow him, but I lost his trail." He winced. "That's never happened before. I thought I knew the wood like I know my own orchard, but not this time. I guess I was too upset."

The dog had disappeared at the same time the house ran off. If the house had gone looking for the Star Oak that night, Evie mused, it was entirely possible that the Thornwood had acted to protect it, covering tracks and obscuring trails so that the Star Oak wouldn't be found by the house or anyone else who'd gone into the wood that night.

Evie had a feeling it was no accident that she'd come upon Snow tonight. The Thornwood had led her to him, perhaps to make amends for getting him lost while trying to protect its own. But why was the Star Oak still hiding? Did it have anything to do with Veld Tapper, the man who had kicked Snow? What had he been doing in the wood? She still found herself with more questions than answers.

"I'm sorry the house scared Snow," Evie said. "I'll do my best to make sure it never happens again."

The man shook his head. "It wasn't your fault, and I'm the one who should be apologizing." His voice was deep and deliberate. A voice of the earth, Evie thought, someone who thinks before they speak. "I was scared for Snow, and that made me angry at the house, and at myself, and the whole world, really," he went on. "I didn't want to speak to anyone while I was like that. But I was unforgivably rude."

"And yet I forgive you," Evie said gently. "It's all right."

"Thank you." He glanced around, as if just then noticing they were still standing outside in the dark. "I know it's late, but would you like to come in for a cup of tea as a proper apology?"

Evie hesitated, glancing over at Thornwood house. There were no lights on, and as she stretched her awareness in that direction, she could feel Ruby's presence and her slow, even breaths. She was still fast asleep on the living room couch.

Safe, just as the house had promised.

Evie had been wanting a chance to speak to Mr. Weaver ever

since they'd arrived. As Amelia Howell's closest neighbor, he likely had insight into the woman that the rest of the villagers lacked. He'd also been in close proximity to Thornwood house for the last six months and might have some idea what was happening to it. And his cottage, though it wasn't sentient, seemed to welcome her in. Light spilling from the hallway behind him revealed aging wood floors and soft rugs, and she caught the fading scent of roast chicken that must have been from his dinner.

The wind chime tinkled between them, drawing Evie's gaze. She remembered Ruby staring at the chime as if she recognized it, but she hadn't said how. Had she seen this moment in one of her visions of Evie's future?

It was no use wandering too far down that path. Evie had never been one to make decisions in her life based on farseeing. The visions were too nebulous, prone to making one second-guess oneself. And anyway, she didn't need magic to tell her that this person could be a friend to her, if she gave him a chance.

So she smiled at her new neighbor and said, "I'd love a cup of tea, Mr. Weaver."

He stepped back and gestured for her to come inside. "Please, call me Gil."

"I wish I could tell you more." Gil set a tea tray on the wood-block coffee table between them. The mugs he'd brought were pine green, big and thick, the kind of mug you needed two hands for. The pleasant scent of chamomile drifted on the air as he poured for her. "It was the night before you arrived. I had just come back from the orchard late when I saw the house pulling itself off its foundation and making for the tree line." The rocking chair he was sitting in creaked as he leaned forward, handing her a mug. "I was away the other times it happened, so it was a shock to see it up close."

"I can imagine." Evie accepted the tea with a grateful smile and shook her head when he offered her the chipped milk cup and sugar bowl.

Gil's living room was a place of comfortable clutter. A couple of shirts draped over the back of the rocker, Snow's bed sitting next to it with toys and tug ropes scattered all around. Bookshelves lined the back wall, but there were at least a dozen more volumes stacked on the floor beneath the windows or on the various end tables. A gray stone fireplace sat to her right. There was no fire lit now, of course, in the heat of summer, but Evie could imagine sitting in front of it in the middle of winter, staring into the dancing flames.

She was seated on the couch, a lumpy brown island in the middle of the room, with a faded yellow quilt thrown over the back. It was one of those couches that had lost any discernible shape long ago, but was so soft that Evie felt she could happily die in its embrace.

"Are you sure you didn't see anything that could have made the house do that?" Evie asked. She took a sip of her tea. "Was there anyone else near the house when it left?"

"No, and I would have known if there had been," Gil said. "I'm not a witch, but I have a pretty good sense of the land around our properties, and Amelia taught me some things." He rubbed the back of his neck and chuckled. "She used to say my skin was too thick for much magic to get in, except when it came to apples and wind chimes."

"Wind chimes?" Evie was intrigued. "Did you make the one by your front door?"

He nodded. "It doesn't just respond to the wind. I hear its music other times too, when people are near. The chimes are different for each person. I can tell you, it's come in handy over the years."

Like the day she and Ruby had arrived, Evie thought. He must have heard a new chime then. She wondered what it had sounded like to him.

"If your magic was keeping watch, then I suppose it couldn't have been a person that made the house run away the last time," Evie mused, "but Veld Tapper had to have been in the Thornwood for a reason."

"I'll be having a conversation with him in the morning, so I'll be sure to ask him," Gil said, his expression darkening. He'd been furious when Evie told him what she'd seen through the dog's eyes.

He reached down beside the rocking chair to run the back of his hand over Snow's soft coat. The dog had been too tired for a bath and was now fast asleep, snuffling in the midst of some dream. "It shouldn't surprise me that it was Tapper," he went on, "but I never thought he'd stoop to kicking an animal like that. I don't understand why Ignatius hired him. Maybe it's because Tapper worked for his father, so he leaned on the family connection."

"I actually met Ignatius yesterday," Evie said. It wasn't an encounter she was eager to repeat. "Cinda told me about his being trained and then passed over as Amelia's successor. He didn't seem too happy about it."

"It isn't a normal day unless Ignatius Smythe is unhappy about something," Gil said. "Don't get me wrong, he does all right by the village. Like I said, he hired the crew working on the library, and he's supervising everything personally, even though it's not his job. When his parents were alive, the family always tried to take care of Iskendra, funding projects and helping the community thrive, but most of the time I think Ignatius would prefer to be left alone with his books and magic. He can't seem to get enough of either."

An unsettling thought occurred to Evie. Could that be why Amelia had made her decision not to name Ignatius her successor? Had he found out in the course of his training that there was a Star Oak growing in the Thornwood, so he'd sent his crew in after hours to look for it? She didn't want to think it. Ignatius hadn't been friendly, but that didn't mean he was after anything more than the caretaker position.

But a Star Oak—what a temptation that would be, even to the most honorable witch.

She looked across at Gil, weighing how much to tell him and how much he might already know about Thornwood house and its magic. It sounded like he and Amelia had been friends, though Evie was beginning to wonder if the old witch, with all her secrets, had truly been close to anyone in the village.

That isn't what I want, she thought, remembering the Green family's invitation to dinner, the mayor's warm welcome, and shopping for bicycles with Gemma Gray. She didn't want to close herself off to the villagers the way it seemed Amelia had.

Gil's soft chuckle interrupted her thoughts. "What is it?" she asked.

"You get a very intent look on your face when you're thinking," he said. He touched his index finger to the center of his forehead. "You've got a deep crease, just there, from a lifetime of that, I imagine."

Evie tried to smooth her features into a neutral expression. "Maybe I'm just focusing on my tea," she said.

"Oh, I admit, my chamomile is delicious, but it's not *that* good," he replied. "So, what are you thinking, new witch?"

"New witch?" Evie raised a brow. "What kind of a nickname is that?"

He shrugged. "Amelia never cared for formality. She liked it when I called her 'old witch.' I meant it affectionately, of course. But that obviously doesn't fit you."

Now it was Evie's turn to chuckle. "You could just call me 'Evie,'" she pointed out.

"All right—Evie—what are you thinking?"

She hesitated. New friend or not, she wasn't sure how to proceed here. Gil wasn't a witch, but that didn't mean he couldn't make use of a Star Oak's powers. If she revealed her suspicions that there was a Star Oak in the wood, could she trust him to keep the tree's existence a secret?

On the other hand, if she truly wanted to make a home here, she was going to have to trust *someone*. Gil Weaver, who loved his dog and crafted musical, magical wind chimes, gave her a good feeling. It was a place to start.

With that thought in mind, Evie put her cards on the table. "Tell me, Gil," she coaxed, turning that intent gaze on him, "did you know that Thornwood house was constructed from a Star Oak?"

Gil sat back in the rocker, letting out a long, slow breath. "I'll be damned," he said. "The old witch was right. She told me her successor would figure it out. 'If she's worth her salt as a witch, she'll know right off.' I shouldn't have doubted her."

"Amelia told you that?" Evie was taken aback. Risky for the old witch to leave a test like that for her, especially when it involved the house's welfare. What if she'd been wrong, and Evie hadn't figured it out? What if Ruby hadn't been there with her visions to help? "Then you already know that there's a Star Oak in the Thornwood?" she pressed.

"N-no, I didn't know that." Gil blinked. "I thought the Star Oaks were all gone, especially from around here. Is that what the house is after?"

"I think that's part of it," she agreed, though it still didn't explain why the house had gone into the village those other times. "I also think there's a chance Veld Tapper was looking for the Star Oak as well, either on his own or on Ignatius's behalf. Maybe he was hoping the house would lead him to it." She leaned forward. "Is there anyone else in the village besides Ignatius who might have known about the Star Oak's existence? Any other witches or people who might have knowledge of the history of the Thornwood?"

Gil scratched his beard in thought. "A couple of the librarians are witches, and there are several families who have been here a long time, like the Fullers and the Niemlans. Some of them have a bit of magic, but nothing overly powerful. My family's been here almost as long as the Smythes, and I've never heard about a Star Oak in the wood."

"I met Gemma Gray yesterday too," Evie said thoughtfully. She made a mental note to pay the library a visit, stock up on those books Gemma had suggested. "I take it neither of the sisters was interested in the caretaker position?"

"Oh, no," Gil said with a laugh. "The Gray sisters are too attached to their library and to the past."

"I see." Evie shifted, making herself more comfortable. "Well, thank you for the insight." She gave him a meaningful look. "I have to ask that you keep what I told you about the Star Oak in confidence. No one else can know about its existence."

"I won't tell anyone."

He gave her the promise easily. Evie hoped her instincts were right about him.

Gil finished his tea and ran his hand over Snow's flank again. There was a thin, raised scar crossing the knuckle of his index finger. "What will you do now?" he asked.

It was an excellent question. Evie had hoped to locate the Star Oak and ask it to use its power to help the house, but at least for now, it seemed the tree didn't want to be found. Which meant not only did she have to get Thornwood house to trust her, she also had to think of a way to gain the Star Oak's trust as well.

"I won't stop looking for the tree, but I think the best thing to do right now is to focus on convincing the house to bond with me." That way, it could heal itself using her own magic. Evie's mouth twisted. "So far, it's refused to bond with anyone."

"You've gotten farther than the others," Gil said. "One witch showed up at dawn, and by midmorning, the house had punted every bit of her luggage over the wall and into the wood. Took her hours to find all the bags. She was gone by sundown."

"I suppose that's reassuring, in a way," Evie said, chuckling, but her humor faded quickly. "If the house doesn't accept us, Ruby and I will have to go back to Dorna City."

Evie had promised her daughter they wouldn't leave, but she'd never realized how hard it would be to keep that promise. Foolishly, she'd convinced herself that she was different from all the other witches who'd tried to bond with Thornwood house. And though she'd gotten in the front door, there were still secrets alive and well in that house. Doors that wouldn't open. She'd gotten farther than the others, but she still might not be enough.

Gil was watching her closely. "You could still live here, though, couldn't you?" he asked. "Be something other than a caretaker?"

Not if the ECRA had their way, but Evie didn't want to tell him that. Even if she'd had the option, could she really stay in the village and watch someone else become caretaker in her place? See the life she'd wanted to build for herself lived out in front of her? The thought of it gave her a sudden, sharp empathy for Ignatius Smythe, unpleasant as he was.

"It wasn't a bad place, where we came from. We were happy there sometimes."

"But you still left." He picked up the teapot and refilled their mugs.

"Yes." She met his eyes. "Because I want to believe we can do better than only being happy 'sometimes.'"

He smiled. "Then you will."

They sipped their tea in silence after that, but it wasn't an uncomfortable quiet. Evie was surprised at how serene she felt sitting on the old couch with her legs tucked underneath her. A cool night breeze blew the scent of ease lilies in through the open windows, and she could hear the tinkling wind chime on the front porch.

Evie put her mug back on the tea tray and reluctantly stood. "I should be going," she said. "I need to check on Ruby and try to get some sleep."

Gil rose with her. "I hope you won't be a stranger, Evie," he said seriously. "I'm sorry we got a rough start, but I'm determined to make it up to you, show you what a good neighbor I can be."

"Be careful making promises like that," Evie teased as he led her to the door. "Ruby and I are getting ready to tackle repairs on the upstairs part of the house tomorrow—er, later today, I should say. You're welcome to come and help."

She'd been joking, but Gil, to her surprise, was already nodding. "Of course. I'll come early and bring my tools." He held out his hand, his expression softening. "Good night, Evie, and thank you again. Truly, I'll never forget what you did for Snow and me."

"You're welcome." Touched, she clasped his hand. "Good night, Gil."

The tinkling whisper of the wind chime accompanied her all the way back to the house.

TWELVE

"He has a *dog*?" Ruby sat up on the couch, throwing off her blanket and crawling over to sit closer to Evie. "Do you think he'll bring him over when he comes?"

"I expect he will," Evie said, ruffling Ruby's tangled hair fondly. She'd been filling her in on her adventures in the night. She'd also accurately predicted that the existence of Gil Weaver's dog would be the thing that thrilled her daughter the most about the whole experience. "He's coming over sometime after breakfast, so why don't you get dressed, and we'll get this day started."

Ruby didn't immediately move. A pensive expression settled on her small face. "I had a vision about Mr. Weaver once," she admitted. "It was a couple of years ago, before I stopped being able to look into your future."

"I wondered if that might be the case," Evie said carefully. "Do you want to tell me about it? You don't have to."

This was still a tender subject. When Ruby's abilities had first asserted themselves, Evie had warned her that there were only so many times a farseer could look into someone's future. They followed the threads of a person's choices and actions in order to see glimpses of the outcomes. But each time they traveled those fragile cords, the burden of their power pulled the threads tighter and tighter, until finally they snapped, leaving no pathway for the farseer to follow.

At the time, Ruby took the warning to heart, but she was human, and she was an orphan whose guardian and teacher had been in a dangerous job. It was an impossible temptation when she awoke frightened in the night.

Just one more look. One look, so I can go back to sleep.

It was a lesson most farseers had to learn the hard way, and so had Ruby.

"I didn't know the man in the vision was Mr. Weaver, not at first," Ruby said. She picked at a corner of her quilt. "It wasn't until I recognized the wind chime on his front porch. Then I knew. In my vision, there was no wind, but it was chiming anyway. Isn't that weird?"

"Not at all," Evie said, remembering Gil's description of the wind chime's magic. Morning light striped the floor in gold at their feet. Evie edged her toes into the warmth. "Anything else you want me to know?"

Ruby was quiet for a long moment. It felt as if the two of them stood at a tipping point, uncertain which way they would fall. What if Evie's instincts about Gil had been wrong, and Ruby had seen something in her vision that she didn't like? It almost made Evie tell her daughter to keep the vision a secret, that she didn't really want to know.

Finally, Ruby leaned against Evie's shoulder and whispered, "He's a good person."

Evie smiled, and the tension inside her eased. It sounded like Gil could be a friend after all. "I'm happy to hear that," she whispered back. "Go and get dressed now, because we have a lot to do today."

"Okay." Ruby whipped off the quilt and hopped up. "I'll go check the mail too!"

"It's probably too early yet for that," Evie called after her, but the front door was already slamming shut.

Evie tipped her head back against the couch cushions. She wished she could stop Ruby from worrying about the ECRA contacting them during their time here. But how could she ask her to forget about them, when the same kernel of worry was ever present at the back of Evie's mind? If it made Ruby feel better to monitor the mail every day, Evie wasn't going to dissuade her.

While Ruby was getting ready, Evie dug out a bowl from one of the moving boxes and went out into the back garden to pick some strawberries to go with their breakfast. When she came around the corner of the house, her gaze was immediately snared by the glasshouse. Well, you couldn't really call it a glasshouse now—all the panes were gone, leaving only the rusted iron frame standing like a lonely sentinel.

Evie set her bowl on the ground. She looked up at the house, shielding her eyes against the early-morning sun. Her power was fully replenished, swirling inside her like a vortex of heat and light, tendrils of it reaching out to the land around her, drawing the heads of daisies and blades of saw grass toward her the same way they'd stretch toward the sun.

"Will you let me help you some more?" Evie entreated the house. "It isn't the same as a Star Oak, but I know I can help you heal, if you give me a chance."

Evie couldn't see the turret from where she stood, but she still felt the house's attention. Wind hissed through the glasshouse's iron skeleton, and a swell of emotions overtook her. There was hope and longing, briefly bringing the scent of stove-warmed chocolate to Evie's nose. But it was tempered by wariness, and the comforting scent quickly vanished, leaving an indecisive silence.

Evie's heart twisted. She couldn't make the house trust her, so she bent and picked up her bowl, walking over to the strawberry patch to pick some of the ripe red berries.

Out of the corner of her eye, she noticed the jitter bells shivering in the mood garden, their tubular petals shifting from pink to coral as they absorbed the house's nervousness. If she picked the flowers now, she could brew them in a tea to give her energy. Evie resisted the urge to put her herbalist skills to the test and instead moved even farther away from the house, keeping her back to it and giving it space to make up its mind.

After a few minutes, there came a soft creaking sound.

Evie stilled, a large berry resting in the middle of her palm. She felt the house leaning subtly toward her, nudging her with the barest hint of power, like someone coming up behind her and tapping her on the shoulder.

Smiling to herself, Evie bent and brushed off her skirt before turning to face the house again. She held her arms out from her sides, palms turned toward the ground. In response, the grass chittered and the earth stirred beneath her. Evie's skin tingled as power coursed through her body. Dew sprang from the grass blades. An old, ruffle-feathered crow cawed from the top of the garden wall. Insects buzzed in the air, and all around her, the flowers in the garden, both magical and mundane, seemed to sigh in contentment as magic touched them.

It was an intimate, serene moment, one that even the wind stood still for. And through it all, the attention of the Thornwood was firmly fixed on her, as if to see how the scene would unfold.

As the power continued to gather, visible now as sparks of green and gold light drifting on the air, Evie channeled the magic. She didn't put the offering into wildflowers this time. There was too much; it would overwhelm and kill the poor things. But the house could bear it easily, so she funneled her magic toward the glasshouse instead.

Power flowed, and the rust clinging to the iron structure flaked away. Metal that had been bent and twisted now straightened with an earsplitting shriek. Glistening threads wove between the structure's ribs like spider silk, thickening and spreading into new panes of glass that caught the sunlight and cast brilliant rainbows on the back wall of the house.

At last, at the peak of the glasshouse, the stained-glass panel reformed. Shards flew into place like puzzle pieces. The colors shone, liquid and vibrant, and Evie was finally able to see what the scene depicted.

She shouldn't have been surprised. A Star Oak's gnarled trunk and silver branches appeared before her in the panel. Blunt-edged leaves unfurled, like blue hands cradling bunches of silver acorns. There wasn't just one shade of blue either. Lapis, azure, indigo, and teal blended together in a gorgeous representation that made Evie ache to see the real tree in person.

It had to be out there. She just needed to find it.

The sparks of light faded, and Evie dropped her arms heavily to her sides. It felt like she'd been running for miles, though she hadn't taken a single step. She took a moment to center herself, adjusting to the depletion of magic, then stepped cautiously toward the glasshouse.

A door at the back of the structure swung open at her approach. Evie stepped inside and immediately gasped. She'd been so focused on repairing the exterior of the structure, she hadn't noticed what had been restored and replenished within.

Dozens of magical flowers and herbs grew in pots near the glass walls. Witch-light fronds for making ever-burning candles. Rose tears to restore clarity of thought. Night violets to keep away bad dreams. There was even a creeping onyx vine to quell pain. A wooden slab balanced on two sawhorses divided the interior in half. Garden gloves, shears, pots, and potion vials, along with a host of other cultivating tools, filled the table, unused and waiting for her.

Evie picked up the garden gloves, running her fingers over the smooth, sturdy fabric. Once again, she was swamped with longing, but this time the feeling wasn't coming from the house.

This was exactly the space she would have designed for herself, as if the house had read her heart as surely as it had absorbed her power. Was that what the bond between house and witch could be like? If the house accepted her, would they come to know each other as well as they knew themselves?

She could feel the house's presence hovering just over her shoulder, tentative yet excited, waiting to see if she was pleased.

"It's beautiful," Evie whispered. "I love it."

She spent the next few minutes cataloging the various magical plants in her head. Her hands itched for pencil and paper to make a detailed inventory, but she didn't want to leave even for a moment before she'd thoroughly explored the place. Later, there would be time to write everything down. For now, she would just get an idea of what ingredients needed to be harvested in the next few days, in addition to what was out in the mood garden. There was so much here, and they weren't just plants for healing; she didn't want any of it to go to waste.

There were whimsy magics, like the chameleon fronds. Their tiny leaves, when held under the tongue, could change the color of a person's hair from blond to blue, or brown to green, even black to silver, depending on their size. She'd heard that redheads got rainbow colors, though she'd never seen it for herself. The leaves could do the same for clothing, when sewn just right into the hem, but they didn't last through many washes. They were used often by traveling performers.

There were weightier magics too. The ridged red-and-white-striped petals of paradise let you recall your sweetest memories with perfect clarity. A trio of pots in the north corner contained bushes heavy with silver-tongue berries. The pink bramble fruit could make even the most nervous speaker into an eloquent poet up to a day after consuming them—but they also compelled the orator to tell the absolute truth.

Evie was surprised to find there was even a parcel of poisons, clearly marked in hanging baskets suspended high off the floor.

None of them were lethal, but neither were they to be treated lightly. The tiny sorrow peaches could be crushed, boiled, and hardened into candies that would make you hideously sick to your stomach—useful for when a child ate something they shouldn't and needed to vomit it up in a hurry. The crushed stem of a widow's wail, when burned in a candle's flame, would create a scent that could make a person sleep like the dead for a day. And the filament of the tiger's breath, when treated the same way, could blind a person temporarily. Evie had known both to be used by people to defend themselves—and for more nefarious purposes.

When she'd finished making a circuit of the glasshouse, Evie approached the other door connecting the small building to the rest of the house. But when she went to open it, the knob wouldn't turn. The door was locked.

Puzzled, Evie searched around for a key. She noticed a small nail driven into the wall next to the door. Faint black streaks covered the wall beneath it where something had rubbed the paint away. Had there once been a key hanging there? Evie wondered. If so, why had the house not brought it back?

She turned back to the door, reaching for the knob again, then stopped. In her mind, she pictured the layout of the downstairs and the position of the glasshouse. The back of her neck prickled.

This door led into the same room the house had tried to conceal from her.

Evie glanced over her shoulder at the magical plants covering the tables. She pictured Amelia Howell as she might have been in her younger years, moving through the glasshouse, pruning bushes, collecting seeds, and meticulously harvesting the ingredients for her magical concoctions.

Taking them from the glasshouse straight into her study.

Evie looked back at the door. She hadn't wanted to consider the possibility before, but with a sinking feeling, she knew what the hidden room must contain. "It *is* her study, isn't it?" she asked aloud. "Amelia's sanctuary—the heart of the house. That's where you don't want us to go."

A chill breeze, bitter with regret, wafted over the back of her neck. It was nothing like the anger Evie had felt before when she'd tried to get into the room. If anything, it nearly felt like the house was apologizing to her.

As she stood there outside the door, the tang of magical herbs suddenly gave way to a rich, earthen smell that filled Evie's nostrils. Overwhelmed, she closed her eyes and took a step back. This was ancient magic, deep and powerful, as intoxicating as a bottle of whiskey.

This must be the remnants of Amelia Howell's magic.

Evie pulled away, unwilling to reach for the power. It wasn't hers to touch, and she wasn't sure she was prepared to handle it if she tried.

"I shouldn't have pried," she apologized, opening her eyes. "Of course you want to protect her space."

Evie had given it power, and the house had given her a gift in return, but that didn't mean the two were bonded. Maybe that was a condition Amelia had set with the house before she died—the only person allowed in her study was the caretaker.

As much as Evie might long for it, this place wasn't really hers yet, and it might never be. The realization was like a bucket of ice water poured over her earlier excitement.

Evie walked back to the other door and exited the glasshouse into the garden. With the study closed to her for now, she also wouldn't be able to read the instructions Amelia had left in her diary. Quelling the sharp bite of disappointment, she collected the bowl of strawberries she'd left in the yard and walked briskly around to the front of the house.

Traces of regret trailed behind her, carrying the scent of a cut flower beginning to wilt, but Evie didn't look back.

THIRTEEN

Evie was prepared to settle into a bad mood for at least the rest of the morning. Stew in her frustrations, pout a little, that sort of thing. Then she walked into the sun-warmed kitchen to see that Ruby had dug out their warped, ancient skillet and was hard at work making pancakes.

The smell of bubbling batter and the hiss of heated butter smoothed over her rough edges at the same time they made her stomach growl. Evie lingered in the doorway for a moment, just soaking up the scene of her daughter smiling, tapping her slippered feet, and humming to herself as she flipped the pancakes one by one into a crooked stack.

Things always seem worse when you're tired and hungry, Evie reminded herself as she carried the bowl of strawberries to the sink to wash them. She sliced up several for some pancake toppings and then brewed a pot of strong coffee to help clear the cobwebs from her mind. She joined Ruby at the kitchen table, and they dug into the food.

Yes, there were places the house wanted to keep to itself. That didn't mean it would feel that way forever. It was frustrating, but she just needed to give it time.

After breakfast, she and Ruby walked into the foyer, only to be hit with another surprise.

"Look at that!" Ruby grabbed her arm, shaking it excitedly.

Evie couldn't believe it. While they'd been busy in the kitchen, the house had used more of her magical offering to repair the staircase to the second floor.

And what a job it had done.

The two jagged halves had been brought together and mended. The polished wood banister now ended in two beautifully carved newel-posts, while a burgundy rug flowed down the stairs, held in place by gleaming brass rods.

A hopeful breeze stirred the dust motes in beams of sunshine coming from the front windows. It was as if the house was saying, *Look here—I'm trying. I'll meet you halfway.*

All right, then, so will I, Evie thought determinedly. It was time to get back to work.

"We'll find some old drop cloths and padding to protect the stairs while we haul out the rest of the debris from upstairs," Evie decided, laying her hand on the banister. "I don't want anything to damage this. It's too beautiful."

As they stood admiring the stairs, there was a knock at the front door, accompanied by a loud, enthusiastic bark.

"He's here! And you're right—he brought his dog!" Ruby

jumped up and down, clapping her hands before running to open the door.

Gil and Snow stood on the porch. As he'd promised, Gil carried a large green toolbox at his side. Snow squirmed with excitement, and as soon as the dog laid eyes on Ruby, he shot inside and threw himself ecstatically at her feet, tail whipping back and forth along the floor.

"Oh, you're so pretty!" Ruby cooed, dropping to her knees so she could rub the dog's belly.

Since returning from his adventure, Snow had had a bath. His fluffy white coat shone in all its glory in the morning sun. The dog's tongue lolled out the side of his mouth, his eyes going half-closed under the barrage of Ruby's affection.

"He's going to be spoiled for the rest of his days," Gil predicted, looking down at the two of them fondly before meeting Evie's eyes. "Sorry I couldn't come sooner. It took longer than I thought to get Snow cleaned up."

"We're just getting started," Evie said, beckoning to him. "Come in, please."

For a second, Gil hesitated, glancing around the room as if waiting for some sign or reaction from the house. When nothing happened, he stepped over the threshold, closing the door behind him. Once again, Evie could feel the house's attention fixed on them, but it made no objection to Gil's presence, nor did she sense any unease coming from it. It was a good sign; Evie felt another hurdle had been silently crossed.

Before she could make introductions, Ruby bounded to her feet, locking eyes with Gil in that hyperfocused way she sometimes got when she was recalling one of her visions. If Gil was unnerved by the scrutiny, he didn't show it. He held her gaze steadily, waiting for her assessment to be complete.

After a moment, Ruby nodded, as if she'd decided something, and held out her hand. "It's nice to meet you, Mr. Weaver," she said. "I'm Ruby."

"A pleasure to meet you as well, Ruby." He took her hand in his big, calloused palm. "Please call me Gil. You have your mother's eyes."

"They're the same color blue, but I'm adopted," Ruby said matter-of-factly, as if they were discussing the weather. "Evie adopted me right before we moved here."

Evie blinked.

To his credit, Gil recovered fast. "Is that so?" He smiled and put his toolbox down. "Would you like to help me check the plumbing in the upstairs bathroom? That old faucet up there has always had a leak, but Amelia would never let me near it. She said an orchard keeper had no business puttering around with the plumbing."

Ruby grinned and nodded. She whirled to face Evie. "Can I go up and pick out my bedroom too?" she asked, her eyes shining with excitement.

Evie nodded, watching as Ruby pounded up the newly repaired steps to go exploring. Snow followed her, as if the two of them had been best friends forever. "Be careful," she called out. "There might be more broken glass. Keep your shoes on, and look after Snow."

"I will!"

Evie turned back to Gil, who was squatting next to his toolbox. He pulled out a hammer and wrench and set them aside. He looked up at her, his eyes kind. "You all right?" he asked. "You look a little stunned."

"I'm not sure what just happened," Evie admitted. "I didn't expect her to say that to a stranger." Then again, Gil was hardly a stranger to her, Evie reminded herself. Ruby had had a vision of him over two years ago.

Gil stood up, tools in hand. "I'm sorry," he said, "if the adoption was something I wasn't supposed to know about."

"It's not a secret," Evie said, sorting through her feelings with an effort. "The only reason I didn't mention it last night was that it never came up. But I'm happy that she told you. I'm just surprised. The adoption was something we'd both wanted for so long, but because of what I used to do for a living, it was . . . very difficult to make it happen." And it wasn't entirely certain yet. "Ruby doesn't like to talk about it, what we had to go through."

Maybe it meant Ruby was beginning to feel more settled. Safe. It was a hopeful sign, even if it had caught Evie off guard.

Gil's brow furrowed. "How would working for the ECRA make it hard to adopt a child?" At Evie's raised eyebrows—she hadn't mentioned to him what she used to do for a living—he cleared his throat and looked away. "I might have, um, asked Cinda about you before you came here." He glanced back at her. "I know I shouldn't have pried, but curiosity has always been a weakness of mine."

"I'll remember that." Evie considered him. She wanted to be a part of this community, but doing that meant letting people in, opening herself and her past to scrutiny.

Ruby had already taken that step with Gil. And Evie had taken him into her confidence about the Star Oak. Maybe she could do this too.

"How much do you know about the ECRA?" she asked.

"'Environmental Crisis Response' is pretty self-explanatory," he pointed out, "and we're not so far out in the wilderness that we haven't heard all the stories of the disaster relief they've provided around the world."

He wasn't wrong. Back when it started, the ECRA dealt *solely* with disaster relief. But by the time Evie had joined, they'd expanded their reach and mission to provide magical oversight for most countries in the world—save for the Quiet Lands, where it wasn't needed. With that reach came more power, and that was when corruption had started to take hold.

"Ruby became my apprentice and ward through one of their teaching programs," Evie explained. "She was seven." She took a calming breath and let it out before continuing. "Because of their involvement in that process, the ECRA felt they had the right to coordinate the adoption as well."

"I've heard the ECRA doesn't exactly have a reputation for making things easy in the magical community." Gil leaned against the newel-post. "What happened?"

"Mr. Tansling, the advocate assigned to our case, expressed concern that my inexperience, my immaturity, and the dangers that went along with my position within the agency would make me a poor candidate to adopt." Evie parroted the words the committee had burned into her mind.

It had grown a little easier over the last few weeks to quell the flare of anger and pain those memories brought up, but it would always be there. When she'd made her deal with the ECRA committee, Evie had believed that was the end of the agency trying to exploit her and Ruby.

How wrong she'd been.

She glanced at Gil curiously. "Did Cinda tell you? What I used to do for the agency?"

Gil shook his head, though there was a spark of humor in his eyes. "She just warned me it wouldn't be wise to cross you."

"I wouldn't go that far." Evie laughed. The humor made it easier to talk about this. "I was one of their earthwalkers," she went on, "a first responder of sorts, to mitigate natural disasters and the damage they cause."

Gil's eyes widened, and he gave a low whistle. "Aren't earthwalkers considered to be among the most powerful land witches in the world?"

"The most powerful in the ECRA," Evie corrected him. Thankfully, the world was much larger and more varied than one organization.

"Still," Gil said, "I'm surprised they tried to deny you anything."

"I don't believe they were ever worried about my job being dangerous," Evie scoffed. "Their true concern in letting me adopt was losing influence over a farseer witch. They wanted Ruby's loyalty to be to the agency so that she would join them one day."

If Ruby were to have family ties of her own, it would give her more options and make her less dependent on the ECRA. It was one of the things Evie would never forgive them for. The battle she'd had to fight for Ruby was the beginning of the end of her time with an organization she'd already come to despise.

"In response to their concerns, I told the ECRA I was seeking a new position, one with much less danger," she said. "They weren't happy, but they approved the adoption—conditionally. And then Mr. Tansling and the head of the committee, Mr. Cinton, conducted a closing interview with Ruby, out of my presence." She didn't think Mrs. Shields had been involved in that, though she couldn't be sure.

Gil heard the change in her voice. "What did they say to her?" he asked, his brows lowering. Evie could feel the house listening as well. Its presence thickened the air, the newel-posts shivering in indignation.

Evie sat down on the stairs, resting her palm on the burgundy carpet in a calming gesture. "They tried to get her to sign an advance contract." Mr. Tansling would have acted as her advocate, of course. So amiable, so helpful, was Mr. Tansling. "Effective the day she came of age, it would tie her to the ECRA for a period of not less than ten years. They hinted—it would have been a criminal charge if they'd lied and said it outright—that the adoption approval hinged on her compliance."

The house contracted around them. Wood creaked and groaned, and the sunlight streaming through the windows darkened as the glass panes flushed crimson.

Gil swore. "I'd have wanted to tear the building down."

When she'd found out, Evie almost had. She would have taken great pleasure in unleashing the full force of her powers on the men who'd dared to threaten her daughter's future.

But in the end, fear won out over anger, fear that if she confronted them, the ECRA would rescind the deal they'd made with Evie. "Fortunately, the committee members underestimated how intelligent Ruby is," she said.

"She didn't sign the contract?"

"No." Evie waited until the house's joists relaxed and the windowpanes lightened before continuing. "She refused, but the experience left its mark. Ruby still worries the agency will make us come back to the fold, that they'll take away this chance they've given us. She checks the mailbox every day, just to make sure they haven't tried to contact us, and she doesn't like to talk about the adoption process."

"I'm sorry you both had to go through that." Gil bent, offering a hand to help her up. "But I'm happy that Ruby took me into her confidence."

"Yes, it means she trusts you already." Evie took his outstretched hand and let him pull her to her feet.

Gil smiled. "Well then, this has already been a productive morning, if I've managed to gain the trust of one of the witches here. Now I just have to work on the other one."

"You did offer to fix the plumbing." Evie's lips twitched. "That will go a long way toward endearing you to the other witch in the house."

"Good to know," Gil noted. "Is there anything else I can do to—"

Suddenly, the floorboard beneath his left foot buckled. Gil stumbled back but regained his balance quickly. "Hey now, what was that for?" he demanded, giving the ceiling a look of mock hurt. "Six months since I've been allowed to set foot in this house, and *now* you want some attention?" He laid a hand on the carved newel-post. "But it's nice to be here again, old friend. I've missed you."

A wave of affection flowed like warm honey through the room, strong enough to ripple the balusters on their footings.

"Careful," Evie admonished the house. "I think you've tested the repairs enough for one day. But I'm glad that the two of you could reconnect."

"And not a moment too soon." Gil gestured with his hammer and wrench in the direction of the upstairs. "Shall we go see what's in store for us up there?"

As they ascended the steps, Evie felt lighter, as if a painful knot had been worked loose inside of her. The bad memories weren't gone, but it had felt good to share them with Gil, to confide in someone who listened and understood. It made her realize that she'd never truly felt that connection with anyone in the ECRA. She'd enjoyed her relationships with the other witches she'd worked with, but they'd never felt like more than colleagues.

Things were going to be different here, Evie promised herself. The house was trying to meet her halfway, and she wanted to do the same with Iskendra and its people. Both of them had work to do.

Fourteen

The upstairs portion of Thornwood house was a jarring sight after all the cleaning and magical repairs they'd made to the first floor. There were three bedrooms and an additional bathroom, but, as expected, all four rooms had suffered significant damage during the house's wanderings. There were gaping cracks in the walls, more broken furniture, and shattered windows. A thick coating of plaster dust covered every surface and even drifted on the air, making them all cough.

The leaky faucet that Gil had been worried about turned out to be the least of their problems in the bathroom. The entire sink had been torn off the wall and now lay in pieces on the floor. The tub had overturned and cracked, and there was evidence that one of the pipes had burst. The house had sealed the leak with some of Evie's magic, but not before there'd been significant flooding, which had stained the bathroom tiles and ruined the carpet in the adjoining bedroom. A thick, mildewy scent permeated the air.

"I should have brought more tools," Gil lamented as he and Evie stood in the upstairs hall, surveying the damage.

"I can fix the worst of it with magic." Evie sighed. "But it's going to take time."

At least Ruby was having fun. She'd chosen the room at the end of the hall to be her bedroom, one of two that overlooked the back garden and glasshouse. The windows were cracked and dirty, the floors stained and uneven, but there were some salvageable beauties here and there as well. A white canopy bed frame sat on the opposite side of the room, along with a brass light fixture in the shape of an old sailing ship, complete with a mermaid as its figurehead. Magical light filled its sails, casting lacy shadows upon the walls.

They took what they had and worked for a full day. Gil came back again the next, and the next, all through the rest of the week. With a third pair of hands, Evie was able to take time to tend to the plants in the glasshouse and garden, harvesting the magical ingredients before they withered, drying and preparing them for potions, creams, and other remedies.

Inside, she used her magic wherever she could, repairing pipes and structural damage, offering the house a continual source of strength. They spent the rest of the time doing the manual labor—hauling debris and any unsalvageable furniture downstairs, cleaning and fixing what they could, and rescuing the front garden from the worst of the weeds.

Gil repaired and reattached the kitchen cabinets and added some shelves by the windows for potted herbs and plants. He reinforced the bed frame in Ruby's room to make sure it would hold the weight of a mattress and did some repairs on the window trim so that Evie wouldn't have to use as much of her magic to fix it.

Some days, the three of them talked and laughed as they worked, and other days they were quiet, because the work was hard, and they needed every bit of their energy. But the progress was noticeable and satisfying, so much so that Evie didn't even mind the daily aches in her back and shoulders, or the sore muscles in her legs after her hundredth trip up the stairs.

Through it all, she kept her senses open to check on the house, making sure that it wasn't upset by any of the work they were doing or the changes they made. So far, Evie had sensed no other hidden rooms or concealing magic upstairs, which was a good sign. Thornwood house was opening itself to them, slowly, and far from being upset by their actions, the house felt . . . serene. Evie swore the rooms grew lighter and brighter the longer they worked to clean them, and it wasn't just from their efforts at scrubbing the dirt away.

Maybe the house was shedding some burdens of its own, Evie thought as she wrung out her dirty mop in a bucket of water. She tucked some loose strands of her hair behind her ear. She hadn't had a chance yet to continue her search for the Star Oak, but she could feel she was making progress earning the house's trust, which in turn would help it heal.

She was absorbed by the work, but Evie hadn't forgotten about Shara Green's invitation to dinner. Evie had been in and out of the village several times since that first day, meeting people when she could. She was on a first-name basis with Ira Plinton at the general store, and they'd dropped into the café a few times so Ruby could talk to Trin, though most of their time had been spent focusing on the house.

Now that the work was coming along, it was time to change that.

The night of the dinner, she and Ruby had just enough time to get ready while Gil finished replacing some rotten boards on the upstairs doorframes. He let himself out afterward, Snow at his heels, promising he'd come back as soon as he could.

It felt so natural, as if Gil had been a part of their lives for a year instead of just a week. Another step in the journey of putting down roots here.

After they'd cleaned up and changed, Evie dug into one of the moving boxes—they still hadn't managed to unpack everything—until she found a heavy object bundled in brown paper. She tore the wrapping away and pulled out a fist-size chunk of onyx that gleamed in the late afternoon light. She could feel the subtle magic radiating from the mineral.

She'd been planning its use ever since her first trip into the village, though she wasn't sure how it would be received.

"Worth a try," she murmured.

She slid the onyx into her pocket and then picked up one of the small potted plants she'd had shipped in a specially enchanted chest. Tiny purple berries grew in colorful clusters all over the plant, whose leaves were furred like velvet. She tucked it in the crook of her arm, then she and Ruby set out for the village on foot.

Evie had chosen a pair of sage pants that brought out small flecks of green in her blue eyes and a sleeveless shirt of white lace to wear to dinner. Ruby was dressed in a flowy red skirt and beaded vest that she'd decorated herself, and painted her nails to match. Evie had braided her hair, though it was already coming loose as Ruby skipped along in her sandals.

"There was no mail from the agency today," Ruby said, glancing back at her. "I checked."

"Just as we hoped," Evie said. "Are you happy, little seer?"

Ruby's smile was radiant. "Yes. Did you know Trin keeps chickens in her backyard?"

"I didn't." Evie adjusted her grip on the plant. The berries gave off a sweet, pungent scent when pulverized with a mortar and pestle, but they also lost their efficacy soon after, so she didn't want to accidentally crush them.

"Her mom has this big old coop," Ruby told her, "and Trin said she'd give me some of the chicks the next time she had them so I could start a coop of my own!"

"That's generous of her," Evie said, raising an eyebrow. "Out of curiosity, where are we keeping this future chicken farm?"

"I thought we could put it on the other side of the willow tree," Ruby suggested, "near the pond. Maybe we could get some ducks too." She looked up at Evie hopefully. "Witches like us should have familiars, shouldn't we?"

Evie cocked her head. "I suppose there's nothing wrong with having ducks and chickens for familiars." It wouldn't take much magic, she thought, to make a chicken coop in the spot Ruby had suggested. It was a good place. Keeping chickens was something they would never have been able to manage in the city. "But I thought you might have your heart set on a kitten."

Ruby swung round. "I can have a kitten *too*?"

Walked right into that one, Evie thought. "We'll talk about it once we're all the way moved in," she said, affectionately tugging Ruby's braid.

When they reached the outskirts of the village, Evie noticed a young woman heading in their direction. Her silky, straight brown hair was gathered into a messy bun, wisps of it escaping around her oval face. She looked vaguely familiar, but Evie couldn't place her until she saw the basket of library books the woman was carrying. That was when the resemblance registered—this must be Gemma Gray's sister, the other librarian in Iskendra.

Evie caught the woman's eye and nodded a greeting. She opened her mouth to ask about the books, but the woman averted her gaze and hurried past them without a word. Her magic left a faint trail of indigo sparks behind her that quickly faded.

"She didn't even say hello," Ruby muttered, as the woman disappeared around a bend in the street.

Evie's good mood dimmed. It was the first time they'd been openly snubbed since she'd had the encounter with Caleb Bearn that first day. She understood why he and Ignatius Smythe were annoyed with her, but why would Gemma Gray's sister avoid her in the street?

"Maybe she was preoccupied," Evie said, ushering Ruby forward. She knew how weak that excuse sounded, but she didn't want to give her daughter cause to worry.

Luckily, they were only a couple of blocks from the Green family's café. Shara had told them to come around to the backyard if the weather was fine, and it certainly was. As the sun dipped toward the horizon, the heat of the day slowly burned off, and the breeze blew cool but not cold against Evie's cheeks. The air was rich with the scent of cooking food: fried chicken mixed with the sweet tang of lemonade, blending with the pungent smell of roses from the flower beds bordering the street.

They turned down the lane to the café and walked around the side of the building, past a wall of ivy to a tall wooden fence and gate. The image of a boot had been carved into the wood just above the latch. Evie raised her hand to knock but hesitated.

What if the woman's snub was a sign of things to come for the rest of the evening? What if the people behind this gate were going to look at her and Ruby and see nothing but a pair of outsiders? Evie's stomach twisted into painful knots at the thought.

"Are you okay?" Ruby asked.

Evie looked down at her daughter. Ruby's eyes were still lit with excitement, but she could see the doubt creeping in at the edges. Evie couldn't stand that, so she forced a bright smile onto her face.

"I'm fine," she said, knocking firmly on the wood. "Let's do this."

Shara's voice called out, "Come on back!"

Evie pulled open the gate, and the two of them stepped into the backyard. A row of tall white peonies greeted them alongside the fence to her left. The thick flowers were already beginning to shed their petals in white flakes onto the ground. Beyond them, at the back of the garden, was the chicken coop Ruby had mentioned.

On the opposite side of the expansive yard, there were criss-crossing strings of fairy lights. They flickered softly above two picnic tables that had been laid with green cloths, matching the ivy snaking around the back wall of the building.

Both tables were loaded with food. Platters of that fried chicken she'd smelled earlier, bowls of creamed corn, potato salad, and fluffy greens sat alongside trays of fruit, nuts, and bright, crumbly cheeses. Glasses of wine and lemonade were just being poured and handed out.

Six people lounged at or milled around the picnic tables. Some of them Evie recognized, but others were strangers to her. Cinda was there, holding a black cat with white paws in her lap. Trin sat next to her, petting the cat and talking nonstop while the mayor smiled down at her indulgently. Jamie Green straddled the opposite bench, munching on a chicken leg and looking clear-eyed and completely recovered from his fever.

At the other table was a lanky man with straw-colored hair and a wide mouth, whose legs were so long they had a hard time fitting in the space beneath the picnic table. He wore the café's signature apron, so Evie guessed this must be Shara's husband, Ben. He was talking to an elderly man and woman whom Evie didn't know.

Then Shara was coming toward them across the yard. When she reached Evie, she smiled and held out her hands, her own apron slightly askew over her flower-print sundress.

Evie carefully passed the potted plant off to Ruby. The nerves that had been building inside her vanished as soon as the woman's warm hands clasped hers. "What a beautiful garden," she told Shara. "Thank you so much for having us."

"We're all happy you could make it," Shara welcomed them. "So many things to do already moving into a new house—cooking shouldn't be one of them, so we have plenty of food, and there will be baskets of leftovers for you to take home with you, along with pie and three different kinds of cookies." She winked at Ruby. "Speaking of which, you should go talk to Trin. She'll sneak you one before dinner from the stash she thinks I don't know about."

Ruby giggled. She handed Evie back the potted plant and took off to greet her friend.

"You're a lifesaver with the food," Evie confided in a stage whisper, which made Shara laugh. It was a boisterous, unselfconscious sound that chased away the last of Evie's trepidation. She held out the plant to the woman. "These are trypsen berries," she explained. "I've cultivated a few varieties over the years, but this one is the best for syrups. They give a sweet kick to teas and coffees, and they also help relieve an unsettled stomach."

"Why, it's beautiful." Shara cupped one of the purple clusters carefully in her hand. "I've never seen this type of berry before. Where does it come from?"

"The Meeravin Forest, in northern Angletyr," Evie said. "I got them from a time witch I visited there about five years ago."

It was one of the most unique experiences Evie had ever had. She'd felt as awestruck as Ruby when she'd watched Gemma Gray's magic slow the turning pages of a book. The most powerful time witches could still their minds and spiral back to invisibly witness history for days or even weeks at a time. But the witch Evie had met in Angletyr had managed to stay rooted in the past for three years, a feat no one else like her had ever accomplished.

"The woman amassed an impressive body of knowledge about plants and lost herbal remedies by observing a hidden monastery garden dating from about a hundred years ago," Evie said. "The trypsen berries were one of her discoveries."

She'd been very remote when Evie had spoken to her, as if her mind was no longer able to fully occupy the present, but she said she had no regrets, that retrieving lost knowledge was her calling.

Shara's eyebrows rose. "Then I'm all the more grateful to you for sharing them," she said, "and the Meeravin Forest has such a rich history." She sighed wistfully. "Oh, I would love to travel someplace like that. You have to tell me more stories when you can."

She shifted the plant to the crook of her arm and drew Evie over to the picnic tables to join the others. "Listen up, everyone." She whistled to catch the children's attention, with a skill and volume that said she'd done it many times. "This is Evie Sharpe, and that's her daughter, Ruby." She pointed to the table where Ruby was now seated in Cinda's place, cradling the sleepy cat in her arms. "They're our witches now, and it's time we introduced ourselves properly. Go to it, and then we'll eat."

The lanky man unfolded his long body from the picnic table and loped over to Evie, trailed by the elderly couple. "I'm Ben, Shara's husband," he said, shaking her hand. His fingers were long and spindly like the rest of him, and he towered over his wife. He ushered the elderly woman forward and said, "Allow me to introduce Agnes Fuller, the village butcher."

The woman shook Evie's hand in a firm, bony grip that bordered on painful. Her face was seamed by countless wrinkles, eggshell skin slightly flushed from the wine, but her milky blue eyes were sharp. "Cinda tells us you're a land witch, like Amelia was," she said, her tone matter-of-fact. "I'm going to be coming to you next week for some herbs for my dry rubs and some lotion for my hands. Or was it the other way around? Ah, well, whatever does the job."

Evie's lips twitched. "Delsitra leaves," she said. "They can be used in both, if you want to be efficient."

Agnes cackled, the wrinkles around her eyes deepening. She raised her voice. "I can see why that fool Ignatius was all in a twist, Cinda," she called out to the mayor. "This one's smart, well traveled"—she nodded at the trypsen berry plant—"and she's pretty to boot. He's not got a chance against her."

"Oh, Agnes, let's not talk about the Smythes before dinner," pleaded the bald man standing behind her. His twinkling eyes were sunk deep in folds of brown skin. He wore suspenders and a crisp white shirt with a yellow bow tie, and the hand he held out to Evie bore a tattoo of three small, diving swallows done in black. His smile was wide and mischievous. "I swear it gives me indigestion. I'm Malcolm Jent, postmaster."

Evie shook his hand, thoroughly charmed by the pair of them. "It's a pleasure," she said. "Is there anything I can prepare for you, Mr. Jent?"

"Malcolm, please," he said, waving a hand. "I'm mostly still kicking at the same pace I was ten years ago"—he winked at her—"but if you've got anything for achy joints, I'd appreciate it."

"I'm sure I can help with that," Evie said, making mental notes for both their orders.

Shara brought her nephew over to introduce him to Evie, since the two of them hadn't met properly the last time she'd seen him. Then she began shooing everyone back to the tables, where Ben was passing out plates, napkins, and forks. Evie soon found herself with a glass of wine in hand, sandwiched between Shara and Ben on one side of a picnic table, eating the best fried chicken she'd ever tasted.

The conversation flowed easily as Agnes, Malcolm, and the Greens told them more about the village and its residents. Agnes's daughter was a teacher at the school Ruby would be attending in the fall, and the woman offered to take Ruby to meet her before classes started. In turn, Evie and Ruby shared their moving adventures and described some of the changes Thornwood house had undergone since they'd arrived. The sun set lazily, drawing a curtain of ripe orange across the sky, the perfect backdrop to the party. When the deep-blue night finally descended, the fairy lights shimmering above their heads created a pocket of warmth, an intimate atmosphere within the dark garden.

"I never understood why you need magic to renovate a house," Agnes was saying as Ben passed out plates of strawberry pie and whipped cream. Evie was trying to figure out where she was going to put the dessert—she was sure she'd never been so full—when the old woman turned to her curiously. "Why can't you just use good old-fashioned wood and nails?"

"You can, and should," Evie said, trying to think how best to explain the process. She took the intimidatingly large piece of pie Ben held out with a smile of thanks. "That kind of work's an important part of it. But sentient houses require more, and Thornwood house in particular needs special care."

"Of course it does," Shara said. She handed a plate each to Jamie, Trin, and Ruby, who took them and disappeared to the other side of the garden for their own adventures. "You don't *renovate* a house that's been through what it has, that can feel what it does, any more than you'd renovate a life that's suffered a great loss. You nurture it, allow it to grieve, and, when it's ready, help it to reimagine itself and what it's going to be moving forward. It won't be the same as it was, but it can still be something amazing."

"Yes, that's it exactly," Evie said, struck by the woman's insight. She'd never been able to articulate the process so well. She gave Shara a curious look. "How did you—"

"Oh, those aren't my words," Shara said quickly, blushing as she spooned a dollop of cream over her pie. "Amelia told me that a long time ago, and it just stuck with me. It's what her own father told her when he passed the caretaker position on." She smiled at Evie. "There's a compassion in that way of thinking that I've always liked, so I figure someone should keep passing it on."

"Yes, I . . . I agree, and thank you." Evie was moved beyond what she could express. With just those few words, Shara had placed her in line with the caretakers in Iskendra who had come before her. It was a level of acceptance that Evie hadn't been expecting, certainly not this soon. It warmed her and gave her the courage to broach a subject she'd been deliberately avoiding. She checked to make sure Ruby was absorbed playing with the other children before she cleared her throat. "On our way here earlier, Ruby and I passed one of the Gray sisters—not Gemma," she clarified. "She seemed bothered by us, for some reason."

"That was Abby," Malcolm said. "She's the younger sister by a couple years. I'm sure you've already heard the Smythe family is funding some expensive renovations to the library, and Ignatius is overseeing the crew that's doing the work. Means they've spent a lot of time together recently, so he's got someone to pour out all his troubles to." He tilted his head meaningfully.

"The girl should have more sense," Agnes said, stabbing a strawberry with her fork. "Last time she came in the shop, I'd just got done skinning a deer, and there was a bit of blood left on my cleavers. Well, she nearly fainted at the sight of it!" The old woman cackled in delight.

"To be fair, no one wants to see your bloody cleavers, Agnes," Malcolm chided her. "The girl's just young, and Ignatius has been filling her head with gossipy nonsense. I'm sure you were a paragon of wisdom when you were that age."

"I can't even remember back that far," Agnes said, shrugging, "so it's no concern to me what I might have been like."

Well, that explained Abby's reaction to her, Evie thought in dismay. Was it possible Ignatius was trying to set the rest of the villagers against her? He'd already been rejected for the position of caretaker. What did he hope to accomplish by sabotaging her, unless it was just out of spite?

Cinda leaned forward, catching her eye. "Don't let it trouble you," she said. "Folks are still getting used to the idea of a stranger as their new witch, but that's what tonight is for, so you can meet more of us. Agnes and Malcolm are old friends, and the Greens are well-known in the village."

"What she means," Agnes clarified, giving the mayor a shrewd look, "is that all of us are shameless, hungry old gossips ourselves, so we're the ones best situated to spread our good opinion of you around the village to counter Ignatius's slander. Always the politician, Cinda is. You'll want to be careful of her."

"I resent that," Cinda huffed. She licked a smear of cream off her thumb. "Your opinions are your own, and I wouldn't dare try to sway them. I'd just be wasting my breath anyway," she muttered.

"You took a risk, though," Evie said, glancing at the mayor. "What if they didn't approve of me?"

Ben laughed. "No chance of that from our corner," he said, "after what you did for our nephew." He put his arm around his wife and rubbed her back.

"And we're not gossips," Shara said primly, leaning into his hand, "but, yes, I might have mentioned to a small handful of customers—"

"It was at least ten," Ben interrupted. "I started counting."

"—that the new land witch is a gift to the village," Shara continued, undeterred. "And so she is. I told no lies."

Evie's cheeks warmed. "Shameless gossips or not, I appreciate the effort," she said. "It sounds like I'm going to need all the help I can get."

"We should have a name for this little conspiracy of ours," Agnes said, holding out her wineglass for Malcolm to refill. "Make things official."

"Isn't the aim of a conspiracy to keep things as *unofficial* as possible?" Malcolm asked, pouring more wine for Agnes and then Ben. "Shouldn't we be operating in secret?"

"Oh, you're no fun," Agnes said, swatting him playfully on the arm.

"I think we should be the Sharpe Contingent," Shara said.

"Hear! Hear!" Agnes raised her wineglass, sloshing liquid down the side.

Evie smiled, raised her own glass, and mentally added a headache remedy to her list for Agnes's order.

FIFTEEN

By the time Evie and Ruby left the garden party, Ruby was asleep on her feet, and Evie was so weighed down with baskets of leftovers, she didn't think she'd be able to get them all back to the house.

But she had another stop she needed to make first, and the warm reception they'd received at the party had given her a renewed sense of courage to do it.

So, hefting the baskets of food, with Ruby trudging sleepily along behind her, Evie paid yet another visit to Caleb Bearn's shop. There was still a light on inside, so Evie knocked on the door.

It was a solid minute before she heard footsteps, but finally the door creaked open.

"Oh, it's you." Caleb sounded disappointed. "What do you want?" A sheen of sweat covered his face. He looked like he'd just come from the furnace.

"I'm sorry to disturb you so late," Evie said. Juggling her baskets, she reached into her pocket and pulled out the chunk of onyx. She offered it to him. "Place this somewhere in the center of your shop. If a piece of glassware or pottery falls within twenty feet of it, it won't shatter."

"It saved all the dishes in our old place," Ruby chimed in, covering a yawn. "Whenever we dropped one, it'd just bounce."

"That so?" But Caleb didn't take the onyx from her. Instead, he stepped back into the shop and returned a moment later with a delicate-looking tulip vase done in bright carnelian. He held up the vase and then looked at her in challenge.

"Go ahead," Evie invited.

Caleb hesitated, his jaw working, then he let the vase slip from his fingers.

It landed on the pavement in front of Evie and bounced end to end with a soft clinking sound. Ruby bent and picked it up before it could roll away. She held it out for Caleb's inspection.

"I'll be damned." Caleb took the vase and turned it over in his hands, but there wasn't a mark to be found on it. He shot Evie a look of suspicion. "This isn't some magic trick of yours?"

"Well, er, technically yes, it is magic," Evie pointed out. "But I'm not trying to trick you."

"Hmph." He looked slightly mollified. "I suppose you'll charge me a king's ransom for it?"

Evie put the stone into his free hand, folding his scarred fingers around it. "It's yours," she said. "I'm sorry for the damage that was done to your shop, but I really think this will help give you peace of mind for the future."

That was all she could do. Whether he used the stone or not was up to him.

Evie had started to turn away when Caleb cleared his throat. "Hang on a minute," he said grudgingly. "Just . . . wait there."

Surprised, Evie waited while Caleb once again disappeared into the depths of his shop. He was gone much longer this time. When he finally returned, he held a larger, fluted vase that was about eight inches tall, done in a lovely shade of seafoam green.

Evie was confused. "Are you going to test the stone again?" she asked, exchanging a glance with Ruby. "It works on larger vases too, I assure you."

Caleb shook his head. "You've proved your point." He thrust the vase at her. "Here. A trade for the stone."

As soon as Evie's fingers touched the vase, she felt the pull of magic set into the glass. It swirled and eddied, a pleasant warmth in her hand. "It's gorgeous," she said.

"Glad someone thinks so." Caleb snorted. "It was part of an order I did a while back," he explained, "fashioning glass to hold a magical charm. This was the prototype I made, only my client said it wasn't big enough. Made me start over. Maybe you can get some use out of it."

"I'm sure I can," Evie said, surprised by the thoughtful gesture. "Thank you so much."

She stared at the vase, feeling the ebb and flow of power as she tried to determine its function. As near as she could tell, it was a protective vessel of some kind. She'd have to study it further if she wanted to learn more. "What sort of project was this for?" she asked. "I might be interested in a similar order."

Caleb's expression shuttered. "I'm sorry, it was a private commission between me and my client," he said. "Now, if you'll excuse me, it's late, and I still need to clean up my shop to get ready for classes tomorrow."

"Of course." Evie concealed her disappointment behind a smile. "Good night, Mr. Bearn, and thank you again."

SOMEHOW, EVIE MANAGED TO GET THEIR BASKETS OF LEFTovers, a magical vase, and one very tired daughter back to Thornwood house about thirty minutes later. She put the food in the refrigerator and sent Ruby to take a hot bath while she went around turning off lights and locking up the house. She even trooped upstairs to check the second floor to make sure Gil hadn't left any of his tools behind.

She stopped on the landing when she noticed a light shining from under Ruby's bedroom door.

Stretching her awareness, she sensed a current of power lingering in the air. Sparkling motes of silver framed the bedroom door, woven with traces of green and gold. The house had used more of her magic in their absence.

Evie went to the door and opened it.

She gasped.

"Ruby," she called, hearing her daughter's footsteps at the bottom of the stairs. "You'd better come up and see this."

"But I'm tired," Ruby whined as she stomped up the stairs. "Can't it wait until—"

Ruby stopped in the doorway, staring at her reimagined bedroom. The white canopy bed that Gil had repaired was the same, but a brand-new mattress had been added to it, and waterfalls of tulle strung with fairy lights draped over the canopy and posts. Ruby's quilt lay folded neatly at the foot of the bed. A white coverlet was turned down at the corner to reveal matching sheets and pillowcases.

A window seat had been added to the back of the room, with lilac and pale-yellow tasseled pillows lined up in neat rows. There was a rolltop desk with a matching chair; the book Evie and Ruby had been reading together lay on the desk. The brass ship fixture that hung from the ceiling had been polished until it shone.

"Is this really mine?" Ruby whispered. She was wide-awake now.

"I think so, little seer," Evie said, ruffling her hair, which was still damp from the bath. "Tell the house thank you and then you can try out the bed."

"This is wonderful." Ruby's voice quavered as she addressed the ceiling. "It's everything I ever wanted." Unable to wait, she ran across the room and launched herself onto the bed. The mattress creaked, and she dove beneath the covers, giggling.

Evie could feel the house puffing with pride. The brass ship fixture swung back and forth, sailing an invisible sea and making the lights dance upon the walls. She put her hand on the doorframe and whispered, "Thank you. You've made her so happy."

She stayed with Ruby for a while longer, continuing the book they'd last read together on the night they camped in the backyard. It was worth the wait. The blue-eyed rabbit and the singing goose pulled off a spectacular heist that provided them with all the carrots and lettuce they could eat for a week.

When Ruby started to nod off, Evie closed the book and tucked her in. She turned off the lights and was almost to the hall when

Ruby's sleepy voice reached her. "Good night, M— Evie," she murmured.

Evie stopped, her heart skipping in her chest. "Good night, Ruby," she managed. She stood there a moment longer, listening to her daughter's quiet breathing as she slipped into sleep.

Sixteen

A few days after the garden party, Evie walked outside early in the morning while Ruby was still asleep. She carried a handful of tools, intending to have a look at the little wooden bridge over the willow pond. It was fast becoming one of Ruby's favorite spots to play. She would often take a sandwich and a book and sit by the water reading in the afternoon sun. Evie wanted to make sure that the bridge was sturdy and safe and give it a fresh coat of paint when she had the time.

As she hauled her tools down the porch steps, she was surprised to see Cinda's bicycle parked out on the road. The mayor stood beside it, talking to Gil. She was gesturing to the Thornwood and talking animatedly about something, though Evie was too far away to hear what she was saying. She didn't seem upset, though, so Evie wasn't immediately concerned.

Gil saw her coming across the yard and waved. "Just the witch we need." He tipped his head in Cinda's direction. "Talk to her, will you? I can't make heads or tails of what she's trying to tell me."

Cinda swatted his arm as Evie set her tools down and came out the gate to join them on the road. "That's because you've got no imagination, Gilderoy Weaver. You've gotten too used to nothing but apple trees all over your property."

"What's going on?" Evie asked, regarding Gil curiously. "And what's this about your name being Gilderoy? You didn't tell me that."

"With good reason," Gil said, scowling at Cinda. "How can I expect the new witch to take me seriously now?" he complained.

"Oh, dearest," Cinda said, draping an arm around Gil's shoulders, "there was never any chance of her taking you seriously." She ignored his groan and turned her attention to Evie. "I *was* actually on my way to see you," the mayor informed her. "A few people around the village this morning told me they'd seen something strange hovering above the trees out in the Thornwood."

"Hovering?" Evie repeated, wanting to make sure she'd heard the woman correctly. "Like a bird, you mean?"

Cinda shook her head. "Reports differed in the details, but everyone I talked to said it definitely wasn't an animal. Said it looked more like something had gotten tangled in the branches at the top of the trees—maybe a weather balloon or something—but they said it looked strange. I thought I'd ask you about it, in case there might be magic involved."

"That description's not much to go on," Evie said, "but I'm happy to check it out, assuming I can find it."

"We might be able to see it from the roof of Thornwood house," Gil said, pointing. "There's a pretty spectacular view of the wood, especially if you stand just to the left of the turret."

Evie glanced over at him. "You've been up there?" The angle of the roof was steep, and it was a long way down to the ground.

Gil shrugged. "Sometimes pocket owls will nest in the nooks and eaves up there, drawn by the house's magic," he said. "They're scarce in this part of the world, so Amelia used to go up and check on them every now and then, make sure their nests weren't being disturbed. Eventually, it got to where she couldn't do it anymore, even with magic and the house to help her, so I took over."

"That's lovely," Evie said. The idea of pocket owls nesting on the property intrigued her. They were smaller than a blackbird but with a similar-colored plumage, and it was said that nesting on pockets of magic—hence the name—naturally strengthened the shells of their eggs. It was a little late in their normal nesting season, but there was a decent chance there might be owlets up there right now.

Evie couldn't pass that up, and she was curious to see what this mysterious "weather balloon" was that was caught in the trees. "Will you show me how you got up there?" she asked Gil. "I'd like to see for myself."

"Of course." Gamely, he followed her back through the gate and across the yard. "I'm assuming you're not afraid of heights, then?"

"Well, I am," Cinda called after them, "so if it's all the same to you, I'll stay down here and you two can tell me what you see." The mayor perched on the wall near the gate, fanning herself with her hat.

"We'll be back in a few minutes," Evie promised, holding open the door for Gil.

Inside, he led the way upstairs and down to the end of the hall, where a small door opened onto a second, much narrower flight of stairs to the attic. Evie had been up here only one other time since she and Ruby had moved in. The space was tiny, dusty, and quiet.

Sunlight stubbornly crept in through a dirt-caked oval window opposite the stairs.

Gil went over to the window and unlatched it, swinging the panel all the way open. It was just large enough to allow them to fit through. In fact, the shape of the opening, and the bright morning sun that suddenly streamed in, reminded Evie of a portal from a fairy tale.

"Watch your step," Gil cautioned as he leaned out the window, putting one foot on a narrow ledge and keeping the other inside the attic. "There are a couple of metal rungs built into the side of the house there, right next to the window. They're sturdy. Just keep a firm grip and climb."

Carefully, he maneuvered himself the rest of the way out of the window and started up. Evie followed his example, getting one foot securely on the ledge. She leaned out and saw the first metal rung immediately. Gripping it with both hands, she pulled herself out onto the ledge. All the while, the house, usually so expressive and movable, was for once holding itself absolutely still, so as not to risk either of them losing their grip.

"You two be careful up there!" Cinda called from below.

Evie glanced down at the mayor, who was fidgeting on the wall, crumpling her hat in her hands as she watched them climb. It was a stomach-swooping height, to be sure, but Evie trusted her magic to be there for her if either she or Gil was about to fall.

As she climbed the makeshift ladder after her neighbor, Evie took a moment just to enjoy the view. Gil had been right—it was a spectacular sight. The Thornwood cupped their two houses like a pair of leafy green hands, and for miles in every direction there was nothing but a vista of swaying trees and deep-blue sky.

"I think I could stay up here forever," Evie sighed as Gil helped her up the last metal rung and onto the roof beside him.

Suddenly, the house sprang into action. One by one, shingles stood straight up like soldiers all along the edge of the roof. Warping and stretching, they formed themselves into a waist-high protective barrier that surrounded Evie and Gil. The chimney bricks rearranged themselves with a loud *ca-chunk, ca-chunk* to plug any gaps. Once that was all done, the house seemed to slump and exhale, as if it had been holding its breath.

"You were worried about us." Evie made her way carefully across the roof to lay her hand on the shingles of the turret. "Thank you," she said. "I promise we'll be careful."

In response, the shingles stood up just a little bit taller in pride.

Gil came to join her by the turret. "I think I see what the villagers were fussing about," he said, pointing west about a quarter mile into the Thornwood, where a spot of bright yellow clung to the tree canopy. From a distance, it did look like a deflated balloon or an overly large kite had caught on the topmost branches of the oaks. But when Evie looked closer, she realized there were dozens, maybe hundreds of individual strands of fabric, like filaments.

"They're moving independently of the wind," Evie said, speaking half to herself. Excitement budded inside her as she realized what she was looking at. "It's not a balloon—it's alive."

"Really?" Gil squinted at the yellow mass. "Do you know what it is? Is it a danger to the trees?"

"It's not dangerous," Evie assured him. "They're sun stalks—quite a few of them, by the looks of it. They drift, sometimes for miles, and attach to treetops or other tall structures in clusters like that in order to better absorb sunlight. Then they just float and sway, like a sea anemone, and periodically release seeds into the air."

"Well, that's efficient," Gil observed. "Did you have them in Dorna City? Floating at the tops of those big old buildings like waving wheat?"

Evie laughed. "I would have loved that. No, you won't see them in the city, and they're fairly rare elsewhere too, but we used to have them in abundance in the land where I grew up." She sighed wistfully. "Sun stalks and helia blossoms—that's what we were known for. The sunners and the singers, they called them in Elerva."

Hearing the name, Gil's eyes widened, then his expression softened into sympathy. "You're from the Quiet Lands."

"That's right." Evie deliberately kept her voice light. She appreciated his sympathy, but she didn't need it. It had happened a long time ago. She hadn't been much older than Ruby.

Elerva, Arettia, and Fylir—the lands where every bit of magic had been used up. According to the ECRA, a confluence of events and mistakes had caused it to happen. The problems started when several prominent and powerful magical families—Evie's included—all decided to settle together in those lands, which were renowned for their natural beauty. Elerva in particular, with its breathtaking mountain ranges and crystal-blue lakes, was unlike any other place in the world. Evie had loved growing up there.

For the first few generations, no one realized how much their combined power was straining the magical resources throughout the area. Land magic, like Evie's, was by its very nature designed to give back to the land, but most other magics were not. Those magics drew and drew on its resources, which were slow to replenish. It had been Evie's grandmother—her namesake, Evelyn Sharpe—who had first discovered that something was wrong. Measures were put in place over the next several years to limit the use of magic, but too many people ignored them, believing that the Sharpes were being unnecessarily alarmist.

Then, to make matters worse, there'd been a dangerous surge in volcanic activity in Arettia, the hook-shaped series of islands just off the coast of Elerva and Fylir. The ECRA were called in to quell it, but the magic they'd had to bring to bear strained all three lands to the breaking point. All of a sudden, the hum and flow of magic, ever present for centuries, simply ceased, leaving behind a preternatural quiet that every witch in those lands had felt.

And they, like Evie, had grieved in the silence.

She'd thought that grief would be the worst part, but she'd been wrong. The worst part came later, after she'd been working for the ECRA for a few years, when she learned that multiple senior witches in the organization had known about the dangerous depletion of magic for years but hadn't reported it. They'd believed the land would replenish itself naturally. Magic, such a powerful and constant force in the world, couldn't possibly disappear forever.

Now the Quiet Lands were paying the price for their inaction, and Evie had been forced to continue to work for an organization that had irrevocably damaged her homeland and taken no responsibility for it.

"I wondered about that," Gil admitted, bringing Evie's attention back to the present. "Why you and Ruby came all the way out here, to a place neither of you had ever been, with no family connections. It seemed odd, but now I think I understand."

"I considered moving back to Elerva," Evie admitted. She watched the sun stalks undulating in a mesmerizing dance above the trees. She hadn't realized how much she'd missed that sight. "My parents would have welcomed us. They started a foundation—named after my late grandmother—to help fund research in the Quiet Lands. They hope to find a way to rejuvenate the magic. I could have helped them instead of joining the ECRA, and sometimes I think I should have, but . . ." She didn't know how to begin to explain it to him.

"You're a land witch," Gil said, stepping closer so he could lean against the turret. His body helped block some of the stronger wind gusts on the roof. "Just like Amelia." His deep voice was gentle. "I know for a fact she would never have been able to live in a place where her connection to the land was severed. It would be suffocating."

Evie stared at him. "Yes," she said. "That's exactly what it felt like."

No one had ever expressed it like that, with such uncomplicated empathy. Even her parents had taken a long time to understand her decision to leave when she came of age. But the warmth in Gil's gaze as he studied her made Evie feel like he knew exactly what she'd gone through and what it had cost her to leave the place that had been her first home.

"Thank you," she said, and because the words felt inadequate, she laid a hand on his arm where it rested against the turret. It was chilly enough up here in the wind to raise goose bumps on his skin.

She lifted her gaze to his. Up close, his eyes were darker than she'd realized. Warm and soft, the color of buckwheat honey. Lovely eyes, and so kind.

Flushing at the thought, Evie released his arm and stepped back. "I think I'm going to go out this afternoon and collect the seeds from the sun stalks," she said, changing the subject. She nodded to the drifting yellow filaments. "They can be crushed into powder and sprinkled around the foundation of our houses to help keep away drafts. It would be smart to put some away for winter." She hesitated, then added, "You could join me, if you like. Climbing trees for the harvesting can be fun, and I've already learned you're not afraid of heights."

Gil didn't immediately reply. When she glanced back at him, he was looking out over the Thornwood, a distant expression on his face. His fingers trailed over the spot on his arm where she'd touched him.

Embarrassed, Evie took another step back. She was suddenly more than ready to get off this roof. "It was just a thought," she said. "If you don't want—"

"I'd like to come with you," Gil interrupted, making Evie pause. "I was just lost in thought." His lips curved. "Remember, I'm a born and bred orchard boy. I've climbed my share of trees to get at their prizes."

Evie's heart thumped. Lovely eyes, and a nice smile too.

They made their way back toward the ladder, while the house slowly dropped its shingles back into place. Evie winced at the creaks and groans the house made during the process and resolved to feed some more magic into it as soon as she was able. The last thing she needed was for the roof to spring a leak.

Crouching at the edge, Evie prepared to climb down, but before she could take that first step, she froze.

"Are you all right?" Gil asked, immediately crouching next to her. "Finding your footing on the way down is the hardest. I—"

He cut himself off as he followed her gaze. He'd seen it too.

In the back corner of the roof, there was a half-hidden nook situated between the eaves and the brick chimney. Peeking out from the shadows there were three sets of beady black eyes and three hooked yellow beaks. Tufts of light-gray feathers lay scattered around a bulky nest of sticks and mud. It would be a few more weeks before the feathers darkened to black as the owlets matured, but they were already adorable, huddling together in the nest as they watched Evie and Gil warily.

"I can't believe it," Evie whispered. An unexpected swell of emotion made her eyes sting. "We had sun stalks and helia blossoms, but even in Elerva, we never had those." She shook her head. "This place hides little wonders everywhere, doesn't it? Just when you think you've uncovered them all, you find more."

"It's full of surprises," Gil murmured in agreement, his head bent close to hers so as not to disturb the owlets. He added softly, "But then, so are you, new witch."

A shiver traveled over Evie's skin. "I don't know what you—"

"Are you two ever coming down from there?" Cinda bellowed suddenly from below. "I'm dying from old age and curiosity here. What did you see?"

Evie startled, and Gil dipped his head, shoulders shaking with sudden, helpless laughter. The sound rolled over her in a pleasant rumble. The moment, and the tension it had brought, was gone, but she carried that feeling with her all the way back down to the ground.

Seventeen

Ruby was awake and eating a bowl of oatmeal at the table when Evie came into the kitchen a few minutes later. Evie poured tea and made a bowl for herself while she told her daughter how she'd spent her early-morning hours. At first, Ruby was grumpy about having missed Evie and Gil's adventures up on the roof and their encounter with the owlets, but Evie assured her they'd be seeing the birds leaving the nest and going out for their first hunts very soon.

"Are you going to collect the sun stalk seeds?" Ruby asked, scraping her spoon through the bowl to get the last of the oatmeal.

"Gil and I are going right after I drop you off in the village," Evie confirmed. She smiled when Ruby's eyes lit up. "What? Did you think I forgot what day it is?"

Evie had spent some time talking to Shara at the garden party about Ruby and Trin's growing friendship. She'd confided to her that there hadn't been many other students Ruby's age at the ECRA campus, and she knew Ruby had been lonely there. It was one of the many things Evie had hoped to change by moving to Iskendra. But she'd never dreamed Ruby would find someone like Trin, who was the perfect antidote to that loneliness. Evie was thrilled to see the effect it had already had on her daughter.

Shara had felt the same, and so they'd arranged for the girls to spend the day together at the café, helping Shara with some pie baking for the upcoming market day. The fact that Shara would make such a gesture, that she cared about getting to know Ruby better and wanted to encourage the friendship between their daughters, made Evie want to move the world for the woman.

She poured Ruby some orange juice and joined her at the table, cradling her mug of tea between her hands as she inhaled the fragrant steam. They sat in silence for a while, Ruby glancing out the window every now and then with a thoughtful look on her face. Sipping her tea, Evie waited patiently to see if her daughter was going to share what was on her mind.

Finally, Ruby looked at her. "Do you think there are helia blossoms in the Thornwood?" she asked. "Since there are sun stalks, I mean?"

Evie had been expecting another story about Trin and their plans for today, so the sudden shift in topic surprised her. "There might be," she said, "but they're still fairly rare, and just because one plant grows in a place doesn't necessarily mean we'll see the other."

"But it would be nice," Ruby observed, turning her gaze back to the window, as if she could see through the trees and into the deepest part of the wood. "It would be like you were home, wouldn't it?"

Evie considered that. Her feelings on this subject were complicated, and sometimes painful, but she'd long ago made a promise to herself to share them honestly with Ruby whenever she could, because she wanted Ruby to feel she could do the same—even when it was difficult. "It would be welcome," she admitted, "because it would remind me of a place and a time in my life that were important, and that helped make me who I am." She traced a finger around the rim of her mug. "But that place isn't my home anymore, and hasn't been for a long time."

It had stopped being her home the day the magic went away, though Evie hadn't been able to admit it to herself at first. She hadn't known she could lose something so precious so quickly, and it had torn at her spirit.

"You'd better go get dressed," Evie said, tugging at the sleeve of the fuzzy robe Ruby had on over her nightgown. "We need to leave soon."

"I'll be ready!" Ruby grabbed her orange juice and downed the rest of it in one gulp, *thunking* the glass on the table before scampering for the stairs. Evie watched her go, noting how the house sprang to accommodate her passing, smoothing out wrinkles in the floor rugs so she wouldn't trip, opening and closing doors as she barreled through.

"Don't spoil her too much," Evie said, smiling fondly as she walked back into the kitchen to finish the dishes. "A scraped knee here and there is to be expected."

She waited for some reply and chuckled when she realized the house was pretending not to hear her.

After she'd dropped Ruby off at the Greens' café, Evie took her time coming back. She rode her bike to several different vantage points throughout the village to get a good look at the sun stalks and plot her route to finding them in the wood.

By the time she arrived back at Thornwood house, Gil was already waiting for her. He was tossing a stick for Snow, but as soon as the dog saw her coming, he bounded over for some pats, which Evie was more than happy to give. She left her bike in the yard, grabbed a large basket from a hook on the kitchen wall, and joined Gil on the road.

"Sorry I'm late," Evie said, as Gil whistled for Snow to return and stay in his own yard, "but I think I know where we need to go to find the sun stalks."

"I'm glad one of us does." Gil grinned as he gestured toward the wood. "Lead on, new witch. I'm looking forward to seeing them up close."

"It'll be worth it," Evie promised him, though she found herself distracted, remembering the moment they'd shared on the roof, and by that smile of his. Had she truly never noticed it before? Or the way the sun caught the red streaks in his beard? He was a handsome one, perceptive, and kind, and the more she noticed those things, the more she was going to have to be careful. It wasn't that the feelings he stirred in her were unwelcome—quite the opposite, actually. She did long for a partner, someone she could trust her heart with, and someone who would trust her in return. It was a precious thing. But so many things in her life right now felt conditional, not quite hers to grasp yet.

Fortunately, Gil seemed not to notice the direction of her

thoughts. The tension she'd felt between them earlier had faded, and he walked beside her in comfortable silence. It was another hot day, so stepping into the cool shade of the Thornwood was a welcome reprieve. Evie forced herself to focus on the task at hand, weaving a path through the trees even as she reached out with her magic, seeking the pulse of the sun stalks drifting somewhere high above them.

It wasn't long before she sensed them. A cloud of warmth encircled her questing magic, and she heard the familiar tinkling of the reedy stalks knocking gently against one another in the air above the canopy. It was like hearing the call of an old friend she hadn't seen in years.

Gil cocked his head, listening. "Sounds a little bit like my wind chimes." Then he noticed the old oak tree where they'd stopped. Its lowest branches were far up, out of their reach. "I should have brought a ladder," he lamented. "And here I bragged about being a professional climber."

"Don't worry," Evie said. "We'll get up there, but this time, we'll do it my way."

And with that, she lifted her arms, sending out tendrils of power like a greeting, and a request, to the branches swaying above their heads. She could feel Gil watching her. She wondered what he was thinking. Had he seen Amelia work similar magic in her time as caretaker? Or would this be a new experience for him?

It took a moment for the old oak to turn its attention to her, but Evie felt the brush of affection and assent, followed by a soft creaking as the oak bent its branches in her direction.

Gil murmured something under his breath that Evie didn't catch. She shifted her attention to him in time to see another branch angling down toward him, coming to a stop like an outstretched arm at chest level in front of him.

"Go ahead," she coaxed when Gil looked at her, a question in his eyes. A new experience for him, then. Evie felt a twinge of childlike delight at being able to give him this. And maybe it made her show off, just a little, when another branch came within reach and she leaped upon it, perching lightly among the oak leaves like a queen.

Following her example, Gil climbed up on the branch. With a rustling sigh, the tree lifted them easily, up and up, until they passed above the canopy, and Evie gently used a tendril of magic to make them stop.

The sun stalks drifted all around them, like a golden aurora in the sky. Evie's breath hitched at the sight, and Gil whistled softly in amazement.

"You were right," he murmured, never taking his eyes off the drifting golden stalks, which, up close, they could see were attached at the base to the very top of the oak, "this was more than worth it."

"Told you." Evie settled her basket into her lap and reached out for the nearest stalk. She pulled it closer, tugging gently like she would a balloon string. Gil, sitting a few feet away, began to gather more of them together in a bouquet to hand to her. He watched Evie use her index finger to slide the seeds from the open stalks like peas from a pod. But these were larger, the size of grapes, and they plunked into her basket in a nest of gold.

She left a few seeds in the stalk and released it to drift back with the others. Gil handed her the next one, and she repeated the process. She could sense the orchard keeper's gaze on her as she worked.

"You're not like Amelia," he commented after a moment, which made Evie glance over at him curiously. "Your power," he amended.

"Granted, I haven't known many land witches, but Amelia's magic—it felt different. Why is that?"

His thoughtful expression reminded Evie of how he'd looked on the roof earlier. It was almost like she was an equation he was trying to solve. "Every witch expresses their power differently," she told him, dropping more of the seeds into her basket. "They even put their focus on different parts of the land they care for. I take it Amelia never climbed trees this way?"

He chuckled. "I don't think you could call this climbing," he said, patting the branch he was seated on. Smaller branches and leaves clustered behind him like the back of a chair. "And no, I never saw her magic do anything like this." His voice dropped. "It's . . . remarkable."

"Thank you." Evie felt her face heat at the compliment. And as they sat there, side by side, cradled in the branches of the old oak, surrounded by a forest of golden stalks, she reflected that in many ways, this was a new experience for her as well. Most of the time, when she talked about her magic, it was in the service of the ECRA, something that was required for her work.

Talking to Gil this way was different, more intimate. He asked her questions because he was interested in *her*, with no agenda or need to use her power to achieve some goal. It was refreshing, and peaceful in a way Evie wasn't accustomed to.

But she *could* get used to it, very easily. Because part of finding a place that was home was finding people who made you feel like Gil had in that moment. Or like Shara and Trin had, offering their friendship to her and Ruby. They were all pieces of that puzzle, threads in a tapestry she was slowly weaving to shape her future.

The truth of it resonated inside Evie, making her heart thud with a painful longing. The sun stalks quivered and swayed in her grasp, as if they also felt the weight of her emotions. But nothing was certain yet, and none of this was guaranteed. So Evie took a steadying breath and reminded herself again to be careful—with him, and with herself.

EIGHTEEN

It was late afternoon by the time Evie and Gil returned to Thornwood house. Evie hadn't intended to stay in the tree talking to Gil that long. She had just enough time to wash her hands and leave the basket of sun stalk seeds on the kitchen table before grabbing her bike and pedaling to town to pick up Ruby. They returned to the house at dusk and ate a quick dinner of leftovers from the previous night, while Ruby regaled her with stories of her pie-baking adventures with Shara and Trin. Everyone involved had agreed that the blackberry and lemon cream pies would be the envy of all at the market. Evie had to agree; her mouth watered at the thought of the tart lemon, the perfect summer treat.

By the time she and Ruby had cleaned up the dishes, both of them were exhausted, so they agreed to save their bedtime reading for another night, when they could keep their eyes open.

After she'd bid Ruby good night, Evie headed back downstairs to the kitchen, where she'd left the basket of sun stalk seeds. She would take them out to the glasshouse to store them for now, until she could find a good container to keep them in for the winter.

A flash of seafoam green caught Evie's eye as she walked past the window. It was the vase that Caleb Bearn had gifted her with the night of the garden party. Ruby must have put it on the windowsill for decoration. Evie had been so busy with the house and then the sun stalks, she'd forgotten all about it.

She picked up the vase and turned it over in her hands. Magic tingled at her fingertips as she explored it. Yes, it was definitely a protective vessel, as she'd thought, but there was an enhancement property as well, one with a very specific use that she hadn't detected at first.

Curious and no longer tired, Evie took her basket of seeds and the vase and went out the front door and around the side of the house to the glasshouse.

Inside, it was humid and dark. Evie put the basket of seeds on a shelf, lit some candles, and carried the vase to a table in the corner where some medicinal herbs were growing. She bent to examine the sylciria plants. Similar in appearance to rosemary, the black spikes could be pruned, chopped, and used to spice food. When made into a cream, it had the added benefit of helping to ease the itch from skin rashes. There were five seedlings here, but one of them had gotten shoved into a corner where the light couldn't quite reach, and it was beginning to wither.

She picked up the droopy plant and carefully eased it out of its small pot. Cradling the roots, she whispered to it, soothing and supporting it as she transferred it to the magical vase, pressing down the soil until the plant was secure. Then she set it on the worktable and waited.

Immediately, the plant perked up. Its curled spikes straightened and thickened, sprouting new growth. Evie smiled, feeling the vitality return to it. But she was still puzzled by her encounter with Caleb, the fact that some mysterious client had had the glassblower design a vessel in secret to protect and revitalize plants. A design like that would be beneficial to all the magical community. Why wouldn't Caleb want to talk about it?

Evie picked up the vase again, feeling suddenly uneasy. It *was* on the small side, but a slightly larger container than this one would be perfect to preserve another item of magical power—the cut branches from a Star Oak. Then the witch could take their time preparing them to be turned into wands.

Evie couldn't help but return to her earlier suspicion, that Ignatius Smythe was the one looking for the Star Oak. He'd been in a position for a time to know the house's secrets, and Amelia's too, and he could have easily hired Veld Tapper and the rest of his crew to search the Thornwood for the magical tree. He also had some kind of relationship with the glassblower, having offered to repair the man's roof. He could have hired Caleb to create the magical vase for him as well.

Now Ignatius appeared to be conducting a whisper campaign against her. Was he afraid she would learn what he was up to, so he was trying to drive her away?

The details added up, but Evie had no concrete proof, nothing she could report to the ECRA anyway. She had only her speculations, and she didn't want to involve herself with the agency again unless she had no other choice. It would be better to keep this mysterious witch, whoever they were, from finding the tree if she could.

Unless she was too late, and they already had.

Evie shook her head. She couldn't worry about that now. She could only hope that the Star Oak had managed to stay hidden, and that she was doing enough to help Thornwood house heal and re-imagine itself.

Speaking of which, it was time she checked in on it again, just to make sure everything was still proceeding as it should.

Evie set the vase aside and reached out, putting one hand on the wall of the glasshouse, and the other on the table in front of her. The spikes of the sylciria plant snapped and danced as she loosed her power. She let her awareness push outward, encompassing the structure of the house so she could assess its condition.

What she found made her spirits deflate.

Power fizzed at her fingertips, but it was diminished. The magic she'd offered to the house during the past days was almost completely gone. She could no longer feel it coursing through the walls. The structure itself was still sound, so there was no danger in them staying in the house, but the place overall had a brittle feeling to it.

How could that be? They'd worked so hard, and Evie had given so much; the house should have retained more of her power each time she offered it and grown stronger. Instead, it felt like her magic had simply drained away. Behind the sheen of the new repairs, Evie could tell the house was suffering. The feeling tore at her.

Was it because they weren't bonded? Or did the house need the specific magic of a Star Oak to replenish itself?

"You knew the power was fading, but you still used what you could to do Ruby's bedroom, didn't you?" Evie said, running her hand down the windowpane of the glasshouse. Gratitude and exasperation warred inside her. "I know you want to look after her, but you need to take better care of yourself. Let us do more of the work.

You've seen we can manage it, and your friend Gil is helping, so we'll be all right."

A breeze stirred her hair, and Evie felt something that was almost like an affectionate pat on the shoulder before the house's presence receded.

Evie sighed. She was so tired, in body and in heart, but her mind was too active to sleep, so she left the glasshouse and went around to the front of the house. She climbed the steps and sat down on the porch swing, tucking her legs underneath her. The moon overhead was a sliver of white, a curved bow that was so big and close she felt she could reach out and take it into her hand.

There was still so much she didn't know, about the house, the Thornwood, even her role as caretaker. Was all this part of another test Amelia Howell had left for her, a mystery that she couldn't see? Was that why she couldn't get into the study to claim the old witch's diary? And if she couldn't pass this test, how could she hope to protect the Star Oak from those who wanted to exploit its power?

"What more do I need to do?" Evie murmured, but she didn't know if she was talking to herself, the house, or Amelia's spirit, lingering there in the summer night.

And what would happen to Thornwood house if she didn't figure it all out?

Nineteen

Evie slept poorly that night and, consequently, woke early and grumpy the next morning. She'd taken over the couch now that Ruby had her new bedroom, and though it was much better than sleeping on the floor, as she had been doing, she'd still tossed and turned half the night, thinking about the house and the Star Oak.

The sky was gray and heavy, with dark clouds scudding in over the Thornwood, but Evie found she was too restless to stay inside. She dressed quickly and went out to the glasshouse. The smell of rain grew stronger with every gust of wind, but Evie held out hope that she could get some weeding done before the showers settled in for the day.

She filled a belt with garden tools, put on her gloves and a wide-brimmed hat, and resolutely went to work, starting with the vegetable patch in the backyard. It hadn't gotten nearly as much attention as the gardens in front, and it showed.

A spitting rain started after only a few minutes, but Evie ignored it. She hacked at thorny green clumps, thinned encroaching grass so the garden could breathe, and trimmed away some of the dead growth that had accumulated over the past six months. Soon she was sweating and cursing as she yanked and tossed and raked, working off her frustrations while attempting to restore the garden to some semblance of order.

Most of the time, work like this was a source of solace for Evie, something that occupied her physical body with hard and satisfying labor, leaving her mind to roam freely. It was how she'd first learned she was a land witch, in fact.

She'd been four years old, outside "helping" her parents in the garden. After a long day of digging in the dirt and getting her face and romper absolutely filthy, she'd finally settled herself in the pumpkin patch. That was where her mother had found her, squatting in the grass, pumpkin vines twining around her arms like living sleeves. She'd had her eyes squeezed shut, tongue between her teeth, trying to ripen the little green ball clutched in her hands into the impressive orange fruit her mother had shown her in picture books. She'd only had a tiny spark of magic at the time, but she'd poured it all into the plant. By the time she stopped, she was so exhausted, she'd fallen asleep face-first in the garden. Her mother had carried her straight to bed, dirt and all.

The next day, they'd discovered that the pumpkin had not only ripened overnight, it was now too big to be carried by just one person. They'd had to move it with a wheelbarrow. Evie had been ecstatic. After that, she'd gone back to the garden almost every day, and that tiny spark within her began to grow and ripen, just like the pumpkin. Even when she wasn't giving magic to the plants, she felt comfortable there, listening to the chattering grass and the burrowing of roots through the earth.

In Amelia Howell's garden, Evie felt more like a beleaguered princess fighting her way through a briar patch. But the land was still present, taking in her frustrations and bolstering her wherever it could. Evie appreciated the effort, but she didn't want to be soothed right then. She wanted to fight, to wear herself out so her worries and fears wouldn't get the best of her.

Absorbed in her struggles, she didn't realize someone was approaching until she heard a soft chuckle. She turned to see Gil on the other side of the wall between their properties. He leaned a hip against the uneven stones, watching her.

"Sounds dangerous over there," he commented. "Who's winning?"

"So far, it's the weeds," Evie said with a grunt. She set her shears on the ground and stood up straight, stretching the sore muscles in her lower back. "How did Amelia ever manage to keep the gardens from growing wild?"

"That's easy." Gil smiled. "Her secret was she bribed the village children to help her, hid foil-wrapped candies and coins all over the property. You've never seen a more well-tended patch of ground in your life."

"She didn't!" Evie laughed, picturing the clever old witch creeping through the yard, dropping coins and treats in her wake. Peeling off her garden gloves, she strode over to join Gil at the wall. The honeysuckle was bright and blooming, and the occasional hummingbird streaked from blossom to blossom, flashing its ruby throat and iridescent green plumage.

"Amelia had all kinds of tricks like that up her sleeve," Gil said. "You couldn't take your eyes off her for a second."

Well, that was something, Evie thought. If the old witch had needed help to contain her own garden, then she didn't feel quite so inadequate.

"Where are you off to?" she asked, seeing the bag Gil had slung over one shoulder.

"I'm headed to the orchard," he said. "One of the trees was damaged in a storm we had a few weeks back, but I didn't notice it until now. Going to see if I can save it." He spoke casually, but Evie noted the tension around his eyes.

"Is there anything I can do to help?" she asked. "Want me to take a look at the tree?"

He scratched at his beard, looking self-conscious, which just made him more appealing in Evie's eyes. "I didn't want to impose, since I know how much work you've got, but . . ."

"I could use a break." Evie took off her belt and hat and laid them in the grass. The rain had paused, but the sky was still dark, and she knew it would only be a temporary reprieve. "I admit, I'd like to see this orchard of yours. I only saw a bit in passing the day Ruby and I arrived."

His smile broadened. "Then let me give you the grand tour. I'll meet you out in front of my place. Say, five minutes?"

"I'll be there."

THE ORCHARD WAS BIGGER THAN EVIE COULD HAVE GUESSED, having only seen a portion of it from the road. Gil led her around the back of his cottage and down a packed-dirt path through a cluster of dogwood trees. The path ended at a worn gate, but Gil paused to whistle Snow down from the other side of the yard. The dog bounded up to Evie and wagged his tail happily until she bent to pet him.

"You're looking beautiful as always," she said.

"He's started pining for Ruby when he doesn't get to visit," Gil said, shaking his head. "Your daughter's ruined my dog."

"She's talked me into getting a kitten and some chickens." Evie shrugged. "Snow's not the only one she's got wrapped around her little finger."

They passed through the gate and into the orchard proper. Rows of trees enclosed them, branches heavy with green fruit. Just like the pumpkins, if Evie had seen this when she was a child, she wouldn't have been able to resist turning as many of the nascent apples to red as she could reach.

"Couple of months will be picking season," Gil said as they walked. Every few feet, he stopped, laying his hand on a tree trunk or examining the thick green leaves for signs of pests. "I'll have to introduce you to my hard cider when the time comes." He glanced over his shoulder at her. "Old family recipe."

"Sounds wonderful."

"I'll warn you, it has a kick," Gil admitted. "Ask Cinda about that sometime. She still hasn't forgiven me for what she calls the worst morning-after harvest festival she's ever had."

Evie laughed. "Consider me warned."

As they walked, Evie gradually worked out the ache in her back from crouching in the garden. Rain pattered down on them through the leaves, but it was a cool, pleasant sensation on her warm skin. The air was still, and they walked in shade down the rows of trees. Evie reached out with her magic, dipping into that space of quiet serenity, and felt again that sense of presence, of the trees and the land being so very aware of them, tracing their footsteps in the soft grass.

But the apple trees, though they greeted her with polite curiosity, seemed to naturally bend and sway toward Gil. He was their center. Evie could feel their affection in every brush of leaf. She was welcome here, but Gil was a part of this stretch of land, as if he'd sprung fully formed from the soil.

"How long has your family owned this orchard, Gil?" Evie asked. Overhead, the sun broke briefly through the thick cloud cover, the light and dappled shadows playing across his face.

"Since my great-great-grandfather Silas's time," Gil told her. "We were here before that, working the land—we've always been farmers—but it was Silas who finally scraped together the means to make it his own."

"Was Silas a land witch?" she asked curiously.

"No one in my family's ever had the gift, not the way a traditional witch does." Gil shrugged, as if this didn't trouble him. "But we planted the trees, all of them. They took care of us, and we took care of them."

"They adore you," Evie said. She stopped in front of a crooked trunk, a tree shaped like a chalice held up to the sky. A robin was singing in its upper branches. Gil came to stand beside her, and that swell of affection rose around them, a palpable feeling of contentment that the keeper of the orchard was near. "I've rarely seen a person more beloved of the trees." Evie enjoyed the sensation.

"The feeling's mutual." Gil put his hand on the tree, closed his eyes, and breathed deep for a second. When he opened them, his gaze was distant with memory. "I'm an only child, so the orchard was always going to go to me, but my parents surprised me by handing the whole place over about five years ago." He smiled. "They were ready to retire and explore the world, or at least, that's what they told me. But I think they could see how much I was already tied to the land. I had no interest in leaving."

"Not even to see the world?"

He shook his head. "My world is here. I've got no regrets about that. But it's a lot to ask for someone to settle down out here in the middle of nowhere. A lot of the people in Iskendra my age are looking to go elsewhere. Not many people come here to stay." He glanced over at her. "There are some exceptions, of course."

"I would hope so," Evie said. "There's nothing wrong with wanting a quieter life."

"You'll have that here," Gil said as they resumed walking. They were deep in the orchard now. Gil made a right turn and stopped in front of a tree that had had part of its trunk split. Several large branches had fallen nearby and lay in a tangled heap.

Gil went up to the tree and put his hands on the shorn portion. "Nasty split," he murmured. He looked at Evie. "What do you think?"

Evie approached and went down on her knees. She laid her palms flat against the ground and let her magic sink to the roots of the tree, assessing. "It's struggling," she said, "but it's resilient." She looked up at him. "I can lend it some of my own power, give it an edge in its recovery. Would you be all right with that?"

"You're a healer of dogs *and* trees?" He cocked a curious eyebrow at her.

"I can heal any living thing, though not of every ailment," Evie clarified. "Some wounds and sicknesses are beyond my capabilities.

What I do is more along the lines of giving the being in question more strength to aid and quicken its natural healing processes."

Sometimes her power was enough to knit bone or seal a wound, stop a fever or eradicate a mild poison. But direct intervention like that had its costs, so if there was a natural remedy to be found, that was often where Evie started with treatment. It was why land witches tended to make the best healers.

"It sounds similar to what Amelia did," Gil said, "though I never questioned her on the specifics of her powers. I know she sometimes looked after the trees here, though, mostly in my parents' time. What'll it do to you, when you give power to bolster the tree?"

"Nothing serious," Evie assured him. "It will make me a little more tired, that's all."

She started to lean in, reaching for the trunk, but Gil knelt beside her and intercepted her hands. Where their fingers touched, Evie felt the tiniest jolt, not quite an electric shock. It wasn't painful, more like power meeting power.

"Are you sure you don't have magic in you?" Evie asked. His face was close enough to hers that she could pick out flecks of gold in his eyes. She had the sudden urge to reach out, lay the back of her hand on his cheek. Just to see if his beard was as soft as it looked.

"I said I'm not a witch," Gil corrected her with a grin, "but there's some tiny spark in me, I suppose. Amelia always thought so, especially when it came to the trees." He sobered. "You've already been wearing yourself out working on Thornwood house. I don't want you to spread your power too thin helping me here."

"It's what's required," Evie said, drawing back so she wouldn't be distracted by him. "I'm used to it."

"Can you take some of mine instead?" he asked, shifting so that he was sitting cross-legged on the ground.

"Some of—" Ah, of course. His own power. He might not be a land witch himself, but his connection to and love for the orchard were strong and deep—over the years, that bond would have become its own source of magic, a waiting well, even if he hadn't the knowledge or training to use it.

But could *she* tap into that power and act as the conduit to offer it to the tree? Evie had never tried something like that with someone who wasn't a trained witch. She supposed there was only one way to find out.

"Hold out your hand," Evie told him.

Gil obligingly offered it to her. There was a thin coating of dirt beneath his nails and shiny calluses on his palm. She supposed she shouldn't be surprised that she was drawn to him, another gardener like herself.

Evie laid her hand on his, and palm to palm she felt that jolt again, stronger this time. "You have more power than I realized," she murmured.

"Is that a good thing?"

"Yes, particularly for the tree." Evie laid her free hand on the damaged trunk. She closed her eyes and gently reached through the connection between her and Gil. It was like dipping her hand into a cool stream on a midsummer day. His power was mossy green and calming, forest ferns and shaded glens, a reflection of the man himself. She felt she could sink into that connection, flow with the stream and find rest, just as she had while walking with him through the orchard.

Like pulling a pebble from those same waters, she carefully

drew out a tiny fragment of that power. She moved slowly, fearing she'd hurt him if she didn't. "Are you all right?" she asked, checking in as the magic wound around their joined hands like spooled thread.

"Fine," he said, amusement in his voice. "Tickles a bit, but that's all right."

It didn't take much, and at the end, Evie added a bit of her own power, just because she wanted to offer something of her own to the orchard. They were neighbors, and she wanted Gil's land to know her too, to be at ease with the new witch's power and understand that she meant no harm.

Gold and green light settled over the tree trunk, filling up the gash in the wood. As they watched, it slowly healed over with a new skin of bark. The branches above their heads rustled and swayed. Even the trees surrounding them seemed to shift their attention toward the small bubble of power they'd created together.

When it was finished, Evie sat back in the grass, reluctantly letting go of Gil's hand. A tingling sensation lingered inside her, and the smell of apples and rain thickened the air.

"This is amazing," Gil said. He was examining the tree, running his hands over the smooth bark. "It already looks so much better." He shot her a curious look. "Is that something I could do for the trees again, if it became necessary?"

"How do you feel after doing it once?" Evie asked.

"A little tired, as you said, but nothing that's going to slow me down too much."

Satisfied, Evie nodded. "Then, yes, we could do it again, as long as you're careful not to strain yourself. It's easy to give too much of your own vitality if you're not paying attention."

He absorbed that. "I should have asked Amelia more about the things she could do," he said. "I knew she wouldn't be here forever, but I always thought . . . I thought there would be more time." He stood, wiping his hands on his pant legs. "Thank you for this," he said, offering a hand to help her up.

"My pleasure." Evie took his hand and felt that jolt of power again, more strongly, as their fingers touched. It was just a lingering effect of her magic joining with his, she told herself.

And knew it for a lie.

Gil held her gaze as she stood, and Evie knew he'd felt it too. His grip on her tightened fractionally. It was like a slow dance, a dream. Evie moved, tugging his hand, and he followed, until her back was against the tree. She could go no farther.

He leaned over her.

That scent again. Apples and rain.

He's going to kiss me, Evie thought. Had this been in Ruby's vision? When she'd first spoken of it, Evie had been afraid her daughter had seen something unpleasant about Gil, something she wouldn't like. But now she realized Ruby's hesitation might have been for a different reason entirely.

Evie's power rose, a heady whirlwind pushing them together. But as she stood in the eye of the hurricane, ready to surrender, a cold thought intruded.

"Not many people come here to stay."

Wait.

No, she didn't want to think it.

Wait.

Apples and rain. That was what she wanted.

She wanted *this*.

But what if she couldn't keep it? What if she couldn't stay?

Wait.

Suddenly, Gil stepped back, breaking the contact and putting an arm's length of space between them. Evie let out a shaky breath. She was at once relieved, disappointed, and confused. Had she said that last part out loud? Was that why Gil had retreated?

Cold droplets splashed on her bare skin. The rain was picking up. The tree provided some cover, but her clothes were already starting to stick to her, raindrops collecting on her lashes.

"Evie, I—" Gil wore a dazed expression. He raked a hand through his dampening hair. It curled pleasingly at the ends. "We should head back," he said, looking up at the sky. "Storm's about to break."

It already had, Evie thought, as they picked their way carefully back over newly muddied ground. And she wasn't certain either of them was ready for it.

TWENTY

For the next two weeks, Evie and Ruby continued to work on the house, using some magic but mostly relying on manual labor. With Gil's help, they tore out the ruined mildewed carpet upstairs and hauled it out of the house. Then they got down to repairing and replacing the parts of the floor that had sustained the most damage in the flood. It was slow, messy work, but Evie was determined that the house conserve as much magic as possible. She assured it several times that, far from minding the hard work, she enjoyed seeing the small transformations that took place day by day as a result of their efforts.

Of course, the house didn't always listen when she told it to save its power.

One day, Evie climbed the stairs to the second floor, only to discover that all the old light fixtures in the upstairs hall had been replaced, so they no longer had to go stumbling around the dark hallway when they worked late into the night. Gil had been working all day on the windows in the primary bedroom, so she knew it couldn't have been him who'd made the changes.

Like a child caught sneaking a cookie, the house had tried to give off an air of innocence, but Evie had felt the unmistakable waft of guilt—it smelled like burnt toast—when she'd confronted it.

As the days passed, neither she nor Gil brought up the moment they'd almost kissed in the orchard. Then again, there never seemed to be a good opportunity to do so, between Ruby's presence and the mountain of repair work. But the camaraderie of the jobs suited them both, and any awkwardness between them slowly faded.

That was for the best, Evie told herself. She needed to focus on the house, the search for the Star Oak, and making a place for herself and Ruby among the villagers. What she might want beyond that didn't matter right now.

At the end of the second week came market day, and Evie called a temporary halt to the repair work so she and Ruby could take some of the potions, creams, teas, tonics, and other remedies Evie had been working on to the village. The Greens had offered to share a corner of their market stall until Evie got her own stall going, so early that morning, she and Ruby packed up their wares and loaded them into their bike baskets, and when those were full, they stuffed the rest in bags that they slung over their shoulders while they rode into the village.

Even though it was the hottest day yet since they'd arrived in Iskendra, the market was crowded and boisterous, so much so that Evie and Ruby barely had a moment to sit down. It seemed many of the villagers had been waiting for the chance to meet the new witch, and now they had the perfect opportunity.

Fortunately, Evie had prepared accordingly. She'd selected a combination of flowers from the mood garden and assembled them into several dozen nosegays. Together they would draw attention by adding a spot of brilliant white amid the more colorful booths in the market. But that wasn't their only purpose. Evie had chosen stalks of brittle hearts and ruffled winter glories, ice vines and even some ease lilies—all plants that thrived on calm, quiet temperaments. With a little bit of extra magic from Evie, they would act as a breath of winter, cloaking anyone who held them in cool air, like a bite of vanilla ice cream.

The villagers couldn't get enough of them.

Over the next several hours, Evie shook dozens of hands, learned and forgot dozens more names, and ended up running out of everything they'd brought. The entire afternoon passed in a whirlwind.

Despite her best efforts, it wasn't all wonderful. There had been a few snubs and some narrow-eyed looks, but Shara's full-throated laughter had taken the sting out of them, and every few minutes, it seemed, Ben would produce something new from the market for them all to try. Evie sipped blackberry iced tea, nibbled on plump caper berries, and sampled golden honey in dripping streams straight out of the jar.

When the market had settled down enough for her to escape for a few minutes, Evie took a lap around the various vendors, collecting a bouquet of lilacs and some more herbs for the front garden. She waved to Gil, who was back at his stand with Snow and surrounded by a group of people. His face lit up when he saw her, and he quickly motioned her over. Through him, she met one of the town councilors and discovered that she had a cat that was due to have a litter of kittens soon. The woman was more than happy to promise one to her for Ruby. Evie tucked the information away to surprise her daughter later.

The chicken coop would have to wait, at least for now. Evie didn't want the house expending any more magic unless it was absolutely necessary. Maybe she could get Gil to help her with that project eventually, or she would tackle it herself after talking to one of the farmers.

When the market ended, she'd intended to head over to the library to talk to Gemma Gray, see if she'd had any luck procuring books on sentient houses. Evie had already done a considerable amount of research while they were in Dorna City, so she didn't hold out a lot of hope that she'd learn anything new, but she was still determined to try.

As it turned out, she didn't need to track Gemma down. The time witch caught up with her as she was heading back toward the Greens' stall.

"You're the most popular attraction at the market today!" Gemma declared, squirming through the crowd and nearly losing her straw hat before falling into step beside Evie. "I came by the stall intending to look at your tea selection, and everything was gone!" She grinned. "So I thought I'd come straight to the source."

Evie laughed. "I have more at home. You should come by sometime, and I'll show you what I've got."

"Oh, I can barely get away from the library right now." Gemma let out a dramatic sigh. "It's been a disaster! We had a wall come down yesterday, did you hear? Of course you heard, it's a small village. An entire wall! Luckily, it wasn't load bearing, but still, when Abby told me about it, I nearly had a heart attack."

"Sounds like you have your hands full," Evie sympathized. "I probably shouldn't ask, then, if you've had a chance to track down those books you mentioned."

"Of course I did." Gemma reached into the basket she was carrying. "I always have time for books, whether the walls are falling down or not. That's the other reason I was coming to talk to you." She fished out a slender volume and handed it over. "Most of the information I found was very general, and you probably already know it, but there are some firsthand accounts of sentient houses through history, written by their caretakers. Some of the information in there might apply to your situation. It's worth a shot."

"That's wonderful," Evie said, feeling her hopes rising as she took the book and flipped through it. "Thank you so much."

"Anytime." Gemma steered them away from the crowds and into the relative quiet of the park. She sat down on the grass and gestured for Evie to join her. "The shade feels heavenly," she sighed. "I like the energy of the market, but give me a cool, quiet study room any day of the week."

"Mmm," Evie answered, distracted by the book in her hands. The first story she'd flipped to was an account of a sentient house built from stones quarried deep in the Helindriak Mountains.

"I've lost you now, haven't I?" Gemma said. "It's my own fault for putting a good book in your hands. I should have learned that lesson by now, being a librarian and all."

"What?" Evie looked up to see Gemma fanning herself with her hat and laughing. "I'm sorry!" She closed the book. "I didn't mean to be rude, it's just I've been wrestling with a mystery for weeks, and I'm no closer to solving it."

Gemma hummed sympathetically. "If it helps, I've already read the book. Couldn't resist. What mystery are you trying to unravel?"

"Magical replenishment," Evie said, grateful to have another witch to bounce ideas off of. "From what I've read, all sentient houses need it periodically—it's how the caretaker relationship came to be. But what if that magic doesn't take? Does there need to be a magical bond in place? Because I still haven't been able to bond with the house."

Though she was tempted, she didn't mention the Star Oak or its role in the process. She'd confided in Gil, and she hoped she could eventually do the same with Gemma, but she didn't feel she knew the woman well enough yet to bring her into her confidence. Not when it came to magic so powerful and rare.

"From my reading, the magic itself should be enough," Gemma said. "The caretaker bond represents a promise more than anything. 'I'll take care of you, and you'll watch over me.' Those are just words; powerful, yes, but they don't make the magic any stronger." She cocked her head. "Unless there's something special about Thornwood house that I don't know about. Did Amelia leave anything behind that might give you some insight into the house's needs?"

Evie couldn't quite hide her wince.

"What?" Gemma prodded.

"She might have, but the house isn't letting me see it," Evie confided. "Amelia's study is sealed off."

Gemma stopped fanning herself. She set her hat in the grass and turned more fully toward Evie. Her expression was troubled. "Why would it do such a thing?"

"Grief? A desire to preserve something of Amelia's? I wish I knew." Evie ran her fingers through the grass restlessly. The soil pressed against her hand like a clasp, as if the land was instinctively trying to soothe her.

"Have you used your magic to try to get inside?" Gemma asked.

Evie shook her head emphatically. "I won't do that, the same way I won't force a bond on the house." It would be cruel to do something the house didn't want, and Evie intended to respect its desires.

"Even if it puts the house at risk?"

Evie glanced at Gemma sharply. "Risk of what? I know the house is struggling, but—"

"If the house loses its ability to replenish itself, it could lose its sentience," Gemma said bluntly. She tapped the book in Evie's hands. "More than one of the houses described in there ended just that way. Either their caretakers died or they abandoned the houses. As you can imagine, they're not happy stories."

A weight like a stone settled in Evie's stomach. Deep down, she'd been afraid of this, but somehow, talking about it here in the light of day made it all seem so much more immediate. Palms sweaty, she rubbed her hands over her knees. "If that's the case, I don't know how much longer we can go on as we have been," she said quietly.

Something had to change. Either Evie needed to make a breakthrough with the house . . . or someone else had to take over the caretaker position. But could Cinda even find someone in time? And what would happen to the Star Oak?

Gemma put her hand on Evie's shoulder. "I think you need to get into that room," she said gently.

A second denial rose automatically to Evie's lips, but she held it back this time, thinking. "It could break what trust I've managed to build with the house," she said at last.

"Or it could be the push the house needs to move forward," Gemma countered. "Sometimes grief can paralyze us, wear us down like rocks by the shore until there's nothing left. Maybe the house needs you to lift it out of that fog, Evie." She tucked her knees up to her chest, clasping them with her arms. "I'm not a caretaker, but I've spent enough time observing the past to see people make the same mistakes over and over again, have the same regrets year after year. I wish I could tell them to make different choices, follow other paths, but the past is set. It's damn frustrating at times."

Evie glanced over at Gemma. Her expression was distant, and bent toward sadness. "Why do you spend so much time in the past, if that's all you see?" she asked.

"Oh, I never said it was *all*," Gemma corrected her. "I also know there's power and value in actually seeing what came before with your own eyes, not just reading about it in the pages of a book. If more people could learn from the past the way that time witches do, by experiencing it directly, we'd all be better caretakers of our future."

Evie couldn't argue with that. "Thank you for getting me the book." She stood up, brushing the grass off her pants. "And thank you for the rest of it too." Her mouth twisted. "Even if I didn't want to hear it, I'll think about what you said."

"That's all I ask." Gemma stood up too, putting on her hat. "Look, there's Ignatius," she said, pointing to a flower stand at one end of the market. Ignatius lingered at the edge of the crowd, trying to find an opening to shoulder his way through. "He's been a bit of a thorn in my side lately."

"Really?" Evie said dryly. "I thought I was the only one."

"Yes, I heard about that," Gemma said. "Which reminds me, I should apologize for my sister's behavior. That's part of the problem, you see. Abby's infatuated with Ignatius." Gemma rolled her eyes. "I'll grant you, he's smart and good-looking—shame about his personality—but I think she can do better, so I'm hoping it will pass."

"Depends, I suppose," Evie said. "Does Ignatius know how she feels?"

"That's a good point." Gemma shot her a wicked grin. "I never asked." Cupping her hands around her mouth, she shouted across the park. "Hey! Ignatius! I know you can hear me! Over here! You buying flowers for my sister? She likes daisies best!"

Heads turned all over the market, and Ignatius's face burned red as he pivoted and aimed a death glare in Gemma's direction.

"That never gets old—yes, he knows all about it," Gemma said, smiling sweetly as she waved at Ignatius. She nudged Evie in the ribs. "That was for you. I hope it cheers you up."

Evie couldn't help but laugh. "You know, it really does."

Twenty-One

The lift in Evie's spirits that Gemma had provided was quick to fade when she and Ruby got back to the house that evening. They had a peaceful dinner and washed the dishes, and then Ruby went upstairs to collapse in bed. Evie had settled on the couch with the book the time witch had given her.

She laid it aside an hour later and flopped onto her back, rubbing her tired eyes. Despite being exhausted from the long day, she knew she wouldn't be able to settle down, let alone sleep, not after what she'd read.

She considered going for a walk to help clear her head. She rose and even put on her shoes, fully intending to head right out the front door. Instead, her footsteps took her down the back hall, straight to the door to Amelia's study. Evie stopped several feet away, hands fisted at her sides, as Gemma's warning echoed in her thoughts.

None of the stories about sentient houses that had lost their magic had ended happily. Gemma had been right about that. Evie had read the accounts for herself, and they were heartbreaking. She couldn't just stand by, doing nothing, while Thornwood house got weaker by the day, not when the answers she needed might be right behind this door.

It would only take a bit of power to force it open, whispered a voice at the back of Evie's mind. The house would be angry, but it had been angry at her before, and the feeling had always passed. Surely, it would forgive her if the outcome was for its own good.

She wasn't crossing the line.

She took a jerky step forward but aborted it at the last second, which made her stumble and bang her shoulder on the wall. Bracing herself clumsily, Evie turned and practically ran across the hall into the bathroom. She slammed the door and leaned back against it. Her shoulder throbbed, and she felt like an idiot.

What in the world was wrong with her? Groaning, Evie slid to the floor and leaned her head back against the wood. Was she really hiding? In her own house? You couldn't hide from a sentient house anyway. That was ridiculous.

The whole situation was ridiculous and frustrating, and for the first time since Evie had arrived here to find Thornwood house had picked itself up and run off, she had the urge to cry.

Was she really going to betray the house's trust by forcing her way into Amelia's study? But what was the alternative? Wait to see if grief caused the house to waste away until it lost its sense of self? Until she and Ruby had to leave? Were those really the only options?

Distantly, Evie heard an owl hooting in the Thornwood. It was probably one of the pocket owls, or their owlets, out to hunt or explore the wood. She listened to its intermittent, haunting call for a moment, then deliberately pushed herself to her feet. She opened the bathroom door and walked out, down the hall to the front room. Pausing at the foot of the stairs, she prepared to call out to Ruby, but as she stretched her awareness, she realized her daughter was fast asleep.

Nodding to herself, Evie turned and went out the front door without looking back.

IT WAS WARM IN THE WOOD. NO BREEZE PENETRATED THE THICK canopy of leaves, and the humid air quickly made Evie's blouse stick to her skin. The trees and soil whispered against her, questioning and curious. It was at once pleasant and strange, like voices at the edge of hearing. But she sensed she was welcome, so she pressed on, allowing the sparse moonlight and her magic to guide her steps.

She knew that coming out here had been impulsive; the wood encompassed miles and miles of land. She could never hope to search it all in a month, let alone one night. If the Star Oak didn't want to be found, she wouldn't have a chance.

But she had to try. Thornwood house might not survive unless she found it.

Evie couldn't sustain the house indefinitely with her own magic. She felt it in her bones; she didn't need Amelia's diary to tell her. Bonding with the house would certainly help, but Evie suspected it wouldn't solve the bigger issue. Thornwood house had been looking for the Star Oak because it had been made from a Star Oak. It needed replenishment from the source.

About half a mile into the wood, she slipped into a clearing, following the curve of an oak branch that seemed for an instant to point the way. Or maybe she was tired and it was simply wishful thinking. She felt no call, no presence beckoning her to one path or another.

Absorbed in her thoughts and worries, she didn't immediately notice that in the center of the clearing stood an old stone slab, surrounded by a patch of orange-petaled flowers that gleamed in the moonlight. With a gasp, Evie recognized them.

Helia blossoms. The singers. They did grow here, right along with the sun stalks. Ruby's guess had been right.

Stepping carefully, she approached the thick carpet of flowers, brushing against one with her ankle. The movement was like gently striking a bell. A high, clear sound rang out, one that immediately conjured a memory.

When she was a child, her mother had taken her to the public gardens in Elerva, where the helia gardeners made music at all the major holidays. But it wasn't like any performance Evie had ever seen. The gardeners didn't wear fancy costumes; it was overalls and dirt-stained gloves. They didn't walk through the flowers; they *danced*, their slippered feet tickling the blooms as deftly as fingers on piano keys. There was hardly a discordant note, and the dancers never seemed to tire.

Evie had been entranced.

The day Elerva went quiet, she had run all the way to the helia gardens. Tears streaming down her face, she'd touched hundreds of blossoms. Stained her fingertips yellow with pollen, desperately seeking that familiar, beautiful music. But it was gone. Only its memory was left to be treasured.

Evie listened until the music of the helia blossoms faded. Then she left the clearing, pulling the comfort of her power around her.

Her parents had chosen to stay in the Quiet Lands because it was where their families had lived for generations. They would be patient, they said, and find a way to replenish the magic. They knew they likely wouldn't live to see it return, and probably neither would their children or grandchildren, but eventually, their descendants would hear the singers again.

That wasn't Evie's path. Gil had been right. Being without magic was like living with a vise squeezing her chest. She needed to feel the land; it was a part of her. Her father had been the first to see it, and tell her to go.

"Find a place that sings to you, Evie," he'd said. *"Make a home where you can be happy."*

She'd thought that was what she'd been doing, leaving for Dorna City. Joining the ECRA. She would use her magic to help people and to protect other lands from going quiet. At the time, she'd thought that was where she'd stay forever.

But life had other plans for her.

Her path turned out to be a seven-year-old girl deposited on her doorstep one day by an ECRA representative with instructions to teach the girl to use her magic. An error on the paperwork, of all things, had gotten her incorrectly classified as a land witch. By the time Evie realized the mistake, she'd had no intention of giving the girl up.

One day, she would bring Ruby out here to see the helia blossoms and hear their song. For now, Evie continued on into the wood with the bittersweet memories for company. She'd come a long way since that time, and so had Ruby, but they were both still searching. Needing that place that sang to them the sweetest. She'd started to think it didn't actually exist.

Until they came here.

Evie stopped walking. She closed her eyes and began to gather her power.

Normally, when she did this to sense the people around her or connect with the land, it took very little effort and magic. But this time, Evie called upon more—more magic, and more of herself. When she opened her eyes, the power manifested in the air, a curtain of green and gold, motes of light that, when she looked closely, were pieces of herself.

Tiny glowing leaves of ash and beech, to represent her connection to the Thornwood. Gold-veined feathers, from the sharp-shinned hawks that used to nest in her backyard when she was growing up. The ghosts of the helia blossoms. Even the rosebushes in Dorna City, outside her apartment window. They were all there. Her father's voice wove in and out of the light, vibrating like a plucked harp string. Her mother's lemon perfume filled the air.

Ruby's warmth encompassing it all.

The power coalesced into a single thick strand, hooked at its end in the shape of a shepherd's staff, hovering in the air like an invitation.

"This is me," Evie said, offering the power for any and all to see. "I am laid bare, the wanderer in the wood. Please, guide me to where I need to go."

Evie felt raw and strange. She'd expected to be afraid, exposing herself like this, but instead, the wood seemed to draw close, folding around her like a cloak.

You are safe here. With us.

Emotion welled in her throat, and Evie felt the softest tug on her magic. The crooked strand pulled taut, forming a golden road through the trees.

She didn't hesitate. She stepped into the weave of her own magic, following the gold strand on a path farther into the wood.

She walked for what felt like days and quickly lost track of the miles she must have trod. She could feel every twig and stone pressing against the soles of her shoes, a pressure that became an ache and then a pain when she refused to stop and rest. If she did, the trail might disappear, and she would lose this slender chance.

So she kept walking.

Presently, she became aware of a strange humming sound, like a swarm of distant bees. Evie turned her head left and right. The sound was everywhere. It filled her ears with an intensity that bordered on pain.

It was the trees, she realized. Speaking to one another, or singing—either way, it was a chorus that bombarded her senses. She couldn't make out the words, and even if she could, she wouldn't understand. The language was too old, too far from the human realm.

But she was getting close; she could feel it.

The hairs at the back of Evie's neck lifted with awareness. She had the sudden, overwhelming sensation she was being watched, but this time it wasn't coming from the trees.

She slowed her pace, listening, while at the same time trying to make it appear that she was oblivious.

A shadow moved in the corner of her vision. Evie swung toward it.

"Who's there?" she shouted.

The golden cord of magic, which she'd so carefully built, snapped.

The trees stopped their humming.

Evie was alone, her guide gone.

"Who's there?" Evie repeated, louder, fueled by helpless rage. She'd been so close. "I know someone's out there! Show yourself!"

When there was no response, she flung out a tendril of magic, causing the branches of a nearby tree to bend and stretch in the direction she'd seen the movement. If she was quick enough, she could trap them.

There was a panicked yelp. A figure darted out from behind one of the trees, evading the branches, and took off running. Evie cursed and gave chase, stumbling over the uneven ground. Whoever it was had a good head start on her, and Evie didn't know the wood very well yet. Still, she kept running. Branches whipped by her face, and night birds squawked in alarm as she flew past.

"Stop!" she cried, but if anything, the figure simply ran faster, leaping over fallen logs and sunken hollows. They were too far away and cloaked in shadows for Evie to make out any features; it might have been Ignatius Smythe or Veld Tapper or anyone. If they had magic, they were concealing that as well.

Distracted, Evie caught her toe on a large stone jutting from the ground. It stopped her dead, jarring her whole body. She went sprawling in the brush, rolling through dirt and damp leaves until she came to a stop on her back. She stared dizzily up at the stars peeking through the canopy.

In the distance, the mysterious figure's footsteps grew fainter, until they were gone.

Damn it. Damn everything! She'd lost the trail and her quarry.

She'd come deep in the wood, used so much of her power, and had nothing now to show for it.

She sat up, wincing as her toe throbbed. She didn't think it was broken, but she'd probably have a hell of a bruise there unless she healed herself.

Evie cursed again. If she'd just been a little bit faster . . .

Regrets wouldn't do her any good. Slowly, Evie got to her feet, wiggling her toe and testing her weight to make sure her ankle was all right too. It was going to be a long walk home. Maybe she should heal herself now, just to spare herself some discomfort.

A twig snapped behind her.

Heart thundering, Evie spun. Magic boiled beneath her skin. Her fingers flexed, and the leafy vines twined around the nearest beech tree unwound themselves from the gnarled trunk. She closed her hand into a fist, and they whipped out, ensnaring a second figure that had been coming up behind her. There was a muffled *oomph* as the vines pulled the person against the beech tree and tied them securely to the trunk, arms at their sides.

Got you.

"I surrender," said a dry, familiar voice.

Twenty-Two

"Gil? Is that you?" Cautiously, Evie approached the tree. Sure enough, moonlight filtering through the branches overhead revealed her neighbor, wrapped up like a gift in leafy vines, smiling sheepishly at her. "What are you doing out here?" she demanded.

"I saw you headed into the Thornwood, and I was worried about you running into trouble," Gil said. "Took me this long to track you down."

"You tracked me?" Evie said, trying to wrap her head around the idea that he'd followed her here, this deep in the wood.

"Well, not so much tracking," Gil said, giving her a meaningful look. "I followed the light."

Ah.

The magic had been visible to him. Evie had thought, as she was being led through the wood, in a fever dream of green and gold, that she'd been the only one who could see her power laid bare.

She cupped her elbows with her hands, hugging herself. She

knew it was silly, this sudden self-consciousness. It was her power; she wasn't ashamed of it, or of him seeing it. But there had been something raw and unfettered in what she had done, the merging of past and present, that she'd never experienced before with her magic. Then, in an instant, it had vanished, leaving her senses reeling.

When he noticed her discomfort, Gil's expression instantly went contrite. "I'm sorry," he said. "Obviously, I didn't think things through, and I ended up scaring you. It won't happen again."

"It's all right," Evie said. "I'm on edge; that's all. I thought I was on the path to finding it—the Star Oak—but there was someone else out here too, watching me."

"Who was it?" Gil asked, frowning. "Could you tell?"

"Unfortunately, no," Evie said. "They ran off before I could get a good look." She glanced over at Gil. Should she be suspicious of her neighbor's story? If he'd been the hooded figure, she supposed it was possible he'd circled around while she was lying in the dirt and come up behind her.

Even as she had the thought, she dismissed it. Not because of any physical evidence, but because of what she felt as she looked at him. Her earlier discomfort melted away in the face of a deeper certainty. Where Gil was concerned, she trusted her instincts, and she trusted Ruby. If her daughter said that Gil was a good person, then he was.

Gil chuckled, drawing Evie from her thoughts. "Well, Cinda was right," he said. "You are not a person to be crossed."

Evie smiled in exasperation. "I'm not that scary."

"I beg to differ." He flexed his arms, but the vines held him fast. "Um, do you think you could . . ."

"Of course! I'm so sorry!"

Evie stepped up to him, taking hold of one of the imprisoning vines. This close, Gil smelled like soap and the summer night, and there was a pleasant warmth radiating from his skin. Evie wondered—possibly too late—if this was a good idea. But it was her power that had tied Gil up. Only she could undo it.

Gently, she coaxed the magic flowing through the vine to release its hold. The green strand went limp in her grasp, but it and several others were still wound securely around Gil's arms and torso, so Evie began the slow process of untangling them.

Her fingers brushed his bare arms as she worked. Gooseflesh pebbled his skin, and Gil's chest rose sharply with an indrawn breath.

Evie stilled, looking up at him. "I'm sorry. Did I hurt you?"

"Not exactly," Gil rasped. He stared down at her, his eyes dark pools in the moonlight. The intensity of that gaze made it difficult for Evie to concentrate. With an effort, she forced her attention back to her task, but she could feel him tracking her every move.

One by one, the vines holding his arms fell to the ground and slithered away. Finally, only his torso was still tied. Evie risked another glance up at him, silently asking permission. Gil swallowed and gave a nod.

Her face aflame, skin tingling all over, Evie gently loosened the vines around his waist. Magic crackled in the air between them, green and gold sparks appearing from nothing and then winking out again like fireflies. Evie tried to keep it contained, but she was only human, and it had been a long time since she'd been with anyone.

Her fingers accidentally skated over the hem of Gil's shirt, and he groaned softly.

"Sorry," she said again.

"Don't be."

Then it was done. The last of the vines dropped to the ground and snaked back up the tree where they belonged. Evie felt at once relieved and bereft as she stepped back, putting some space between them.

"There," she declared. "You're free."

"Somehow it doesn't feel that way." Gil brushed some stray leaves off his shirt. He hadn't taken his eyes off her.

"What does that mean?" Evie asked, unsure if she wanted to know the answer.

He sighed and raked a hand through his hair. "Just that I need to confess something to you," he said. "But I'm worried about what will happen if I do."

"Oh?" Evie kept her tone light, even as she braced herself for disappointment. It wasn't as if she'd never been rejected before. She could handle it. "Does this have anything to do with our visit to the orchard the other day?"

"It does." Still, Gil hesitated, not elaborating, and Evie felt her unease deepen.

"I didn't intend for . . . whatever that was . . . to happen," Evie said. She found herself needing to fill the silence, to explain herself. "I wanted—still want to be your friend, because I haven't had that many people I've been close to, definitely not in the ECRA." She sighed. "But I'd be lying if I said I wasn't attracted to you, and that I got swept along by those feelings."

"Swept along," Gil echoed, staring at her with an expression Evie couldn't interpret. "Yes, that's a good way of putting it. If you're feeling that too, then maybe it's time I told you."

"Told me what?" The demand came out sharper than Evie had intended, but she'd already had too many unpleasant surprises tonight. Deliberately, she softened her tone. "What is it, Gil? You can trust me."

Gil shifted, leaning against another tree—one that wasn't covered in vines, Evie noted—before he spoke. "Folks used to say that even though she was a land witch, Amelia Howell had some farsight in her. Did Cinda tell you?"

"She did." A tingle of premonition ran down Evie's spine. "It's not unheard-of, but it is rare."

"I thought it was just a rumor," Gil said. "She'd never used it in my presence—until one night when she did. I was nursing some heartbreak over a village girl, and I think I'd gone on about it a bit too long for Amelia's patience. She was never one to mince words. It was one of the things I adored about her." He smiled, a fond, sad smile that tugged at Evie. She stepped forward and took Gil's hand, giving it a squeeze before letting go.

"Anyway," he said, clearing his throat, "I had a terrible case of puppy love, and Amelia had had enough, so she put down her sewing and said, 'Gilderoy Weaver, I could keel over dead at any moment, so kindly do not waste what time I have left in this world filling my ears with your romantic struggles. They're ponderous and unnecessary. Beth Conrad is not the girl who'll have your heart. A land witch is going to take it, and it'll knock you over the head so quick, heaven hopes you won't have time to get moony and ridiculous.'" He shook his head. "Then she went right back to her sewing, as if nothing had happened."

"You're right," Evie said. "She didn't beat around the bush." Under other circumstances, she might have laughed at Amelia's lecture and Gil's delivery of it, but all she could think about then was Ruby, and the way she'd stared at Gil's wind chime that first day, before they'd even met. "Did you believe her?" she made herself ask.

"I always took everything Amelia said seriously, but I admit that time I was skeptical." Gil chuckled. "Of course, that was before a beautiful, unmarried land witch moved in next door."

Evie's face grew even hotter. "And you knew I was unmarried because . . . Ah, wait, let me guess. Cinda told you that too?"

"Are you kidding? She's been at me constantly," Gil said. "She's ready to plan the wedding if it'll help keep you here in the village."

"Agnes Fuller warned me that Cinda was a consummate politician." Evie sighed. "I guess I should have listened."

"Agnes usually knows what she's about, even if she's a bit too enamored of her meat cleavers." Gil put his hands behind his back. "The thing is, though, I've never liked being pushed in one direction or another, or swept along by anything, even if it's for my own good. Brings out my stubborn side."

"I understand." That was why he'd pulled away in the orchard. Without realizing it, he'd done them both a favor. "I could point out the obvious—that there's no guarantee that I'm the land witch she was talking about," Evie said. "I could also confess that you're not the only one with reason to hesitate here."

Gil cocked his head. "Anything in particular that you're afraid of?"

"I didn't say it was fear." At least not of him. It wasn't fair, she reflected, that she'd sought happiness for so long, only to realize she might not get to keep it. "You remember what I told you the night we met? About what would happen if the house didn't accept me."

The orchard was Gil's whole world. He needed someone whose

future was firmly rooted in Iskendra. Evie couldn't promise him that, not yet. It wouldn't be right to pretend otherwise.

"Fair enough." Gil pushed off the tree. "So, what do we do, then, about this thing that's happening between us?"

"In my experience, the future isn't something that should ever be taken for granted," Evie said, running her hands up and down her arms. "Nothing in life is promised or set in stone. I think we should both take some time to consider that."

"That seems wise," he said thoughtfully. "No expectations, then? Until we want there to be?"

"Agreed."

He grinned. "I'll try not to be moony and ridiculous."

"And I promise not to tie you up in vines again." She reached out to pluck another leaf out of his hair.

As she turned away, she swore she saw him blush fiercely.

Had a summer night ever been so warm? Evie felt like she might burst into flames.

As if in answer, a breeze finally managed to push its way through the trees, bringing welcome relief as it caressed her skin. Evie perked up at the sound of tinkling bells in the distance.

The wind had reached the helia blossoms, causing them to sing.

Twenty-Three

The sun was coming up by the time Evie and Gil walked out of the wood together, back down the gravel path that ran in front of their two houses. Though she'd been up all night, Evie wasn't as tired as she'd expected to be. Maybe it was because she was still on edge, wondering who the mysterious figure in the wood had been, and furious that they'd interrupted her when she'd been so close to finding the Star Oak.

It could have been worse, though. If she hadn't sensed them, she might have led the figure right to the magical tree. The thought sent a shiver through her.

She was grateful for Gil's easy presence beside her. It helped calm her on the long walk back. They didn't talk much, but that was all right. They'd said what they needed to say to each other; they would figure out the rest of it later. Evie was just trying to decide how to say good night—well, good morning now—when she stopped dead on the path.

Ignatius Smythe was standing outside her front gate, scowling up at Thornwood house.

Evie's heart kicked in her chest. She picked up her pace, closing the distance between her and the hearth witch. Gil was right behind her.

Ignatius turned at their approach. "There you are," he said, frowning, as if she'd been keeping him waiting. "I was going to go up and knock on the door, but the house sealed the gate on me." He pushed on the metal latch to demonstrate. It didn't budge. He looked over at her, his gaze disapproving. "I see you haven't done a very good job calming the house."

"What are you doing here, Ignatius?" Evie demanded, ignoring the barb. She glanced over at the house. Other than sealing the gate, it wasn't showing any signs that it was angry or upset by the man's presence, which was a relief, especially since Ruby was still asleep inside.

"I came to check on you," Ignatius said. He looked her up and down in consternation. Only then did Evie realize how disheveled she was from her fall in the wood. Her blouse and pants were dirt- and grass-stained, her hair in disarray. "I saw you come out of the Thornwood," he went on. "Have you been out there all night?"

"We weren't the only ones," Gil said. His tone was mild, but his mouth had flattened in displeasure. "Evie was being followed."

"Followed?" Ignatius looked dubious. "Are you sure? Sometimes the wood can play tricks on the senses. It was probably an animal, or—"

"No, it wasn't." Evie felt the edges of her temper fraying. Maybe she was more tired than she'd thought. "I suspect Veld Tapper. It wouldn't be the first time he's been in the Thornwood late at night."

"Tapper?" Ignatius's jaw tightened. "That's ridiculous. He has no reason to be wandering the wood."

He was lying. Evie was certain of it. "You weren't aware that he was in the Thornwood just a couple of weeks ago? That he hurt Snow?"

Ignatius looked sharply at Gil. "He hurt your dog? Is that true?"

"It is," Gil said. "Tapper denied it when I confronted him, but Evie saw it in Snow's memories when she rescued him."

Out of the corner of her eye, Evie noticed the house's turret had swiveled subtly toward them. It was listening.

"Why didn't you come to me?" Ignatius said. "I would have taken care of it."

"Would you?" Evie asked. "I wonder."

He glared at her. "What's that supposed to mean?"

"It means that I know you've been out in the wood too," Evie said. "Don't bother to deny it."

Ignatius opened his mouth, then hesitated, giving her a calculating look. "The Thornwood is ancient," he said at last. "Of course I go there to learn sometimes. As the last witch of a prominent family, I'm expected to know all I can about the wood, in order to better serve my community. It's what I was raised to do."

"That's very noble of you, Ig," Gil murmured. Evie could hear the amusement in his voice.

Ignatius's eyes narrowed. "Yes, well, we don't all get to choose our calling in life," he said. "Sometimes it gets taken from us."

It would always come back to that, Evie thought wearily. "I'm not your enemy, Ignatius," she said, "though you're determined to make me one. And I know you didn't come out to check on us out of any sense of kindness, so why don't you just tell me what you're doing here?"

"Fine," Ignatius said. "Maybe it's time we put civility aside. You're right, I came out here to check on the *house* and to ask you what game you think you're playing."

Evie blinked. "Excuse me?"

"Don't bother pretending." Ignatius waved a hand. "I know who you really are. Not that it was particularly hard to find out about you. I know people in the ECRA too—my own brother left here as fast as he could in order to work for them. And you . . ." He shook his head, jaw clenched. "You were one of their highest-ranking earthwalkers. No one just up and leaves a prestigious job like yours to come to a tiny village in the middle of nowhere, so what do you really want? Is this just an extended vacation because you were tired of city life?"

Understanding dawned, and Evie almost laughed at the absurdity of it all. She should have seen this coming. Of course Ignatius had spent the last few weeks probing into her background, and he'd found just enough information to confirm whatever assumptions he'd built up in his mind about her and her motives.

"I'm here to be a caretaker, Ignatius," Evie insisted. She had nothing to prove to him, but at least she could try. "Ruby and I want to start over in Iskendra, for reasons that concern no one but ourselves. That's the beginning and end of the story. I care about Thornwood house, and I want what's best for it, just as you do."

Ignatius shook his head. "I don't believe you."

"Shocking."

"I suppose the best I can hope for is that you'll eventually get bored with all this," Ignatius said, "and go back where you belong. If not, the house will see through you sooner or later." He cocked his head, smiling unpleasantly. "Maybe it already has. I don't sense the caretaker bond, so it obviously hasn't accepted you yet."

And with that, Evie's temper finally snapped. "Maybe you're right, Ignatius," she said, her voice quivering with anger. "Maybe Thornwood house will decide I'm unworthy. But until it does, I'm not going anywhere." Her nails dug painfully into her palms. "And I'm going to make sure you never find that Star Oak."

Ignatius recoiled as if she'd slapped him. "W-what?" he stammered. "N-no, you—" He cut himself off and glared. "You don't know what you're talking about."

"Don't I?" Evie squared her shoulders. "I've seen the work Caleb Bearn's been doing for you. The magical vase? Whatever it is you want that Star Oak for, it won't be worth the price you have to pay when the truth comes out."

His gaze darkened. "Are you threatening me?" He drew himself up. "These allegations are ridiculous, and you're slandering the name of one of the most well-respected families in the area. I'd tread carefully if I were you."

Before Evie could reply, the house's turret groaned as it bent ominously downward. Ignatius flinched and backed up several steps.

"I think it might be time for you to leave, Ignatius," Gil put in. "Come back when you've cooled off."

"No need," Ignatius snapped. "I've said all I came to say. I'm done here."

He turned and stormed off back toward the village. When he was gone, Evie leaned against the cool stone wall. The anger drained out of her, leaving her with a bone-deep weariness that she feared even sleep wouldn't cure.

She cast her awareness toward the house, but it had calmed, and thankfully, Ruby was still in bed, safe and oblivious to the scene outside.

Gil leaned against the wall next to her. "Are you all right?" he asked quietly.

Evie nodded. Her mouth twisted in a grimace. "I thought I could get him to back off, leave the Star Oak alone, if I told him what I suspected, but I'm afraid I've only made things worse." She stared after Ignatius. She was still missing something here, and she didn't like it. Now she'd played her hand too soon, revealing what she knew about the Star Oak to Ignatius.

"I shouldn't have let him get to me," she said. "Although he wasn't wrong—the house hasn't accepted me."

"*Yet*," Gil said. "It hasn't accepted you yet, and if I'm not mistaken, it just got very angry with Ignatius on your behalf, so I'd say that's a good sign." He laid his hand over hers on top of the wall. "As for the rest of it, we'll figure it out, one way or another. You're not alone in this."

"Thank you." Evie entwined her fingers with his, letting their warmth soothe her for a moment before letting go. She wasn't going to push him or take more than he offered. Neither of their paths should be dictated solely by magic.

The future was never guaranteed. That was what she'd told Gil. But what she hadn't told him was how *much* she wanted this, all of it. And how she felt it was all slipping through her fingers.

Twenty-Four

The following week, Evie kept busy, focusing on the house during the day and doing her best not to think about Ignatius Smythe. At night, she went into the Thornwood to continue her search for the Star Oak. She walked for hours, letting the land and her magic guide her, until her calves were tight and aching, her ankles blistered. Sometimes she took Gil along with her for company, and when he couldn't get away, he sent Snow. No matter what, he made sure that she never went out alone.

Each night, she came out of the wood having failed.

Evie tried not to let herself get discouraged, but with every day that passed, she worried more about the Star Oak and about Thornwood house. And she couldn't help the thought that kept intruding on her in the night: If she couldn't get the wood or the house to trust her, to show her what they were hiding, did she really belong here?

Fortunately, in the light of day, she could put those fears aside and concentrate on the work. She'd finally begun making headway in the gardens, and between them and the plants in the glasshouse, she now had a collection of teas, powders, salves, ointments, and medicines that was three times as big as she'd been able to cultivate in her tiny personal garden in the city.

But she wasn't done. She went to the mood garden and harvested jitter root and mother's care. She picked the last of the strawberries to make into flavored syrups to sweeten some of the more bitter concoctions. Then she prepared some more herbs that Agnes Fuller had requested and filled orders for people who'd come to see her at the market. All of these she put into a cloth-lined basket, and then she and Ruby headed into the village.

When they entered the butcher shop, Agnes was packaging an order for Mrs. Sweels and her son, Alec, so she introduced them to Evie and Ruby. As it turned out, Alec was also going to be in Ruby's class in the fall.

By the time Evie and Ruby had left the shop, they had given Mrs. Sweels cough syrup for her husband's cold, and Ruby and Alec had made plans to get together at the Greens' café with Trin.

Next, they delivered some pungent burn cream to the glassblower, leaving it with one of Caleb Bearn's assistants, as thanks for the gift of the magical vase. Then it was over to the post office to buy stamps. Malcolm came out from the back, grinning broadly, and introduced her to the customers who'd come in with packages to mail.

By the end of the morning, Evie had made appointments with two of the villagers to come to the house—one to treat an infected cut and the other to get something for his allergies. Just like at the market, there had been a few stares and whispers, but far more people had been kind, curious, and eager to ask her advice on one thing or another.

She'd expected resistance, getting the people to come to Thornwood house, but after their initial hesitation, and a reminder from Evie that she and Ruby had been living in the house for several weeks now without incident, they'd relented. And more than one of them had confessed to being curious to be inside the place again. Almost all of the older folks had played in and around the house as children, and they missed the magic of the place.

Evie hoped that that time might come again, when the villagers and especially the children were welcomed by the house. Maybe the presence of more people would help to ease the house's grief, even if only for a little while.

After they finished their deliveries, Evie and Ruby headed for the library so Evie could return the book she'd borrowed. She'd been fascinated reading accounts of sentient houses all over the world, from the swamps of Herentith to the heart of the Rilkefore archipelago. Each was unique in history and formation, but unfortunately, none of the stories had given her a clue as to how she could help heal Thornwood house.

Evie had decided it was time to take a different approach. She needed to know more about the Star Oaks and their powers. She knew she couldn't ask directly for fear of revealing the tree's existence, but she could at least browse the library's collection of magical tomes. There might be something there she could use.

Evie and Ruby rode their bikes over to the old stone building, which looked more like a castle than a library. A sweeping tower was attached to one side of the building, and rivers of dark moss grew in the cracks between the thick gray stones. Rosebushes flanked the steps leading up to a red door, and ash trees shaded the yard where there were picnic tables and benches set up for reading outside.

Metal scaffolding had been erected around the tower and portions of the back wall, and the Smythe crew were hard at work restoring some portions of the stone that had crumbled and broken away from the building. Evie looked for Veld Tapper among them as she and Ruby went up the steps to the building, but she didn't see him.

Inside the building, it was cool and well lit, with heavy wooden tables and chairs placed throughout the main room. Dark wood shelves arranged in rows held books from floor to ceiling. The smell of aged paper filled the air, and the wisp of turning pages and the occasional cough were the only sounds in the quiet room.

They approached the tall circulation desk, but Evie's resolve faltered when she saw Abby Gray standing behind it like a guard.

The witch did a double take as they approached but managed to school her expression into a flat mask by the time they reached her.

"Can I help you?" she asked in a frosty voice.

"I hope so." Evie offered a friendly smile in the hopes of thawing her. "I'm Evie Sharpe, and this is my daughter, Ruby."

The woman's expression didn't change. "I know who you are, Ms. Sharpe. What can I do for you?"

"We're looking for some books on the history of the village," Evie hedged. "Specifically anything about the Thornwood and its magic."

"We have a local history section on the second floor." Abby pointed to a set of stairs through a doorway in the corner of the room. "But I'm afraid any books relating to the magical properties of the wood are under the purview of the Smythe family."

"Oh?" Evie's brows rose. "And why would that be? Surely the information isn't restricted?"

"I never said that." The woman shuffled some papers behind the desk. "But many of the tomes are on loan from the Smythe family's private collection, and they retain the right to decide who gets to examine them." She removed a piece of paper from a folder and slid it across the desk toward them. "You'll have to submit a form requesting access to the special collections, as well as state your reasons for doing so."

Evie scanned the impressively detailed form and felt her eyes glazing over. "I see." She folded the piece of paper and put it into her pocket. "And how long can I expect to wait for my request to be evaluated?"

"Due to the challenges of the renovations and the staffing issues we've faced in recent months, I'm afraid there is a backlog of requests." Abby shrugged. "Once you return the form, we should have a response for you no later than a month from now."

"You're very kind," Evie said, keeping her smile in place with an effort. "Thank you for your time."

"You're welcome." The librarian walked away, not bothering to hide the satisfied smile curving her lips.

Evie and Ruby exchanged a glance.

"Is it worth it to go upstairs?" Ruby asked. "It sounds like the Smythes took away all the books."

"All the ones *we'll* be interested in, anyway," Evie said. She should have realized Ignatius would see to it that she'd find no useful information on Star Oaks here. Maybe the situation would have been different if Gemma had been behind the desk instead of Abby, but the other time witch was nowhere in sight.

Still, Evie wanted to have a look around. The library was beautiful, and she might find something else of interest in the stacks.

"Come on," she said, "we'll go upstairs and at least enjoy the view from the windows that look out over the park."

They climbed the stairs, their footsteps echoing hollowly on the polished floors. Evie breathed in the scent of the old books and let the quiet wash over her. The library wasn't very crowded, and there were only a few patrons milling around the second floor.

Evie's senses tingled. There was an unmistakable aura of magic coming from the other side of the room. She glanced down at Ruby and found the girl already looking up at her, her mouth slightly open. She'd felt it too.

They rounded a corner and found a glass-paneled door on the south wall that was marked SPECIAL COLLECTIONS. And beneath it: BY APPOINTMENT ONLY. Behind the glass, tall shelves of books filled the room. The magical aura was coming from somewhere within.

"That must be the Smythe family's collection," Evie murmured. She and Ruby drifted over to the door. Evie glanced around before trying the knob. Locked, of course.

Still, she lingered by the door. There was something distinctly familiar about the power she sensed. A rich, earthy feeling, out of place in the tidy library.

A deep and old magic.

The last time she'd sensed it, she'd been standing in the glass-house, at the door to Amelia Howell's study.

An ominous feeling stole over Evie. Had Amelia bequeathed some of her books to the library's collection?

Or had Ignatius stolen them?

Well, now she had a decision to make. Neither Abby Gray nor Ignatius Smythe was going to let her into this room. She supposed it could have been out of spite, but Evie strongly suspected there was something in here they didn't want her to see.

"I'm about to do something I'm not proud of," Evie whispered to Ruby. "I think—"

"Do you want me to create a distraction while you break into the room?" Ruby interrupted. Her eyes were bright with excitement. "Because I absolutely can."

Evie suppressed a groan. She should have guessed that Ruby would be eager to be part of her criminal plot. That was what she got for reading her daughter books about forest animals who planned garden heists. She vowed that after this was all over, she'd be the good parent. She'd volunteer at the school, bake cupcakes, whatever it took to break these habits.

But for now . . .

"No distractions," Evie said firmly. "We're going to keep a low profile." Ruby wilted, but she perked back up when Evie added, "I just want you to keep watch and warn me if anyone's coming."

"Will do!" Ruby crept to the end of a row of shelves and peeked out. "All clear," she whispered over her shoulder.

Evie eyed the lock. Her former profession as an earthwalker hadn't necessitated much breaking and entering, but she'd picked up a trick or two over the years from her fellow witches. On the windowsill a few feet away stood a row of potted plants, mostly violets eagerly soaking up the sunlight from the floor-to-ceiling windows that showed an eastern view of the park below. Evie went to the smallest of the plants and picked up its pot, carrying it back to the door.

Kneeling in front of the lock, she held up the plant and gently stroked a small, curling stem with her fingertip. "Can you help me?" she asked, nudging it with her power.

The violet practically purred in her mind, like a cat getting scritches under its chin. The stem stirred and grew with Evie's magic, coiling once around her finger and then stretching away from its pot and toward the lock.

"That's right," Evie coaxed softly. "I just need a hand."

The little stem pushed into the lock, shifting and wiggling experimentally. Evie held her breath, half expecting the plant would be stopped by a magical ward or some other form of protection. But nothing happened, and a few seconds later, Evie heard a soft click. The stem retracted, and Evie stroked the plant's furry leaves in thanks before returning the pot to its place on the windowsill.

She went back to the door, exchanged one last look with Ruby, then turned the knob and pushed it open.

TWENTY-FIVE

Inside the Special Collections room, it was silent and dim. There were only a couple of windows high on the wall at the opposite end of the room. Evie didn't want to turn on the light for fear of drawing someone's attention, so she made her way quickly along the shelves, scanning with her eyes and with her magic to find the source of Amelia Howell's power that she'd sensed.

It didn't take long. Like a siren, the call was stronger now that she was actually in the room, though there were other sources of magic here too. Of those, the warmth of hearth magic was the strongest. It was a tangible heat on Evie's face, making her eyes water when she walked past certain books. The Smythe family obviously had a strong affinity for fire magic in their line. Still, none of those sources of heat could compare to the old witch's power when Evie finally located it.

She stopped at the end of a row and crouched to reach the bottom shelf. A thick, white, clothbound tome practically fell into her hands, as if the book had been waiting just for her. The binding was loose, and there were streaks of dirt on the cover, smudged fingerprints all over the spine. But it was clearly magical. Evie swallowed a gasp at the pulse of power that emanated from the book when she opened it.

Amelia Howell's diary. It had been here all along.

The pages were old and yellowing, many of them coffee-stained, others torn and mended with tape. The entries were written in several different inks. The hand that had composed them had started out steady, the script flowing effortlessly in clean lines—until the last twenty or so pages, when it became jagged and uneven.

A lifetime's worth of experiences and knowledge, about the house, about magic, and perhaps about the Star Oak as well. All contained in this one volume, a chronicle of a witch's life.

But why was it *here*? Had Ignatius lied when he said he'd left it in Amelia's study? Evie had thought Ignatius and the mayor were the only ones who'd known about the existence of the diary, but maybe that wasn't true. Abby and Gemma were both librarians and witches—one or both of them had to have sensed the diary's magic in the Special Collections room. But maybe they hadn't known what the book was.

Or maybe Abby had known and was keeping it safe for Ignatius, using her magic to hide it from her sister. But she hadn't been able to hide it from Evie, not when the diary was calling to her so strongly with its power.

Evie couldn't risk taking it out of here. She could sense there were powerful magical wards placed on all the books, including the diary, that prevented their removal from the room. That was why it was so easy to pick the lock, she realized. The books were meant to be read here; it would be far harder for them to leave the library.

She didn't have much time, so she flipped to the back of the diary to find the final entry. She hated starting on the last page of the story, and she vowed that someday she would start at the beginning and read every word, to honor the old witch's memory. But for now, she had to know the ending first and work backward from there.

The final entry of Amelia's long life began:

The replenishment continues at a steady pace, but it's taking longer than I imagined to establish the bond. I know now I won't be here for the final part of it. That's all right. The house knows what to do, and the Star Oak sapling is young and strong. It will bond with the house, whether I'm here or not. When my successor arrives, she'll read this and know where she fits, the last piece of the puzzle.

Evie's breath caught, and she sat for a moment in pure shock.

A Star Oak *sapling.*

It should have been impossible. There hadn't been a documented case of a Star Oak sapling surviving in the wild in generations. There just weren't any left.

Suddenly, all the information Evie had been collecting over the past few weeks, the clues she'd gathered, rearranged themselves in her head.

A young tree, not yet fully established—*that* was what the house had needed all along to replenish its magic. Something that could bond with it, the Star Oak growing into a new form as it merged with the house and the power of the ancient tree that had first made the house sentient. That was how both would continue to thrive.

Quickly, Evie flipped back, paging through months of entries, looking for more mentions of the young Star Oak. This was what she'd been missing, the story she'd been looking for.

Eventually, she found the first entry related to the tree, dated six months before Amelia's death:

I thought it would fall to my successor to begin the house's replenishment, but I realize now that's not going to be possible. The process must start soon, as the house's magic is waning, and I'm too old, too sick, and too damn tired now to keep up its strength.

I will go to the Thornwood tonight to petition the Star Oak to give me a sapling so that it can be planted within the house and grow to bond with the structure. The glasshouse would be best, but my study is more secure. Ignatius can help me with the planting. It's time he knew some of the house's secrets, though I'm afraid that it may change his priorities. The boy's still swimming in his own uncertainties, and until he figures out what it is he really wants, I can't risk showing him more. There's too much at stake.

The next entry skipped ahead several weeks.

Ignatius isn't going to be the caretaker.

There was a line break, and a change in the ink color after that. It could have been that her pen simply ran out of ink, but Evie suspected that Amelia had written the words and then walked away for a time to sit with them and come to terms with her decision. None of this had been easy for her. Then she continued:

It's going to hurt the boy, and he already burns with so much anger about being left behind. I didn't want this. It scares me, these changes happening so late in the day, when my time is coming to an end. We're never ready. But. The visions I've been having. The woman. Hair as black as a lightning-struck tree. I keep seeing her face. I hear her voice, echoing through the house. A farsighted child's laughter.

It is both privilege and pain, to hear the footsteps of those who'll come after you, wanting to meet them and knowing you never will.

Who are you, I wonder? What will you bring to this place?

Evie stared at the words on the page. It was as if Amelia Howell's spirit reached out to her, whispering those questions to her in the silence. Was it possible to grieve someone you never met? But even though she'd never spoken to them, Amelia had sensed her and Ruby. She had seen a future where they had come to Thornwood house.

But what had happened to the sapling? To the bonding?

Evie flipped through the rest of the entries, skimming accounts of Amelia bringing the sapling from the Thornwood to the house, of her and Ignatius planting it in her study. From there, everything seemed to go well. The house's power grew, even as Amelia herself began to wane. Evie could feel the sense of melancholy in Amelia's writings, but near the end, there was an acceptance to her words. She'd done what she'd set out to do in her life, and she was ready to move on. There was no indication that anything was amiss with the sapling.

But something had obviously gone very wrong after Amelia died.

Evie wished she had time to read everything, but she knew eventually someone would discover her here. Ruby had already poked her head in the door twice to check on her, and she could tell her daughter was getting anxious.

Reluctantly, Evie closed the diary and put it back in its place on the shelf. She ran her fingers once more over the worn spine to say goodbye. Then she stood up, stretching her cramped muscles, and slipped quietly out of the room.

Ruby was waiting for her, her eyes swimming with questions. Evie nodded in acknowledgment but motioned for her to be silent for now as she closed and relocked the door. She put her arm around Ruby's shoulders and led them back toward the stairs.

Her thoughts were a tangle. All had been well with the Star Oak sapling when Amelia had died, so what had happened afterward? Had the young tree gotten sick? Was that why the house wouldn't let anyone into the study? Had the house gone into the wood looking for the fully grown Star Oak for help to save it?

She needed to get into that room. She had to convince the house to let her in and see what was happening.

Evie was so absorbed in her thoughts and plans that she almost collided with Gemma Gray, coming up the stairs as they descended.

"I'm so sorry," Evie said, sidestepping quickly. "I didn't see you."

"That's all right; I wasn't watching either," Gemma said, laughing as she looked up from the tower of books she was carrying. "I'm just happy you both finally made it here. Can I help you find anything?"

"We were actually just leaving," Evie said, still distracted. "But—"

"Since you're here, let me just put these down, and I'll give you the full tour," Gemma said. She trotted over to the closest table and off-loaded her stack of books.

"Oh, that's not necessary," Evie assured her. "I can see you're busy, and we don't want to take up too much of your time."

She did her best to keep the urgency out of her voice. She didn't want Gemma to think there was anything wrong. Evie didn't know how Amelia's diary had ended up in the Special Collections room, and she didn't want to believe that Gemma or her sister might have been involved somehow, but she wasn't going to take any chances, not until she knew what was really going on with the house and the sapling.

Unfortunately, Gemma wouldn't be put off. "It's no trouble," she said eagerly. "Afterward, we'll get a cup of tea. I just brewed a pot in my office, and it's cool enough to enjoy it outside today."

Evie fixed a smile on her face. She couldn't refuse without appearing rude or suspicious. "That would be lovely," she said.

So, for the next half hour, Gemma took them on a tour of the library. She and her sister had amassed a sizable collection, and the elder time witch told them she had spent much of her training visiting the great libraries of the past and tracking down rare volumes.

After the tour, Gemma brought out cups of tea to the picnic tables on the lawn, and the three of them sat and sipped in the shade while the sounds of the workers echoed from behind the building.

Eventually, Ruby began to squirm, sloshing her tea in her cup and casting glances at Evie every few minutes.

Evie knew her daughter was dying to hear what she had found in the Special Collections room, but if her excitement bubbled up any more, she was liable to let something slip. So Evie sent her off to play among the trees.

"Just stay away from the worksite," Evie cautioned her. "It's not safe around that area."

"I'll be careful!" Ruby called over her shoulder.

"She has so much energy," Gemma said when Ruby had gone. "You can practically feel it radiating off her, can't you?"

Evie laughed. "Honestly, it's exhausting at times."

"Abby was the same way when she was that age," Gemma said. "When her powers first started to manifest, she would daydream herself into the past a lot. It was only for a few minutes at a time, but it drove our parents crazy because her power was so strong and unchecked. We never knew where we'd find her, standing in one place, staring at nothing. I used to worry she'd wander into the street."

Evie had never considered the challenges that might be involved in raising a time witch, but she knew all too well what it was like to deal with magic showing up at unexpected times. When Ruby had come to live and train with her, one of the first things she'd said to Evie was, *"You won't be here forever."* Delivered with the ominous certainty of a seven-year-old. For a minute, Evie had been convinced that Ruby was predicting Evie's death. Then Ruby had clarified that she meant Evie wouldn't live in Dorna City forever. Evie had been relieved at the correction, then skeptical.

But Ruby had been right about that part too.

"I worried about Abby for a long time, even when she was older,"

Gemma went on. "Being a big sister, I couldn't help it. Every time we'd move to a new place, which was fairly often, for our parents' research, I'd look into the past and find safe places for Abby to inhabit. I wanted her to learn, but I didn't want her to see too much, grow up too fast, and miss out on what was happening in the present, you know?"

"I know exactly what you mean," Evie said. Curiosity overcame her as she looked at Gemma. "Did you explore much of the past in this area when you first came here?" she asked carefully. "The Thornwood is ancient. I'd be tempted myself, if I had the ability to see the wood before it became what it is now."

Especially if that meant she would be able to see the Star Oak when it had first taken root in the wood. How long ago would that have been? Hundreds, maybe even a thousand years? Evie couldn't fathom it.

Gemma nodded. "Oh, I have been tempted, believe me. Abby and I had conversations with Amelia about which places in the wood would be the best for glimpsing past events, though Amelia cautioned us to be careful out there."

"Why was that?" Evie asked.

"There was the risk that the Thornwood's power would blend into our own magic," Gemma explained. "It could make us—temporarily at least—strong enough to go much farther into the past than we're usually able to. But the farther a time witch travels from her tether in the present, the easier it is to get lost—and the longer you stay, the easier it is to lose yourself."

"I understand," Evie said. She remembered the time witch who'd given her the trypsen berry plant, how changed she'd been by all the time she'd spent in the past. She'd gained so much knowledge, but she'd no longer been able to fully exist in the present. It would be a fine line to walk, being fascinated by the past and losing yourself in it. "Do you think that—"

She never got a chance to finish. A shout came from one of the renovation crew.

"Look out—get clear!"

Evie's head jerked up at the warning.

Ruby was nowhere in sight.

Evie was off the picnic table and running around to the back of the library before the thought of moving had even occurred to her.

She rounded the corner in time to see the workers scattering. Blocks of heavy stone slammed into the scaffolding where they'd just been working. Some of the wooden planks snapped under the weight and plunged to the ground. Evie looked up to see that more stone had come loose from the wall high above.

And Ruby was crouched in the bushes at the base of the tower, using the meager plants as cover while the stones and planks fell around her.

Evie didn't think, didn't allow the panic to choke her. She lifted her arms and became raw power, a conduit for a flood of magic that surged up through the soil and into her body. She became the roots of the trees, the biting thorns on the rosebushes. Even the wind that blew across the park yielded before the power surging inside her. The magic fed her, and she cast her power outward to envelop the bushes, thickening them into a dense, woody mass of writhing branches and leaves. They curved into a shield that rose above Ruby's body, impenetrable even to the deadly stones.

It was over in seconds. The debris stopped falling, leaving nothing but a cloud of dust lingering in the air. Slowly, the workers drifted back, until someone called out that the area was clear. Still, Evie kept the wall of plants in place above Ruby's head. With another burst of power, she pulled her hands apart. In response, the shield of plants widened, forming a canopy that stretched and curved away from the tower.

Ruby stood on shaky legs and moved beneath the spreading green, using it to protect herself until she was well away from the wall and standing at Evie's side. Only then did Evie let the plants shrink and untangle themselves, returning to their natural size and shape.

"That was amazing!" Ruby cried. "I've never seen you do something like—"

She stopped when Evie turned to stare down at her. Evie wasn't sure what her expression looked like, but she could feel her body shaking, the aftereffects of the magic boiling through her like hot oil.

"I told you to stay away from the worksite," Evie said. Her voice sounded odd, and there was a sharp ringing in her ears. "You could have been hurt. You could have been . . ."

She was grasping Ruby's shoulders now. She wanted to hug the girl, shake her, cry, shout. Her chest was heaving, shallow breaths making her lightheaded.

That had been so close. So very close.

"Evie."

The voice broke through the panic. It was Gemma. The ringing in Evie's ears gradually subsided, and she became aware first of the hot sun beating down on her shoulders, and then of the time witch standing next to her, her hand on Evie's arm. "Are you both all right?" Gemma asked in concern.

"She is. We're fine." With an effort, Evie let go of her daughter and took a step back. Ruby's eyes were huge, and she was hugging herself as she stared at the fallen slabs of stone littering the grass. It appeared to just now be hitting her, how close she'd come to disaster.

The workers were gathering around now, checking in with one another and asking if Ruby was all right. The girl shrank from them. Evie put her arm around Ruby's shoulders and ushered her out of the crowd. She spoke briefly to Gemma, forgetting the words as soon as she said them, but they must have been enough, because the time witch didn't follow them as Evie led Ruby away.

They had the presence of mind to retrieve their bikes, walking them back down the gravel road toward home. Evie didn't think either of them was in any condition to ride.

About a mile down the road—a mile spent in complete silence—Ruby dropped her bike to the ground with a clatter and grabbed Evie's arm.

"Are you mad at me?" she demanded. "E-Evie? Please look at me!"

Evie hadn't realized she'd been staring straight ahead at the road all this time. If she'd been a hearth witch and been this intent, the road would likely have caught fire. She blinked and turned to see Ruby's miserable expression, her eyes filled with tears.

"I'm *sorry*," Ruby said. "I'm so sorry. I—"

Without a word, Evie pulled her daughter into her arms. She held her and let her cry, great heaving sobs, as the fear of the last few minutes came flooding out of both of them. Evie was still wrung out from the magic she'd channeled, sick and weak and so afraid.

In that moment, it had felt like she'd held all the magic of the earth inside herself.

All that power, and still, she'd almost been too late.

"I'm furious," Evie whispered when she could finally speak. "Absolutely furious with you." She hugged Ruby tighter. "Because you terrified me just now. Ruby, if you'd been hurt . . . I don't know what I would have done. You can't . . ." She cleared her throat. "You can't ever do that to me again."

And she knew, with a certainty that had nothing to do with farsight and everything to do with motherhood, that Ruby would absolutely scare her this way again. Probably often. And there were some things that, if she wasn't careful, magic wouldn't be able to fix.

"I'm sorry," Ruby repeated, wiping tears and snot off her face with her sleeve. "I didn't realize I was so close to the building. I should have been paying attention. I'm sorry."

"I know," Evie said, finally pulling back. She smoothed Ruby's tangled hair. "It's all right."

"Is it?" Ruby asked doubtfully. For the first time, Evie noticed how her shoulders were hunched, as if she were pulling into herself. Evie hated to see her daughter try to make herself small, hated that she was the cause of it. "I've never seen you so mad before."

"I—" Evie wanted to deny it, but she realized Ruby was right. She'd never felt so angry, because she'd never been so scared. "It's not you, not really," Evie said, trying to explain. "I was mad because I knew what could have happened. I saw it all so clearly, in those seconds when the stones were falling. I was terrified of losing you, Ruby. I had to protect you. I would have done anything, and I just—I lost myself for a minute."

I had to protect you. I would have done anything.

And suddenly it hit her. Like a lightning bolt, making her skin run hot, then cold. Evie stared at Ruby as memories washed over her, one by one. Memories of the house, its surge of inexplicable anger when she'd first tried the door to Amelia's study. Or when it had gotten upset that first day they'd come back from the village. Shingles and shutters tossed in the yard. At the time, it had reminded her of a child's tantrum, but what if the house had been feeling something completely different?

Feelings Evie hadn't been able to understand or explain, not back then. But now, all of them began slotting into place.

Like the last piece of a puzzle.

"The diary," Evie said, her words barely a whisper. "The sapling. The house's grief. Oh, I've been so blind."

"What?" Ruby tugged her arm. "Evie, what are you talking about?"

"I know what's in the study."

It wasn't just the sapling. There was something else.

Evie crouched, lifting Ruby's bike from the road. She put it in her daughter's hands and then retrieved her own. "Come on, I'll explain everything on the way, but we need to hurry."

Twenty-Six

A half hour later, Evie, Ruby, Gil, and Snow stood in the narrow hall outside Amelia's study. She and Ruby had stopped on their mad dash home just long enough to get the orchard keeper and bring him to the house, filling him in on everything that had happened at the library. Evie thought it might help if the house had someone familiar close by for what she was about to do.

She had another reason as well, but she kept that to herself for now.

Evie's palms were sweaty as she laid them against the study door, letting her magic sink into the wood, seeing what she could sense in the room beyond.

There was that familiar, overwhelming scent of rich, ancient magic. She recognized it for what it was now. It *was* Amelia's magic, but it was also the Star Oak sapling's planting site. They were both wrapped up together, making one nearly indistinguishable from the other.

Around her, the house gave a shudder, rattling the floorboards and making the ceiling beams creak ominously. Snow whined and skittered back from the door. The scent of rotten fruit filled the air as the house realized what Evie was doing. She could feel its warning like hot breath down the back of her neck.

Don't do it. Turn back.

"I know we promised you we wouldn't pry," Evie said, addressing the house, "but that was before I realized the truth. I thought that you were keeping me out of the study because you were angry, grieving, protecting Amelia's memory." She shook her head. "But it wasn't really that at all, was it? You were only angry because you were afraid. I see that now."

"Afraid of what?" Ruby asked. She touched the wall beside the door, running her hand up and down it as if to comfort the house. She turned to Evie. "What's in there?"

"I can't say for certain," Evie admitted. She had her suspicions, but it was too painful to voice them. She needed to be sure. "Whatever it is, I believe it's magical and dangerous, something that's threatening the sapling and affecting the house's power. I think the house has been trying to protect us from it all this time."

Her words hit a nerve. The house recoiled, a chill breeze sweeping down the hallway. The light fixture above her head began to swing back and forth, its tiny crystals shivering.

"Don't be afraid," Evie said, and she aimed the words at Ruby as much as the house. Her daughter was watching her anxiously. Evie had explained to her and Gil before going inside the house what she meant to do. Ruby knew she was taking a risk, but she also understood there was no other way. "Please let us in," Evie went on. "You have to let me check on the sapling. If it's hurt, if it's . . ." "*Dying*," she almost said.

Gil touched the wall beside the door, his expression somber. "Trust us, old friend. We're here to help. Amelia would have wanted us to help."

Ruby drew herself up, glancing at the ceiling. "You've been watching out for us ever since we got here," she said. "Now you should let us look after you."

Another ripple went through the house, stronger this time. It rattled the door beneath Evie's hands, sent tiny cracks into the walls. In its wake, more emotions spiraled out from the house. They saturated the air with a dizzying blend of heat and cold, of mingled scents that assaulted her nose. The outburst was so strong, it took Evie a moment to sort through the tangled feelings.

Frustration. Anger. Fear.

Helplessness. Pain.

Hope.

It was the hope that ultimately drove Evie forward.

She pressed her hands harder against the wood, her magic surging. Almost immediately, she encountered resistance, a force she'd never felt before.

She turned to look at Gil. "There's a barrier," she said. "I don't think it's coming from the house."

"A barrier?" Gil stepped closer, his big body a comforting presence at her side. "Can you break it?"

"Maybe." It wasn't terribly strong and was likely only meant to keep non-witches from entering the room. But without knowing the origin of the barrier, Evie couldn't be sure. The magic might still be dangerous. The safest way to deal with it would be to destroy the door itself. It would take more power than she wanted to use, but she didn't have a better choice.

But Ruby was too close. Evie couldn't do this with her daughter standing right there, especially after what had happened at the library.

That was the other reason she'd brought Gil over. She met his eyes, and then her gaze slid meaningfully to her daughter.

A muscle worked in his jaw, but Gil nodded in understanding. "Ruby, let's give Evie some space to concentrate," he said, holding out one hand to her and snapping his fingers with the other to call his dog to his side. "We'll go out and toss a stick for Snow until she's done."

Ruby hesitated, looking at Evie. "Are you sure?" she asked.

Evie nodded. "I'll be fine."

"We'll come back and check on her in a few minutes," Gil added. To his credit, he sounded completely calm, as if nothing at all were amiss.

Snow bounded up, distracting Ruby by jumping up and nudging her hip. Ruby scratched him between the ears and then reluctantly let Gil lead her outside to the yard.

Once they were gone, Evie turned her full focus on the door. Closing her eyes, she blocked out everything but the sound of her breathing, the rough texture of the wood against her palms. The air thickened with tension as the house braced itself, contracting inward. Drawing on the connection to the house, the gardens, the glasshouse, and beyond—even to the Thornwood itself—Evie found power ready to help her. She felt it in the swaying branches of the ash trees beyond the garden wall. She heard it in the squawk of the blackbirds that had gathered by the pond in the front yard. She even sensed a faint chorus of it drifting over from Gil's orchard, as if the apple trees sensed their keeper was in need.

All those sources, and the wood was the most eager, as if the Thornwood had been waiting for this.

Waiting to set the house free.

Evie worked her magic into the door, urging it to return to the earth, just as she'd coaxed the door to the shed where Snow had been trapped. It wouldn't be so easy this time. This door was newer, sturdier, and it did not want to give itself up. More than that, Evie felt those unfamiliar strands of power weaving themselves through the wood grain, blocking her, reinforcing wherever she tried to break through.

But she was a land witch, and this house was under her protection.

She gritted her teeth and pushed harder.

Sweat broke out on her skin, and her arms began to tremble. Evie opened herself fully, drawing in more power from the Thornwood. She pushed it through her body, blood and bone singing with raw magical energy, riding the conduit she had become between the land and the house. It pulled at her strength, her will, but she forced it through, becoming one with the magic.

And the barrier, though it was stubborn, was not strong enough.

The magic disintegrated, and so did the door. Evie tumbled into Amelia Howell's study, her momentum driving her to her knees. She caught herself, hands slapping hard against the wood floor.

Panting, dizzy, and drained, Evie at first couldn't take in the details of the room around her. When her head finally cleared, the first thing she noticed was that the study was a mess. An old oak desk to her right had been overturned, its front legs crushed. Bookshelves in one corner of the room had been emptied and smashed, the books strewn over the floor in haphazard piles.

At the back of the room, a large section of the floorboards had been removed, leaving a patch of bare, churned earth. The lingering magic coming from the spot was overwhelming to Evie's senses, like incense left burning in a closed room. She crawled closer, a sinking feeling in her gut.

Where she'd expected to find a dead or dying Star Oak, its blue leaves curled and darkening to black, instead she ran her hands through nothing but cool soil.

There was no sapling. It was gone.

At the same moment Evie realized this, she noticed a spark of light in the corner of her vision. Turning toward it, she beheld a bright, moving dot of purple, like a coin spinning in midair. The sphere swelled until it was the size of Evie's fist, then her head, and still it showed no sign of stopping.

Too shocked by the absence of the sapling to react at first, Evie almost let herself be caught by the trap. The sphere launched itself across the room, stretching and spreading into a net of light that shot toward her.

Thornwood house responded, shaking the walls and floor in warning. It was like being in the middle of an earthquake. Evie scrambled back, away from the sphere, leaping to her feet. Arms raised, she drew power from the closest source at hand: the planting site.

The magic slammed into her body, so strong it almost knocked her to the floor again. She sucked in a breath and pushed the power outward, aiming at the net. It swept aside the questing purple strands that were unfurling, reaching for her like the tendrils of a jellyfish.

Time magic, Evie thought faintly. This was time magic.

Her suspicions had been right.

She could feel the strands, their connection to the past, voiceless whispers that surrounded her. She knew magic like this could be weaponized, but she'd never personally had to deal with an attack like this. Still, she knew enough to understand that if those strands touched her, they would imprison her in a moment of time. She wouldn't be able to move or fight back.

And she wouldn't know how to free herself.

With a growl, Evie thrust more power at the strands. Golden light filled the room, and Evie could have sworn the magic took the shape of Star Oak leaves, a shimmering tapestry in the air. It burned away the time magic completely, leaving nothing behind but bits of gray ash that drifted to the study floor. When the last one faded, only then did she release the power back into the ground at her feet.

Then it was quiet. The Thornwood's presence slowly retreated. The house, whose own presence had been hovering anxiously just over her shoulder, exhaled around her, wood groaning and nails popping, as if it was throwing off a pair of shackles it had worn for a very long time.

Evie's chest heaved. She was cold, shaky, her teeth chattering like she had a fever. The sudden rush of power, followed immediately by its absence, had left her hollowed out. She needed to sit down, maybe drink a glass of water.

The room was spinning. She turned toward the door, but her legs were sluggish, and she stumbled. Her vision grayed at the edges. She thought she saw the outline of a figure just outside the room, and a voice calling her name. But they were so distant, and Evie was suddenly very tired.

She was falling again. She tried to raise her arms to catch herself, but they wouldn't move. Not good. She was going to hit the floor hard.

But she didn't. Strong arms caught her and gathered her up. Evie felt herself lifted and carried out of the study, her head nestled against a broad chest. A heartbeat fluttered rapidly beneath her cheek, and the smell of soap and apples filled the air. Evie relaxed into it and let herself sleep.

Twenty-Seven

When she woke, it was dark outside. Evie knew immediately that she was no longer in Thornwood house, though she could feel its presence nearby. Blinking, she stared up at an unfamiliar ceiling, then looked down to see a yellow quilt covering her from chin to feet.

She was lying on Gil's old, lumpy couch. It was just as comfortable as it had been that first night she'd sat here and had tea with him.

Gil. Ruby. Where were they?

Evie tried to sit up, but her head swam, and she slumped back into the couch cushions. Best to take things slow. Her body felt like it had been run over by a wagon and a dozen horses.

"You're awake."

Evie turned her head to see Gil coming around the side of the couch. He was barefoot, holding a cup of steaming tea that smelled of peppermint. There were dark circles under his eyes.

"How long have I been asleep?" Evie asked. It must have been a while, judging by the way her voice croaked.

Gil perched on the edge of the coffee table and set the tea down beside him. "You've been out all day and most of the night," he told her. "It's a little past three in the morning now. Ruby's been here, but I finally got her to go to sleep in the guest room upstairs. Snow's with her."

"Is she all right?" Evie tried to sit up again, slower this time.

Gil leaned forward, supporting her with one arm across her back. "She's fine," he said, but there was a catch in his voice. "She's just worried about you. We were both . . ." He trailed off, swallowing, and dipped his head until his forehead was resting against hers.

There it was again—the scent of apples and soap. Evie breathed it in and felt an involuntary sigh of contentment escape her. She gathered both of his hands in hers, running her fingers over the rough calluses. "I'm sorry I worried you. Thank you for taking care of us both."

He had watched over her daughter while Evie slept. He had been there for her right when she'd needed him the most. And she hadn't had to ask for any of it.

"As if I could do anything else," he murmured. He leaned back just a little, freeing one of his hands to lay it against her cheek. "Do you remember what I said in the wood that night, about not wanting to be pushed into things?"

She was having trouble remembering her own name as his thumb skimmed across her jaw, a featherlight touch. "Yes," she managed.

"Well, I was an idiot, and I don't give a damn about any of that anymore." Gil released a ragged breath that ghosted across her cheek. "I was so worried about having my future set in stone. But you were right. *Nothing* is certain, and tonight I watched that future nearly get snatched away from me, and I couldn't do a thing about it. Please, I . . ."

The "please" moved inside her like quicksilver, seizing her heart. All the protests she might have made, the fears she'd nurtured about getting too close to him, only to have to leave, were no match for that simple, earnest word. She was lost, and yet she'd never felt so safe.

Her lips were a whisper from his. "Can I kiss you?" Evie asked. She added, her heart drumming fiercely, "Please."

"*Yes,*" he breathed, but he didn't move. "As long as you're feeling all right? This is what you want?"

"It is. *You* are."

She squeezed his hand as she said it, and that was all the encouragement Gil needed. His hand slipped from her cheek to curl around her back, drawing her against his chest. Evie's lips met his, and the kiss was gentle at first, as if he were still afraid he might hurt her. His beard was warm and prickly, making her smile against his mouth.

It wasn't enough. Heat danced in her veins, and Evie was suddenly filled with energy. She wound her arms around Gil's neck to pull him closer. He made a sound in his throat, and suddenly his hands were in her hair, then skimming down her back, lips demanding, devouring her in a way she hadn't felt in a very long time.

Their future might not be certain, but everything in Gil's kiss was a promise, a discovery, a new beginning. And Evie let herself be swept away by it, because everything in it felt *right.*

When they finally pulled apart, Evie discovered that Gil was now sitting on the couch, cradling her half in his lap, the quilt tangled around them. They shifted, repositioning themselves so they were sitting side by side, with the blanket covering them both. Evie laid her head against Gil's shoulder as he settled back, offering her the tea he'd prepared.

She took a grateful sip. It had cooled somewhat and was now just the temperature she liked. "Thank you," she said.

"For the tea, or the kiss?" he asked, amusement thick in his voice, though it was still a bit unsteady.

Evie considered. "For everything," she decided. She offered him a sip, and they sat in contemplative silence. It was a tiny, welcome moment of peace after all they'd been through, but it wasn't going to last. Evie's thoughts were already tracing back to what had happened in Amelia's study, the revelations there, and everything that was going to come next.

Things had changed irrevocably, and she had a lot to do.

"What happened over there?" Gil asked, as if sensing the direction her thoughts had taken. "After I took Ruby outside, I saw a flash of purple light. It filled all the windows. Then I got this overwhelming feeling from the house that you were in danger."

"There was a magical trap waiting for me," Evie said, remembering that sphere of light, the strands like spindly fingers reaching for her. "The house was aware of the danger but couldn't stop it." Briefly, she told him about disarming the trap and finding the empty planting site in the study.

"The sapling was stolen?" Gil's expression hardened. "Do you know, that's the first time I've felt glad that Amelia's gone—she doesn't have to see what's become of her student. I never thought Ignatius would do this."

Evie laid a hand on his arm. "Ignatius didn't have anything to do with it," she said. "I'd convinced myself it was him too, and heaven knows he didn't give me much of a reason to think otherwise, but I was wrong. The trap I found was made from time magic."

Gil didn't look convinced. "Just because it was time magic and not fire magic doesn't mean he wasn't involved." His eyes widened. "Abby—Abby Gray could have helped him. She's always liked him—"

"It's not her either," Evie cut him off. "I only started piecing it all together on the way back from the library today. Remember when you and I found Ignatius standing at the gate the other morning?"

"I do," Gil said. "He was acting awfully suspicious, like he wanted to get inside the house."

Evie nodded. She'd thought so too, at the time. "Why would he do that if he'd already stolen the sapling? Why return to the scene of the crime and risk the house's wrath? It wouldn't make sense."

"Fair enough, but then what *was* he doing there?" Gil asked.

Evie thought back to all the conversations she'd had with Ignatius. "I think he was worried all along that something was wrong with the sapling," she reasoned. It could also be why Ignatius had had a vessel made that strengthened plants. She'd suspected him of using it to preserve Star Oak branches, but he might simply have been intending to use it to help the young tree. "All this time, he's known about the sapling," she went on, "about the replenishment of the house's magic. But after Amelia died, the house sealed the study and started uprooting itself and running off. Ignatius knows that's not supposed to happen, not if the replenishment process is going as it should."

"But if he was so worried, why didn't he tell us about the sapling?" Gil asked. "Why would he keep what he was doing a secret?"

Evie winced. "Because he didn't trust me with knowledge of the

Star Oak, any more than I trusted him," she said. "I suspect Amelia might have even sworn him to secrecy until I learned about the tree by reading her diary. I think that was meant to be the test she left behind."

If the new caretaker was accepted by the house, if Evie was allowed into the old witch's private sanctuary, that meant the house trusted her, so Ignatius could too. He was following Amelia's final instructions.

"But the diary wasn't in the study," Gil said, frowning, "so you couldn't have passed the test."

"No, and the house couldn't disarm the magical trap or warn me about it," Evie said. It had grown too weak by that point. All it could do was communicate its fear through anger. It had been trying to keep everyone away, to keep them safe.

All this time, she'd thought the house was pushing people away out of grief, but it had been much more than that. If only she'd seen what was going on sooner . . .

"What is it?" Gil asked, squeezing her hand.

She shook her head, frustrated. "Just that I made so many mistakes. I never questioned why the house was reacting in anger. I just assumed I knew what it was feeling and what it needed. I did the same thing with Ignatius. I assumed that because he didn't want me here, he must be up to something nefarious." She sighed. This last one was the hardest to accept. "And I assumed that just because Gemma Gray gave the appearance of being kind, that meant she was on my side."

"Wait." Gil sat up, turning toward her. "You think *Gemma* set the time magic trap? That she stole the sapling and the diary? Why her and not Abby?"

"I'm not saying Abby is innocent," Evie noted. "She may have known about some or all of what was happening, but it was Gemma's magic in the study. She's the one who did this, the one I chased in the wood that night; I just didn't see it before." Again, it all came back to the house.

"The day I first met Gemma, she said she'd been out to your place to deliver some books, but you weren't home. When Ruby and I got back that afternoon, the house had thrown a bunch of its shingles and shutters into the yard. At the time, I wasn't sure what to make of it—I thought the movers had upset it—but now I think it was the house reacting to Gemma being in the area. It threw things at her to chase her off. The morning that Ignatius visited, it didn't do anything like that. Not once during our argument was the house ever afraid of him." It had only gotten upset when she did.

She'd been angry and suspicious of Ignatius because he treated the house like an object. He didn't truly understand it or its needs. But she'd let those feelings cloud her judgment. If she hadn't, she would have known by the house's behavior that Ignatius's intentions, however flawed, were ultimately good.

"It was also Gemma who advised me to force my way into Amelia's study," Evie went on. She shuddered. She'd almost done it too, because she thought she was following the wisdom of a friend who wanted to help. "I think she was trying to bypass the house's protection and get me to trigger the trap."

"But why?" Gil asked. "Exposing the trap just exposes Gemma, lets everyone know that a time witch stole the sapling."

"Not necessarily," Evie speculated. "It would be my word against Gemma's—there's no evidence. If I'd gone into that study unawares, which was probably what Gemma was expecting, the trap would have caught me and anyone else in the house, freezing us in a moment of time. I imagine the magic was also designed to alert Gemma when it went off. She would have come running, forced her way inside, and 'discovered' that the new caretaker had dug up the sapling and taken it somewhere else."

"I see," Gil said. "With you and anyone else made helpless by the trap, you think she would have tried to frame you for the theft?"

"Yes, and it wouldn't have been hard to frame an outsider, especially if her trap had gone off when I first arrived in the village, when no one knew me or Ruby."

"But the house complicated her plans," Gil said, nodding, as if he could see the shape of it now. "By keeping you away from the study, it gave you time to get to know the villagers, earn their trust, and figure out what was going on."

"Exactly," Evie said. "It made her plan for a frame job harder, but she didn't really have a choice but to continue." The theft would have been discovered eventually, one way or another.

Gil sat back again and put his arm around her. "When you got rid of the trap, it changed something in the house," he said thoughtfully. "I can't explain it, but it was like a pall lifting. There's energy everywhere. Even I could feel it, thick-skinned as I am to magic."

"That's very good news," Evie said, settling against his side.

There was another piece of the puzzle slotting into place, the reason that the house had continued to grow weaker, even after she'd kept offering it magic. The time magic trap had likely been siphoning it away from the house, stealing Evie's own power and using it to sustain itself until the moment she broke into the study. Now that the trap was gone, the house would be able to retain much more of her magic.

But it wasn't enough. "We have to get the sapling back so the house can finish replenishing itself." They'd chosen each other, the sapling and the house. They needed each other. She set her mug on the coffee table. "I'd bet almost any amount of money Gemma's got it hidden in the library."

"Makes sense," Gil said. "It's where she lives and works. I can't believe it's been there all along, right under our noses."

"She probably has powerful wards erected around it, so that other witches can't sense it," Evie said. "I didn't have a clue it was there when Ruby and I visited." Even Abby might not be able to sense it, if Gemma didn't want her sister involved in her plot.

But the house had known, Evie realized. Its connection to the sapling had overridden Gemma's concealment, so it knew the sapling was at the library. *That* was why it had gone into the village those times. It had been moving southwest, toward the back road into the park—heading for the library. It had been trying to get to the sapling, but when it had accidentally damaged Caleb's roof, it had retreated, not wanting to hurt anyone.

If the sapling was at the library, Gemma likely intended to bond it to the building. She wanted its power to sink into the foundations, becoming a part of the structure and strengthening any magic within. As long as Gemma lived there, her magic would continue to grow, giving her more and more power. No one would ever realize the source of that magic.

Evie leaned back against the couch cushions and stared at the ceiling. "What I don't understand is *why* she's doing this. Most witches want more power to fuel their studies, but why would she go that far? Gemma knows about sentient houses. She knew what stealing the sapling would do."

She'd said as much, that day in the park. If it lost enough power, Thornwood house would lose its sentience altogether.

It would die.

Evie just couldn't wrap her head around it. Gemma had seemed so kind, and so committed to her work of preserving and understanding the past. Thornwood house should have been part of those efforts.

"The only thing I can figure is that she doesn't see the house the way the rest of us do," Gil said. "Even Ignatius seems to forget sometimes what he learned as a child—Thornwood house is more than its four walls and its magic. It has a soul." He trailed a hand down Evie's arm affectionately. "You saw that from the beginning. I think Amelia knew you would."

Evie's throat tightened as she remembered what Amelia had written about her in her diary. What *would* the old witch have thought of all this? Had Evie truly lived up to her expectations?

There were some questions she would never have the answers to, just as she would never understand the forces that drove Gemma Gray. All she could do now was move forward with the lessons she'd learned.

On the bright side, her enforced rest had done her and her magic a world of good. Her head felt remarkably clear now, considering how much power she'd expended in the past twenty-four hours.

Evie drew in a deep, calming breath. The ever-present scent of apples filled the house. Sitting there, she felt the pull of Gil, a connection that pulsed like a heartbeat. It was so warm, a particular magic that reminded her of the day they'd spent in the orchard, even though they weren't walking among the trees right now.

Evie turned to him abruptly. "Did you . . . Are you . . ." She tried to find the words. No, it couldn't be. He'd claimed not to have the sensitivity for magic. And yet . . .

He gave her a crooked grin. "Something wrong?"

Evie scowled. "Did you lend me power earlier? The way we did that day in the orchard?"

"What can I say? I've always been a quick learner." His grin fell away. "Or maybe I just needed the proper motivation. Seeing you laid out pale as a ghost on my living room couch was more than enough. If you don't mind, I'd rather not go through that again."

"I'll do my best to make sure you don't." Fascinated, Evie laid her palm flat against his chest, ignoring his swift inhalation. There it was, the magic of the orchard swirling inside him, a power generations in the making. She felt each turn and twist of the roots of dozens of trees, lined up in rows down through the years. Probing deeper, she discovered a fainter echo of that same power inside her. A bite of crisp, juicy apple on a hot summer's day, the taste of it wrapped in magic that sharpened her thoughts and returned strength to her tired limbs.

A power warm and comforting—and uniquely Gil.

Evie laid her head against his chest where her hand had been. "I didn't even realize you were doing it," she said.

He threaded his fingers into her hair. "That's because I'm a hell of a kisser."

"No argument." To remind herself of that fact, she lifted her head and kissed him again. Warmth filled her chest, chasing away the last of the darkness and fear like a sunrise after the hardest hours of the night.

Amelia Howell had known so much, Evie thought as she broke the kiss at last. She'd known what would happen between Evie and Gil.

She'd seen Evie and Ruby take their place in the house. Had she seen Gemma Gray coming as well? Had she thought Evie was the one who'd be able to stop her?

She would, Evie vowed.

First she needed to check on Ruby, and the house, and then she was going to get that sapling back. She might have been deceived before, but her eyes were open now, and she knew exactly what she had to do.

Twenty-Eight

Even with the infusion of magic, Evie needed her rest, and Gil made her do so until dawn. As faint gray light slowly brightened Gil's cozy living room, Evie rose and made her way upstairs to his guest room to wake Ruby. A part of her wanted to let her daughter sleep. She was buried in a pile of blankets, strawberry-blond hair falling across her eyes. Snow lay on the rug at the foot of the bed, alert and on guard. It was a picture of contentment, and for just a moment, Evie was sorely tempted to crawl under the blankets and join her.

In the end, Evie went to the bedside and gently touched Ruby's shoulder. "I'm here," she whispered. "Time to wake up."

Rolling over, Ruby made a sleepy noise. Her lashes fluttered, and she opened her eyes and looked up at Evie blearily. Then she focused and bolted upright.

And burst into tears.

The sun climbed higher in the sky, gilding the rug and the dark wood floors. Evie watched the light move as she curled up on the side of the bed, holding her daughter. She rubbed soothing circles on her back, reassuring them both that everything was going to be all right.

"I didn't see it," Ruby kept murmuring. "I should have seen it in your future, but I used it all up. I was so stupid back then, and now I can't help you with anything!"

"Stop," Evie said gently. "I won't have you talking about yourself that way, ever. You can't see every bad thing coming. You're not meant to. Just as a time witch isn't supposed to linger in the past. We live in the here and now. That's where we make things happen."

When Ruby had calmed a little, Evie told her about Gemma Gray and the magic trap, as well as her suspicions about where the sapling was.

"We're going to gather everyone together," Evie told her daughter. "Cinda and the rest of our friends from the village. We need a plan. But first we have to go home and make sure the house is all right. It's probably worried about us."

"I'm sure it is. It was really upset when you fainted." Ruby hesitated. "We should invite Ignatius to come over too," she said finally.

"Really?" Evie's brows lifted. "What makes you think he would help us? Did you . . . look into his future?"

"Not exactly," Ruby hedged. "It was something I found at home. It's better if I show you."

Gil insisted they have breakfast before they left, so Evie and Ruby sat at his old kitchen table, sipping tea and juice while he cooked pancakes and bacon and dished up fluffy piles of scrambled eggs. Ruby and Gil took turns slipping pieces of bacon to Snow. The dog had set up a vigil underneath the table, his furry body sprawled over Evie's feet. Outside, the wind chime tinkled merrily in a cool morning breeze.

Despite everything that had happened, and everything yet to come, Evie was happy. She wasn't a farseer witch. She was solidly and stubbornly of the land, but even she sometimes had notions, fleeting glimpses of things that might be. There at the breakfast table, she had a notion of Gil and his lumpy brown couch sitting in the middle of the living room at Thornwood house, near the window that looked out on the willow tree. He was reading a book. Light spilled over his face, lighting fires in his chestnut locks and making his eyes shine.

Or maybe they were just her hopes, pieces of a future she wanted to build. If she spoke them aloud, or let herself want them too much, they'd vanish like smoke.

After breakfast, Evie and Ruby headed home. As they approached their gate, Evie slowed her pace, feeling the subtle shift in the air.

Gil had been right. Something fundamental had changed about the house. It was more vibrant, more present, than she'd ever felt before. Only the Thornwood itself was more active, and as Ruby closed the gate behind them and did her daily check of the mail, Evie felt a surge of magic wrap around her. With it came a sense of well-being, and thin tendrils of concern that Evie could almost translate into words.

Are you well?

Were you hurt?

I'm glad you're home.

"We're both fine," Evie assured the house. She and Ruby climbed the stairs to the porch, and Evie sat for a moment on the swing, gathering Ruby next to her, letting her senses expand to encompass the whole of the house, assessing, making sure that it too had suffered no permanent damage from the destruction of the time trap.

What she found this time was staggering.

The house had been reinvigorated. The removal of the trap had allowed her own magic to flow into every beam and plank, each shingle and shutter. And there it stayed.

Evie's heart thudded in a mixture of joy, relief, and regret. "I'm so sorry," she said, gripping the chain that connected the swing to the porch roof. "I'm sorry I didn't see what was happening to you until it was almost too late."

She'd been so focused on proving herself to the villagers, finding the Star Oak, and bonding with the grieving house that she hadn't truly listened to what it had been trying to tell her.

And Evie felt a renewed surge of anger toward the time witch who'd laid the trap.

Gemma Gray had things to answer for.

But the house was all right now, Evie reminded herself, and just then, she felt a wave of reassurance from it, reinforcing her thoughts. Her own magic would be more than enough now to keep its vitality strong until she brought back the sapling.

There was no more time for regret. Evie let the motion of the swing carry her to her feet. She turned to Ruby. "We need to gather the others," she said. "What was it you wanted to show me?"

Ruby jumped up, and Evie trailed behind her into the foyer. The house's attention followed as well when Ruby ducked behind the staircase and pointed to a darkened corner. For the first time, Evie noticed that one section of the wall beneath the stairs hadn't been refurbished or repainted. It was the same sky blue that she vaguely remembered had been on the walls when they first entered the house.

Crouching so she wouldn't hit her head, Evie went to the spot Ruby pointed out. Faded pencil marks covered the walls. There was a name, an age, and a date scrawled in a child's hand beside each line.

Gracie. Finnius. Carlos. Gil. Trin. Conna. Lin. On and on . . .

There were dozens of names, and the lines gradually moved up the wall. Evie ran her hands over the faded pencil scratches and imagined all the village children who Cinda said used to play here, growing taller and taller until their heads would have brushed the back treads of the stairs.

She stopped when she reached a familiar name: Ignatius.

"I found it when I was cleaning back here," Ruby explained. "His brother's name is there too, but it's faded so much you almost can't read it." She pointed farther back into the darkness. Evie had to squint to make out the name she indicated: Arthur.

"How do you know that's Ignatius's brother?" Evie asked.

"Because I touched the name, and I looked," Ruby admitted. "I wasn't going to, but there's something about the names here. They're strong." She hesitated. "It was like you said. The magic was trying to tell me something. I was sure of it this time."

"I believe you," Evie said, squeezing her hand.

The names here were the children who had played in the house, the ones who had helped tend Amelia's gardens, and who therefore had the strongest bond to the house—that included Ignatius. Evie wondered how many of them were still in the village. Had most of them left and gone to Dorna City, or to work for the ECRA, as Ignatius said Arthur had?

Evie backed out from under the stairs and sat on the floor. Ruby plopped down beside her. "I don't know if Ignatius's bond with the house will be enough to convince him to help us," Evie cautioned. "He doesn't like me very much, and he may not believe that Gemma is the sapling thief." She had no proof now that the time trap was gone. "He might accuse us of taking it."

She aimed her words at Ruby, but she was also listening for the house's response.

"Maybe." Ruby shrugged. "But when I touched Arthur's name, I felt a lot of different things." She spoke slowly, as if she were trying to untangle a complicated knot. "Arthur loved Thornwood house, but he's not going to come back to live in the village. Ignatius cares about the house too, and he's going to stay, but he hates that his brother left him behind."

At those words, Evie felt a rising melancholy from the house. She tried to put herself in Ignatius's shoes, imagining what it must have felt like to lose his brother to a life in the city and a job with the ECRA. And then to spend all that time training with Amelia Howell, thinking he was going to take over caring for the house, only to be rejected.

"He must have felt like everyone in his life was abandoning him," Evie murmured. She'd been so worried about the house, and being accepted by the villagers, that she hadn't seen what Ignatius was going through. But her job as caretaker was to tend to *all* the villagers, not just the ones who supported her. She'd left Ignatius out of that.

She looked up at the ceiling, addressing the house directly. "It still doesn't explain why Amelia didn't choose him," she said. "If Ignatius did care about you, if he wanted to be caretaker—"

"I don't think he did," Ruby interjected. "His brother went to the city because he wanted to, and Ignatius was the only one left. I think he was doing what he thought he was supposed to do."

"Carrying on his family's responsibilities in the village," Evie said, understanding, "whether he wanted to or not." Hadn't she felt that same sense of responsibility to her own family, who were working so hard to protect and restore magic to the Quiet Lands? And she'd carried the weight of guilt when she left them to make her own way in the world.

She felt the brush of regret from the house, and the faint sound of children's laughter that lingered at the edges of her hearing. "I see," she said. "Neither you nor Amelia wanted to put Ignatius somewhere he wasn't supposed to be." Just like Evie's father, when he'd told her to go, to find the place that sang to her—the place where she belonged.

She and Ignatius had more in common than she'd ever realized.

But his place *was* still in this house, Evie realized. He didn't need to live here to protect it and Amelia's legacy. She had a feeling Amelia would have approved of that. Evie just needed to convince him.

No easy task there.

"What are you going to do?" Ruby asked.

"I'm going to do exactly what my wise farseer suggests," Evie said, smiling. "I'm going to get Ignatius involved in our plans." Of course, she would have to get him to the house first. Evie decided to ask Cinda to do the honors there. Ignatius was more likely to respond favorably to someone he knew, no matter how contentious their relationship. "I'll also ask the Greens to come, and a few others." Her smile turned wicked. "And then we're going to plan something nefarious."

TWENTY-NINE

The Greens arrived first, coming later in the afternoon when the café was done serving lunch. All four of them—Shara, Ben, Jamie, and Trin—gathered outside the gate, where they lingered, watching the house with a hesitant curiosity.

"Thank you so much for coming!" Evie called out to them with a bright smile as she trotted down the porch steps. She checked in with the house one last time, just to make sure it was still all right with having so many guests at once.

She felt a hovering sensation at her back, like the shy, budding excitement of a child peering around a parent. It was a bittersweet pang, knowing that the house had probably missed having the company of the villagers these past several months.

"It's all right," she said, opening the gate and ushering them all inside. She took Shara's hand and gave it a squeeze. "The house has been waiting for everyone. We have a lot to talk about."

"Oh, my goodness!" Shara's head was on a swivel as Ruby led

them through the foyer to the kitchen. "I love what you've done in here. It's beautiful."

"It was a group effort," Evie said, putting an arm around Ruby's shoulders and laying a hand on the doorframe. "Gil's been a tremendous help too."

"He's so thoughtful that way," Shara said, with a knowing smile that made Evie's face flame.

Ruby served the tea, and Shara had brought biscuits and blackberry jam, which Evie arranged on a plate. Gil arrived a few minutes later with Snow, who was barking and wiggling all over at seeing all the extra people available to give him belly rubs. They ate and made small talk in the kitchen, as Cinda was still conspicuously absent.

She had the hardest job of all, convincing Ignatius to put in an appearance. But Evie had no doubt that if anyone could drag the stubborn man here, it was the equally implacable mayor.

In the meantime, Evie just enjoyed the sense of contentment and happiness radiating from Thornwood house. There were traces of it everywhere. The steam rising from the teakettle blew and twisted into the shapes of flowers and stars before fading away. A tiny, happy vibration passed through the kitchen floor when Ben laughed at a joke Ruby told him. And Evie swore the lights on the iron chandelier flickered and danced every time Ruby, Jamie, or Trin passed underneath it.

No doubt about it—Thornwood house loved the children most of all.

As she poured fresh cups of tea for everyone, Evie's gaze strayed out the kitchen window to the front yard. She did a double take at what she saw.

Cinda was striding up the path like a general on a mission, arms pumping, her yellow hat sitting slightly askew on her head.

Ignatius Smythe trailed sullenly behind her.

He fixed a calculating gaze on the house, but Evie saw the moment he realized that something had changed. His steps faltered, and his brow creased in a frown. As if he felt her watching him, he turned toward the kitchen window, and their eyes met. Ignatius flushed, glared, and walked away, out of her sight.

This definitely wasn't going to be easy.

But Evie reminded herself of everything Ignatius had been going through. In the end, his behavior hadn't been so very different from the house's. He'd been angry, but it was an anger rooted in fear. She had to overcome that, just as she'd done with Thornwood house.

She met Cinda at the door. The mayor was wiping her boots on the mat and grumbling to herself.

"Stubborn, pouting child," she muttered as Evie came up to take a basket of cookies from her hands. Cinda removed her hat and smoothed her steel gray hair down. "Good luck with that one," she said, looking at Evie askance. "I can't decide whether you're brilliant or mad for inviting him."

"We'll find out soon enough." Evie sniffed the basket and moaned. "These smell amazing. Everyone's in the kitchen."

She looked over Cinda's shoulder, expecting to see Ignatius appear, but there was no sign of the man.

A quick breeze at the nape of her neck made her turn instinctively toward the rear of the house. He must have gone to the backyard, Evie thought, though she couldn't imagine why.

Ruby darted into the room just then, drawn by the smell of

cookies. Evie handed her the basket and told her to take Cinda into the kitchen to join the others. Then Evie went out the front door and down the steps, going around the side of the house until she reached the glasshouse.

Ignatius stood looking at the restored structure, his gaze lingering on the stained-glass image of the Star Oak. He wasn't smiling, and his shoulders were slightly hunched, hands dug deep in his pockets. He either hadn't heard her approach, or he was ignoring her.

I have to try, Evie reminded herself.

"I thought about putting a bench at the edge of the mood garden," she called out to him. "Someplace to sit and relax. What do you think?"

Stiff as a statue, Ignatius turned toward her, following her gaze to the expressive plants. Several clusters of flowers swayed and reached in his direction, creating a sense of movement through the garden. A churning patch, Evie thought, remembering the old nursery story—*"watch for the churning patch, when the wind is still, and a conflicted soul comes near."* Ignatius was feeling lots of different things right now, and Evie found she could read his emotions simply by watching the flowers change.

The burning heart stalks were tipping from pink to red, which meant he was still angry. No great surprise there. Nor was the confusion and uncertainty that made the green calyxes flex on the hesitants. He didn't know why he'd been invited, and he was likely suspicious that it was a trick. But Evie wasn't expecting to see the stems of the aching stars shiver and grow when Ignatius stepped in that direction.

They only did that when flooded with loneliness.

Evie looked away. She couldn't help but feel as if she were trespassing in a private place, even though all she'd done was look at the flowers.

"A gazebo would look nice," Ignatius said at last, backing away from the garden. "There used to be one back here a long time ago, but a storm knocked it down. We used some of the wood to build the bridge over the pond in front."

"You know a lot about the history of this house," Evie said, walking over to stand beside him. "The stories you could tell—"

"Cinda said that the sapling was stolen, that Gemma Gray has it," Ignatius interrupted her. "Is that true?"

"It is," Evie confirmed. "You can see for yourself if you like."

Without waiting for him to reply, she led the way through the glasshouse to the door to Amelia's study. She paused when she saw the brand-new key dangling from a cord hung on the wall next to the door.

"Why are you smiling?" Ignatius asked irritably, as she took the key and inserted it into the lock.

"No particular reason." Evie went inside and held the door open for him.

She and Ruby had spent part of the day tidying the study and repairing some of the damaged furniture and shelves. They'd get to the rest eventually. But there was nothing to be done about the bare, disturbed earth in the middle of the floor where the sapling had been.

Ignatius went at once to the spot, dropping to his knees to run his fingers through the soil. His perpetual scowl crumpled into sorrow and anguish.

The change was startling. It was the first time in their short acquaintance Evie had seen him vulnerable. It made him appear much younger than he actually was.

"Why?" Ignatius accused, his voice brittle. It took Evie a moment to realize he was addressing the house, not her. "Why didn't you find a way to tell me what happened? I could have helped you!"

A soft breeze wafted through the room, bringing with it the lingering scent of Amelia's magic, of fresh earth and old books. Ignatius closed his eyes and breathed in the scents. His shoulders dipped, and he sat back on his heels.

"Are you all right?" Evie asked.

Ignatius looked up at her, his expression turning sour. "That old witch knew what she was doing after all," he said. "She obviously needed someone more powerful than me to untangle this trap. I guess that makes you feel pretty good about yourself."

"Do you think that's why I brought you here, Ignatius?" Evie crossed her arms. "To gloat? I came within a hair's breadth of being frozen in a time trap more powerful than I've ever seen. And if it had happened any sooner, it would have caught Ruby too."

What was it like, being in a trap made from time magic? Would it have sent her mind careening into the past, holding her for hours? Or maybe it would have frozen her limbs and stolen her memories. When used with malice, *any* magic was dangerous, but the idea of time being used against her daughter in such ways was unthinkable.

"I never realized Gemma Gray had that kind of power," Ignatius admitted. "She hides it well. When do you plan to confront her?"

"I don't," Evie said. It would be foolish to do so in the library anyway. It was Gemma's sanctuary, the place where she was most powerful, even more so since the sapling had been growing in the building for months now. It might even be integrated into the renovations, making it difficult to reach. "I brought you here with the others because of the sapling. I need your help to get it back."

"*My* help?" he said, incredulous. "I've done nothing but try to undermine you since you came here."

"I know, and it's been a hurtful distraction that's contributed to the situation we're now in." Evie held up a hand before he could argue. "If we hadn't spent so much time mistrusting each other, we might have discovered what Gemma was doing sooner, and we could have saved Thornwood house a lot of suffering. We're both to blame for this, Ignatius."

He chewed on that for a moment, and Evie was relieved to see some of the indignance leave his posture. He raked a hand through his blond hair, jostling his glasses. "You're right," he said. He gave a humorless laugh. "I've been so angry—at Amelia, at the house, and at—" He cut himself off. "Then you breezed in here, and I thought surely you weren't going to take the job seriously. That was the last straw." His eyes took on a faraway cast. "I think what got me the most was that I thought I was doing everyone such a favor with this." He made a gesture that encompassed the room, and perhaps the whole house. "I was doing what was expected, and then when the old witch told me I wasn't going to be the one . . ." He shook his head. "She saw right through me, made the decision I couldn't. I guess I should have thanked her, but I didn't. I just stayed angry." He swallowed. "And she died."

Evie sat down on the floor next to the bare patch of earth, careful to give him space. She didn't know Ignatius well enough to know how to comfort him, but she felt she had to say something. "This will always be the house you grew up in," she reminded him. "Amelia will always be a part of you. But even if she was doing what she thought was best for you, no one wants to feel rejected by the people they love."

"What can *you* know about rejection?" He glanced up at her sharply. "You had a position of power most witches would kill for, and you just threw it away. I still can't understand that."

"That type of power comes with a cost," Evie countered, "and the ECRA isn't always the noble organization it makes itself out to be." She bit her lip, trying to decide how much of her personal life she was comfortable sharing with him. "Look, when all this is over, if you still want to know, I'll tell you why Ruby and I left the ECRA, and what we had to go through to do it. But right now, we need to focus on getting the sapling back. That's the most important thing."

"Don't worry, I can leverage my family's power against Gemma," Ignatius said, some of his arrogance reasserting itself. "We don't have enough proof to bring official charges against her, but all it would take is some well-placed threats to get her to turn over the sapling."

"Or she'll take it and run," Evie said. "If she does that, we may never find her, and the sapling will be lost. Do you really want to take that chance?"

Ignatius didn't have an answer for that. "Do you have a plan, then?" he asked reluctantly.

"I do." Evie tucked her knees against her chest, smiling. "We're going to steal the sapling back."

Thirty

"This is ridiculous," Ignatius said, taking a bite of one of Cinda's cookies and chewing aggressively.

"They're oatmeal raisin," Cinda said with a sniff, "and you never used to complain about them."

"Not the cookie." Ignatius glared as the mayor covered her mouth to hide a grin. "This whole notion. I can't believe we're considering this." He stabbed a crumb-crusted finger at Evie, who was sitting across the kitchen table from him. "I blame you for all of it."

"I figured you might." Evie lifted one shoulder in a shrug. "I can live with it."

Ruby and the rest of the kids had gone outside to play with Snow, leaving Evie, Cinda, Shara, Ben, Gil, and Ignatius in the kitchen. Ignatius dunked the remains of his cookie in his tea as if he were trying to drown the treat.

"So it doesn't bother you that we're essentially organizing a magical heist in front of the mayor of Iskendra?" Ignatius demanded.

Cinda snorted. "Politician, remember? We're all corrupt."

"It's true," Gil said. "She has been for years."

Over the last couple of hours, Evie had told Cinda and the others everything that had happened and everything she'd learned about the house since coming here. She'd told them about the Star Oak, about Gemma's theft of the sapling, and she'd laid out her plan to take it back.

"The way I see it," Shara said, reaching for another biscuit, "we're not actually *stealing* anything. We're simply recovering what rightfully belongs to Thornwood house. I don't mind being involved in that."

"I appreciate the help, even though I wish we didn't have to do it this way," Evie said.

Sneaking in at night when the library was deserted would be easiest. Unfortunately, with Gemma and Abby living in the apartment in the library's old belfry, Evie didn't like her chances of breaking in while the witches were upstairs.

"Gemma and her sister always come into the café at the end of the week to have dinner together," Ben said, leaning his elbows on the table. "We'll just find a way to keep them there talking for as long as you need to get the sapling. It's not a problem."

"I'll be there to help too," Cinda added. "We'll keep her distracted. It's you and Ignatius who have the hard part."

"I'm aware," Ignatius groused. He glanced at Evie. "Gemma's not stupid. She'll have wards securing the renovation site."

"Of course," Evie said. "She's also concealing the sapling's presence, which takes a great deal of magic. But I believe the two of us together can break the wards and find it."

"Better to have two of you anyway, to keep a lookout," Cinda said. "One person alone gets snared by her time magic, and it's over."

She was right. And if they failed, Gemma would take the sapling and run. "It's a risk, even with two of us," Evie admitted, "but we have to do this, for the house's sake."

Beneath the table, Gil laid a hand lightly on her knee. "I'll be outside the library with Snow. If Gemma does manage to head back while you two are still inside, I can make sure you're warned."

"Does that mean you're going to make me a wind chime?" Evie asked curiously. "I won't be very quiet carrying it."

"Trust me," Gil said, "this one will be special. It'll only chime if there's danger, and you'll be the only one to hear it."

Evie laid her hand over his. "That would be amazing. Thank you."

"Speaking of danger," Cinda said thoughtfully, "should we be worried that Gemma will see this coming?" The mayor glanced at Evie. "Will she be able to sense that you've disarmed her trap without being caught in it?"

"I've been thinking about that," Evie mused. "I can't be sure, but I believe that since I destroyed the magic before it could trap me, that means it wouldn't have had a chance to alert her. It depends on the conditions of the magic that she put in place, of course, but I think if she were aware of what happened, she would have shown up here by now." She glanced at Gil. "Your wind chime hasn't gone off, has it?"

Gil shook his head. "It's been quiet, except for when the people here arrived," he confirmed.

"Hopefully, that means she thinks the trap is still in place, so she has no reason to suspect what we're about to do," Shara said. She wore a grim expression. "I still can't believe Gemma, of all people, would do something like that to Thornwood house. She's always been kind to Trin and me whenever we visited the library, always eager to help."

"It's the Star Oak," Ignatius said. He stared down at the table, tracing circles on the wood with his thumb. "That kind of power is rare and . . . difficult to resist."

No one knew what to say to that, so the table fell quiet, except for the clink of cups in saucers.

Finally, Ignatius looked up and cleared his throat. "All right, if we're really going to do this, I'll use the renovations as a cover," he said. "I'll make some excuse to stay late at the library, conduct an inspection or something. I've done it before, so it won't seem out of the ordinary, and Gemma has no reason to suspect me." He glanced at Evie. "As soon as it's dark, come to the back door, and I'll let you in. That'll be the easy part."

Easy, though it also meant trusting Ignatius to carry out his part of the plan. But Evie had come this far on a leap of faith. She wasn't going to turn back. "That sounds good," she said. "If all goes well, we'll bring the sapling home and replant it immediately."

She felt a sudden swell of hope from the house, so strong that it rattled the teacups in their saucers. Ben and Shara let out exclamations of surprise. Cinda and Gil exchanged a smile.

"*We'll* bring it back here?" Ignatius said. "Are you saying you want me to help you replant the sapling? You, with all your expertise, want help from—"

Cinda put her hand over Ignatius's mouth. "Let me stop you before you say something I hope you'd regret later."

Ignatius irritably batted her hand away.

"Yes, I want you to help me," Evie said patiently. "You don't always understand it or its needs, but Thornwood house still cares about you, Ignatius. I think it and Amelia would have wanted you to be a part of its renewal." She had no proof of this, of course, other than a feeling. Evie had sensed genuine regret in the words Amelia had written in her diary about Ignatius. There was more in this house that needed to be set right, and this was the only way Evie knew to do it.

She was even more certain when another breeze swept through the kitchen, strong enough to lift the curtains at the window. One of them swatted playfully at Ignatius's cheek. The young man jumped and stared at the curtain in bewilderment.

"You could have said so before," he grumbled, his face flushing as he realized he was addressing a curtain as if it could talk back to him.

They were really going to do this, Evie thought. This could actually work.

They talked some more, and planned some more, but the tea eventually ran out, and everyone had learned the parts they had to play. One by one, her guests departed, until only Ignatius was left sitting at the table. Evie would have guessed he'd be among the first to leave once their plans were in place, but he stayed, toying with his empty mug.

Evie turned from where she'd been washing dishes at the sink. She saw out the window that Ruby was still playing in the yard. She turned her attention to Ignatius.

"There's something I need to ask you," she said, "and I hope you'll tell me the truth."

He glanced up at her, his expression guarded. "What is it?"

"You *have* been going into the Thornwood at night to search for the Star Oak, haven't you?" Evie asked. "And you've taken some of your crew with you to help search."

His jaw worked, but he didn't deny it. "I didn't know about Veld Tapper hurting Gil's dog," he said. "After you told me, I let him go the next day. But yes, I did make the offer to the crew that if they wanted to search in their off-hours, there'd be a bonus in it for them if they found anything." He looked out the window, frustration etched into his features. "Amelia would never tell me where it was. I don't think she trusted that I wouldn't try to take something of the tree for myself. She knew how much my magical research meant to me and . . ." He huffed. "I guess she really did know me better than I know myself."

"What would you do with the Star Oak's power, if you had it?" Evie asked.

"You don't understand," he said. "It's not about making myself stronger. I don't want to pick it apart piece by piece. I just want to study the tree's power. Magic of that kind—so ancient, so rare—and it's right *there*." He gestured out the window, toward the Thornwood. "It's so close, but I can't find it. I can't get the tree to show itself to me."

"If it makes you feel any better, it wouldn't show itself to me either," Evie said. "But I think part of *your* problem is the company you keep."

"You're right." Ignatius sighed. "I didn't know Veld well enough before I hired him. I just trusted his connection to my family."

"I don't want him in the wood anymore," Evie said firmly.

He looked at her, his brows lifting. "Is that the word of the caretaker of Thornwood house?" he asked, but for once, there was no mockery in his tone.

"It is," Evie said. "If I lose my position, then you can do as you please, but while Ruby and I are here, I want the wood to be a safe haven, not a place where an innocent animal can be kicked in the dark."

Ignatius didn't reply as he took all that in. Evie thought he was going to argue, but in the end he simply nodded. "All right."

He kept his gaze locked on hers, studying her, until Evie had to ask, "What is it?"

"You have no reason to trust me in all this," Ignatius said. "So why are you?"

"Because Ruby wants to give you a chance," Evie told him. "I trust her judgment, and the house's. I believe Amelia trusted you more than you think, even if she didn't tell you about the Star Oak's location. So I'm choosing to follow their example."

They would find out soon enough if that trust was warranted.

Thirty-One

Evie spent most of the following day in the glasshouse, readying the things she would need for the heist. In some ways, it felt like the old days with the ECRA, when she would prepare for missions that would take her into the heart of an earthquake-stricken town or a forest fire. But her preparations for this task were much more geared toward stealth than protection.

She spread her best cloak on the worktable and laid her sewing kit beside it. To make herself more at home in the darkness, she needed the plants that thrived outside of the light. So she went to the lower shelves and clipped a handful of black thorns from the anterra roses and crushed them with a mortar and pestle, sewing the remnants into a pocket in the hood of her cloak. They couldn't conceal her presence, but their magic had a repelling effect that drew on people's fear of the dark. It would make strangers naturally turn away when she came near, without really knowing why they were doing so.

Next, she cut several lengths of midnight's gaze, a dark-blue ivy with feathered edges as delicate as eyelashes. She pressed these into the cloak's inner lining, using her magic to coax the plant to seal itself tight to the fabric. It would make her steps and movements softer, lighter, so that she barely disturbed the grass and earth when she walked.

Finally, she plucked a few petals from a gasping trillium, fastening them to the clasp that held her cloak closed. She ran her fingers over their velvety softness to bring their magic closer to the surface. When she needed them, they would quiet her voice and the voices of anyone near her.

With these tools in place, she would be little more than a walking shadow, a specter in the dark that would frighten people away. Not a pleasant thought, and certainly not an image she would ever cultivate normally, but right now, it was necessary.

Later that evening, once the sun had disappeared on the horizon, Evie set off on foot toward the village. In addition to her cloak, she had a bag draped over one shoulder, with a small spade tucked inside. Ruby had agreed to stay and watch over Thornwood house, and Evie trusted the house to guard her. Not only could Evie feel her own magic strengthening it, but she also sensed the house's power, poised and ready to keep her child safe.

Now it was up to Evie to do what she could to make sure the house was safe and protected for many years to come. If this worked, the sapling would be reunited with the house, and then perhaps Evie could finally solidify her place as caretaker.

True, she hadn't yet broached the subject of bonding with Thornwood house, but that would come. Once the sapling was back in place and the replenishment complete, the house would be healed. When that happened, and with Gemma's trap gone, Evie hoped the house would be ready to accept her. She hoped that the Star Oak might show itself to her as well, so that she could protect it from Gemma and anyone else who would abuse its power.

But she still needed to ask for those things, and to earn them. And a small part of her feared rejection, even now.

That was a worry for another day.

By the time she reached the outskirts of Iskendra, it was full dark. Evie pulled up her cloak hood and made her way quietly along the village streets. She cut across the park to take advantage of the natural cover provided by the oak and beech trees. With her magic, she softly coaxed the low-hanging branches to arch over and hide her, to work with her cloak to keep her concealed.

And the land, always so attentive, even when she wasn't in the Thornwood, responded to her call.

Presently, Evie glimpsed the tall stone tower of the library looming out of the darkness. It was an imposing edifice at night, solid and watchful against a backdrop of trees and pinprick stars. Evie slowed her pace as she circled the building in search of the back door. She let her senses reach into the building, digging for information, for some sign of the sapling.

She didn't sense it, but when she went deeper, she was swamped by Gemma's purple time magic. It was overwhelming. There was so much power here that, given enough time for the sapling to grow, the library itself could potentially become sentient one day.

Was that what Gemma was ultimately after? It wouldn't in itself be a bad thing, Evie thought as she drew back her awareness. A sentient library would be a wonder, in fact. But Star Oak saplings had to be given freely, and the one they sought had chosen Thornwood house. It was a bond that should never have been tampered with.

Rounding a corner, Evie found the back door, situated at the top of a short flight of stone steps. She went up and tapped lightly on the wood, at the same time reaching her other hand to her belt, where she'd hung the tiny wind chime Gil had given her as a warning system. It swayed silently in the folds of her skirt. No sign of danger.

Evie hadn't seen Gil or Snow when she'd made her way through the park, but she had no doubt they were out there somewhere, watching for trouble. The thought of that strengthened her resolve.

But the seconds passed, and still Ignatius didn't come to the door.

Telling herself not to panic, Evie reached out and tried the knob. It turned, but the door wouldn't open. It thrummed with a familiar barrier magic, one that she'd last sensed in the door to Amelia Howell's study, though this was much stronger.

Gemma's magic. The time witch had known that Ignatius would be conducting an inspection of the renovations. Had she placed a barrier here in case someone other than Ignatius tried to get into the library? Was it strong enough to alert her if Ignatius let Evie in? Maybe that was why he was hesitating. Once again, Evie let her awareness press into the building, but this time, she met a slight resistance. No, not resistance, just another magic, another power drifting up to meet hers. It was working on disabling the barrier from the other side of the door.

Ignatius. It had to be. There was the familiar woodsmoke tang that she remembered from their meeting in the café, with an underlying heat that surrounded the door, making Gemma's magic stand out in sharp relief.

Using that magic as a foundation, Evie called on the land to lend her power.

Strands of green and gold light emerged from the ground around her, rising like thin fingers that pushed into the door. Guiding them, Evie gently unwound the threads of time magic. She took each purple strand individually and pulled it away, careful not to make a disturbance that would alert the spider in the center of the web.

After a moment, she had them all, collected like a bouquet of phantom lilacs that flared in her hands and then dissipated. The door swung open.

Ignatius was standing on the other side, moonlight catching on the lenses of his glasses. "Finally," he said, exhaling a noisy breath. "I've been trying to melt that ward for the last hour. How did you get past it?" He looked at her suspiciously. "Are you sure you don't have some time magic in you as well?"

"I'm fairly sure I don't," Evie said, stepping inside and easing the door shut behind her. Moonlight shining through the back windows gave her just enough light to see that they were in a back room, not one of the public areas of the library. "Your magic acted in tandem with mine. It was as if your power was shining a light on the barrier, allowing me to see the magic better."

Ignatius blinked at her. "So you're saying our magics work well together?"

"Looks that way."

He groaned. "Cinda's going to be absolutely insufferable when she hears that. And Amelia's probably looking down on me and cackling."

"Are you really so determined to dislike me?" Evie said, half-amused and half-exasperated as Ignatius led the way through the dusty storage area of the library. Racks of tools stood against one wall, left behind by the crew doing the renovation work.

"If it makes you feel any better, it's getting harder and harder," he mumbled.

They came to another door, this one made of metal and with an even brighter glow of time magic emanating from it. "Does this lead to the basement?" she asked.

Ignatius nodded. "My crew are working on the foundation down there. That's probably where Gemma will have put the sapling, at the heart of the structure. It doesn't need sunlight like a regular oak tree would. It'll be drawing on Gemma's magic instead as it bonds to the building."

Then this was the area that would be most heavily protected. And the sapling was so young, not yet fully aware of itself or its surroundings, that it would continue to try to bond with the library, not realizing that it had been removed from where it had first grown roots. They needed to get it home.

Evie approached the door and bent down, examining the lock. "Can you use your magic alongside mine again?" she asked.

"I can try," Ignatius said, laying his palm against the door. His skin reddened and glowed, as if lit from within. "I'm not entirely sure what I did last time to help you."

Evie waited for him to center himself, then she felt his power flowing over the door, a swelling heat that illuminated the protective ward in crimson, rust, and carmine. "That's it," she said. "Just keep doing that."

It took longer, but, working with Ignatius's power as a base to steady her, Evie once again unraveled the magic sealing the door, strand by strand. A moment later, it swung open with a creak that was louder than Evie would have liked.

Ignatius grabbed a nearby chair and propped the door open. "I don't want it to relock behind us," he explained. Then he held out a hand, and small orange flames kindled at each of his fingertips, illuminating a staircase leading down.

"Ready," he said.

Evie led the way down the basement stairs, Ignatius following with the light. It was cooler down here. Smells of damp stone mingled with fresh-cut wood from the builders' work. A roped-off area in one corner marked the site where the crew had been repairing the foundation.

The stone jutted out slightly in that section of the wall, and all along it, Evie sensed Gemma's power. She drew back instinctively. This was more than a barrier. If she focused, she could make out thick tendrils of time magic coursing through the stone in vibrant purple rivers. They weren't as concentrated as the magic hiding in Amelia's study, but Evie had no doubt that if she or Ignatius touched them, it would trigger a similar trap, and Gemma would sense it.

"This is going to be much harder to undo," Evie said, taking it all in.

"Especially with the sapling boosting her magic," Ignatius agreed. He sniffed in derision. "Just look at all that magic. She could never sustain so much on her own. It would drain her to a husk."

"I don't sense Abby's magic anywhere down here," Evie said, scanning the wall for those familiar indigo sparks she'd glimpsed when she'd first encountered the woman. "I wondered before, but I'm starting to think she has no idea what Gemma's been up to." She glanced at Ignatius, knowing the younger witch had a crush on him.

"Abby would never be part of this," Ignatius said.

The certainty in his tone surprised Evie. "How do you—"

Ignatius cut her off. "I don't want to talk about it. We need to get this done. The sapling must be behind that wall," he added, nodding to the rivers of time magic and the jutting stone.

He was probably right, but Evie still couldn't sense its presence. She stepped closer and lifted a hand, hovering it in the air. She didn't dare touch the stone wall with the trap in place, but she wanted to see if— Wait, *there*.

A faint pulse, and the smell of fresh earth, of a garden just after the rain. Buried behind the stone, but it was unmistakable.

"I feel it," Evie said, "sealed in a pocket behind the wall. How did your crew not notice it when they were working?"

Ignatius came over to her. "Gemma may have stripped certain memories from them," he said grimly. "Stealing a few moments here and there—if she was careful, and used the sapling to help, they wouldn't have noticed. It's highly illegal, of course, but not unheard-of."

They exchanged a glance, and Evie shuddered. Magic like that was the most intrusive kind of theft—the theft of time.

"We'd better get to work," Evie said. It was going to take a lot of magic to dismantle the traps, and they would have to proceed slowly. She hoped Shara, Ben, and Cinda could keep Gemma and Abby at the café long enough.

Ignatius stood next to her and raised his hands, waiting for her to take the lead. Closing her eyes, Evie concentrated, coaxing a single strand of magic to lift from the wall and come to her. Thin and taut as a harp string, it glittered in her mind's eye. Evie reached for it with her power, feeling Ignatius's magic supporting her own.

Immediately, she met resistance. She pushed, careful not to go too far, too fast, and finally managed to snag one end of a glowing strand of purple magic. In her mind, she held it, purple entwining with gold, vibrating to the point of pain against her skin.

Slowly, so slowly, she wove her magic securely around the strand, stripping it away from the stone wall. She moved on to the next, thinking it would be easier the second time, but Gemma's magic was stubborn. It had been embedded there for a long time, and it wasn't going to be removed easily.

Beads of sweat broke out on Evie's forehead. Beside her, she could hear Ignatius breathing heavily as his magic wrapped around hers, a red radiance mixing with the gold and green. Fire and earth could find common ground here, and a good thing too. Evie didn't think either of them could have managed the intricate work alone.

Finally, after several minutes, they'd cleared a large enough section of the wall to work with, making the stone safe to touch. Evie let her magic go and took a step back from the wall, bending to put her hands on her knees.

Ignatius sank to the floor, panting. "That was awful," he said. "I never want to do anything like that ever again."

"Some of those strands were at least a year old," Evie said. "She's been planning this for a long time." She looked over at Ignatius. "How did Gemma even find out about the sapling?"

"I didn't tell her, or Abby, if that's what you're thinking," Ignatius said, taking off his glasses to wipe the sweat from his face. "Neither did Amelia, as far as I know."

"She must have seen it in the house's past," Evie mused. "If she went back far enough, even for a short time, she could have seen the Star Oak that first formed the house."

And from that she would have been able to calculate when the house would need to be renewed with a sapling. Evie examined the cleared space of wall. She would have bided her time, arranging a space for it down here. Gemma might have even damaged the wall on purpose, requiring renovations that she could then make to her specifications, all to hold the sapling.

"How are you going to break through?" Ignatius asked. "The mortar is set; those stones are solid."

"I know," Evie said. She ran her hands over the cool stone, hoping for weak points, but there were none. "Your crew did good work here. Too good."

"Thanks?" Ignatius huffed a laugh.

"If we punch a hole in the stone with magical force, it'll make too much noise," Evie said, "and we risk damaging the sapling in the process. I think I'm going to have to disintegrate a small section of the wall, and we'll work to get the sapling through the hole."

Ignatius's mouth dropped open. "You're going to disintegrate a whole section of newly mortared stone? It's not possible. You'll hollow yourself out, and then I'll have to drag your unconscious body back up those stairs."

"How gallant," Evie said dryly. "Fortunately, I've had my power bolstered recently, so that will help." She sent a silent thanks to Gil and the roots of his orchard. "But you're right, I'll need more." She shot him a pointed look.

"Wait, you . . . are you serious? You want to siphon my magic?" He shook his head. "Why can't I just help you the way I have been?"

"Because it won't be enough," Evie said. "I need the raw power of fire, something that will feed and alter my own magic. It won't take much," she assured him, "but I think it's the only way."

Ignatius stared at the wall for several seconds, not responding, as if he could simply will the stone to fall apart with his formidable glare. "Fine," he said at last. "Let's get this over with. And don't siphon too much," he warned. "I'm pulling back at the first sign you're taking advantage."

"You have my word that I won't." Evie made space for him to once again stand next to her in front of the wall. Together they placed their hands on the stone, and Evie prayed her plan would work.

Thirty-Two

Evie exhaled and concentrated. Ignatius's power hovered at the edges of her consciousness, like pins and needles on her skin. It wasn't the comforting pulse of Gil's power, but it was substantial, and she would need it. The cold stone beneath her hands was strong and unyielding.

Closing her eyes again, Evie began to draw power from Ignatius. It came as a trickle of heat at first, then steadied as the man relaxed and allowed himself to trust her. She felt the moment he gave in, bringing down his walls so she could draw the hearth magic into herself, nestling it in her chest like a hot coal.

If someone had told her weeks ago that she would be accepting a voluntary offering of power from the same man who'd been determined to drive her out of the village, she wouldn't have believed it. Yet, here they were.

As Evie felt the magic build, she drove it slowly and carefully into the wall, boring a hole straight through stone and mortar. Dust sifted through her fingers, the wall becoming soft beneath her hands as the magic wore it away. Her shoulders were tense, muscles quivering with the effort of channeling the power. She tried to ignore the ringing in her ears and the ache building in her skull. Beside her, Ignatius sucked in a labored breath.

"Are you all right?" Evie asked in a strained whisper. "I think we're almost through."

"Keep going," he said through gritted teeth. "I can give a little more."

No, he couldn't, Evie realized. He was fading, his power stuttering like a candle flame about to go out. She drew away, letting go of his magic, and instead focused all her own will on the wall.

Finally, just when she was starting to get lightheaded, her hands plunged through the stone and met empty air. Gasping, Evie somehow kept her balance and forced her grit-covered hands apart, widening the hole as much as she dared.

They'd done it.

Evie dropped to her knees, and with an *oof,* Ignatius did the same.

Then things got interesting.

As if a dam had burst, a flood of magic erupted from the hole and swept over them both. The full effect of the sapling's magic was suddenly revealed, no longer hidden by stone and hindered by Gemma's power.

And what a magic it was.

Evie's eyes snapped open, and she peered into the hole, which was barely wider than her shoulders.

The sapling was stunning. It grew from a patch of earth at the base of the outer wall, its bark shining a brilliant silver. Tiny blue leaves sprouted from the branches, each no larger than the pad of her thumb. The branches swayed, though there was no breeze, automatically reaching for Evie, as one magic called to another. That rich, earthen scent enveloped her, stealing away all the aches and pains in her body as if they had never been there.

No wonder people were drawn to the power of these trees like moths to a flame; it was difficult to resist that glittering magic. The sapling was so young, eager, and curious—and so inexperienced in the greed of witches. It couldn't help but bolster and soothe anything that came within its reach.

Evie sat back, reluctantly pulling away from the hole in the wall. "It's amazing," she whispered.

"I forgot you'd never seen it in person before," Ignatius said, crowding next to her to get a glimpse of the sapling. He let out a relieved sigh. "Good, it looks as strong as it did the day we planted it in Amelia's study. We should hurry, though. We've been at this too long already."

He reached into the hole.

"Wait!" Evie cried, but she was too late.

Two tendrils of purple magic snaked out from behind the sapling and speared straight at Ignatius.

The man reared back. His reflexes were quick; he almost escaped the hidden trap. But he banged his shoulder on the jagged stones surrounding the gap in the wall, and one of the tendrils wrapped around his left wrist. It slowed him, allowing the other tendril to encircle his throat.

Ignatius froze.

"No!" Evie grabbed his shoulder, but she could already feel his skin going cold beneath her hand. The sensation frightened her. "Ignatius, fight it. Use your power and burn away the magic!"

He couldn't hear her. Ignatius was half turned toward her, but the magic had given his eyes a glazed look, his skin turning dull and gray. This was what it looked like to be frozen in a moment of time. The trap would hold him immobile for however long its power lasted, or until Gemma came to free him.

Unless Evie could break him out of it.

Cautiously, she bent to examine the purple thread of time magic wrapped around his wrist, digging into his skin like a wire. It hummed with power, creating a static charge in the air that thrummed in Evie's skull. She could feel it getting stronger by the second.

Like a signal, Evie realized, traveling to alert Gemma that one of her traps had been triggered.

No time to waste, then. She took the small spade from her bag and reached into the hole in the wall. Not wanting to be caught by another trap, she took a moment to quickly explore around the sapling for any lingering time magic that might ensnare her. When she was satisfied that the area was safe, she began to dig.

Fortunately, the soil was loose, but the sapling's roots had already run deep into the ground. They had been steadily growing into the earth and into the library's walls for months now. It was also difficult to dig through the small opening. Evie's arms and shoulders were soon burning, and she hadn't made much progress. The whole time, she was conscious of Ignatius frozen beside her, held by the trap.

After a moment, she tossed her spade aside in frustration and reached as far into the hole as she could. She grasped the sapling with both hands, letting the loose soil run through her fingers as she connected with the land.

"Please, help me," she murmured. "Let your roots come free. This isn't your home. Your home is waiting for you at Thornwood house. Please, let me take you there."

She opened her mind, allowing the sapling to feel her connection to the land and her love for the house. It wasn't a caretaker bond, not yet, but Evie hoped it would be enough for the sapling to recognize that she spoke the truth, that she meant no harm.

The tree's small leaves fluttered like wings. Evie caught her breath as its branches arched toward her in a silver crescent, sending out a pulse of warmth. Slowly, she felt the sapling's roots draw inward, retreating from the library's wall and loosening their grip on the soil. When she felt them give, she eased the sapling out of the ground, shaking off the lingering clumps of soil. The scent of rich earth filled her nostrils. Evie savored it, using it to calm her racing heart.

All the while, the power of the sapling flowed over her. A whisper came to her ears, so soft, but she felt the greeting in it.

Hello.

I feel you.

"Yes." Evie smiled and carefully laid the sapling on the ground near Ignatius.

We're going home.

"We are." Evie reached out, her fingers brushing the sapling's blue leaves, the silvered bark. "But I need your help to get us there."

She faced Ignatius. He was still frozen in that same pose, eyes wide in shock and fear. No need to worry about being subtle anymore. Gemma had been alerted and was no doubt on her way here right now. Evie would just have to sever the strands of power quickly and cleanly.

As if on cue, the wind chime at her belt sounded a warning, a high and urgent note, a sound that only she could hear.

Evie forced herself to remain calm. She held her hand palm up and asked for power from the sapling. And the young tree, so eager to help, gave its magic to her freely. Gave and gave, until it was almost too much. Evie grunted as she stemmed the tide, channeling the power, shaping it into a glowing golden knife with an ivy handle that materialized in her outstretched hand.

She grasped the blade and, before she could second-guess herself, made two quick slices in the air. The sapling's power held true. The time magic came apart, the bindings falling away from Ignatius's wrist and throat, leaving behind angry red marks on his skin. The magic drifted to the ground harmlessly and faded.

Ignatius came out of his trance with a jerk. Gasping, still on his knees, he lost his balance and would have fallen if Evie hadn't been there to grab his shoulder.

"It's all right," she said, low and urgent. "You're going to be fine, but we have to get out of here now. Gemma's coming."

"I— All right." He blinked, disoriented but otherwise unhurt. He looked into the hole at the empty spot where the sapling had been, then down to where it rested at Evie's feet. He scooped it gently into his arms.

"How long was I trapped?" he asked as he stood up.

Evie was already heading for the stairs. "Just a few minutes," she assured him.

"Really? It felt like no time at all." He shuddered as he moved past her.

They came out of the basement and moved quickly and quietly to the back door. Evie closed it behind them and pulled up the hood of her cloak, and together they made their way as stealthily as possible across the park. Evie again drew the tree branches down so they could hide in their cover, at the same time doing her best to shield the sapling with her power. The young tree would give off magic like a beacon to anyone nearby, and she didn't want Gemma to find them that way. She could feel the red tide of Ignatius's power helping her.

They left the park behind and soon reached the edge of the village, taking the gravel track back toward Thornwood house. Ignatius looked over his shoulder, but there was no one following them.

"We did it," he said in wonder. "We actually got away with stealing back the sapling." He glanced sidelong at her. "You could have left me there, you know."

Evie stared at him. He was cradling the sapling against his chest as if it were a newborn. Its power flowed over him, automatically reaching to soothe the effects of the time trap. The grayish cast to his skin was gone, and the red marks on his wrist and throat had also disappeared.

"Did you actually think I would do that?" she asked.

He avoided her gaze. "I guess not, but I probably deserved it. I did try to set the village against you."

"True. Are you going to *keep* trying to turn them against me?"

He laughed. "I don't think I can after tonight. We're partners in crime." He shook his head, as if he still couldn't quite believe it. "Generations of Smythes are rolling in their graves right now, thanks to me."

Evie reached out, patting him on the shoulder. "A little rebellion is a good thing," she said. "Embrace it."

Thirty-Three

When they arrived back at Thornwood house, Evie breathed a sigh of relief. Though the road was dark, it looked like every light was on in the house as they approached. Ruby met them on the front porch, bouncing excitedly on the balls of her bare feet.

"You got it!" she cried. "I can't believe you got it!"

"Have a little faith," Ignatius told her, as Ruby danced around him, examining the sapling from every angle. "Of course we got it."

Evie smiled at the two of them, but she was really waiting for the house's reaction to this homecoming.

She wasn't disappointed.

Thornwood house quaked as soon as Ignatius crossed the threshold with the sapling in his arms. The overhead lights flickered, and the pictures on the walls rattled in their frames. Its excitement continued to grow as they moved through the house, so that even the floorboards vibrated as Evie led the way to the back hall where Amelia's study waited.

In response, the sapling's branches shimmered and reached past Ignatius's shoulders, its small leaves brushing the walls. It sought contact with the house. The sapling was home, back in the place it was meant to be, and it was just as excited as Thornwood house.

In Amelia's study, the books on the bookshelves were trembling, pages fluttering as a delighted breeze blew through the room. The faded rugs rippled across the floor, nearly tripping Ignatius as he came into the room.

"Here, take this"—Ignatius thrust the sapling at Evie—"before the house makes me fall and break my neck."

But there was no heat in the words, and out of the corner of her eye, Evie saw Ignatius put his hand on the doorframe and give a nod, acknowledging the house's excitement. An answering breeze ruffled his blond hair.

"Are we going to replant it now?" Ruby asked, crouching by the patch of earth. "Can I help?"

"Of course," Evie said. She glanced around the room thoughtfully. "I think we're going to need Gil as well, to help us keep watch while we replant. Could you run and get him, Ruby? He should be home by now, if he left the park around the same time we did."

"I'll be right back!" Ruby tore out of the room, shouting over her shoulder, "Don't start without me!"

Evie carefully set the sapling down next to the bare patch of earth. She took out her spade and began to dig, widening and deepening the existing hole to accommodate how much the sapling had grown over the last few months.

"Do you think Gemma will come here?" Ignatius asked, crouching next to her to scoop out handfuls of loose dirt from the hole. "Once she realizes the sapling is gone?"

"I don't know if she'll risk confronting us directly, but I'm not going to take any chances," Evie said, as a pulse of anxiety whipped through the house. "Gil and his wind chime will act as an early warning system, but I want to put some wards up as well." She glanced over at him. "I have some sun stalk seeds. Will you use them to make some hearth protections?"

"Of course."

They finished with the hole, then Evie went out through the study door to the glasshouse. She grabbed the basket of sun stalk seeds and selected three large ones. They were warm to the touch. She held them out to Ignatius. "Will this be enough?" she asked. "We'll use the hearth downstairs."

"It should be," he said, taking them gently into his hands so he wouldn't crush them before it was time.

They made their way back inside to the living room to stand in front of the stone fireplace. Evie had swept it clean during the move in, but there were still a few small dustings of ash from old fires. Ignatius scooped up a handful and crushed it and the sun stalk seeds between his palms.

There was a flash of red between his splayed fingers. Heat stirred the air around Evie's shoulders as Ignatius scattered the seeds and ash in the cold hearth. Then he laid both hands on the mantel and closed his eyes. Red tendrils of power flowed outward, disappearing into the walls and ceiling.

A good hearth ward, Evie thought. Those who wished the house well would feel the welcoming heat of Ignatius's magic when they came near the property. For those who meant harm, it would be like a blistering inferno. A harsh and effective deterrent, but it would also be short-lived, the magic burning away when triggered.

No matter. Evie would add her own protections soon enough.

They returned to the study to check on the sapling. Beside the hole, the young tree glowed, an entrancing silver light against the blue leaves. It looked much bigger in the small space of the study than it had in the library's basement. Evie marveled at the fact that in just a few months, it would fill the room, reaching nearly to the ceiling.

Ruby returned a few minutes later with Gil and Snow on her heels. Evie drew him in for a hug. Gil nodded to Ignatius but stopped short when he saw the sapling glittering at the back of the room.

"It's beautiful," he murmured. "I don't know what I was expecting a Star Oak to look like—I saw the image in the stained glass at the top of the glasshouse—but this is even more vibrant than I thought it would be."

"Imagine a full-grown Star Oak that's been in the Thornwood for centuries," Ignatius said, an edge of wistfulness in his voice. "Wouldn't that be a vision?"

"Maybe someday you'll get to see it," Evie said, as the four of them arranged themselves around the widened hole.

"Maybe," Ignatius said doubtfully. "It doesn't matter right now. Let's get the sapling replanted."

Before she reached for the tree, Evie sent out a questing strand of magic to the house. It was time to put her own set of wards in place, something she'd never attempted to do before. It required the house's cooperation, and she hadn't wanted to push things too far too fast. But now it was important that she know as soon as possible if Gemma was headed this way. The sapling had to be protected.

The house met her at once, like one hand clasping another. It pulled on her magic, sending it all throughout the house. To Evie's eyes, it was a gold and green layer over the red of Ignatius's ward. If Gemma tried to enter Thornwood house now, she would be met by a manifestation of Evie's magic, a literal wall of thorns that she hoped even Gemma's time magic wouldn't be able to breach.

When she pulled away, Evie felt lightheaded again. Even with the sapling's power helping her, she'd channeled a lot of magic tonight. She needed to rest.

Soon, but not yet. Not until the sapling was back where it belonged.

"Are you all right?" Gil was kneeling next to her. His warm brown eyes were full of concern.

"Just tired," Evie said, "but I can't stop now." This was what she'd been working toward, a way to help the house, ever since she'd first laid eyes on it hunched by the edge of the river.

Carefully, she lifted the sapling and lowered it into the hole. The roots stirred and sank into the soil, disappearing from view. A frisson went through the tree, and with it a ripple of power passed through Evie, lending her strength and vitality as the sapling connected with the land and in turn acted as a conduit to her. She closed her eyes briefly, grateful for the bolstering gift.

She supported the tree while Gil, Ignatius, and Ruby all bent forward and scooped dirt into the hole. They carefully built it up around the sapling, until Evie was able to let go and sit back on her heels. She patted the dirt into place, making sure the sapling was secure.

The bark flashed silver, dazzling Evie's eyes. Before she could react, the branches began to grow, snaking up the back wall of the study between the bookshelves. Some of the branches passed into the wall itself, and around them the house shuddered again. Magic hummed in the air, so thick Evie could taste it.

Suddenly, another wave of power flooded Evie, lighting her from within. She gasped, but the magic wasn't coming from the sapling this time.

This was the house.

The power wove through her and passed into the sapling, silver radiance that vibrated with pure joy, and a sense of homecoming that brought tears to Evie's eyes.

The sapling was back, and the house was welcoming it.

Overhead, the light fixtures danced again, flaring with power. The room shook, and a crack formed over the door, snaking toward the ceiling. The house groaned beneath the sheer force of the magic.

It was too much power all at once. Evie leaned forward, putting her hands on the sapling. "Help me," she entreated the others, who also put their hands on the silver bark. "Easy, now," she said, coaxing the sapling and the house to slow down. "It's not like the library basement, with all that stone like a castle. There's more wood and glass here, and Thornwood house has been weak without you. You have to be gentle with each other."

She let the power sift through their hands, slowing the tidal wave of magic. Ruby looked up, her eyes gleaming as she met Evie's. "This is amazing," she said.

"Let the power flow through you, but don't try to hold it all at once," Evie advised her daughter. "It will make your visions stronger, and it may trigger them when you don't want them."

Ruby nodded, shutting her eyes so she could focus. They continued like that, the four of them all acting as channels. The minutes stretched into an hour as they worked. Evie's neck was stiff, her arms sore from holding them in one place, but she didn't dare let go until she was sure the house could handle the strain.

Thankfully, it became easier as the night wore on, and the flood of magic gradually began to slow. Evie eventually pulled the others back and assigned them to individual shifts in the study, so that some of them could rest while the others kept guiding the sapling and the house.

When the clock struck three in the morning, Evie got up from the living room couch and went to relieve Ignatius. Ruby was upstairs, and Gil and Snow were sound asleep on the living room floor near the windows.

"You should go home," she said, noting Ignatius's rumpled hair and the dark circles under his eyes when she walked into the room. "I'll take the last shift until dawn."

"Are you sure?" Ignatius stood from where he'd been crouching beside the sapling, but he lingered in the study, looking for all the world like a mother hen hovering over her nest. "I can stay a while longer."

"I think we're nearing the end—the rest will be up to the sapling and the house," Evie said. She reached out, checking on their condition. She could feel the bond between the house and the sapling solidifying. It was strong, but that didn't mean it couldn't be severed again. The Star Oak would still need to be protected, from Gemma and anyone else who might want to come for it.

The house itself had gone silent during the bonding process, as if it were sleeping. Dormancy, the condition was called. It would stay that way through the rest of the replenishment, unable to communicate with anyone, but afterward, it would come back stronger than ever.

At last.

Still, Ignatius hesitated. Evie smiled and made a shooing motion.

"I have a feeling you're going to be needed at the library come morning," she pointed out, "once your crew arrives and sees the damage we left behind."

Ignatius winced. "You're right." He rubbed his eyes beneath his glasses. "I should probably go and try to catch a couple of hours' sleep until then."

He moved past her but paused, placing his hand on the doorframe. He closed his eyes. Evie could imagine him reaching out to the house, checking on it one last time. It was quick, and when Ignatius opened his eyes and looked back at her, Evie once again glimpsed a vulnerability in his expression.

"I misjudged you," he said quietly. "Amelia was right; you're the right person to be here, to bond with the house. I won't stand in your way any longer."

"I'm glad to hear it." Evie smiled. "You're always welcome here. You grew up in this house, and it still needs you."

"Thank you." He gave a nod and left, his footsteps echoing on the hardwood floor. A moment later, she heard the sound of the front door closing quietly behind him.

Evie yawned, stretched, and made her way over to the sapling. The tree had stopped its growth about halfway up the wall, but several more leaves had sprouted from the branches, and here and there, silver acorns glinted like jewels.

As Evie settled herself on the floor beside the sapling, in her mind's eye, she pictured the study as it might one day look, reimagined. The sapling would become a full-grown Star Oak, its trunk and branches weaving in and out of the walls of the house. New, built-in bookshelves would nestle around those branches, accommodating wherever the tree wanted to grow and spread. There would be a desk on the opposite wall, and a chair and footstool where she could read or work late into the night.

She glanced over at the door to the glasshouse. On fair days, when there was a cool breeze, she would leave the door open, so she could smell the plants and feel connected to that space and the garden out back, even when she was indoors.

Maybe Ignatius was right, and she should build a gazebo by the mood garden . . .

She let her mind wander, keeping one hand on the sapling to channel its power, and one part of her attention fixed on the wards now surrounding the house.

At dawn she felt a soft tap against them, like a bird pecking at seed.

Thirty-Four

Instantly alert, Evie stood, drawing away from the sapling and fixing all her magic on the wards.

"Gil," she called, and a moment later heard a stirring as Gil rose from his puddle of blankets on the living room floor. He ambled into the study, rubbing his eyes and yawning. "Everything all right?" he asked, his voice sandpapery from sleep.

"Can you stay here? Someone's testing the wards." Evie was already moving toward the front door. She glanced upstairs, sensing Ruby was still asleep and safe in her bed. "I won't be long," she said, closing the front door behind her before Gil could argue.

Mist clung to the grass in thready clouds. The air was damp and crisp. Evie made her way barefoot across the lawn to the wall, where a figure stood on the gravel road.

Gemma Gray looked as if she hadn't slept either. All traces of friendliness were gone from her expression. Her eyes were cold and calculating as she took in Evie, then lifted her gaze to Thornwood house behind her. Evie felt her prodding at the wards, like a child plucking the strings of an instrument she didn't know how to play.

With a stab of irritation, Evie pushed back, feeding more of her power into the wards, letting it snap against Gemma's magic like a whip crack. The woman cursed and retreated a step as Evie approached.

"You're stronger than I gave you credit for," Gemma observed, "and bolder. I never thought you'd break into my sanctuary."

"I don't know what you're talking about," Evie said with a polite smile, "but you'll be happy to hear that Thornwood house is on its way to a full recovery now that it and the sapling have been reunited. I remember how concerned you were about its well-being, so I thought you'd want to know."

Gemma laughed, but there was no humor in it. "I also underestimated how many of the villagers would flock to help you—especially Ignatius." She crossed her arms. "How did you manage to thaw him?"

"It helped that he never pretended to be anything but what he was," Evie said. "It's harder with people who hide their venom behind a kind smile."

"I never had any ill will toward *you*," Gemma insisted, "or any of the others who came here before you. I didn't want to have to involve them in my plans at all, and at first, it looked like I wouldn't have to, since the house chased everyone away to keep them safe from my trap. My hope was that it would keep doing that until it exhausted all its magic."

"You were willing to kill a sentient house, one that's been part of Iskendra and the Thornwood for centuries, so you could have a Star Oak sapling." Anger surged in Evie. "What you did violates everything we stand for!"

"Do you really believe that?" Gemma challenged. "That the

magic of the Star Oak would have been put to better use in Thornwood house than *my* library, bolstering the power of knowledge? Don't you remember what I told you that day at the market?"

Evie thought back. "You said that if more people had the power to see into the past, they would be better caretakers of the future."

"Exactly," Gemma said. "Imagine it—a sentient library, curated by time witches, magically enhanced by a Star Oak sapling. With those resources at our disposal, we could eventually develop the power to send *anyone's* mind into the past. What if they could bear witness to history just by touching a book? How much better would we be as people if we could see and experience what's come before, so we don't repeat our mistakes?"

She swept a hand toward the house, making Evie tense. "Compared to that, what is Thornwood house's purpose—and yours, for that matter, as its caretaker? What are you accomplishing here?" She shook her head. "Admit it, this house is not truly useful to this community or to the wider world."

"Something doesn't need to be *useful*," Evie said, "to justify its existence." Her voice shook. "This house is a place that is loved. It has seen generations come and go within its walls, lives that matter. And if I have anything to say about it, it will see many more. Being a part of that is more than enough accomplishment for my lifetime."

Even as she spoke, Evie knew she would never get the time witch to understand. Gemma looked at the house, but she saw nothing beyond the power and potential of the Star Oak.

"The Thornwood will never show you where the Star Oak is hidden," Evie went on, "and the sapling is back where it belongs. Whatever it takes, I will protect them from you, so you'd be wise not to pursue this any further."

"There's the earthwalker in you talking." Gemma cocked her head. "Did you know I looked into your past when you came here? I didn't go far, but even the last few months told me a lot about you, your old life, and the deal you made with the ECRA to make a new one." She smiled unpleasantly. "You may have wanted to be a caretaker, but that doesn't mean your place here is assured. Do you really believe you'll be allowed to stay?"

Evie flushed. "You don't know anything about me," she snapped. "Look to your own future, Gemma. Leave the past where it is."

"Oh, don't worry." Gemma turned, strolling off down the gravel road, as if she hadn't a care in the world. "I've already mapped out my future, and it's looking very bright. Have a nice day, Evie."

Evie watched Gemma until she disappeared around a curve in the path. Her stomach churned with an inexplicable sense of dread. But there was nothing Gemma could do to them now, Evie assured herself. Mentioning the ECRA was an empty threat. If Gemma tried to bring them down on Evie and Ruby, it would risk revealing Gemma's own theft of the sapling.

No, she'd just been posturing, trying to get under Evie's skin because her plans had been thwarted. But Evie couldn't rule out the possibility that Gemma might try to hurt one of her friends in revenge for helping her. She would warn Gil, Cinda, and the Greens to keep an eye out, and Evie would place some temporary wards around their properties, just in case.

But for the moment, she needed to stay with the house, make sure everything was all right.

She headed back up the porch steps to find Gil standing in the open doorway, watching her. "You doing okay?" he asked, opening his arms as she came close.

"Fine." Evie walked right into them and laid her head against Gil's chest, listening to the reassuring thump of his heartbeat. "Just tying up some loose ends."

"Do you think she'll leave well enough alone?" he murmured into her hair.

"No, I don't," Evie said. "But I swayed more of the villagers to my side than she was expecting, and now I've got Ignatius Smythe in my corner. She's outnumbered, and I've warded the house against her, which means she'll probably go back to searching the wood for the Star Oak."

She would have to keep a close watch on the Thornwood, make sure Gemma didn't try anything drastic to find the hidden tree. Being caretaker here was going to keep her very busy for a while.

It swept over her afresh, the notion—the hope—that they were staying. That this was all really happening—the new life she'd wanted for herself and Ruby.

She tightened her arms around Gil's waist, leaning back to look up at him. He smiled down at her. "By the way, during the night, before it went dormant, I heard some suspicious noises coming from the house," he told her. "I think it might have been doing some work upstairs."

"Is Ruby all right?" In the chaos, Evie had completely forgotten about the half-finished projects upstairs.

"I took a quick peek, and she's sound asleep." Gil chuckled. "I think that kid could sleep through an earthquake."

"Tell me about it."

Reluctantly, Evie stepped out of Gil's arms and headed back inside. Up the stairs, she stuck her head in the bathroom first. Where there had once been bare wood, pristine white tile now covered the floor, leading her gaze across the room to the impressively large claw-foot bathtub. A rack of fluffy towels was situated next to the tub, and a sink and vanity with a silver-framed mirror sat on the opposite side of the room. Evie took a moment to imagine a long, hot soak in that tub, which she fully intended to take advantage of later that day.

Leaving the bathroom, she cautiously approached the primary bedroom. For some reason, she felt a fluttering of nerves in her stomach, though she had no idea why. She hadn't made any definite plans for what she'd wanted her bedroom to look like, so whatever the house came up with should be just . . .

Evie halted in the doorway, aware that her mouth was hanging open, but she couldn't seem to help it.

The room had been done in beautiful earth tones. Forest-green walls and dark wood floors beneath the exposed ceiling beams made the space feel tucked away and cozy. Soft rugs had been arranged throughout the room. The biggest of these spread before a large stone fireplace against the far wall. A comfy chair and footstool waited in front of it. A chest of drawers sat near the door.

The bed was to her right, a large four-poster like Ruby's, this one done in dark wood, the posts intricately carved with helia blossoms, of all things. But what finally drew Evie to step into the room was the wall of windows overlooking the garden and the glasshouse. She could even see the stained-glass Star Oak from where she stood, which meant her bedroom was directly above the study where the sapling grew.

Evie stretched out her awareness and, yes, there it was, the pulse of power directly beneath her feet. She could feel the sapling at the heart of the house, strengthening it and spreading its power over the entire property. Eventually, it would grow into the bedroom as well, bringing a piece of the land and the Thornwood into this sanctuary.

She didn't need to help them anymore. The house and the sapling were one. So Evie stood in front of those gorgeous windows for a few minutes, enjoying the view and soaking up the sunrise.

"Thank you," she murmured, addressing the house, even though she knew it was dormant and wouldn't be able to hear. "I love it."

It would have been the perfect peaceful moment, standing there in her reimagined bedroom. But as hard as she tried, Evie still couldn't quite get Gemma Gray's taunting words out of her head.

Thirty-Five

Over the next couple of days, Evie made good on her vow to set up magical protections for the Greens, Cinda, and Gil, weaving her magic around their properties so that she would know if anything was amiss. None of the people involved questioned her actions, though all of them hoped that Gemma wouldn't try to hurt anyone out of revenge. In fact, there had been no sign of the witch in the village since the morning Evie had spoken to her outside Thornwood house.

That absence bothered Evie more than if Gemma had threatened her or confronted her again. Evie had seen the cold anger in her eyes that day outside the house. She had been prepared to use her magic to defend the house and Ruby and Gil, to call up every power at her disposal.

But Gemma had just walked away, and she'd seemed . . . content. Like she knew something Evie didn't.

It unsettled her, so she kept watch, trying to stay vigilant for whatever came.

Even so, when the worst finally did happen, Evie found herself woefully unprepared.

As she stood in the kitchen one evening, washing the dishes after supper, she heard Ruby dash out the front door.

"I forgot to get the mail earlier!" she called when Evie asked her where she was going. A few minutes later, she darted back inside and slammed the door behind her.

"Be gentle with that door," Evie admonished her, as Ruby burst into the kitchen like a miniature tornado. "We finally got all the repairs done, and I don't feel like doing any more for a long—" She stopped at the look on Ruby's face. "What is it?"

Her daughter didn't immediately reply. She was holding a piece of paper and the torn remnants of an envelope that had a return address Evie knew all too well.

"Ruby—" she began, but didn't get any further.

"It's from the ECRA," Ruby said, her voice dull, even as her eyes filled with tears. "They're saying we have to come back to Dorna City." She squeezed the paper in her fists. "Your trial period as caretaker is being t-terminated, effective immediately."

A heavy silence fell in the kitchen as Evie tried to process what Ruby had said. No, it had to be a mistake. The ECRA couldn't terminate their agreement. In her haste, Ruby had just misread the letter.

"Can I see that?"

Evie took the paper from Ruby's limp hand. She noticed at once that it was signed by Mr. Cinton.

It wasn't a mistake.

"They're citing the fact that I've been unable to control the house," Evie read, a hollowness taking her over as she parsed the justification the committee had used. "They think it poses a danger to the community."

"How could they know about that?" Ruby demanded, her voice high and constricted by a sob. "The ECRA aren't here. There's no way they could know what's been happening with the house!"

Dread coiled in her stomach as Evie thought back to her conversation with Gemma that day they'd spoken at the market. She'd told the witch that she wouldn't force the house to bond with her, that it would be cruel to do so.

"Gemma knew," Evie admitted. "She must have written to the ECRA right after I told her I didn't want to break into Amelia's study."

She said she'd looked into Evie's past, had seen the deal Evie made before they came here. It had provided her with the perfect backup plan, a way to get rid of them that didn't involve framing Evie for the theft of the sapling. She just needed to give the ECRA an excuse to summon her back.

All it took was a letter to Cinton, letting him know that Evie had failed to bond with the house. Gemma had probably expressed her concerns about the house running off and damaging property. How long would it be until the house hurt someone? Evie couldn't get it under control. She was better off back where she belonged.

And then the ECRA would say Ruby would be better off without her.

As Evie's thoughts continued to spiral, there came a knock at the front door, and then Gil's voice, alongside Snow giving a happy bark. It was jarring. "Anyone home?" he called. "I brought those paint samples you were asking about last week."

"We're in here," Evie called dully.

Footsteps sounded, and then Gil poked his head into the kitchen. His smile wavered and disappeared as he saw the two of them standing silent, Ruby with tears shining in her eyes. "What is it?" he demanded. "Did something happen to the sapling?"

Evie shook her head. "The sapling's fine, and the house is still dormant and healing. It's just . . ." Her throat closed. She couldn't explain it, so she handed him the letter at the same time Ruby bolted for the door. "Wait!" Evie called after her.

"It's not fair!" Ruby hurled open the front door. She looked over her shoulder at Evie as the tears started to fall. "They can't force us to go back! I'm going to make sure they can't!"

She ran out of the house, slamming the door behind her. Evie automatically went after her, but she caught herself. She knew her daughter. Ruby needed time to collect herself, and if she was being truthful, so did Evie. A few minutes storming around the yard would help Ruby calm down.

In a fog, Evie walked back to the kitchen, where she found Gil sitting at the table, the letter in front of him. He scrubbed a hand over his beard and looked up at her.

"You can get around this," he said, with a certainty that gripped Evie's heart.

"How?" Evie sank into the seat across from him. She glanced out the window to see Ruby throwing rocks into the pond beneath the willow tree. Snow danced around her, trying and failing to get her attention.

"Simple—bond with Thornwood house. You're both ready."

Evie looked around the silent kitchen, feeling the muted presence of the house as it slept. "I can't," she said, "not while it's still healing itself. It's not even aware of what's happening right now. The bond wouldn't work."

Gil crossed his arms. "Wait a few days," he suggested. "It'll come out of this phase, and you'll bond. Then the ECRA can't summon you back."

"We can't know how long Thornwood house will be in this state," she argued. "It could be days, weeks, or even months, and the ECRA won't wait. If I don't respond, they'll send someone."

"Let them." Gil's face settled into a stony scowl. "You can stop this, Evie."

"This?" Evie grabbed the letter in her fist, crumpling the paper. "*This* is just the beginning." She flung the letter aside. "They'll take Ruby next, because obviously if I can't control a house, they'll declare I was never fit to be her parent. And if they come here, they'll find out about the Star Oak sapling and the one hidden in the Thornwood." She strove for calm, even as the inevitable conclusion played out like a nightmare in her mind. "They'll take *everything*, Gil, just like they always do, gobble it up for power and make themselves into something even scarier than they are now."

"Surely not." Gil sat back in his chair, shifting agitatedly. "They don't have a basis for any of that. It's illegal!"

"It doesn't matter!" Evie exploded. "The ECRA always rewrite the rules in their favor when it comes to witches and anything powerful in the magical community. They'll just do it again here, with us!"

Laws hadn't stopped the ECRA from stripping her homeland of its magic. They hadn't stopped them from ensnaring her in a contract that had come to define her life. Somehow, the ECRA would find a way to justify their actions.

"So fight them," Gil declared, as if that were the end of it.

Evie stared at him incredulously. "Have you been listening to anything I've said? The ECRA hold all the cards. I tried to outplay them once. When I heard about the position as caretaker here, I didn't even think. I just wrote to Cinda and told her I'd do it." She gave a bleak laugh, staring up at the ceiling the way she often did when she spoke to the house. "I thought, how hard could it be? How difficult could an aging, sentient house be to manage? I would bond with it quickly, and the ECRA would give up on getting us back."

Her chest constricted, as if the weight of everything she'd been carrying was finally going to pull her under. "Nothing turned out the way I thought," she whispered. "I never expected to fall in love with this place the way I did. I had so much magic to share with it, but I wasn't prepared for the house to need more. I wasn't prepared to have to protect something as rare and precious as a Star Oak. I tried to be enough, but—" Evie shook her head. "Now I've failed the house, the Star Oak, and worst of all, I've failed Ruby, because I couldn't keep my promise that we would stay together."

"To hell with that, and with the ECRA."

Surprised by his vehemence, Evie leaned forward as Gil laid his hand over hers. "The ECRA may have carved that doubt into you," he said, "but they're wrong. You saved the house, and you did it with a power greater than magic. It didn't happen by accident. You can protect the Star Oaks from the ECRA too, and make your place here with Ruby. Fight for what you want, Evie. Fight for your home."

"And just how many people do you think have gone up against the ECRA and won?" Evie countered. "That's why they keep growing in power and influence."

"All the more reason someone needs to challenge them," Gil said. "I'd put my money on you any day." He squeezed her hand.

Oh, how Evie wanted to believe him. She wanted desperately to think that this was all going to work out somehow, that she wasn't going to lose her daughter, the happiness the two of them had been building here.

Or the feelings she had for Gil, so new and fragile she hardly dared put a name to them.

Gil gently swiped a tear from her face, his hand lingering to cup her cheek. "You're not alone in this," he said quietly. "I'm not just talking about myself. I mean the villagers too. So many of them care about you. I hope you can see that."

"I do," Evie managed. "I want—" But the words wouldn't come, so she sat back, pressing her hands to her aching temples. "I need to figure this out, and I have to talk to Ruby." She wanted to give her daughter space, but Evie also didn't want her to be alone and hurting right now. She had to tell her something, give her some hope, even if she didn't have a plan for their next move.

She glanced out the window, but Ruby was no longer standing by the pond. Evie thought she'd probably gotten tired of throwing rocks and had gone around back. She'd taken to playing by the glasshouse and in the mood garden the last few days; she could empty her rage into the burning heart stalks to make their crimson flowers bloom.

But when Evie went out the glasshouse door to check, Ruby wasn't in the backyard either. A stirring of unease gripped her. She returned to the kitchen and looked out the window again. "Do you see Ruby?" she asked Gil.

Gil stood, pushing back his chair. "Snow was out there with her. I'm sure she's just out of sight."

They went out to the porch. Gil whistled for Snow and Evie called Ruby's name, but there was no response from either of them. Evie jogged around the house, calling out again, Gil at her heels.

"Where is she?" Evie spoke half to herself, urgently sending her awareness all around the house, inside and out, searching for Ruby's familiar pink aura. This couldn't be happening. "She wouldn't have run off. Ruby doesn't do that. She knows it would make me worry." At any other time, the house might have been able to give her a clue, might have seen where her daughter had gone, but it was still dormant and wouldn't be able to respond.

"Snow!" Gil shouted, and finally, in the distance, there was an answering bark.

It was coming from the Thornwood.

Thirty-Six

"She's in the wood." Evie's heart hammered in her chest as certainty closed around her. She recalled the last thing Ruby had said before she'd run out the door.

"They can't force us to go back! I'm going to make sure they can't!"

"She's gone to look for the Star Oak."

"The Star Oak?" Gil echoed. "But why?"

"Probably because she thinks its power can help her somehow, maybe help her see a future where we finally get away from the ECRA." Evie shot out through the gate to the gravel path. When Gil joined her, she shut the gate and spun another protective ward around the house.

"There's a storm coming in." Gil pointed to the darkening western sky. Lightning danced between the low-hanging clouds, and a chill wind stirred up the willow tree branches over the pond.

The dread Evie had been feeling intensified as she sent her magic toward the Thornwood. Green and gold light spun from her fingers, faltering as it approached the trees and met a familiar, unwelcome purple magic.

"No!" Evie cried. "Gemma's in the wood too! With Ruby!" She broke into a run, Gil right behind her.

"Slow down," Gil cautioned her as they reached the tree line. "If you fall and break your neck, you'll be no good to Ruby."

"I shouldn't have let her leave the house, shouldn't have let her out of my sight," Evie babbled. "I should have known . . ."

"That Gemma would be in the wood?" Gil pushed a branch out of the way as they ducked into the trees. "You couldn't have known, and we don't know that Ruby is anywhere near her. She could have gone in a completely different direction."

Evie wished she could believe that, but the fear, the instinct that something was terribly wrong, wouldn't leave her.

The storm rolled in fast, cutting off the light as they pushed deeper into the wood. Thunder rumbled overhead, and moments later, thick raindrops pattered on the leaves, a sound that quickly turned to a roar as sheets of water poured down on them. The ground became a disaster of wet leaves and slippery mud. It was difficult to see more than a few feet ahead of them.

And there was something wrong with her magic.

The farther they ventured into the wood, the more Evie's sense of Ruby became distorted. She knew her daughter was somewhere nearby, but she couldn't gauge the distance. When she turned west, she felt Ruby's presence, but she also felt it in the opposite direction. The more she tried to pinpoint her daughter's location, the more Evie was like a compass with the needle just spinning and spinning, refusing to point to her true north.

It had to be Gemma's doing.

Evie stopped in the middle of the wood, grasping Gil's arm.

"Did you hear something?" he asked.

"Gemma's magic is strong here," Evie said. "I think she laid traps in the wood. They're distorting my sense of time in ways I can't parse, but I know they're keeping me from finding Ruby."

Gil made a noise of dismay. "What happens if we run into one of those traps?"

"Nothing good." Evie looked over at him, at the raindrops glistening in his hair. "Do you trust me?"

His gaze softened. "You have to ask?" When she only continued to look at him steadily, he nodded. "Yes, I trust you."

"We need to stay together." Evie slid her hand into his, guiding her magic to wind around their joined hands. Glowing green leaves and golden feathers swirled across their skin. "I'm grounding you to the earth with me," she explained, as the light flared and faded. Only a tingling warmth remained.

"What does that mean?"

"The best way to describe it is that it's a ward created just for you, spun directly from my magic," Evie said. "As long as you're with me, it will make it harder for you to be incapacitated by Gemma's time magic." Her mouth quirked. "A side effect is that you won't be able to let go of my hand for a while."

"Not complaining," he said with a chuckle.

Feeling steadier, Evie started moving through the wood again, Gil keeping close to her side. It was cooler now, in the deep shade of the trees. The relentless rain didn't help.

With her free hand, Evie let her magic curl toward the trees. If she couldn't sense her daughter directly, she would reach out to the Thornwood to see if it might have better luck. "Where is she?" she asked aloud, stopping to press her palm to one of the moss-covered trees. "Can you tell me where Ruby's gone?"

At first, there was no response but the constant, pounding rain. It dripped down Evie's face, leaving her hair hanging in dark, drenched ropes across her shoulders. She pushed away the discomfort and concentrated.

"Please," she whispered. "Please, just help me find her. Help me pierce Gemma's magic."

This time, there came a faint response, barely discernible amid the roaring rain. The Thornwood was trying to answer, but it was like hearing a voice when she was deep underwater. The call was muffled, indistinct.

Gemma had been busy here. That was why she hadn't come after Evie or any of her friends. She'd been spreading her time magic all through the wood, subtly weaving the strands through the trees, confusing the Thornwood's power and swamping it with her own.

Why hadn't Evie sensed it? Her focus had been on the house, it was true, but the Thornwood was so close, surely she would have detected Gemma's magic at work.

But she'd also been spreading herself thin, protecting all her friends and the house. Obviously, she hadn't had enough magic left to properly monitor the wood.

Another mistake.

"Gemma's trying to find the Star Oak," Evie said, stepping away from the tree. "She's saturating the wood with her power, hoping to break whatever protections the Thornwood has spun around the tree's location. She's not even trying to be subtle."

"Her secret's out now," Gil said. "People know what she's been up to, so she has no reason to hide what she's doing."

"I don't know if my magic will be enough to undo this and stop her," Evie said. They pushed on, but it felt like she was walking through molasses. The mud slowed them down, but it shouldn't be hampering them this much.

Magic designed to delay, to trap and hold—it was everywhere.

"We'll find Ruby first, then we'll worry about Gemma," Gil said. "Remember, the Star Oak is powerful too, and it's no friend to her."

He was right. If there were ever a time when Evie might be able to get the Star Oak to help her, it was now.

Tightening her grip on Gil's hand, she stepped around a cluster of trees. Suddenly, a flash of purple rose in front of her, a sphere of light that bobbed in midair like a will-o'-the-wisp. Cords of purple light whipped out, encircling her and Gil, weaving themselves together into a net.

"Watch out!" Evie tugged Gil close, pressing against his chest. He wrapped his free arm around her just as the purple strands started to contract. Evie concentrated, and a sphere of golden light blossomed between their joined hands, expanding until it covered their bodies in a protective bubble.

The edges of Evie's magic met the strands of the net and sizzled. Evie flinched but held her power steady, even as the purple strands fractured and transformed into long, thin needles that plunged inward, trying to pierce the golden barrier.

"Are you all right?" Gil asked, looking down at her.

"So far," Evie grunted, bracing herself as the needles stabbed her magic. "We stepped in something nasty, though."

"What's it doing to you?"

"Exerting pressure—trying to break the barrier by force," Evie said through gritted teeth.

Gil pulled her closer, as if to make a shield of his own body. "What can I do?"

Evie considered their options. She could break them out of this, but it would take a significant amount of magic. If they ran into too many of these traps, it would drain her power before she could confront Gemma.

Which was exactly what the time witch was hoping for, no doubt.

"I need more power," Evie admitted.

Gil raised their linked hands, laid them against his chest. "Take what you need," he urged her. "We have to find Ruby."

She looked up into his face, knowing he was sincere. He'd give up any amount of his own strength to find and protect her daughter. If Evie had had any doubt before that she was falling for this man, all of it would have vanished with that simple declaration.

Raising her free hand, she drew him down to her and kissed him, the softest brush of lips, but there was power in it.

Green and gold light flared around them. Evie's magic flowed outward to engulf the needles, burning them away one by one. It left her briefly lightheaded, but Gil's power was there to steady her, wrapping her up as tightly as his arms held her. She didn't stagger.

When the last needle vanished, they stepped apart, but she kept hold of his hand. The rain, held at bay by her barrier, came back on them in a rush. Evie swiped her hand across her eyes to wipe the water away.

Was it her imagination, or had it grown darker while they were in the trap? It could have been the storm, Evie reasoned, bringing a false night. The thunder and lightning were right on top of them now. Or it could have been that the trap had distorted their sense of time, making them think that only a few minutes had passed, when really, Evie had no idea how long they had taken to free themselves.

She clenched her hand into a fist at her side. They were being toyed with.

Riding the wave of her anger, Evie sent a spike of power weaving through the trees, lighting up the whole area like the dawn. Gil gave a shout of surprise, but she squeezed his hand reassuringly.

"It's just me," she said, leading him along the rope of light. It drifted ahead of them like a guide. "So we can see where we're going."

The rain kept up its onslaught as they moved through the wood. Evie's boots were heavy with mud, and Gil's pants were now caked to the knees. They both stumbled, supporting each other, and all the while, Evie kept trying to sense Ruby's presence.

Still, there was nothing.

She tried to quell the panic growing inside her like a poison seed. Where was her daughter? Did Gemma have Ruby in one of her time traps, just as she'd snared Evie and Gil? The thought of that made Evie's power blaze bright with fury.

"You're shaking," Gil said, tugging on her hand to make her slow down.

"I'm all right," Evie insisted. "Or I will be, once I find Ruby." She tried another call to the Thornwood, hoping to reach the Star Oak.

"Are you out there?" she murmured, letting her power touch the trees, passing through each vein of leaf and curl of bark, searching for the ancient power, something older than the rest. "Can you help us?" Evie pressed. "Gemma won't rest until she has your power. I'm afraid you can't hide from her forever. We need to stop her now."

Her magic broke the tree line, stopping abruptly at the edge of the river. Evie hadn't realized they were so close. Cautiously, she led Gil to the water. The river was up, rushing past as another flash of lightning lit the sky. In the distance, there was a loud boom as the bolt struck a tree. Shards of wood exploded above the canopy, and a shower of leaves and smoking branches came tumbling down. The wind howled, whipping Evie's hair into her eyes.

"This storm gets any worse, we'll need to find shelter," Gil said. He pointed ahead of them. "We're near the footbridge. We could get underneath there and regroup, and you can try to reach the Star Oak again."

It was worth a shot. Jamie Green had been fishing beneath that very bridge when he'd wandered off and found the Star Oak. Maybe they were close and didn't even realize it.

They moved along the gray ribbon of rushing water, stepping carefully on the uneven embankment. Out of the corner of her eye, Evie caught a flash, and for a second, she thought it was more lightning. Too late, she reacted, throwing up a golden barrier as the second time trap rose in front of them, this time from the river itself. She hadn't been expecting that. It spun out between her and Gil, neatly severing the magical tether that bound them together.

Gil gave a warning shout and reached for her, but his hand tangled in spreading purple strands. Evie tried to pull him free, but another strand grabbed her at the waist and yanked her back, into the river. The shock of the cold water made her lose her grip on her magic.

The last thing she saw before the time magic pulled her under was Gil, his eyes wide and unblinking, frozen in place beside the river.

THIRTY-SEVEN

The water was so cold.

Evie's arms were leaden. She looked down to see those telltale purple cords wrapped around her, the time trap pulling her toward the bottom of the river. Furious, she curled into herself, summoning a burst of power. She flexed her arms, and golden light filled the space around her, incinerating the cords. At the same time, her booted feet hit the muddy bottom of the river.

Evie swam, kicking her legs to propel herself back to the surface. Her clothes and boots weighed her down, and the current dragged at her body, but she'd been in more dangerous waters than these when she'd worked for the ECRA. She'd once been shipwrecked off the coast of Andelea when she and a group of earthwalkers had strayed too close to a tropical storm. *That* time she'd almost drowned.

Still, when her head finally broke the surface, Evie sucked in air gratefully. She swam for the bank, at the same time looking around frantically for Gil.

He was nowhere in sight. Either she'd been swept farther downstream than she'd realized, or Gemma had taken him.

Evie dragged herself out of the water, tripped as her boots sank in the mud, and fell to her knees on the uneven bank. Strands of icy wet hair clung to her face and neck, making her shiver. She was cold and tired, and her magic was slowly being leeched by the time traps.

Now Gemma had taken two of the people she cared about most.

Fury burned away the cold, an inferno Evie had to tamp down with all her strength. Not yet, she thought. She would save her rage. She doubted Gemma had ever seen what an unleashed land witch could do with her powers.

But she was about to find out.

Evie pushed herself to her feet. She kicked off her boots and removed her socks so that she was barefoot on the bank. She sank her toes into the mud and sand, savoring the direct connection between her body and the earth.

"I need power," she whispered, beseeching the Thornwood. "Help me. Please."

Evie waited, and once again, she heard that muted voice, as if a force stood poised on the other side of a wall, desperately trying to call out to her. Evie let the gold and green strands of her power rise. She pulled them toward her chest, built upon them, shaping them into a pointed spear. Thrusting her hands forward, she released it, punching through the invisible barrier of Gemma's time magic.

A loud, thrumming *boom* reverberated through the ground. Evie's ears popped, and the trees closest to her shuddered, shedding a curtain of leaves. She dropped to her knees again, body trembling with the aftereffects of so much magic released at once.

But that spike of power had done its job. Something had changed.

The muted voice reaching out to her was suddenly a roar in her ears. It pounded at her in time with each drop of sheeting rain. Evie put her hands over her ears to block the worst of the punishing noise.

"Slower," she gasped. "Softer, please."

The wall of sound retreated. Evie took a second to gather herself, then opened her mind again. With a surge of hope, she realized this was a thing apart from the familiar friendliness of the Thornwood. An ancient voice, thick and rough from disuse, but powerful. It drew away even as she reached for it, as if it were afraid of hurting her. She thought she'd heard a whisper of it the night she'd been chased in the Thornwood.

It was the Star Oak. It had to be.

Evie pushed herself back to her feet, fighting a wave of dizziness. She half climbed, half crawled her way up the steep embankment and plunged into the trees again, following that immense force of power. She didn't know how long she walked, but she was forced to stop suddenly as a cloak of darkness fell around her.

The rain stopped falling.

Evie looked around anxiously. What was happening now? Had she stepped into yet another time trap?

Then, from overhead, moonlight pierced the curtaining dark, revealing a small clearing. The sky was black and star filled, and as Evie looked down at herself, she realized she was no longer soaking wet. The light painted her skin in silver, and a sense of safety and well-being descended over her.

Was she still in the Thornwood? The trees around her were bathed in moonlight, just as she was, but they were so tall, arching overhead in a beautiful blue canopy . . .

Blue.

Gasping, Evie turned in a circle, taking in the stand of oaks. It wasn't moonlight shining on their bark, as she'd first thought. The bark *itself* glittered silver, with acorns dangling from the tree branches like bells. The clusters of leaves were indigo, cerulean, lapis, every shade of blue one could imagine, weaving among one another at their tops so that it was impossible to tell where one tree ended and another began.

Awestruck, Evie realized the truth.

She hadn't left the Thornwood at all. But the wood was finally showing her its true face.

She peered through the grove—the entire *grove*—of Star Oaks, trying to see how large it was, for to her eyes it appeared to stretch all the way to the horizon.

All this time, she'd been looking for a single tree, the last remnant of a dying species that had offered its precious sapling to Thornwood house. But the truth was that the Star Oaks here hadn't died out at all. They'd simply been in hiding, free to grow in safety, in a wood in the middle of nowhere.

Now, after all this time, they had decided to show themselves.

To her.

Evie approached the nearest tree, her steps tentative. Its bark glowed like starlight, so beautiful it was almost painful. She lifted her hand to one of the branches and was delighted when it curved downward to meet her, with a tinkling sound like one of Gil's wind chimes. When the velvety blue leaves touched her skin, Evie felt a presence at the edge of her consciousness. It was as tentative as she, but she sensed the power behind it, the great age and wisdom.

We're here, it seemed to say. *We see you.*

Evie felt a humming in the back of her skull. It wasn't a painful sensation like earlier. It was instead as if the trees had collectively come together and lowered their voices, speaking in a way she could comprehend.

So many questions crowded Evie's mind. An entire grove of Star Oaks! How long had they been here, hiding themselves in the Thornwood? How had they managed to conceal their power and presence from the witches who had lived here? Had Amelia known about them all?

The implications were overwhelming. This was bigger than Gemma, bigger than the ECRA even—a revelation that would be felt throughout the world.

Under different circumstances, Evie would have sat down before the trees and asked them everything she wanted to know. The possibilities, the knowledge and power of trees that were easily a thousand years old—she could see why Ignatius and Gemma had wanted that so badly for themselves. It was a tantalizing notion, to have your heart's desire so close.

But in the end, there was only one question that Evie needed the answer to, one desire that filled her heart as those blue leaves grazed her fingertips and pulled away. "Where are Ruby and Gil?" she implored. "I have to find them."

A soft breeze stirred the silver branches and rustled the dangling acorns. Evie thought she heard a hint of words mixed in with the sounds. It felt as if the trees were speaking to one another, communicating just beyond her senses. But their answer, when it came, was clear enough.

They're nearby. Safe . . . for now.

For now.

Evie's skin went cold, fury rising to tangle with fear.

The trees answered at once, a susurration meant to calm her. *Don't act rashly. Her traps are numerous.*

"Can you show them to me," Evie asked, "so I can destroy them?"

There are too many. They pull at us.

"I'll stop her," Evie promised. "Just show me where she is, and I'll stop her."

The grove started to reach for her, drawing in its power like a breath, but then it hesitated, wavering between one moment and the next.

What was it waiting for?

"You can trust me." Evie reached out to touch the trunk of another tree. The bark was warm beneath her fingers. "I promise, I won't reveal your secret, and I won't misuse your power."

Silence reigned in the grove—a considering silence, but it still made Evie uneasy. What could she do to convince the grove to help her?

We stand ready, the trees whispered finally, in a chorus of swishing leaves. *Where do you stand?*

The question caught Evie off guard. Where did *she* stand?

"What do you mean?"

She was here in the wood, standing against Gemma and her time magic, searching for the ones she loved. Wasn't that enough?

Before Evie could communicate that, the Star Oaks' magic

swelled around her. Memories flew through her mind, summoned without warning, but they were as sharp in clarity as the day she'd lived them . . .

Stepping off the train after escaping the ECRA, the sun hot and bright in her eyes.

Walking in the wood as the trees reached out to greet her.

Her first sight of Thornwood house, crouching fearfully by the river.

Iskendra, and the faces of all the people she and Ruby had met.

Gil, opening his door to her in the middle of the night.

The images passed through her thoughts, an ephemeral collection of all her experiences since coming to this place. Her head throbbed with the force of it. Last of all, she saw the Star Oaks themselves, and a memory that was not her own, but one she was sure would live in her forever. Every one of the great trees, hidden away in the wood these long years, loneliness growing on them like an impenetrable skin, while the world carried on and forgot them.

Where do you stand?

Evie put her hands over her ears until the echo of sound faded. She couldn't hold the force of all the voices in her mind, but she'd heard them. And she thought she finally understood.

Where did she stand? What was her place in this tapestry she'd woven?

Where was her home?

The Star Oak grove wasn't questioning whether she was worthy; it was simply *waiting* for her, willing her to accept her role as caretaker. Not just of the village and of Thornwood house.

It was asking her to be the caretaker of the wood and the Star Oak grove, to help it find its place again in the world.

There it was, all along—the true test Amelia Howell had left for her successor. The task she couldn't communicate, even in her diary; the responsibility that had always been waiting here.

The enormity of it washed over Evie, and she almost pulled back from the tree. Surely she could never take on something so immense. Gil had told her to fight, but that wasn't why she'd come here. She'd come to Iskendra to escape. She hadn't understood what she was getting herself into. And now the ECRA was trying to pull her back in. She had to find Ruby. *That* was her responsibility. That was what was most important. She had to—

Stop.

The soothing, whispered word echoed in Evie's mind. She wasn't sure whether the voice came from the trees or from her.

She stopped.

Breathing slow and deep, she blocked every stray thought and doubt and just stood there among the trees, letting their presence calm her and letting the truth unfurl within her like the helia blossoms that sang to her in childhood.

She was so tired.

Tired of running, of not being certain where she belonged, or if she could keep this new life she and Ruby had sought.

She *wanted* to belong at Thornwood house. She could be its caretaker. She *wanted* to be Ruby's mother, despite all the uncertainties and mistakes she was bound to make. She wanted to shout it to the world.

She was enough.

She was enough.

But that wasn't all. She wanted more.

Evie yearned for dreamy nights in the mood garden, days spent working in the glasshouse, listening to the birdsong and reveling in the presence of all the wild things of the wood. That was her place. She wanted to be with Gil, to raise Ruby among the friends they'd made in this community.

And she wanted to protect the Star Oak grove, to end its loneliness and use the full force of her magic to help it endure.

"Find a place that sings to you," her father had said. He'd been right. Everything inside Evie had come alive and was singing now. Her hopes and desires surged through her like the tide rushing toward shore.

The ECRA and its demands were nothing at all compared to those feelings. They were small and petty, pale specters before an ancient grove of sentient trees that were all reaching out to her, calling on her to choose them, to choose her home.

So Evie chose.

Thirty-Eight

Evie opened her mind and let in the magic of the Star Oaks.

It was unlike anything she'd ever experienced. Like starlight flowing through her veins, filling her with magic, yet she remained lighter than air. If she tipped her face to the sky, she felt she could have taken flight. Within the gold and green light of her power, blue leaves now floated alongside feathers and berries and helia blossoms, seashells, sun stalks, and rose petals. The Star Oaks were a part of her now, weaving seamlessly into the fabric of her life.

When it was done, Evie gathered her magic back into her body, drawing on her connection to the land to ground her, to remind her that despite the power she now wielded, she was still human. She belonged in the human world.

She blinked and looked around. The Star Oaks surrounding her had replaced their masks, appearing as simple oak trees once more. But when she reached out to them, she found she could trace the boundary of the grove in her mind. It didn't encompass the entirety of the Thornwood, but she counted over a hundred Star Oaks within it.

It was hard to imagine that much magic in one place. Evie knew it needed to be protected, and its secret needed to be guarded too.

Following the grove's guidance, she moved through the wood, identifying and incinerating the magical traps Gemma had laid whenever she could. There were so many; it would take time to find them all. When this was over, she would get Ignatius to help her.

She could sense Gemma's presence now, with the Star Oaks bolstering her. Gemma had stopped in a clearing not far from the shed where Evie had found Snow trapped. The time witch paced back and forth among the trees, agitated and completely unaware that she stood in the middle of the Star Oaks that she'd long been searching for.

Evie didn't care about that. She was focused on the other presences in the clearing. They were muted but very much alive and, thankfully, unhurt.

Evie didn't bother to try to conceal her approach. Gemma had baited her hook and was now waiting for Evie to spring her last trap. She could likely sense Evie as clearly as Evie could sense her.

The rain had slowed to a trickle by the time Evie stepped into the clearing. Streaks of faint orange lit the sky above them, heralding what would no doubt be a glorious sunset now that the storm had finally passed.

The first thing Evie saw was Gil, standing in the center of the clearing, presented by Gemma like a trophy. Ropes of purple magic swirled around his body, draining him of color and vitality. His expression was vacant. He stood rigid, unaware of anything happening around him. Snow sat at his feet, whimpering and pawing ineffectually at his leg.

Evie clenched her jaw, forcing her expression into a neutral mask.

Then she saw Ruby.

She was standing a few feet away from Gil. Gemma stood next to her, her hand on the girl's shoulder in a deceptively affectionate pose. She hadn't restrained her with time magic, but Evie saw the tension in every line of her daughter's body.

Ruby looked up, meeting Evie's gaze with an expression of misery. "Don't come any closer," she begged. "She'll trap you too and—"

"Now, now." Gemma's hand dug into Ruby's shoulder. "We're all going to be calm and reasonable. Didn't I help guide you here when you were lost in the wood?" Gemma looked at Evie, flinching at whatever she read in her face. "I haven't harmed either of them," she assured her. "But they've given me an opportunity that I couldn't pass up."

"I see," Evie said, her voice flat. She kept herself under control, but it took a supreme effort of will. "You know, Gemma, when I stopped to think about it, I realized you were right about me."

"Oh?" Gemma regarded her warily. She shifted her position as Evie stepped closer, so that Ruby stood between them like a shield.

"When you questioned my place here," Evie clarified. "You were right. I had good intentions when I came to Iskendra, but I didn't truly understand what it meant to be a caretaker." She met Ruby's gaze and held it. "I had no idea if I was the right person to handle something so rare and precious. What if I messed it up?" Her throat tightened. "I was afraid, and I didn't always trust myself."

She tore her gaze away from Ruby and looked at Gemma, letting her power gather around her like a contained storm, so the time witch would be sure to feel it. "But I'm not afraid anymore," she said. "Take your hand off my daughter, Gemma. Right now."

Gemma pursed her lips, her expression set, though Evie could see the uncertainty creeping into her eyes. She removed her hand from Ruby's shoulder and gestured to Gil. "I'll release them both to you," she said. "All I want in return is for you to tell me where the Star Oak is. I know you know—I sense its power has touched you. If you don't tell me . . ." She let the threat hang in the air.

"If you hurt them, I and the ECRA will come down on you harder than you can possibly imagine," Evie promised. "Let them go, and we'll keep this in the village. The mayor can settle on an appropriate punishment for what you've done."

Gemma laughed, though there was an edge of wildness to it. "We're far beyond that now," she said. "And don't worry, my magic won't hurt them, at least not physically." For the first time, a malicious light entered her eyes. "But that doesn't mean I can't make them suffer in other ways. I can seal Gil within a moment of fear, make him experience it over and over, while no time at all passes for the rest of us. He'll believe he's been trapped in the wood, lost for weeks, because I've distorted his view of time. That's all it takes, using the leftover power of the sapling."

Evie's expression remained fixed, betraying nothing. She wouldn't give Gemma the satisfaction of knowing how her heart pounded, how she fought to stay calm.

"I'm disappointed in you." Evie stalled as she gathered the Star Oaks' power to her. "Is that what your magic has come to mean—making the villagers suffer? The same people who welcomed you here?"

"You forced me to this!" Gemma snapped. "If you'd just left the sapling where it was, everything would have been fine!"

"Is that what you think?" Evie mused. She gave Ruby a significant look. "Do you think that everything would have worked out just the way Gemma wanted it?"

Ruby met her eyes and stilled. Then she gave a minute nod, and her expression went vacant.

"What are you doing?" Gemma demanded, looking between mother and daughter suspiciously. "If this is a trick—"

"She's a farseer, Gemma," Evie said. "She looks into people's futures just as easily as you see into their pasts. It's a shame. If things had been different, you could have learned from each other."

Gemma's expression twisted into something that was almost fear. "Stop!" she commanded, but Ruby was deep into her power now and wouldn't be distracted.

"Why are you afraid to have a glimpse of your own future?" Evie asked. "Is it because the past is safer? It's set and unchangeable, whereas the future—that's something well beyond your power."

"You have no idea what I'm capable of," Gemma growled, but suddenly, Ruby jerked, coming out of her brief trance.

"It wouldn't have worked," Ruby said, banishing whatever vision she'd just experienced. She looked back at Gemma. "The sapling would have eventually died if you'd left it buried in the library's walls."

"No!" The denial burst out of Gemma. "Why should I believe a word you say?"

"Because deep down, you know it's true," Evie said. "You read the same book I did about sentient houses. You must realize the Star Oak sapling would never have bonded with the library in the same way it did with Thornwood house."

"That's right," Ruby said. "The two of them were meant to be together. The sapling chose the house, and the house chose the sapling."

"Be quiet!" Gemma shouted, making Ruby flinch.

And that was the moment when Evie had had enough.

She stepped forward and sent a blast of her gathered magic across the clearing. It manifested as an explosion of roots, weeds, and grasses, tangling around Gemma's legs, yanking her off her feet.

Ruby bolted across the clearing and into Evie's arms.

"Mom!" she sobbed. "Mom, I—"

"I'm here," Evie whispered, trembling with relief and joy. "You're safe. We're okay."

Evie stroked Ruby's hair, murmuring wordless sounds of comfort as she raised a ward around her daughter, sealing it with a crack of power that sizzled in the air.

But she had no time to rest. She turned to Gil next and sent a flood of power to him. It wrapped around the time magic strands holding him in place, snuffing out the purple light, leaving nothing but her own magic. When it faded, Gil dropped to the ground, which Evie had softened under him. His eyes fluttered closed. Snow crouched next to him, whining and licking his face.

"Get off me!" Gemma was thrashing, trying to free her legs from the twining grasses, the thick dandelion stems, and the brambles that pulled at her clothing.

While she was occupied, Evie went over and crouched next to Gil, still keeping one arm around Ruby. Gently, she nudged Snow aside and put her hand against Gil's cheek. His skin was warm, and he breathed slow and deep. He was asleep, no longer affected by Gemma's power.

Safe. They were both safe.

"Will you stay with him?" Evie asked Ruby. She extended the ward to cover Gil and Snow as well, building a wall with power freely given from the hidden Star Oaks. "Try to wake him if you can, but go slow. He'll be disoriented."

Ruby nodded, though she pressed hard against Evie's side. "Be careful," she whispered.

"I will."

Evie stood, turning in time to see Gemma gain her feet. She was still restrained, but she'd torn through some of the grasping roots and grasses with a string of purple that she'd shaped into a scythe. Evie stepped in front of Ruby and Gil just as Gemma aimed a flick of power in their direction. Evie raised her hands, but she was a second too slow, and the magic wrapped around her wrist and clung.

So cold. Cold enough to burn.

Evie staggered as Gemma raised her other hand, eyes blazing with fury, and a second whip of power wrapped around Evie's waist.

Evie tried to focus her magic, to bring it to bear on Gemma, but her head was swimming. The wood around them warped and twisted, the trees turning to nightmarish shadows, the ground to churning mud, and Evie was slowly sinking in it.

Distantly, she heard Ruby call out to her, and Evie held on to her daughter's voice, using it like an anchor. She tried to reach for the Star Oaks' power but found only a void instead. She fought panic. How had she been cut off from the power source? Had the trees rescinded it?

No. They wouldn't do that. Evie struggled to focus through the fog slowly creeping into her mind. She looked down at the whips of power wound around her wrist and waist. They were distorting time around her, making her disoriented, just as Gemma had done to Gil.

Evie grabbed the strand wound around her wrist. The slender cord left a searing red mark branded across her palm. Evie ignored the pain and pulled.

Gemma grunted at the sudden resistance to her magic. Evie kept going. She hated this feeling, this helplessness that threatened to overwhelm her. Gemma's magic was repellent. She wanted to tear the strands away, but she yanked on them instead, using the time witch's own power to pull herself closer to Gemma, keeping her off balance until she could reach out and snag her arm.

"Let it go." Up close, she could see how hard Gemma strained to hold her in place, to keep Evie's magic in check. Sweat poured down her face, and the arm she held was shaking, muscles taut. "You can't hold me, Gemma. You have to let go, or you'll hurt yourself."

Gemma's eyes glittered with anger. "How are you still resisting?" she snarled, trying and failing to pull free of Evie's grip. "How are you not trapped?"

Evie looked over Gemma's shoulder, her gaze snared by a luminous column emerging from the shadows. One of the Star Oaks stood behind the time witch, seeming to appear out of nowhere, though it must have been there all along. Its silver bark shimmered, and a dark hollow appeared in the tree, shaped roughly like a door.

Come, the Star Oak invited. *Come inside.*

"This has to stop," Evie told Gemma, her voice strained by the pain in her body, the terrible cold of the time magic distorting her perceptions. She gathered her strength for what she needed to do. "You have to—"

She didn't get a chance to finish. Suddenly, there came a great rumbling and crashing through the trees, as if a lumbering giant were running at full speed through the wood toward them. Evie felt a second of bewilderment before she realized what the source of the sound was.

Because she'd heard it before.

Oh, no.

Held in the grip of Gemma's magic, with Gemma still restrained by the underbrush and grasses, Evie twisted in time to see the trees part. They shifted aside as easily as a towering crowd making way for a child to run through.

Thornwood house burst into the clearing, striding on its chicken feet, tearing up clumps of grass and spraying dirt in all directions. It came to a juddering halt just behind Ruby and Gil, who was now sitting up and gazing blearily at the scene as if he couldn't quite tell whether he was awake or dreaming.

Evie didn't blame him. She stood staring in disbelief at the house, which had been utterly dormant the last time she'd seen it. Now it was awake, and after all they'd done to heal, repair, and reimagine it, the very first thing it had done was uproot itself all over again and dash out into the Thornwood, doing who knew what kind of damage to itself and—

Then she felt it.

Radiating like a beacon, a brilliant silver tether emerged from the heart of the house. It descended upon Evie all at once, its power spinning into a shape that was like a helia blossom and a Star Oak leaf entwined, but made of pure magic. It hovered above her head like an offering.

A bond.

Evie opened her mind to it on instinct, and the image disappeared as soon as she accepted the power. The pain and cold of Gemma's magic were swept away by the sheer force of it.

Just like that, it was done, and the bond was everything Evie had imagined. It was like coming home, a sense of joy and well-being that made her eyes burn with unshed tears. The house had chosen the sapling, and now it had chosen *her*.

As if that weren't enough, as Thornwood house towered over the scene, its shingles raised like hackles, its turret bent toward Gemma in a furious glower, the front door of the house sprang open. Ignatius Smythe pounded down the dangling front steps. He jumped the last few feet to the ground, fell on his hands and knees, and then came upright, adjusting his glasses before turning triumphantly to Evie and the others.

"We're here to rescue you," Ignatius declared.

One of the shutters on the upstairs windows snapped off and banged to the ground, frightening a rabbit out of its hole.

"I—I can't tell you how glad I am to see you both," Evie said, her voice caught between a laugh and a sob. Checking to make sure her magic still held Gemma securely, she nodded to Ruby, who helped Gil to his feet, and together, the two of them and Snow made their way over to the house. It bent forward to lay its steps close enough to the ground for them to climb up onto the porch, which was surprisingly still intact, considering the house had just made a mad dash through the Thornwood. Evie couldn't imagine what the inside must look like at the moment.

But it rose smoothly on its wooden feet, drawing Ruby, Gil, and Snow safely out of reach of Gemma, who seemed to be expending all her power trying to keep Evie in check. Evie felt another burden lift from her shoulders.

Ignatius pointed at Gemma. "This ends now," he said imperiously. "Let Evie go, and maybe you won't be banished from Iskendra permanently."

"Are you serious?" Gemma gave an incredulous laugh. "Do you think I care about this backwater village? Your family can have it, as far as I'm concerned. I've only ever been here for the Star Oak." She turned her attention to Evie, her magic flaring. "And you're going to give it to me, or I'll never stop trying to take it. My traps are all over the wood. Neither you nor the Thornwood will have a moment's peace."

Despite the threat, Evie felt a brief jolt of pity for Gemma. She'd had so much more time in Iskendra than Evie. She'd had so many opportunities to get to know the villagers, to make friends with them and see all that they had to offer, just as Evie had begun to do over these last several weeks.

Just as Gemma had made friends with Evie. Except it had all been a lie, a means to an end, and now everything was crumbling around her.

But she was still dangerous, and she needed to be dealt with.

Evie reached out to the Star Oak that still loomed unseen behind the time witch. Its presence filled the clearing, invisible to all except Evie, though she noticed that Ignatius kept stealing glances in its direction, as if he sensed something but wasn't quite sure what it was.

When Evie connected to the great tree with her power, she recognized at once that this Star Oak was older than any of the others she'd had contact with. It was large and gentle, but removed from the world, as if all the fuss and magic in the clearing were just a fluttering cloud of gnats to it.

And with a certainty she couldn't explain, Evie knew this was the Star Oak that had offered a sapling to Thornwood house.

Evie sensed the tree was also willing to give Gemma the knowledge and wisdom of the Star Oaks she desired. She recoiled from that thought. What would happen after? Would Gemma try to take their power? Would the Thornwood be safe? She sent the question and her trepidation to the tree and received a flood of warmth and confidence in return.

All will be well.

Evie readied herself. She released Gemma's arm and yanked on the cord of power attached to her wrist. It threw Gemma off balance again. Before she could recover, Evie grabbed her by the shoulder and pushed her back against the tree.

Ignatius, Ruby, and Gil all cried out an exclamation as Gemma's body passed *into* the suddenly visible tree. And vanished. They cried out again, louder, when Evie followed, disappearing inside the massive, ancient Star Oak.

Thirty-Nine

Evie found herself standing at the edge of a silver lake. Star Oaks surrounded the water's still surface, reflecting back hundreds of the ancient trees. It felt as if she were standing in an in-between place, somewhere that was not quite her own world but a mirror of it.

Was this how the Star Oaks had remained hidden for so long? Had they removed themselves to this place, a wood that was between worlds?

In the center of the lake, Gemma stood on a hillock of land covered in night lilies. The anger and malice she'd exuded before were gone. She turned in a slow circle, her mouth open and eyes wide with shock as she beheld the gathering of ancient trees.

When her gaze fell on Evie, she gasped. "Is this a dream? It has to be, doesn't it?" Evie heard her voice as clearly as if they were standing next to each other. Gemma put a trembling hand against her mouth. "In a million years, I never would have thought . . . a whole *grove* of Star Oaks?"

"It's not a dream," Evie said, unable to quell her uneasiness. She'd had no idea the Star Oak intended to reveal the existence of the entire grove to Gemma.

"No wonder it hid itself so well." Gemma stepped to the edge of the island. Suddenly, another Star Oak appeared, rising from the lake itself, dripping water on her like rain. Its gleaming column of silver half hid her from Evie's sight.

Gemma smiled and reached for the tree, her hand held out in greeting, but her fingertips passed through the bark like smoke. Frowning, she turned and approached the water on the other side of the tiny island.

A second tree rose before her, blocking her path.

"Is this a test?" Gemma asked, glancing over at Evie, as if she could pull the curtain back on these mysteries. "What does it want from me?"

Evie watched silently as Gemma tried again to touch the tree. This time, at the last second, her body met an invisible wall. She raised her hands, pressing them against the barrier. Her arms trembled as she strained, pouring out her magic in purple waves to try to break through.

Her magic won't pass, the trees whispered in Evie's ear. *She must let it go.*

Evie relaxed as she began to understand. The trees knew what they were doing. Gemma could have what she most desired, but she would have to pay a price.

Striding to the edge of the lake, Evie waited while Gemma

continued to try to force her way to the tree. Finally, the time witch cursed in frustration and spun toward her. "What is this?" she demanded. "Why won't they let me touch them? What do they want?"

"You have to choose," Evie said. She lifted a hand and wasn't surprised when the Star Oak nearest her allowed her to press her palm to the silver bark, to comb her fingers through the leaves of the low-hanging branches. "You can leave the island and this place." She hesitated, listening to the sigh of the Star Oaks as their message came through. "Or you can stay, and learn. But if you remain, you give up your power."

Gemma went silent at Evie's words. She sank to the ground at the edge of the lake, drawing her knees up to her chest. It struck Evie—the scene was a surreal echo of their conversation in the park on market day. With everything that had happened since, that day felt like years ago, a moment gone forever as Gemma stared at the mirror-bright surface of the lake in contemplation.

Evie watched her, trying to divine her thoughts. She'd half expected Gemma to get angry, to curse her and beat against the barrier again, declaring how unfair the terms of the Star Oaks' agreement were. But as she continued to sit silently, pondering the trees and the lake, occasionally looking out across the water, Evie realized with a pang what she was going to choose.

"Do you really want the Star Oaks' knowledge so badly?" Evie asked. "You'll leave everything behind. Your sister too. I don't know how long they'll keep you here."

Long enough to teach her better ways, the trees had told her. But Evie had no idea whether that meant a month, a year, or the span of a life, as the Star Oaks reckoned time.

"Abby will get along well enough without me," Gemma said, sounding only a bit regretful. "Give her a message for me, will you?" she implored Evie. "I know I wronged you, and you owe me nothing, but I'm asking you anyway. Abby didn't have anything to do with any of this, I swear it. I kept it all from her, to protect her."

"Go ahead," Evie said. "I'll do what you ask—for your sister."

Gemma nodded. "Please tell her it's time for her to stand on her own—just like I told her she'd have to, one day. That way she'll know that this was my choice." Gemma smiled sadly. "And tell her she can always look to our shared past to find me. Memories are carved in time, and I treasured every one of them I had with her."

"But surely—"

"You can't understand, not really," Gemma said. "You'd have to be a time witch to realize what a gift I'm being offered. I'm gaining all the knowledge I could ever want from the past. It's not what I planned, but in some ways, it's so much more." She looked at the Star Oaks with reverence. "Everything they have ever seen, I'll see too. Whatever sacrifice I have to make now is worth it. Abby will understand."

Evie considered that. Maybe, for time witches like Gemma and her sister, exploring and learning from the past *was* everything. It was what fed them, just as Evie's connection to the land sustained her and guided her purpose.

"I hope you find what you're looking for" was all Evie could say, as Gemma stood and walked to the edge of the lake once more, stopping just out of reach of the water.

"Thank you." Gemma looked at Evie, and there was another flash of regret in her eyes. "I really did want to be your friend," she said. "That part wasn't a lie. In a different world, we might have . . ." She trailed off helplessly.

"We might," Evie said. She raised her hand in farewell.

Gemma waved back and smiled. Then she stepped into the lake and vanished, leaving only the faintest ripple on the water, a shape that reminded Evie of the rings of a cut tree.

Alone, Evie closed her eyes and tipped her head back, listening to the murmur of the Star Oaks, feeling their power swirl around her. If she concentrated, she could feel the entirety of the Thornwood spread across the land. She was a part of it and removed from it. She was a caretaker, and she was cared for.

And she heard voices calling to her.

Ruby.

Gil.

Thornwood house, its gentle whisper coaxing her to come home.

Home.

Evie lifted her arms and stepped forward.

When she opened her eyes, familiar hands had taken hold of her, pulling her from the tree. She came out from the silver bark into the rain-scented clearing, shaking off bits of leaf and acorn, as if for a time she'd been part of the tree itself. Then she was free, and Ruby's and Gil's arms were around her, enveloping her in their familiar scents.

"Got you," Gil said, holding her tightly.

"We thought you weren't coming back!" Ruby cried, and Gil put his arm around her while Evie cupped Ruby's face in her hands and wiped away her tears.

"I'm fine," she murmured. "Gemma's all right too, but . . . I'll explain later, but I promise, everything's all right now."

She felt Thornwood house's presence against her back, cloaking her in a sense of well-being and relief. Snow ran circles around them, barking happily. She could have stayed in that lovely cocoon for hours, but she became aware that Ignatius was pacing the clearing, tugging at his hair, his glasses askew, muttering to himself.

"Not possible," he was saying. "It was supposed to be one tree. *One* tree! Not a . . . not a . . ."

Evie looked around. "Oh, my," she breathed.

The Star Oaks had chosen to show themselves. They ringed the group protectively, shining in all their silver and blue glory. Ignatius just kept circling the clearing, trying to take it all in.

"Did you know about this?" He pointed at Evie. "Did you . . . but how could you? *Did* you?"

"Not at first," Evie told him. "It's as much a surprise to me as to you that the grove has chosen to show itself. But it's going to need protection." She glanced at Ruby as she spoke.

Hope lit her daughter's face like a beacon. "Does that mean we can stay?" she whispered.

Behind them, the house leaned in with a distinctly possessive air.

Evie laughed. "Oh, yes, we're staying," she said. "I'd already decided that. And now Thornwood house and I have bonded. It's chosen its caretaker, and so have the Star Oaks, which makes things much easier."

Ruby let out a joyful shriek and threw her arms around Evie's neck.

"That's wonderful news," Gil said, his voice rough with emotion.

Evie held his gaze as she hugged her daughter. "Yes, it is."

Ignatius stopped his pacing and looked at the three of them incredulously. "Of course you're staying," he bleated. "But someone's going to have to explain all this to the ECRA. A Star Oak grove hiding in plain sight all these years!" He shook his head. "They won't believe it."

"They'll have to," Evie said, pulling back to look at Ignatius. "But I'm not the only caretaker of the Star Oak grove." She gestured to the towering trees. "This is too much for any one person to handle. I'm going to need help."

Ignatius caught her look and froze. "Do you . . . do you mean that?"

"Yes," Evie said, "and you'll have to start work here immediately, because you're right. Someone's going to have to go and explain this new situation to the ECRA."

Ruby stiffened. "You can't!" She tightened her grip on Evie to the edge of pain. "They'll find a way to make you stay if you do."

"No, they won't." Evie gently eased out of Ruby's death grip. "Listen to me," she said, holding the girl's hands. "We're done running and being afraid. You were right; we decided to be a family, and that means that *you* are my home. We chose each other. And no matter what happens, no one can take away the bond between us. Because no magic in this world could match how much I love you, Ruby."

"I love you too, Mom." Ruby's eyes filled with tears again, and Evie hugged her close. The house hovered over them like a mother hen.

"Thornwood house isn't going to give you up now," Gil said,

glancing back at the house. There was that familiar twinkle of mischief in his eye. "The rest of Iskendra won't either."

"Yes, yes, we've established that they're staying," Ignatius said impatiently, "but the *grove*! We have so much work to do!"

Evie laughed. "Then we'd better get started."

FORTY

"I'm going to need you to start again at the beginning, Ms. Sharpe," said Mr. Cinton, sounding displeased as usual. He'd spent the last two hours taking down Evie's statement in regard to her time in Iskendra and the days leading up to the discovery of the Star Oak grove. He'd gone through at least two ink pens in his furious scribblings, but it seemed he still hadn't gotten enough.

Next to him, Mr. Tansling was checking his own notes, but Mrs. Shields hadn't written a thing. Instead, she'd been listening intently, her chin resting in her wrinkled hand.

At the far end of the table sat Arthur Smythe, Ignatius's brother. He'd been an unexpected, last-minute addition to the meeting. Evie couldn't help shooting glances at the man every now and then out of the corner of her eye. She guessed he was maybe five or six years older than Ignatius, and she had no trouble picking out the resemblance between him and his younger brother. They had the same pointed chin and blond hair, though Arthur's was a much darker shade. Unlike his brother, he did not wear glasses, and dressed casually in a collared shirt with the sleeves rolled to his forearms. He'd yet to speak or make much reaction during the meeting, so Evie couldn't get a sense of his personality.

"I can certainly do that, Mr. Cinton," Evie said patiently, returning her attention to the committee chairman, "although this process has already taken quite some time this morning, and none of us have had a break. I can hear Mr. Tansling's stomach growling from all the way over here, so maybe we should take a brief recess?"

"There will be time for that soon enough." Mr. Cinton took off his glasses, scrubbed the lenses with a tissue, then put them back on slightly askew. "I simply find it hard to believe, Ms. Sharpe, that there exists an entire grove of Star Oaks in the immediate vicinity of Iskendra, and no one had any prior knowledge of them, including yourself."

Evie lifted her hands. "And yet, I suspect you've already received confirmation that that is indeed the case." When Mr. Cinton fidgeted in his seat, Evie smiled. "The ECRA has its own field team for investigating the resurgence of magical resources, one that was likely dispatched the moment you received my letter. We probably passed each other at the train station. And you've kept me here, cooling my heels for days now, while you were waiting for the team's report." She leaned forward, resting her elbows on the table. "So I've no doubt you know that everything I've said is true."

"We know that the grove exists," Mr. Cinton admitted, "but every attempt we've made to map its borders and judge its age has met with . . ." He trailed off, glancing at the other committee members for help.

Mrs. Shields stepped in. "It appears the Thornwood doesn't want the field team there," she said, and Evie thought she heard a smile in her voice, though she kept her expression carefully blank. "It's been changing its terrain, dropping spots of fog and darkness, leading our witches back out to the main road whenever they try to locate the grove. The Star Oaks have made themselves known, but they've also made it clear that they'll accept no one but the caretaker and her associates within its borders."

Now it was Evie's turn to school her expression. "Is that so?"

"Oh, please," Mr. Cinton said, rapping his knuckles on the tabletop. "You can't pretend you didn't plan for this to happen."

"*Plan* for this?" Evie echoed, genuinely taken aback. "I don't know what you mean."

"What Mr. Cinton is saying is that it's 'terribly convenient,'" quoted Mrs. Shields, "that you left your position as a powerful earthwalker and moved to a 'backwater village'—"

Arthur Smythe gently cleared his throat.

"My apologies," Mrs. Shields said, giving him a nod. "These are Mr. Cinton's views, not my own. Iskendra is certainly *not* a backwater." Her focus returned to Evie, and her lips twitched. "Whereupon you discovered a powerful grove of ancient magical trees, and those same trees selected you as their guardian and caretaker, effectively granting you a position more prestigious than any you might have hoped to achieve here within the ECRA."

It was, Evie had to admit, an improbable series of events when summed up like that. "If you're suggesting that I knew about the existence of the Star Oak grove before I took the position in Iskendra, I can assure you, I did not. As for the grove choosing me, this committee knows perfectly well that no witch can engineer such a choice or control the whims and desires of such powerful entities."

"Be that as it may," Mr. Cinton interjected, color rising in his pale cheeks, "we are assessing everything about your conduct in this situation, Ms. Sharpe, and once again, I find it questionable."

Cinton was watching her like a cat convinced that it's trapped the mouse. Mrs. Shields simply looked tired of him. Arthur Smythe had his head cocked in Evie's direction and was wearing an expression she couldn't interpret. Through it all, Mr. Tansling continued to take notes. Since Ruby wasn't there for him to question, he seemed to be merely going through the motions for his reports.

When she was a teenager, Evie had been in awe of the ECRA. As she grew older, she'd learned to mistrust and fear them. But in the end, they were just people. Together they might present an intimidating front, but that was all it was. An act, to keep other witches in check and to make themselves feel more powerful. For a time, they'd had a weapon they could use against her, but that was gone now.

Evie wasn't going to be intimidated anymore, and there were things she needed to get off her chest.

"If we're going to speak of conduct," she said, raising her voice, "then I'd like to remind this committee and the ECRA at large that they've done far more damage in this situation than I ever could." She caught Mr. Tansling's eye and stared him down, unflinching. "The handling of my daughter's adoption was outrageous and exploitative, unbecoming of this organization and everything that it *should* stand for."

Mr. Tansling's permanent waxy smile slid off his face, and he stiffened in indignation. "Now, wait just a minute—"

"No, you're going to wait," Evie cut him off with an upraised hand. "I believe I'm entitled to continue my statement."

"You are indeed, Ms. Sharpe," Arthur Smythe spoke up. He wore a faint smile.

Mr. Tansling sat back in his seat, grumbling under his breath.

"Thank you." Evie speared Mr. Tansling with a glare. "You used coercive tactics on a young, inexperienced witch, when you should have been acting as a guardian of her future and her choices. I could say I was surprised, but the ECRA did the same thing to me when I was only a little older than her." She lifted her chin. "But now, forces older than this organization have made their own choice. You know as well as I do that I had no part in engineering this. You're simply angry that you aren't getting what you want, which is control over the Star Oak grove. But if you need to punish someone, focus on me. You're done acting on my daughter's behalf."

Silence fell in the room. She'd expected him to argue, but Mr. Tansling actually ducked his head, cowed by her speech. Mr. Cinton was red-faced, his jaw working, but before he could speak, Mrs. Shields took control again. "No one in this room will punish you for your actions, Ms. Sharpe," she said, shooting a pointed glance at Mr. Cinton. "On the contrary, in my opinion, you have proven yourself more than capable of taking on the role of caretaker for both Thornwood house and the Star Oak grove." She acknowledged Arthur Smythe again with a nod. "Mr. Ignatius Smythe, representative of the Smythe family, the oldest in Iskendra, concurs with our assessment. He passed along his regards via his brother, our head of Magical Artifacts Division."

"I appreciate that vote of confidence," Evie said. Especially since she'd once thought there would never come a time when she and Ignatius saw eye to eye on anything. How things had changed.

Mrs. Shields's expression softened then. "I'm not able to speak for the other members of the committee, but I can say for myself that I apologize wholeheartedly for the pain caused to you and your daughter. The ECRA acted outside its authority, and we paid the price by losing one of our best, and losing the chance to nurture one of the first farseers to come up through the agency. We'll be feeling the effects of that for a long time." She folded her hands on the table. "I *am* empowered to tell you—and I'm sure Mr. Cinton was just getting around to it—that you are hereby discharged from all further service and obligations to the ECRA. Your contract has been dissolved, your adoption of Ruby Keeler has been officially finalized, and you carry all honors and accolades you've earned from this agency into your next position. We thank you for your service."

"Yes, I *was* getting to that," Mr. Cinton said sourly. "But there are still matters that need to be addressed. The location of Gemma Gray, for instance. After her disappearance two weeks ago, Ms. Gray's sister requested an inquiry into what happened, but only a day later, she asked that it be closed. Can you explain that?"

Evie nodded. "I spoke to Gemma's sister and shared a message that Gemma left before her disappearance, so her sister would know that she made the choice to join with the Star Oaks of her own free will. Where that journey has taken her, I can't say, but I believe it's to a place none of us can reach. I told Abby Gray as much." She gave him a look. "The rest of our conversation is private, and Gemma's sister should be allowed to grieve in peace."

Mr. Cinton made a note on his papers, then finally tossed down his pen. "Well, I suppose this concludes matters, though the committee remains unsatisfied on several points."

"The committee would like to take a recess sometime in the near future," Mrs. Shields said. "Let it go, Cinton. A Star Oak grove has been found in the world, which is a cause for celebration. It has a capable land witch caretaker *and* a farseer to watch over it.

Thornwood house was saved from destruction by their efforts as well. It's time to adjourn."

"Very well." Still looking displeased, Mr. Cinton gathered his papers and stood. "You are dismissed, Ms. Sharpe. May you find satisfaction in the path you've chosen, for you will not be welcomed back to the ECRA."

With that pronouncement ringing in the air, the meeting broke up. Evie's tense shoulders relaxed as she stood and stepped away from the table. Arthur Smythe also rose from his seat and came over to her. He offered his hand, and she shook it.

"I'm sorry I didn't get a chance to introduce myself to you earlier," he said, with a genuine warmth that immediately put Evie at ease. "Call me Arthur, please."

"A pleasure to meet you," Evie said. "You look very much like your brother."

"Heaven help us both," he said with a chuckle. He lowered his voice. "I also apologize for crashing the meeting this way, but Ignatius felt—and I agreed—that considering what the committee had already put you and your daughter through, it would be nice if there was someone on the other side of that table who had your back."

Evie was momentarily at a loss for words. "I—thank you," she said, touched by Ignatius's concern, and by his brother's support, even though she was a stranger to him.

Mrs. Shields joined them. "Good luck to you, Evie," the older woman said. She nodded after Mr. Cinton. "You know you can't get rid of us that easily, though. The ECRA will expect regular reports on the health of the grove."

"I thought as much," Evie said. It would be a headache, but nothing she couldn't handle.

"Know also that the ECRA will stand ready to help defend the grove, should anything threaten it that is beyond your power," Mrs. Shields said. "Despite our rocky past, I think we can all agree that protecting the grove is vital. If you're willing, Mr. Smythe and I can be your liaisons in that regard."

That was unexpected, but Evie found she was pleased. If she had to work with someone in the ECRA, she could do a lot worse than Mrs. Shields. And having Arthur involved might just help the brothers' relationship in the long run. "I am willing," she said, addressing them both. "I think we can work together."

"Excellent." Mrs. Shields patted her arm. "Go home and tell your daughter the good news." She walked away, leaning on her cane.

When she was gone, Arthur turned to Evie. "How is my brother doing?" he asked. "We've exchanged a few letters, but they can only say so much. I mean, I imagine, with the discovery of the Star Oak grove, he must be ecstatic?" His voice was deceptively casual, but the look on his face told Evie he was anxious to hear her answer.

"He was very . . . enthusiastic, and he's been working hard to learn everything he can about the grove," Evie assured him.

The day she'd left for Dorna City, Ignatius had been sprawled on the kitchen floor of Thornwood house, chewing a pencil down to the nub, with a map of the area spread out in front of him. He'd been systematically marking the exact location of every Star Oak he'd seen, occasionally looking up and shouting, "There are just so many!" in a tone of absolute glee.

Eventually, Evie had gotten used to the outbursts.

And the grove had never had a single qualm about letting Ignatius in to explore it.

"That's wonderful," Arthur said. "I'm glad to hear it." He cleared his throat and seemed to relax a bit.

Evie hesitated but decided to take a chance. "You should come see for yourself when you're able," she suggested. "I'm sure Ignatius would be happy for you to visit."

"I— Well, I mean—" He cut himself off and met her eyes. A moment of understanding passed between them before he slowly nodded. "Maybe I'll do that. I never thought there'd be anything that would draw me back to Iskendra, but now . . . You can never really predict what brings you home, can you?"

"Doesn't stop any of us from trying," Evie said.

Epilogue

The months passed quickly once Evie returned to Iskendra. As the summer wound down, the heralds of fall arrived with crisp days and cool nights. It was as if a great painter's brush swept through the trees of the wood overnight, leaving the first tinges of yellow and orange on the leaves.

To celebrate the change of seasons, Evie and Ruby decided to hold a garden party at Thornwood house.

Even after their trials in the wood, it had taken Evie less than a week to set Thornwood house to rights again. She'd been worried at first, but the sapling was still comfortably bonded with the house. Drawing on that ample power and her own, Evie was able to repair the damage that had occurred from the house picking itself up and running off again into the Thornwood.

Once the repairs were complete, she'd felt a sensation of settling from the house, like the long, slow sigh of contentment that comes after a time of hard work and upheaval.

The feeling of finally knowing peace.

It washed over Evie in turn, and she knew that the house's days of wandering—much like her own—were over. As if to prove it, the house coaxed the ivy and honeysuckle to again climb its walls, letting the flowers twine around its bones and reach for the sun.

Evie and Ruby spent their late-summer days sitting on the porch swing, listening to the soft creaks of the house, reading Amelia Howell's diary to learn more about her life, and planning their party. Which mostly consisted of them trying to figure out how they were going to fit all the villagers on their property.

In the end, Gil assured them that people would come and go, and he promised to open up his own yard to accommodate the overflow. Everyone would come, at some point. They were all eager to return to the house where they'd spent part of their childhoods, to reassure themselves that all was well.

The day of the party, Evie could feel the house vibrating with the excitement of a child on holiday. Cinda arrived early in the morning, bringing extra chairs and tables to set up in the front and backyard and around the pond. The Greens arrived shortly after, loaded down with so much food, Evie wasn't sure where they would put it all. Ruby, Jamie, and Trin decorated the porch railing, the bridge over the pond, and the newly constructed chicken coop, using brightly colored ribbons and bows. There were no chickens yet, but those were coming.

First they needed to get the kitten settled in.

Ruby had named her Cinder, for her coat was pure black, so that when she and Snow ran round and round the yard they were blurs of shadow and frost against the colorful scenery. Thankfully, the two had gotten along from the start, and Evie sometimes even caught Cinder curled up napping on Snow's back like an ink dot.

During the party preparations, she was content to ride around draped across Ruby's shoulders, mewling whenever anyone went by with a platter of food, as if she hadn't ever been fed properly.

Evie's magical awareness continued to expand. She was becoming acquainted with every Star Oak in the Thornwood, one by one, just as she was sensing the presence of all the villagers, feeling their beating hearts right alongside her own. It had been a strange, crowded sensation at first, but then it had settled, much like everything else, into a familiar rhythm, just another part of her new life.

The villagers started to trickle down the road toward the house a little before noon, just as Evie and Gil were finishing pouring cups of punch and arranging them on tables on the front porch. The air was soon full of chatter and exclamations of excitement as Evie invited people in to tour the reimagined house.

She took them to the back of the staircase first, so they could find their names, right where they'd written them when they were children. Some of them had children of their own now to measure, and Evie felt the house preening at their presence.

"It's going to be as spoiled as the kitten at this rate," Evie whispered to Gil during one of the rare quiet moments, while the guests roamed the house or gathered in groups in the gardens.

Gil chuckled. "I've no doubt about that." He leaned down and stole a kiss as they stood at the top of the staircase.

Ruby trotted up the stairs just then and caught them. "Gross," she declared, but she was grinning. She tugged on Gil's arm. "Can

Snow spend the night here again?" she pleaded. "Cinder really likes it when he stays."

Gil cocked an eyebrow. "*Cinder* likes it, does she?" He shook his head at Evie. "I see how it's going to be. You two are going to steal my dog and leave me all alone." He put on a forlorn look that made Ruby giggle.

"I'm pretty sure your toolbox has taken up a permanent spot in the glasshouse," Evie pointed out, "and I noticed the house has started putting out your favorite coffee mug every morning for you." A breeze swept up the stairs as she spoke, ruffling Gil's hair affectionately. Evie smiled. "I don't think Snow's the only one who's going to be spending more time here."

"Well, that's a relief," Gil said. Their gazes met and held, and Evie had that notion again, the same one she'd had before, of Gil sitting on his lumpy old couch in her living room, reading a book in the sun. It made her magic stir, green and gold warmth humming in her veins.

Later, after the guests had left and the cleanup was done, Snow and Cinder curled up together on the living room floor next to Gil, who'd dozed off in a chair. Tiptoeing around them, Evie and Ruby slipped out the back door. They padded through the glasshouse in their slippers and continued out into the mood garden. The evening had turned chilly, so they were wrapped in chunky sweaters, and each carried a mug of hot cocoa, curls of steam warming their faces.

They settled on the bench that Evie had built and placed in the heart of the mood garden, just as she'd imagined on their first night here. The gazebo would come later, probably the following spring, when the garden emerged from its winter sleep.

There was no rush.

The house was a serene presence nearby, and Evie could feel the Star Oak's power extending around them, holding them in its orbit. She sighed, leaning back into the magic as she took a sip of rich chocolate.

Ruby blew on her cocoa to cool it, rippling the marshmallows on the liquid's surface. "Did you bring it?" she asked excitedly.

"I did." Evie pulled the book out of one of the large, baggy pockets of her sweater. She squinted at it. "I'm not sure there's enough light to read by." The nights came on quicker now, and it was a new moon.

In response, the lights in the windows at the backside of the house flared brighter, casting a warm glow over the yard and the mood garden. Evie smiled at the house in thanks as Ruby scooted closer on the bench, tucking against her side. Evie leaned over and kissed the top of her daughter's head.

At the foot of the bench, the coral yearns opened their star-shaped petals, and the house leaned in to listen with Ruby as Evie opened the book, ready to start a new story.

Acknowledgments

I wanted this book badly. I've wanted them all, but this one burned inside me, which is an odd thing to say of a cozy story, but it's true. My thanks go to everyone who helped bring that fire out. To the entire team at Ace who championed this book, you are incredible. And to my editor, Mary Baker, you understood this book and pointed to all the places in the story that brushed against my own heart. Working on this with you has been a fairy tale. To my agent, Sara Megibow, our mantra is always "onward," but I want to stop, just this once, and cherish this moment with you. To Susan Morris, because you said the book made you cry (in a good way, I hope), and because you're always there to cheer me on. To Joe, my brother-in-law and an amazing home builder and designer, who patiently answered all my questions about old houses, and who I hope won't be too scandalized by all the ways in which I've bent and broken the rules of construction and good sense.

Acknowledgments

This book turned out to be a strange alchemy of things I needed to write to comfort myself during hard times, and gifts I wanted to give to other people. To my family and friends, for the backyard picnics on warm summer nights, and especially to Jeff and Tim, because I wrote this always thinking of both of you. Jeff, I hope it makes you cry in a good way too.